To Anne
Best w
Mary Crowley
28/9/18

A SWEET SMELL OF STRAWBERRIES

by

Mary Crowley

A Sweet Smell of Strawberries

All rights © Mary Crowley 2018

Paperback ISBN 9781983333132

All characters and events featured in this book, other than those clearly in the public domain, are entirely fictitious and any resemblance to any person living or dead, organisation or event, is purely coincidental.

Copyright & Related Rights Act 2000. These moral rights are: the paternity right of Mary Crowley to be identified as the author of A Sweet Smell of Strawberries the integrity right (the right to prevent mutilation, distortion or other derogatory alteration of the work) and the right of false attribution.

Acknowledgements

I would like to give recognition and thanks to my husband John and our three children Damon, Steven and Katie, who have been a wonderful support and my reason for never giving up. Even when the end seemed impossible, you never let me falter and put up with my divided attention. Thank you to my sister-in-law Jayne for reading the manuscript and sorting my commas, your support means the world. Lastly, to everyone who has been supportive of this journey, giving me the courage to publish. Thank You

About the Author

Mary Crowley lives in County Waterford, on the South East Coast of Ireland with her husband John and children Damon, Steven and Katie. Winner of the Waterford Writers Weekend Short Story Competition in 2016, with her entry "The Three Sisters." She also has publications in Writing.ie, Woman's Way and Flash Fiction Magazine.

Mary likes nothing more than spending time with her family, travelling to new places in her beloved VW Camper. It was a trip to the North West of Ireland last year, exploring the beautiful scenery along The Wild Atlantic Way, which inspired the setting for, "A Sweet Smell of Strawberries."

writeinspirationblog.wordpress.com
twitter.com/authormarycrowley

Chapter 1

The sky is lit up in breath-taking deep reds streaked with shades of orange and pinks, ebbing its way up from the horizon framing a beautiful backdrop against, the clear blue ocean. Shoving her bare feet into the thick golden sand, Sarah gazes at the Atlantic watching ripples dance and glisten in the early morning summer sunshine. It is peaceful here, a place where she can fully embrace the natural beauty surrounding her, while hiding from the constraints of reality. A flock of seagulls fly over-head, their timeless raucous call ringing off the cliff face, depicting a mirror of her inner cries as they disappear towards the harbour.

Reluctant to leave the lure of the private cove on the family's farmland behind for now, with one of the most wonderful views of the coastline, curved as though drawn by an artist's hand. Sarah rises, shaking sand off her dress and picking up her surfboard. Having planned on catching a few waves but the stillness of the water let her down. Being a day like any other, she would go to work wearing a perfected smile, the one that never truly reaches her eyes or deceives those who know her well. She tries though for the sake of her father, because he is the person who has gotten her through, making each day one to get out of bed for.

Yet, there is a simmering feeling of gloom and discontent niggling in the back of her mind. Like the depiction of the sky, she fears all is not as simple as it appears on this glorious summer's morning. Reminded of a saying. "Red sky at night, Shepherd's delight. Red sky in the morning Shepherd's warning." It's hard to imagine such beauty could bring gloom in its wake.

As a child, she would question her father regarding this logic. "Why Shepherd's Da, as a farmer would you not agree with the prediction?" She would ask with a quizzical stare. Expecting the answer to be confirmation of her father's, professional knowledge when it comes to such matters. Paddy would give his youngest child an affectionate smile in return, with an analytical response. "Always wanting to analyse and question Sarah, like your beautiful mother, god rest her soul. You should become a solicitor, or even a barrister when you grow up girleen." Would come his reply. Her lips twitch, breaking into a wistful smile at the memory.

'I knew you'd be pleased to see me.' Her lover's familiar husky tone catches her by surprise, bringing her back to the present. 'God you look sexy with your hair wet. It's been too long since we've done this.' The comment met with a warm embrace, and Sarah is taken in as usual by his charismatic ways.

'What are you doing sneaking around at this early hour?' She giggles like a teenager, while melting into his arms with ease. 'You're all hot and sweaty.' She adds in fake protest, reluctant to pull away from the comfort of his embrace.

'How else can I escape to be with you?' He replies, giving her one of his alluring smiles. As always she is putty in his hands, allowing him steer her into the old wooden barn situated halfway between the beach and the farmhouse. How many times have they slipped in here, gripped in immoral lust over the years? Sarah a prisoner to his charm, his touch.

'Tommy or me, Da could catch us you know.' She points out as he is undoing the buttons of her light summer dress, slipping it with ease down over her tanned shoulders. The surfboard she had been carrying, recklessly discarded outside leaving evidence of their presence to anyone who might pass by.

'That's what draws me to you Sarah,' he whispers nuzzling her neck, sending shivers down her spine. 'After all these years, you still manage to make me feel like a teenager.' Words making her smile inwardly, reminding her of the fact Jack had been conceived in this very barn. The heady euphoria of their lovemaking is suddenly whisked away, reminded, Jack no longer exists in this world. Had been cruelly taken from her along with who she once was. Losing a child in tragic circumstances leaves a bitter taste in your mouth, a sense of unjust and no one knows this better than Sarah.

'I should get back.' She roughly shoves him away, grabbing her clothes.

'What the hell?' He questions, disbelief etched on his tanned face. 'You can't build me up, then take off. I'm the one, who's taking a risk coming here. Had to take up running just to have an excuse to get out of the house, for Christ's sake.'

'Are you for real,' she retorts, annoyed by his thoughtless words cutting deeper into her already mangled heart. 'You really don't think do you? This is wrong, I have to go.' She flees from the barn picking up her surfboard, and in her haste does not notice someone is watching them, hidden by the side of the barn.

Nor does she hear car tyres crunch on the gravel outside, once inside the traditional homely farmhouse kitchen. Distracted by having been met by the sweet scent of freshly picked strawberries on entering, Sarah indulges in happier memories.

Closing her eyes allows her to picture her son Jack's cheeky smile. His face slathered in red juice, baby blue eyes inherited from his mother glistening mischievously aware he'd been caught. One hand remaining poised in the air, hovering, contemplating whisking another strawberry from one of the cartons neatly stacked on the table, ready to be brought over to the farm shop. Her lips curl into a bemused smile, heart filling with love for her darling little boy. Naturally, she would have scolded him pretending to be cross while struggling to keep a straight face. Forgetting herself, Sarah reaches out to brush back one of Jack's loose dark curls, wildly flopping down over his forehead. When her hand swoops through dead air reality kicks in reminding her, he is no longer alive. It is these beautiful memories which hurt the most, and time is no great healer.

◆◆◆

On the other side of Kilmer Cove, Agnes Shanahan is also in her kitchen, sitting at the table nursing a mug of coffee, which has long gone cold clutched in her hands. Also indulging in happier memories, she is gazing dreamily at a montage of photographs clustered on the wall depicting a perfect family life. Christenings, communions and graduations, amongst a mixture of casual pictures of her two sons' beaming happily for the camera.

Her husband Ger enters the room, a small heavy man wearing a permanent scowl on his rounded face, as though she isn't there he goes about his business. Slipping on a light jacket to take Roxy, their aged terrier for her early morning walk.

There was a time he would have walked Roxy in the evening, stopping at the Nook Bar for a pint of Guinness on his way home. A routine he had abandoned over five years ago, after an embarrassing refusal to be served by Kitty Kearney, the owner. Walking at this early hour means getting out and back, before the rest of Kilmer Cove have thrown back their duvets and switched off their alarms.

'Hey, girl.' He ruffles the terrier's ears, giving more affection to the scruffy little mongrel, than he has shown his wife in their thirty years of marriage. Clipping the lead onto the dog's collar, he opens the back door to be caught short by Agnes.

'Are you sure ya can't take even an hour off?' His wife pleads in vain, aware of what the answer will be before it comes.

'It's alright for you woman, ta think I'm being unfair but who keeps a roof over our heads eh?' Ger replies without meeting her expectant gaze. 'Sure, can't he get a bus like most other people have ta?' The subject is ended with a slam of the door in his wake. Agnes left with no other option than having to catch a bus to Donegal, then another, along with paying for a taxi to complete the latter part of the journey to Castlerea Prison. She checks her purse, contemplating having to forgo the leg of lamb planned for their dinner. Desmond's first night back home would not be the celebratory occasion she'd envisioned, forced to consider cooking something little less costly to facilitate the cost of her travel.

The journey itself takes over three hours, due to having to stand around waiting for the second bus and not being able to find a taxi straight away. Desmond is about to get into a car with his parole officer, when Agnes finally arrives outside the prison.

'Ma what are you doing here?' Des expresses delight in seeing her, by throwing his arms around her, giving a well-needed hug. 'Don't tell me you had to get a taxi all the way here, it'll have cost you an arm and a leg.'

'No love, I got the bus.' Agnes responds, discretely brushing away a stray tear. 'I couldn't have you coming out and no one here for you.'

'Thanks Ma, you know I appreciate all your support.' Des replies pulling her into a second hug to show his gratitude, his own eyes filling up.

'Mrs. S.' Gary greets Agnes with a warm handshake. He is a tall thin man in his early thirties, scruffily dressed in an un-ironed shirt and beige chinos. Agnes can only assume, this casual attire is to appear on the same level as the prisoners' he works with, as wearing a suit might alienate them. In truth, Gary is not the suit wearing kind, more unorganised seeing clothes as essential rather than a fashion statement. 'I should have rang ya and offered a lift. I'm so sorry. Didn't think, that's my problem you see. Come,' he waves a hand in the direction of the car, which has seen better days. 'I'll drop you both home. Des can pop into my office tomorrow, I hope to have some news by then about a job. We'll have you all back on track Mrs. S, no worries at all...Des will have his life again.'

◆◆◆

As Desmond opens the car door to allow his mother, slip into the passenger seat of Gary's old Volvo, Evelyn Priestly is thinking about him for the first time in five and a half years. She is sitting at a dressing table in the bedroom of the council house, she shares with her son Danny and boyfriend Brian.

Evelyn is carefully placing concealer around her temple, flinching where it is tender to touch. When the effect is not as she would like, she resorts to styling her long strawberry blonde hair differently in an attempt to cover the bruise which is still shining like a beacon, an ugly reminder of the earlier affliction she'd endured.

Happier with the result, she picks up her mobile to take a selfie. With a few adjustments to doctor the picture and the addition of a quirky caption, she posts it to her followers on Instagram. She doesn't know why, but sometimes it is nice to be someone else, the person she dreams of becoming. The life she nearly had, though not as rich and glamorous as her fake persona on social media.

To her eighteen thousand followers, she is Lynn Priestly fashion designer, living in a plush apartment in Dublin when she is home in Ireland, whilst also owning an apartment in Paris and a studio flat in London to accommodate her working schedule. Her fictional boyfriend Nick, a writer and director treats her like a princess, lavishing her with gifts and worshipping the ground she walks on. His caring personality eerily similar to Desmond.

Hearing the front door slam shut, Evelyn hastily shoves her phone in the top drawer under some clothes, an action she has carried out many a time before. The sound of his footsteps on the stairs causing her heart to pound in her chest, Evelyn closes her eyes in anticipation, as the bedroom door swings open.

'Why the fuck, didn't ya answer me. What are ya wearing?' He growls, referring to the pretty pink top she had pulled from the back of her drawer. One bought years ago, when there was ample money to indulge in retail therapy on a regular basis. One of a few decent tops she has left to use for her selfies. 'Why aren't you workin today?' Brian continues to throw questions without waiting for an answer. 'Fecking lazy bitch, am I the only wan bringin in a wage here?' A laughable statement since Brian doesn't work. Instead living off benefits, claiming disability for an ailment he doesn't have, not that Evelyn can make out anyway, though would not dare question the details of his supposed affliction for fear of the backlash she'd receive. On wobbly legs, she makes an attempt to leave the room. 'Have you been at my stuff?' Brian barks, searching through bottles and jars on the dressing table, managing to throw some of her precious makeup on the ground.

'No I haven't.' She snaps in return becoming tired of his recent bad humour getting her down.

'Don't you get lippy with me, I had some pills here by the bed in a little bag and they're gone.'

'You shouldn't go leaving pills lying around.' She replies with more courage than she is feeling, due to fear of their son accidently swallowing one or more of the lethal pills, Brian often has around the house. 'Danny could pick them up.'

'That little bollix better not be in here at my stuff, I'll tell ya....ah here they are.'

'Can you pick Danny up from school at two? I have to work a late shift today.'

'Get yer mother ta pick him up, I'm busy.' Brian retorts pushing passed her. Coming to a halt on the landing, he adds. 'Instead of sitting on yer arse, wouldn't ya want ta give this place a clean it's like a feckin pigsty. An ya wonder why, I get pissed off.' Without waiting for a reply he pounds his way back down the stairs, slamming the front door on the way out leaving Evelyn alone once more. Only now, she is sadly aware of reality and the life she lives, all fantasy banished from her mind. Sighing heavily, she glances around taking in the dirty finger marks on the walls and flaking paint on the skirting boards. Okay, so the house is a bit grubby, but she has long given up caring as any previous attempt at making the place homely is diminished by Brian bringing his friends in trampling around the place and messing it up again.

Deflated, she returns to the bedroom swapping her pale pink top for the ghastly mustard coloured uniform she must wear for her shift at Roaster's fast food.

Catching a glimpse of her appearance in the mirror, as she passes by. What would her Instagram followers think, if they saw how she really lives her life? Then again does anyone really care?

Half an hour later, Evelyn parks her car outside her mother's house, situated on the next street over it has the same layout as Evelyn's only beautifully decorated and spotlessly clean.

'Hey love, you look a bit peaky, yer not pregnant are ya?' Gillian asks, narrowing her eyes as she scrutinises her daughter's appearance.

'Why do you do that?' Evelyn responds crossly, desperately needing her mother to expunge the gloom she is feeling inside, not frighten the life out of her with a suggestion which would be the worst thing in the world to happen.

'What?' Gillian, practically an older version of her daughter appears genuinely surprised by Evelyn's rebuff.

'Always ask if I'm pregnant.' Evelyn walks into the kitchen switching on the kettle. Something she loves doing as it gives her a feeling of still living in the bosom of her family home.

'Ya look like shit recently that's why.' Gillian shakes her head, visibly concerned by her daughter's ghostly appearance. 'I thought it might be morning sickness.'

'I'd rather die.' Evelyn mumbles under her breath. 'Can you pick Danny up from school? I've to do a late shift.'

'Of course, you know I love having him.' Gillian's face immediately lights up at the prospect of having her grandson for the evening. 'I'll give him his tea, sur he may as well stay over an, I'll drop him to school in the morning. There's plenty clean clothes in his room upstairs. Don't suppose Brian will object.'

'That'd be great, thanks mam.' Evelyn purposely not commenting on whether she thinks Brian would mind. Positive, Gillian is aware he would only be delighted at not having to take care of his own son. Changing the subject, she adds. 'I ordered the cake for Danny's birthday party next week. Kelly Briggs is doing it, Lexi at work says she's really good. Did a Dinosaur for her Aaron's birthday and it looked fantastic, the real deal.'

'As long as it's edible...what have you ordered then?'

'A formula one racing car in red and white with a number five on the badge. He's really into watching it on the telly...like fascinated you know.' Evelyn's eyes, light up for the first time since her arrival indicating her excitement for it to be demolished by her mother's negative response.

'Have you considered Brian's reaction when he sees it? Cause if he picks it up the wrong way, you'll have ta ask Jenny to give ya a fringe next time she cuts your hair, if you get my meaning.' Gillian's reply, a cold reminder of the type of relationship Evelyn is in. Tears sting Evelyn's eyes, as she considers the truth in her mother's response, it's not that she intentionally tries to rile Brian, it happens without her realising. If only, she could have the sense to stop and think before acting, it would save a lot of heartache. 'Here.' Gillian wraps her arms around Evelyn in a gesture of support. 'I don't mean to snap love...it's...I worry about you and Danny....you deserve so much better.'

'I don't mam...not after what I have done.' Evelyn sniffs wiping away tears, she opens her bag taking out pressed powder to re-apply her makeup.

'What do you mean?'

'Nothing...I didn't...I'm tired, an bein silly, that's all.'

'Here sit down, an I'll make ya something to eat before work. Can't be living on that stuff in Roaster's all the time. It'd be detrimental to your skin, love.'

Feeling better after a plate of her mother's homemade Lasagne, Evelyn drudges through a very busy eight hour shift. Returning home later in the evening to be met by a cloud of cigarette smoke and a buzz of voices in the lounge, as she pushes open the front door.

All she wants is to put her feet up and watch television for a while, having sent a text to her mother before leaving work to receive a reply saying, Danny is already in bed fast asleep. In recent times, she's been wondering if Danny would be better off staying with Gillian, knowing he would be cared for properly. Giving her a chance to go and get a decent job, save up and possibly get an education, to eventually offer Danny a better life than the one they have now. She would miss him too much if apart, Danny being her only reason for getting up on bad days.

Through the cloudy haze, she can make out Brian laid out on an armchair, his leg thrown across its arm. His best friend Jimmy is flaked on Danny's bean bag, with Jackson sprawled on the couch next to his current girlfriend Collette and another girl, Evelyn doesn't know.

'Evie, babe...come in chill.' Brian beckons her, knowing she hates being called this. She ignores his advances, used to him acting like the perfect boyfriend when his friends are over, either that or whatever he is smoking mellowing his mood.

'Hi Evelyn, how's it goin?' Jimmy says wearing one of his customary goofy grins

'Grand Jimmy.' She replies, before turning to leave the room. He is not the worst, not like Jackson and his ever-changing entourage of female friends making her house, a constant drop in.

In the kitchen she flicks the switch on the kettle, not having the same effect as it does in her mother's home. Brian slinks into the room behind her snaking his arms around her thin waist.

'Hey babe.' He whispers nuzzling her neck. 'Where's your car, who dropped you home?'

'My car wouldn't start so I got a lift with Lexi.' She replies heart sinking at the thought of upsetting him, expecting a negative reaction in return. Instead, he surprises her by swinging her round to face him.

'How about, I send Jimmy to take a look at your car. Then we'd be alone and can head upstairs. Sur, hasn't your Ma got Danny for the night.' He kisses her cheek, then her forehead.

'Ouch.' She flinches quickly pulling away. 'Brian, it's barely nine in the evening. Besides, there's more than Jimmy in there.' She nods in the direction of the other room.

'I'm sorry babe, it won't happen again…You know I don't mean it.' His voice is laced with remorse. 'I love you, you mean everything to me, Evie.' He pulls her close, planting soft kisses on her neck. 'I'll get rid of 'em all, then it'll be just you an me.' It's all it takes for her to believe him and melt into his arms.

Chapter 2

Sarah kicks off her shoes, feet aching from being on them all day. With her father not home yet, it gives her time to switch on the laptop and check her emails. A habit, she has fallen into of an evening wanting to check if Roz the other administrator of, "The Justice for Road victims' group," has posted anything new on their, website or Facebook page. They first met when Roz had contacted Sarah three years previously, having watched her on the news talking to a reporter about the injustice of Desmond's sentencing. It was the beginning of a friendship through shared grief and understanding. A bond, Sarah could never share with her friend, Maggie or even her sister-in-law, Lily. Two women, brought together through the loss of their children and a deep understanding of each other's grief. With nothing new of interest to read, she closes the laptop rising to fill the kettle deciding what to cook for their tea.

From the window, she catches a glimpse of her father walking slowly across the yard towards the house. Shoulders slumped, slowly dragging one foot in front of the other. The sight causing her catch her breath, barely recognising him; this ageing man who has been both a father and mother. His strength and devotion in bringing up his children singlehanded incomparable. The earlier gloom which had unnerved her, sitting unnaturally across her shoulders once again.

'Bloody fence is broken in the top field.' Patrick Connolly complains, kicking off his muddy wellies inside the back door. 'Tommy is not best pleased, I tell you. We've been trying to patch it up an, I'm bloody starving. He'll have to go into town and get new wood.' Sarah could only imagine her brother Tommy's, annoyance over an expenditure they could ill afford.

'I'd wondered where you'd got to, though I'm only in myself we had a last minute rush. Just as, Lily and I were about to close a coachload of hungry tourists pulled up, their driver had taken a wrong turn. They were meant to be visiting Fanad Head lighthouse, and ended up at Kilmer Cove lighthouse. The hotel they are booked into tonight is in Letterkenny, sur they'd have missed their evening meal by the time they drove all the way there, we had to help them out. Mind, they were delighted and said they'd give us good reviews on the website. One woman declared it was the best food she'd had in a long time.' Sarah says, referring to the business she has built up with her sister-in-law, Lily. At one time a small farm shop selling home-grown produce and fresh home baked goods to boost the farms income, now a thriving shop and café due to its idyll position on the Wild Atlantic Way. 'I'll have to make do with cooking you a fry, anything else will take too long.' Sarah informs him, lines forming on her brow as she eyes Paddy skeptically, his pallor is paler than normal. 'Where would Tommy get wood at this hour, anyway?' All the hardware shops will be long closed.' She adds fetching a frying pan, trying to shake off her worry over Paddy.

'Ah...Tommy rang, Eamon Molloy and made arrangements to call to the house, went tearing off there now with a vengeance.'

'Do you think, the damage is caused by fishermen cutting through to get to the cove?' Sarah enquires, catching sight of the mud he'd brought in all over the clean flagstone floor.

'Nah, it's those fellows coming from town, coursing or lamping, or whatever the hell they call it. Ted O'Neil told me, he lost a couple of his calves over the cliff last week, cause they opened one of his gates and never closed it again. Don't get me started on their bloody dogs frightening animals, foxes are less of a threat. We'd want to get Maggie, to look into catchin 'em, we can't afford for it to keep happening.'

'Easier said than done, somehow I don't think the Garda would be happy to sit out in a ditch all night, for the sake of our livestock or otherwise.' Sarah replies, searching through the fridge for some sausages to cook.

'Ah, I'd sit out there meself and stick a shot up their arses. Bloody townies coming out from Carraigbrin, I'd say, no respect for other people's property.' Paddy shakes his head in dismay. Sarah catches glimpse of his stiff appearance through the corner of her eye, as he shuffles across the kitchen to sit at the big oak table dominating the centre of the room.

'It'll be more than a shot up the arse they'll get, if Tommy gets hold of em.' Lily says joining them, nearly tripping over the discarded wellies on her way in. 'He's not even had his tea, gone tearing into Carraigbrin to Eamon Molloy to see if he can get a couple of stakes and slats of wood. A cost we could do without again.' Lily reiterates, Paddy's earlier comments showing her own anguish over the situation.

'Aye, I'd like to catch the beggars who broke it, I tell you.' Paddy adds. Sarah throws her eyes to heaven, concerned by her father carrying out too much physical work at his age. The sooner, she and Lily expand their existing business and increase the farms finances the better, then Paddy wouldn't have to be doing any heavy work around the place, she surmises without voicing her concern.

'Have you time for a cuppa?' Sarah absently asks Lily, while reading an incoming text on her mobile. 'I'm making a pot anyway.' She adds, deleting the message before anyone notices.

'No, I'm in a rush have to drop Rachel into Carraigbrin, she's meeting a friend. They're going to some new nightclub...ah, I can't think what she called it. Anyway, she wasn't ready when Tommy left and of course he was not in the mood to wait. I'm only dropping in this bread and some of, Lena's delicious Sernik. I'm surprised we had any left, was tempted myself but it'd go straight to my bloody hips and I'll never get into that new dress for Lauren's graduation.' Lily quips, referring to her two young adult daughters, the apples of her eye.

'Clubbing on a Monday night?' Sarah questions, intrigued but Lily doesn't get a chance to reply.

'What's this Ser...what's it called?' Paddy asks cutting in.

'Lena, calls it Sernik, Da, a recipe from her home country. It's a baked cheesecake with chocolate glazing and vanilla essence, delicious but not good for the waistline.' Sarah shouts, battling against the background sound of the television, he has just switched on.

'Huh, not something I'd be worried about.' He bellows back in reply. Lily throws, Sarah a knowing wink and smile, Sarah responds by shaking her head in dismay. Paddy being a man of routine always turning on the television early, waiting to hear the ten o'clock news, no matter what.

'I'll see ye later so.' Lily says as she disappears out the door, quicker than she had appeared. Sarah places a plate of sausages, beans and fried egg, along with a plate of bread generously spread with butter and a mug of tea on the table.

'Are ya not eating yourself?'

'Not at this hour, it'd sit in me stomach all night an I'd never sleep.' Sarah replies, placing a generous slice of Lena's cheesecake on a plate for him.

'By god, that is lovely.' Paddy licks his lips as he glances up catching his daughter staring out of the kitchen window, eyes glazed, gone far beyond the yard outside. 'Are ya alright, love?' He asks, worry etched on his aged face. The lines on either side of his eyes from the laughter his children and grandchildren have brought. Deep ones, carved on his forehead from concern over the past five and a half years. Having watched his daughter, fall into a very dark place after Jack's death, a time that had been very difficult to get through for all the family.

'I'm fine Dad, little weary today that's all.' She refrains from saying, something is making her feel particularly uneasy it would be of no benefit to worry him unnecessarily.

'Sarah, you're a grown woman and I can't tell you how to live your life, but...well, I saw Himself making his way up to the barn this morning.' Paddy studies her, visibly anxious for his once bubbly daughter.

'I'm fine Dad,' she reiterates trying not to sound impatient. 'Do you want another piece of that cheesecake it won't keep?' Changing the subject knowing, she should have better disguised her unrest as it would worry, Paddy and rightfully so.

'Might as well.' He takes the bait with ease reaching for the newspaper, he'd not managed to finish reading earlier in the day. 'Says here, they are bringing in new laws regarding roadside drug testing?'

'Well let's hope, the Garda implement it.'

'I'm sure Maggie will, she's a tough gal and competent at her job. Wouldn't let anyone away with much.' Paddy adds in a matter-of-fact tone, studying the article in the paper. Sarah deliberately turns her back to him, busying herself filling the dishwasher while hiding a silent tear which has finally escaped down her cheek. Discretely wiping it away with the back of her hand resenting the fact, she is having one of those hard to keep up the pretence days.

'I forgot to give, Lily a list I'd made up for the cash and carry.' Sarah says absently. 'Mind you she won't be going til the morning, I should catch her before then.' Paddy glances up from the paper eyeing her suspiciously. Before he gets a chance to speak his mind, they are joined by another visitor. Garda Maggie O'Driscoll bursts through the back door, as though the place is on fire.

'I'm glad to have caught you both together, I was worried you'd be already gone out, Sarah.' Maggie's freckled face an unusually ashen in colour. Sarah crinkles her brow over Maggie's comment, wondering where on earth she would expect her to be gone to at this late hour but Maggie's uncomfortable demeanour prevents Sarah from asking.

'Ah come in, Maggie tis always good to see the friendly face of the law.' Paddy's voice, light and welcoming as always when anyone visits the farmhouse. 'Is it a social call, have you time for an aul cup of tea?' The fact, she is wearing Garda uniform of little significance, 'or has Tommy been on to you about the fence?' Paddy's question receiving a quizzical look in return. Maggie gingerly moves further into the room green eyes darting between, father and daughter. The intensity she has brought into the house in her wake revealing, she has something on her mind and it isn't damaged fences. The fear that has sat like a stone in the pit of Sarah's stomach all day beginning to rise.

'No thanks, Paddy unfortunately this is not a social call.' Maggie announces in a stoic tone. 'I have some news which I'd rather not be giving, but with the power of social media these days and some mouths in Kilmer Cove, faster than the power of tweeting, I thought you should hear this from me.' Maggie's words a source of bemusement as no one enjoys gossip more than Maggie, as for tweeting she is right up there with the, president of the United States. 'God, I wish there was an easy way of saying this.' Maggie's hesitation and unusual behaviour, setting alarm bells off in Sarah's head. A bitter reminder of the morning Maggie had arrived in a panic with the news Jack had been involved in an accident. Maggie's face had been ghostly pale, it had taken all her strength to utter the words which shattered Sarah's world completely. Whatever Maggie needed to say, Sarah wished she would just get on with it.

'Maggie what the hell are you trying to tell us?' Sarah almost screeches, bile rising in her mouth.

'I couldn't believe it myself when I heard...thought it was a sick joke to be honest. Driving over here, I worried about how I'd break it to you and unfortunately there is no easy way of putting it.' Maggie rattles on barely taking a breath.

'Jesus, girl spit it out.' Paddy gasps in a barely audible tone. His paling face becoming a mask of anguish, indicating something is wrong apart from Maggie's abnormal babbling.

'Desmond Shanahan is to be released early from his sentence on parole....' There is more to this statement, her dithering clearly indicating this fact.

'When?' Paddy asks the question Sarah cannot bring herself to. The awaited answer lies heavy in the air, as though a thick fog has descended. Leaving Sarah with a feeling of being suffocated as though the room is crashing in around her. Finally, Maggie conveys what is far worse than Sarah's imagination had allowed. Tiny beads of perspiration form on Paddy's forehead, his gaze firmly fixed on Maggie, while feeling around in the pocket of his old tweed jacket for a handkerchief.

'He was released earlier today.' The words gush from her quivering lips and bounce off the four walls, echoing back round. Then everything in the room comes to an eerie standstill, Sarah is trying to digest Maggie's words, yet they are not completely sinking in. 'I...am...so sorry, Sarah we only got told literally half an hour ago when I arrived in for my shift. I couldn't believe it, even Sergeant Collins said, he got no prior warning until the paperwork arrived in on his desk. Shanahan has to sign in at the station once a week for the next three months.' Maggie informs them. 'I can only apologise for the crap justice system we are part of. I'll make sure to be around for him coming in to sign, I can tell you. I'll be watching his every move an looking for the slightest excuse, to put that lout back behind bars.'

'But....he shouldn't be allowed to....I...it's not fair Maggie. In retrospect it means, he didn't even serve his shitty sentence and now he is free to get his life back. Jack can't have his life back, he is lying in a grave and I am the one serving the life sentence. Where is the justice do they not care about my son?' Sarah says searching Maggie's face for some sort of confirmation she'd heard wrong, that there has been a terrible mistake. When Maggie's dark green eyes stare back filled only with empathy, Sarah snaps finally engaging the extent of what is happening. The thought of Desmond being home and in close proximity, for her the nightmare is beginning all over again. 'He murdered a child, my child, something like that never goes away. Just because he has been in prison....he needn't think....Jesus, I can't believe this is happening. Ya have to question is there a god when he lets this happen.' Anger surging through every vein in her body. Jack had been sixteen years old, out running at half-six in the morning when, Desmond Shanahan's car mounted the pavement at over seventy kilometres, in a thirty zone. Jack receiving no warning, no chance to jump out of the way, Sarah can only imagine how terrifying it must have been. He died an hour later in hospital from the horrific injuries he received. Sarah tries not to think of all the milestones Jack has been robbed of and she has been denied over the past five and a half years. His graduation and the probability he would have competed in the Rio Olympics last August, his twenty-first birthday earlier this year.

'Sarah, love.' Paddy pleads, eyes filling with unshed tears. Seeing her father's distress only adding to Sarah's resentment of Desmond Shanahan. His anguish embellished face having become waxen looking. 'Though...I cannot believe... they have... allowed him... to be released early.' He adds, taking short breaths in between words. 'Considering.... the lenient sentence.... he received in the first place.' It had been a particularly difficult time for the family, coping with their loss while waiting for a trial date, until finally nearly a year after burying Jack, a date was set. Then sitting through the case having to relive the final moments of Jack's life once more. The details of the injuries he had sustained, while learning Desmond had been intoxicated when he got behind the wheel of his car. The Judge felt Desmond was remorseful for his actions and sentenced him to five years in prison for, Dangerous Driving causing Death along with a ten year driving ban. There had been no apology, no evidence of remorse on his sullen thin face for the life he had taken.

'I couldn't agree with you more Paddy.' Maggie says, voicing her bewilderment regarding the judicial system. 'Unfortunately I'm at a loss myself, we can only catch the criminals and charge them, after that as you know things are out of our hands.'

'He has barely served what....not even four years for taking a person's life, it doesn't make sense. I'd like to bloody meet the person who decided Desmond should be freed. How would they like it if it was their child?' Sarah spits venomously, anger reaching boiling point. Losing a child under tragic circumstances changes a person, without realising it you become a different person to the one you were before. Hard and unfeeling, viewing the world with a detached persona. When Sarah sees her own reflection in a mirror, she barely recognises the woman she's become. There are times she does not like what she sees, the emptiness behind her eyes and a cold stern expression with nothing left but a cold empty void, and a desperation for vengeance. 'I won't let this lie.' She whispers under her breath, all colour draining from her face, as she is unable to digest the fact Desmond Shanahan is free to live a normal life, to walk the streets her son had once walked. Nothing is more unbearable than knowing, he is be celebrating freedom while her son is lying in Kilmer Cove cemetery.

'Sarah, I don't know what to say without it sounding patronising. He should never have been given such a lenient sentence in the first place.' Maggie's face revealing more than words as to the extent of her remorse. Having been close friends from the moment Maggie moved to Kilmer Cove, after marrying her husband Finn. Their immediate bond, due to both women being pregnant and their babies being born eight weeks apart. 'Sit down, I'll make us all a cup of tea.' Maggie soothes. 'I promise you Sarah, I'll make sure an be there when Desmond comes into the station and if he steps sideways, if there is the slightest hint he has violated the conditions of his parole....' Maggie continues with promises to make Desmond aware, he is not as free as he might think. Sarah turns to gaze out of the window, eyes glazing over, mind drifting, anger draining from her body until there is nothing but an excruciating numbness. Maggie carries on speaking whilst pouring boiling water into a teapot. It falls from her hands, smashing on the flagstone floor. 'Paddy....Sarah call an ambulance....Sarah.' Maggie shouts out in an unusually high pitched tone.

Paddy slips from the chair onto the floor clutching his chest, Sarah thrusts the mobile at Maggie to rush to her father's side.

Everything seems to happen fast, Dr. O'Brien the local G.P and the ambulance from Carraigbrin arrive within minutes of each other attending to Paddy.

'It's his heart.' The aged G.P informs her in the usual soft singsong voice used over the years to sound amiable towards the young and comforting to the old. 'I'll go with him in the ambulance.' The urgency to get Paddy to the hospital, a clear indication of the seriousness of his condition.

'Come on, we'll follow behind, I'll put the siren on.' Maggie says, grabbing Sarah's arm and guiding her to the patrol car parked outside. Sarah unable to fully grasp the magnitude of what is happening, simply allows her. Sitting rigidly, staring at the rear of the ambulance travelling in front of them, as they drive out of the yard.

Lights flashing, sirens blaring, they pick up speed sweeping along the small main street of Kilmer Cove which overlooks the Atlantic Ocean, a view Sarah or any of the locals could never grow tired of, being steeped in natural beauty giving the town a unique outlook. She should phone Tommy and Lily, Sarah realises searching in her pockets for her mobile.

'Shit.'

'What's up?'

'I've left my phone in the kitchen, I should ring Tommy and Lily, maybe even Martin.'

'Here...I still have it, must of shoved it in my pocket unthinking with all the commotion.' Maggie hands over the mobile. Sarah tries her bother Tommy first getting no answer, Lily's phone goes straight to mailbox as does her brother

Martin's. 'It's probably best not to worry them until we know for sure. I can try them again for you once we are at the hospital.'

'Thanks Mags.' Sarah turns to look out of the passenger window, houses give way to the sculpted coastline which passes in a blur. Clenching her hands together until the knuckles turn white, nails digging into her skin. As though enduring physical pain could quash any emotional pain. She asks the question, which is bubbling in her mind as they speed along the scenic coast road. 'Do you think he'll...?' She hesitates, not want to hear a negative response.

'Don't.' Maggie replies. 'Your Da will be fine.'

In what feels like forever, within twenty minutes they arrive in A&E where, Paddy is immediately rushed through. Maggie wraps a comforting arm around Sarah's shoulder leading her into a small but private waiting room. A routine they have performed before, prompting Sarah to recognise her surroundings as soon as they sit on one of the, plastic Formica chairs. Magnolia walls with one small frosted-glass window, so high up it makes no difference to the suffocation the room depicts. A stand on the far side of the room holding the same, leaflets as the last time she had sat there, unprotected sex and STD's, unexpected pregnancy and where to get advice because you are not alone. She wanted Jack, had loved her son with all her heart even when she realised his father would not be part of their life, she embraced bringing her baby up alone. Now, she feels desperately alone each day hurting without Jack's presence, she couldn't bear to lose her father too. That's when it hits her, the horrible feeling of déjà vu and the need to throw up. Instead, Sarah swallows back rising bile, the air thinning around her and for a moment she imagines the walls are closing in on her. Trapped in a nightmare, which cannot be stopped from playing out.

'Here, I know you don't like sugar but maybe you should drink this anyway.' Maggie says, thrusting a polystyrene cup of hot tea into her hand. Sarah glances at her friend as if seeing her for the first time. 'I rang Tommy's mobile but only got a recorded message, so I rang Lily. I didn't know whether you'd want me to try, Martin again until we know more?'

'No...no, you're right...there's no need to go worrying everyone unnecessarily.' Sarah replies, trying to assure herself as much as, Maggie.

'What about Conor...would you like him here?'

'Conor...no there's no need for him to be here.'

'If you're sure...anyway you need people around you so, I called the station to let them know. I'm good to stay as long as you need.' Maggie places her hand on Sarah's giving it a tight squeeze.

'What would I do without you?' Sarah asks, managing a weak smile of gratitude.

'You'd survive, you're tougher than you think and so is your Da, so don't go worrying he'll be fine.' Maggie replies, but Sarah is not convinced and she has every right to be. Moments later, Dr. O'Brien opens the door, all his years as a family practitioner in a small town meaning becoming unethically emotionally attached to his patients, making it hard for him to detach in situations like this. It is the sympathetic look in his eyes giving him away, Sarah knows before he speaks as their family G.P, he has volunteered to be the one to break the news. The solemn expression on his face revealing words he has not yet managed to utter. This coupled with the woman standing behind him, whom Sarah recognises instantly as, Angela Downing the hospital grievance councillor. It's not that she dislikes the woman more her status in the hospital, making her the last person you want to see. Tommy and Lily arrive at the hospital as Dr. O'Brien is escorting Sarah down the corridor, to say a final goodbye to their beloved father. Gauging them coming towards her opens a floodgate of grief, Sarah witnessing her brother a big strong proud man, crumble and cry like a child. It crosses Sarah's mind, Desmond Shanahan has come back into their lives once again causing pain and devastation. It has been why she's been feeling anxious, her life spiralling out of control once again by a man, she would rather see lying on a slab than her father.

Chapter 3

Sarah is not alone in her desire for Desmond to be far from Kilmer Cove, Des is feeling far more incarcerated in his parents' house, than he had been in Castlerea Prison, as he lies on his childhood single bed staring up at the ceiling with a cold realisation the life he had before prison is long gone.

Nothing has been changed in this room or the rest of the house for that matter, since he'd lived here before. Having remained the same as the day he moved to Donegal, nearly ten years previously to start his apprenticeship aged seventeen. Model aeroplanes he had made in school, still hanging from the ceiling covered with a film of dust making a perfect platform for spiders to spin their webs from. Along one wall a collection of posters intermittently disguise the drab blue striped wallpaper, displaying pictures of his dream cars, the Impreza WRX and Toyota Supra. From a young age, he'd been fascinated with cars and how they worked. From classics to supercars, Desmond's mind an encyclopedia of information on any make or model. His heart plummeting from the knowledge, it would be a long time before he would sit behind the wheel of any car. The soft hum of the engine and smell of leather upholstery, his pride and joy a WRX in world rally blue pearl had been scrapped by the insurance company after the accident.

Trying to erase painful memories, he pulls himself up walking over to the window where he gazes out at the quiet street watching a cat saunter across the road, its eyes shining in the dim orangey glow of the street light. Desmond tilts his head to take a closer look at a little Corsa, parked directly across the road from the house. The Corsa isn't new, even if he couldn't see the registration he would have worked out that it is nearly ten years old, a skill he proudly picked up over the years. Knowing a car's make by the shape or lights, though newer cars all look blandly similar.

'Des.' His mother's voice gently calls from the hallway, followed with a timid knock on the bedroom door. He pulls back from the window quickly closing the curtain before she enters, in his haste almost tripping over the knapsack he had thrown there earlier, lying waiting to be unpacked. 'I'm making some tea.' Agnes says. 'I thought you might like a sandwich, you didn't eat much earlier.'

'I'm grand, Ma thanks.' Des replies noticing fine lines on her face, eyes dull and lifeless. She appears to have aged severely since his incarceration and it saddens him to think, he could be somewhat to blame. Though in the back of his mind he holds his father and brother partly responsible too, both having been far from supportive to either himself or Agnes.

'If you're sure.' She hesitates, 'its...well, dad's popped out for a bit to take Roxy for a walk. It would be nice to sit and have a chat while we are alone.' How could he refuse, his mother has been the only person to stick by his side, to believe his version of what had happened.

'Okay Ma, you put the kettle on and I'll join you in a second, maybe have a bit of your homemade fruit cake.' Des throws her a wink, knowing this would please her. It does, Agnes's face brightens considerably worried prison might have changed her son, made him hard and cold.

'What time are you meeting with Gary in the morning?' Agnes asks, as they sit in the small but cosy kitchen nursing mugs of tea. Desmond first met his parole officer, Gary Swift three months before his release, instantly warming to his laid back attitude during their sessions as they prepared for this day. Inside, everyone had been on an even tally, had broken the law and were paying the price mainly wanting to keep their noses clean until release. The prison guards weren't the friendliest, but it was to be expected. Desmond quickly learned not to be perturbed by the aggressive way they dealt with the prisoners. Keeping his head down had been his main objective. It was Gary, who suggested Desmond live with his parents for the period of his parole, giving him a better chance of being granted early release.

'Eleven, I'll need to get the nine twenty bus but I have to sign in at the Garda Station first.' He replies, feeling the strain of conversation, Agnes trying too hard to please and Desmond unsure of what to say or how to act. The awkwardness increased by the fear of, Ger walking through the door at any moment wearing the same disapproving scowl, he had worn on returning from work earlier.

'He seems a nice chap Gary, not a bit what I expected, I suppose.' Agnes offers in way of conversation. 'Very kind of him to have given us a lift and suggest helping getting fixed up with a job, don't you think. Did Charlie visit you in prison?' She takes a sip of her tea, eyes never leaving Desmond.

'No, you were my only visitor.' Des replies, playing with a teaspoon. 'I wouldn't have expected Charlie to come to be honest. I'll give him a shout tomorrow when I'm in the town, let him know I'm available to work again. I'm sure it will be fine, he was happy for me to work until...anyway there'll be no need for Gary to find me something....You know it's only for three months Ma, I'll move on as soon as my probation period is up.' Seeing the hurt expression on her face, Desmond immediately regrets his words, it had been the wrong thing to say.

'Dessie, I have no problem with you being here, it's a relief to have you home safe love. It will be good to have a bit of life in the house again...don't shut me out, it's all I ask. Dad...well he doesn't mean to be so distant it's his way, you understand that don't you? As for your brother Phillip...well...he's like your father proud and stubborn. You were different, sensitive and kind hearted and I'd hate to think...' Agnes wipes away a stray tear. 'I'm being silly.' She quickly stands up. Desmond is about to hug her until they are interrupted by Ger, bursting in the back door like a tornado.

'A man has no sanctity, not even in his own home.' Ger bristles, unclipping Roxy's lead with a sharp tug, the little dog whimpers before quickly scarpering to her bed by the warm stove, where she precedes to nuzzle under a fleece blanket placing a white fluffy paw over her nose. Desmond smirks, even Roxy knows when the old man starts it is safer to keep out of his line of fire. Face as red as a beetroot, Ger proceeds to remove his flimsy blue jacket, hanging it on a hook by the door. 'There is only so much a person can put up with.' He continues, while glaring at Desmond. A silent stand down ensues between the two men, in retrospect there would be no satisfaction in rising to the older man, it would be easier to follow Roxy's way of dealing with the situation. In light of this, Des stands up without finishing his tea, averting his gaze from a forlorn looking Agnes. The bedroom may be gloomy and isolated but it is better to be alone than in his father's company. 'That's it, walk away. We are the ones who have had to put up with being shunned in our home town for the past five years.' Ger taunts accusingly.

'Gerald, please you promised,' Agnes pleads. 'Desmond was hardly holidaying, he has paid severely for what happened.' Agnes's voice is strained, eyes darting between her husband and son.

'Do you want to be the one to go out there and tell Sarah Connolly?' He points in the direction of the door, nostrils flared indicating the level of his fury. 'Eh...Cause she is parked outside our house like some mad woman. Not a day goes by when I am not reminded of the devastation he has brought about....How on god's earth, I ended up with such a failure for a son is beyond me.' Ger has gone too far, said what has always been there niggling yet previously unsaid. It is of no surprise to Desmond this is how his father views him, sadly the revelation doesn't hurt, not anymore, not since he declined to support Des by refusing to attend the court case.

'Des.' Agnes calls as he leaves the room. He cannot bear to turn around and see the hurt expression on her face. Instead, he climbs the stairs returning to the sanctity of his bedroom, whereupon closing the door firmly presses his back against it, wanting to shut out the world. To shut out the muffled sound of his parents arguing in the kitchen below bringing back childhood memories, he had long buried in the recess of his mind. The only difference as the years have passed, Agnes has learned to stand her ground and give as good as she gets. Her assertiveness of no use, Ger would never back down, he isn't that type of man.

When he braves checking, the car has gone from outside. Knowing, the person sitting outside the house had been Sarah Connolly, unnerving him a little. She had sat in the courtroom eyeing him with contempt, while he endured answering the questions thrown at him on the stand. He would have never deliberately driven recklessly, but she just couldn't see it. Turning away from the window he undresses slipping under the duvet but sleep evades him.

Eventually, the morning sun breaks through a gap in the curtains where they have not been closed properly, bringing a sharp reminder of the previous night's events. Des waits in his room until hearing the back door slam giving a clear indication, his father has left for work. Des slips downstairs to find the kitchen is empty apart from Roxy, who is eyeing him with interest from the comfort of her bed. He should call out to Agnes, check if she is okay, instead Des quietly slips out the door into the bright sunlight.

A sharp wind whips in off the sea, bringing with it a strong smell of salty seaweed as he briskly walks the short distance to the Garda station, arriving at five to nine. Of course, it is too much to hope she would not be there, expression stern, colder and harder than any of the prison guards, her hair pulled into a neat bun, green eyes piercing him, narrowed into slits, bringing back vivid memories of the morning *She* arrested him.

'You're early,' she says, before Des has a chance to speak. It becomes clear she has purposefully made sure to be here. Desmond, remembering being forcefully questioned after the accident, she had been cold and harsh back then, and obviously hasn't defrosted in the interim. He is aware, she is a close friend of Sarah Connolly. 'I'll go find your paperwork.' Her tone harsh and abrupt. Twenty minutes later she returns, floating back into the reception area as though time is of no importance. Agitated, Desmond will not give her the satisfaction of retaliating. He simply smiles. 'Right, sign here.' She will be here every Tuesday waiting, of that he is sure, watching for him to make the slightest slip up. It will be a battle of wills for the next three months, a challenge he is open to. She will not break him no matter how hard she tries.

It takes a sprint to the bus stop, where he barely makes it in time before the bus pulls away, Desmond silently cursing the red headed Garda under his breath. As he slips into a seat, relieved to be getting away from the suffocation the small town depicts, his mobile buzzes, a text from Gary. The parole officer is deeply sorry, his wife's car wouldn't start. He will be an hour late for their meeting, as he has to drop the children to school.

With over an hour to wait on arriving in Donegal, Desmond seizes the opportunity to visit his old boss, heading in the direction of Charlie's Classic Autos with a bounce in his step. Walking into the garage is a true coming home for Des, everything familiar, everything he has missed. A gleaming, 1989 20v Audi Quattro in tornado red catches his eye. Des gently runs his hand over the front wing as though he is caressing a woman, admiring her classic beauty and treating her with the respect she deserves. The 2226cc engine capable of reaching a top speed of 140 mph, can get from nought to sixty in less than six and a half seconds, with its 220bhp, twin three-way catalytic converter. Desmond can imagine cruising on a motorway, hands clasped around the leather steering wheel, body comfortably cushioned into the seat. Of all the Quattro's, this rare beauty the quickest to drive over the older models. More trustworthy than any woman, this machine would not let him down.

'Des!' Charlie appears, whipping Des back to reality with a jolt.

'Hey Charlie, good to see you pal.' Desmond's face lights up with a genuine smile for the first time since his release. Charlie had been a great guy to work for, taught Desmond all there is to know about cars. He had started as an apprentice when he left school at seventeen, learning how to take an engine apart and put it back together, until he could do it in his sleep. Once familiar with the inside of a car, he moved onto the bodywork. For over four years he had been under Charlie's guise, holding unmeasurable respect for the man.

'I didn't know you were...out.' Charlie's voice revealing his amazement, while deflecting from the eager gaze of the younger man. He picks up a dirty towel to wipe his hands containing more oil on it than on his hands, Des doesn't seem to notice Charlie's discomfort.

'They allowed me out early for good behaviour.' Des beams proudly. 'I did a couple of courses while I was inside, kept my head down...you know.'

'That's great, I'm pleased for you.' Charlie scratches his head, shifting uncomfortably from one foot to the other. Desmond is not perturbed by Charlie's aloof manner, jumping in a little too eagerly.

'I am hoping, I might be able to get my old job back.' The question, shoots bluntly from his lips, possibly sounding a little naive. Charlie may have been a good and fair employer, but he is also a business man with a reputation he is keen to keep as polished, as the condition of the cars he delivers back to customers. Still taken in by the Audi and oblivious to Charlie's discomfort, Des rattles on. 'It feels so good walking in here and this little beaut, is she yours? A rare treasure she is immaculate, I would only love to feel the power under her bonnet.' He whistles, caressing the paintwork again. Enthusiasm dying as he finally grasps his ex-bosses glum expression, recognising it as the same look Charlie would use, when a customer wanted a car done which is beyond restoration. Its panels and chassis so rusty, you could stick your fingers through them and they'd crumble.

'Jesus no, she's belong to a client.' Charlie blusters, visibly relieved to discuss the car rather than the prospect of employing Des again. 'Worth at least one hundred K...I could only dream of owning it.' Charlie's tone is flat, as though the air has been left out of his tyres. Left with no choice, he braces the inevitable. 'Look Des,' he explains. 'I would love to have you back, you were a first class panel beater and hard worker, but business is quiet mate. I've barely enough work for myself at the moment...Are you driving again, did they quash your ban as well?'

'No...the judge gave ten years. He told me it stands from when I was sentenced, so I've still five and a half left.'

'I'm sorry mate that makes it awkward in this profession. You wouldn't be able to collect or deliver cars for me. Anyway, like I said, things are quiet. Government incentives and car dealers offering finance deals, means most people are buying new cars. You were well aware, it was the other jobs which kept us ticking by before and not just the restorations, it's the downfall of this business.'

'You of all people, I expect to be honest.' Desmond respond's as he looks Charlie straight in the eye.

'I am being honest.' Charlie frowns, abruptly walking away to indicate the conversation is over. He pauses, turning his head to look back at a disillusioned Des. 'Though I have to say man, I can't get my head round you being high on drugs and driving.' Charlie shakes his head in dismay, walking to the back of the garage.

'Neither can I.' Des calls after him, making Charlie stop in his tracks, though he does not turn to face him. Des speaks to his back. 'I swear, I've never taken anything in my life, not even a painkiller. That whole episode doesn't make sense to me. Why, I was even in Kilmer Cove at that time of the morning. As for the drugs in my system, the whole thing is one big blur. It was an accident, I'd never hurt anyone.' It is the first time since the trial he defends his actions. Wondering if this is how life will be from now on, having to explain. Guessing nine times out of ten, the other person won't believe him. Judging by Charlie's expression as he finally turns to face him again, he is still on the fence.

'Look, if things pick up I'll give you a call.' Charlie offers by way of a slight reprieve.

'Sure.' Des walks away, aware Charlie is being polite. There will be no call, no chance of ever working in Charlie's Auto's ever again.

By the time Desmond reaches Gary's pokey little office, on the fourth floor of an old building with peeling grey paint, he has become very despondent. Thought's beginning to crowd his head, at the age of twenty-six does he no longer have a future to look forward to? People judging him over an accident, he had no control over, if he allowed it, it would drive him mad. For weeks after, every time he closed his eyes at night, he saw Jack Connolly's face. Pale blue eyes wide with fear or shock, possibly both, tufts of his dark hair caught in the radiator of the car. Des gives a little knock on the door before going in, the floor to ceiling window behind Gary's desk which faces a grey wall, is the only positive feature in the room. On the desk sits a desktop computer and stack of files, along with an assortment of pens and paperclips. The only other furniture in the room, a row of metal filing cabinets in the same dull grey as the walls. On one of the cabinets sits a cactus which has seen better days. On the rest are piles of papers, possibly waiting to be filed away. Gary looks extremely relaxed and at home in the small cluttered space, leaning back on a chair behind the desk.

'Come in, come in, have a seat. Sorry bout this morning. Jen's aul banger finally gave up. Try telling a pregnant woman with two children to get to school, we can't afford a new car. Sorry...' Gary waves his pen in the air, 'you don't need to hear my problems.'

'I could have a look at the car for you, if you like.' Des offers, gripping the chance to take a look under the bonnet and feel useful.

'I couldn't accept...it would be unethical.' Gary sits forward, putting on his glasses and picking up a sheet of paper. 'Let's get you sorted, I have some good news. I spoke to a Mr. O'Dowd yesterday after dropping you home. O'Dowd Fisheries and Salmon Farm in Kilmer Cove, I'm sure you've heard of it. He has offered a job in the factory starting next Monday.' Gary's face animated with excitement in contrast to Des sitting poker still, his hands becoming clammy.

'The fish factory?' Des questions.

'Yes, isn't that great...sure you won't have to worry about travel. I'd say it's what...ten minutes' walk from your parents' house. Here I've written down the details,' he hands Des the sheet of paper. 'You start next Monday morning, eight thirty sharp. Mr. O'Dowd put his mobile number on there, lovely guy, I'd say he'd be a fair boss to work for. Give him a ring to show your gratitude and arrange for a meet before Monday.'

'Sorry did you say Mr. O'Dowd, as in Conor O'Dowd does he still own the factory and has offered me a job?'

'Yes, is there a problem?' Gary asks, in a tone indicating he is not used to being questioned, or rather how could Des possibly rebuff this offer.

'No...no.' Des takes the piece of paper from Gary.

Outside the grey building, Des stands on the pavement clutching the piece of paper Gary has handed him. It would be a tough three months to get through. A summer living under the same roof as his father, working in a dead end job for Sarah Connolly's ex-fiancée.

A horn sounds. Desmond walks steadily along the street towards the shopping centre not wanting to go home yet. The horn sounds again.

'Des...Dessie Shanahan...hey man...When did you get out?' The voice familiar. 'Where ya headed, want a lift?' Jimmy Duggan is on the opposite side of the road, head poking out of the driver's window of a white Glanza in a queue of traffic.

'Jesus...do I ever, you are a sight for sore eyes Duggan...like the wheels man.' Des eyes the gold rims in admiration as he crosses the street, eagerly jumping into the passenger side of the car. Jimmy revs the engine spinning the tyres as they pull away from the kerb.

Chapter 4

'Are you excited about your party?' Evelyn questions her son Danny, as she folds a large pile of laundry. Trying not to become irritated by the fact he is pushing the chicken nuggets she cooked, around the plate. Not to mention the fact he has completely covered them with tomato ketchup.

'Mammy, will we be having a bouncy castle for the party?' The little boy asks staring at her expectantly. Bold blue eyes framed with thick lashes, the sort Evelyn herself would love to have.

'No darling,' she responds, steeling herself from grabbing the fork out of his hand. 'We wouldn't be able to fit it into our garden.' Aware, Danny is no pushover and will see through the lie, she quickly adds. 'I have a wonderful surprise, you will love your cake and I got one of those Piñata things like Stephanie next door got last year.' When there is no response, she adds, 'I've filled it with loads of sweets.' Her voice filled with enthusiasm, only to be disappointed by her attempts falling on deaf ears, as Danny is evidently not bought. Instead, he stabs a nugget with the fork, wearing the same scowl his father would when things weren't going his way.

'Nathan told me, he had a bouncy castle for his party and if we've nothing to do it'll be boring, and he won't come.' His bottom lip begins to quiver, fueling Evelyn's angst. Placing the t-shirt she'd been folding on the counter, she proceeds to absently bite her non-existent nails. Fully aware, Nathan Murphy's father is a loan shark, along with running several illegitimate and highly illegal businesses, a gangster who takes advantage of vulnerable people. His house is the only one on the estate with walled gardens, cameras and electric gates, patrolled by two mean looking Rottweiler dogs. Nathan Murphy is not someone, Evelyn wants Danny hanging around with. He'd have him stealing cars and drug running for his father before his sixth birthday. Evelyn bristles, having gone to a lot of trouble to make Danny's birthday party special, wanting nothing putting a dark cloud over his big day.

'We'll have lots to do.' She says with a conviction that she is not feeling inside. 'We'll have games like Pass the Parcel and Pin the Tail on the Donkey...and the Piñata.' When he doesn't seem to take the bait, she adds, 'you'll have lots of other friends coming to the party, you won't need Nathan.' Biting her tongue before adding, "Bloody Murphy" so as not to swear in front of Danny. There is also the element of fear he could repeat this back to Nathan, and then Janine Murphy would come pounding on her door. It has been known in the past. No one on the estate would cross the Murphy family in any way, not if they knew what was good for them. At least if, Nathan choose not to come the rebuff would be on their part, not hers.

'He's *me* best friend.' Danny whines, grating on her nerves. 'I want Nathan here, I don't want to play stupid games like Pass the Parcel. It's lame.' The quivering lip develops into full on wails. Evelyn's resolve frays, tired after working a double shift again for the third time this week, to cover the electric and pay for Danny's party. It all becomes too much and she snaps.

'Danny don't be so bloody ungrateful, I've gone to a lot of bother for your feckin party. *If* Nathan was a real friend...' she stops realising how unfair her words are. He is only five, not even five yet and what about not crossing the Murphy's? Evelyn sighs heavily, fighting back the urge to cry she returns to folding the laundry.

It is not the end of the subject as she might have wished. Fuelled with anger, Danny pushes his plate away knocking his glass of juice all over the floor.

'I hate nuggets, it's all you ever cook, Nanna makes real food.' He protests. Evelyn throws down the jumper she'd been folding. Her cooking skills may be lacking in comparison to her mother, but she does make an effort, only things either end up burnt or raw in the middle. Chicken nuggets and fish fingers are her safety net, both taking twenty minutes in the oven.

'Then go and live with her then.' She retorts, immediately regretting her harsh words. Danny makes a dash for the door to be cut short by his father coming in.

'Hey, buddy what's up?' He asks, appearing to be in a rare good humour.

'Mammy said, I can't have a bouncy castle for me party. Nathan won't come an he's, *me* best friend. Everyone at school will think I'm not cool and I hate feckin chicken nuggets.' He wails barely taking a breath.

'Danny, don't bloody swear.' Evelyn shouts, her face flushing with anger and the unfairness of it all, as she's been doing her best. She doesn't know whether to be relieved or more exasperated, when Brian surprises her by resolving the situation.

'It's okay babe, take it easy I've got this. Right, well I'll have no one thinking my son is not cool. I'll get ya a bouncy castle for yer party, an anything else ya want. Can't have the Murphy's or anyone else round here thinkin, I can't provide for me family. We're as good as any of them.' He lifts the little boy up, showing uncharacteristic affection by placing him on his shoulders, and horsing around the kitchen. Evelyn watches in awe, her lips twitching into a smile followed by heartfelt laughter.

'Can we order pizza and get it delivered from Max's.' Danny asks, bouncing up and down on his father's shoulders. 'An get one of those sweet carts where the man gives everyone ice cream?' Danny's eyes dance with excitement as his father swings him back down onto the floor, giving him a high five.

'Danny, I don't think-' Evelyn tries to intervene to be cut off by Brian.

'You can have all that and a magician. I always wanted a magician for me birthday. We'll have a fabulous day, an yer mam can get herself something nice to wear.' He takes a wad of notes from his pocket waving them around. Danny throws his head back, giggling uncontrollably. 'Business is doin good, babe.' He ruffles Danny's hair, before grabbing Evelyn and swinging her around until she is almost dizzy. Kissing her hard on the lips, he adds. 'Me and you are goin out tonight to celebrate get your Ma to babysit. Then we will clean this place up, have it looking great. I'll get Jimmy ta help me, we'll do a right job, new telly an maybe a nice coffee machine...I'll get me brother to do the garden for ya, Danny's birthday is goin to be the best party this street has ever seen, an all his little buddies from school, he'll be the coolest kid in the class. I want people to pass this house an think, Brian Lennon is doin good. I want respect around here like the Murphy's get.' Brian declares, sending alarm bells ringing in Evelyn's head, over hearing their name mentioned for the second time within the space of half an hour, especially coming from Brian. However, Brian's unusual good humour soon quashes any qualms she might have in the back of her mind, along with seeing Danny full of renewed excitement over his big day. 'Now take this.' Brian hands her a couple of hundred euro. 'Drop him off at yer Ma's, head into town an get somethin nice to wear.'

Evelyn doesn't need telling twice, the opportunity to go and buy new clothes thrilling her, Danny willingly goes to his grandmother just as Gillian is happy, as always to take him for the night.

'Me dad's getting me a bouncy castle an a magician for me party.' He beams, before averting his attention. 'Nanna, are you cookin tatoes and ham?' He stares wide eyed at the pans bubbling on the cooker. 'Sure am, Danny bear.' Gillian replies.

'Go wash your hands, yer dinner will be ready in ten minutes.' She fluffs his blonde hair before he darts up the stairs. 'Brian have a flutter at the dogs or somethin?....On second thoughts, I don't want to know.' Gillian says, once Danny is safely out of earshot. 'You be careful, my girl. It's all well and good when he is on a high, but the fall can be a long way down.' The added warning dampening Evelyn's good humour.

'Why do you always think badly of him?' Evelyn questions, her earlier smile replaced with a mask of annoyance.

'Because I've known men like Brian Lennon, what his type are like and I hate the way he builds you up, acting like the great man this week an next week you're all black and blue. I'm not stupid Evelyn, I know what goes on.' Gillian retorts, unable to keep her opinion to herself any longer.

'I'll pick Danny up in the morning.' Evelyn replies, turning to leave.

'There's no rush, he'll be fine here with me.' Gillian replies to her daughter's back. Evelyn waits to give Danny a hug as he bounds back down the stairs, then rushes out to her car driving into town, knowing her mother is right, but wanting to enjoy the high while it lasts.

If there is one thing she has learned to do in recent years is to shop clever. After buying a stunning backless cerise dress with spaghetti straps in Charisa boutique, she drops into Primark to buy a couple of tops, a pair of silver stiletto sandals and matching silver bag. Then she heads down to the charity shop, picking up a designer label shimmering cowl dress in cream, perfect for her Instagram selfies. She also bags a couple of necklaces to finish off her style to perfection.

On her way back to the car, an unexplainable urge causes Evelyn to stop outside a haberdashery, and without thought she pushes open the creaky old door. Inside the tiny shop, rows of material in every colour call out to her. Drawn to a collection of glittering clear gems in a glass cabinet, she visualises sewing them onto the dress she had long ago designed. The one she planned to wear on her wedding day.

'Hello.' The elderly lady behind the counter says, peering at Evelyn over her glasses. 'Can I help you dear?'

'Ah...I'm...' Evelyn babbles, regretting having come in until her eyes rest on the most beautiful material in an ivory white silk. The perfect material for her dress, imagining hand sewing each gem with care then slipping the finished dress on. The soft material clinging in all the right places sprinkling her skin with soft sensual kisses, like a lover enticing, stimulating, it almost makes her cry.

'Forgive me, I didn't recognise you immediately...you've....changed since the last time you were in here.' The woman declares, causing Evelyn to flush with embarrassment. 'I thought you must have moved away, went to university did you? Surprised you came back here after getting your degree.' The words coming like a punch in the stomach. Evelyn would have her degree now, if her life had played out the way it should have. She remembers telling this woman of all her plans, hopes and dreams. If she knew what has become of her and the reason why, she would not be so kind.

'Ah...yeah.' Evelyn finds herself playing along with the charade. 'I'm home visiting my mother and was passing, had to drop in an see this place once more.' The lie flowing easily once she started. 'You know, before I head to New York next week to start my new job.' Realising she has never asked this woman her name and can't ask now. Sad, considering the hours she had spent in here all those years ago, discussing her design plans and Des....

'Oh, I am so pleased for you.' The woman's eyes light up as she rounds the counter to give Evelyn an unexpected hug, resulting in Evelyn's nose tingling from impending tears threatening to spill. It takes all her resolve to fight the urge to cry, wishing the dream were true. 'If anyone deserves it you do.' The woman continues to fuss, glasses almost slipping off her nose with excitement. 'Here let me offer you a few yards of this material as my gift to you. It's similar to the one you always admired if memory serves me right, sure it's how I remembered you. Your hair was different back then...and...anyway, I'm sorry I didn't recognise you right away.' The older woman's reluctance to say what is on her mind clear, as two pink dots appear on her withered cheeks.

'Oh I couldn't accept.' Evelyn protests, also flushing. Only her embarrassment is from the shame of her lies.

'Nonsense I insist. When you make a beautiful dress that either you, or some famous model will wear, you can give my humble shop here in the north west of Ireland a plug.' She smiles taking the material, measuring and cutting off a very generous piece. Evelyn simply accepts the gift, buying the gems and some dainty buttons to go with it. Along with some less expensive material, and a couple of zips and pieces of trimming.

By the time she returns to her car, she wonders what on earth she will do with it all. Pulling the silk material from its bag and caressing it, her hands tingle with a desire to make the dress. To design and make clothes as she once had, sitting in the little spare room of the apartment she and Des used to rent. How excited she had been back then when they set up her work room, with a giant pin board on one wall for ideas and swatches of material. Her desk and chair, where she would sit and create new designs. An adjustable dress form, her parents proudly turned up with one day and the large old wooden table, Des had bought in a charity shop. Sanding it down and painting it, making a perfect large platform for cutting material and creating her designs. Reminded of the fact, her sewing machine and dress form are still in her mother's spare room. Maybe just maybe. She starts up the car feeling giddy and light hearted at the thought, suddenly locked in a whirl of revived ideas and enthusiasm.

An hour later, Evelyn hums showing her light mood as she dresses and carefully applies fresh makeup after a long luxurious shower. The material now safely locked in the boot of her car, ready to be dropped at Gillian's when she picks Danny up in the morning. Taking the opportunity whilst dressed eloquently for a quick selfie, since Brian is downstairs. Posting it on Instagram, with the caption. "Heading out for a night on the town with my beau. Dining at the Ritz, Paris." In reality, her dining experience is a Chinese takeaway Brian had ordered while she was upstairs getting ready. As soon as the delivery man arrives, her momentum drops off cloud nine with a massive thump.

'I thought we're going out.' Evelyn protests, in the same fashion Danny had complained about not getting a bouncy castle earlier.

'We are after we've eaten.' Brian replies, oblivious to the disappointment Evelyn is feeling. 'Thought we'd head into that new club in town, Crystal. You look hot babe, maybe we should stay in.' He waggles his eyebrows suggestively, at the same time forking noodles into his mouth.

'Brian, I didn't go to all this effort just to stay in an watch telly for the night.' Evelyn protests further, turning her nose up when he offers her a spare rib.

'Alright, keep yer knickers on.' He guffaws at his own joke. 'That's if you're wearing any.' He winks. 'I hope not.'

'Jesus, Brian of course I'm wearin knickers.' She replies trying to keep a straight face.

'Really...well not for long.' He grabs her playfully pulling her onto the couch, food abandoned due to his sexual appetite taking sudden precedence. Evelyn is aware her relationship with Brian, is far from perfect but he is her addiction. Her body easily responds to his embrace intoxicated by euphoria, nothing else matters only the magical escape of his touch as he slides easily inside her. Their bodies begin to move as one, he whispers her name making her feel loved. For now it's all she needs, cocooned in being desired.

Later that evening, they saunter into Crystal Club, arms wrapped around each other's waist, looking for all the world a celebrity couple making a grand entrance. Evelyn having retouched her makeup, and perched a pair of sunglasses on her head.

As they stride across the floor Evelyn smiles inwardly, her already fanciful imagination taking over, drinking in illusory admiring stares from every man who looks up, knowing jealousy would drive Brian wild turning him on. Imagining, manifested envious glares from every woman as she hangs on the arm of the sexiest man in the room. Lynn Priestly is acting out her fantasy world.

'Yer asking for trouble flirtin like that?' Jimmy issues a stern warning, as she joins their friends at a table by the dancefloor. Brian safely out of earshot having gone to the bar to get their drinks.

'He knows I wouldn't touch another man,' Evelyn declares throwing a sultry glance in Brian's direction, as she pushes past Jackson and his latest flame. Evelyn doesn't seem to notice, Jackson's eyes follow her as she squeezes in next to Jimmy. Brian, however does on approach and slams a gin and tonic on the table in front of Evelyn.

'Be back in a second, have a bit of business to see to.' Brian says louder than needed, taking a swig from his bottle of beer, before bending to kiss her full on the lips. 'Just remember you're mine.' He whispers in her ear in a menacing tone, before straightening to his full six foot two. Evelyn becomes rigid, fear coursing through her veins for fear of further repercussions later, like the time they'd bumped into Paul Quilty, a friend of Desmond's. Paul had innocently struck up conversation asking how she was keeping. Brian then questioned her over and over when they got home, unaccepting of her denial of never having slept with Paul. The outer scars and bruises always heal, but the brokenness inside her never will, yet somehow she manages to convince herself, he only does this because he cares and is scared of losing her love. She lifts her glass with a shaky hand, almost draining the straight gin completely to calm her nerves. 'Isn't life great? Out on a weeknight with my woman.' Brian declares waving his arm to address the rest of the table. 'Keep an eye on her Jim, make sure she's alright.' He adds, throwing Jimmy a wink before sauntering away to be swallowed up in the crowded room.

'Ya look good tonight Eve, nice dress.' Jackson comments. Something he would not dare to do, if Brian was still in their company. Jackson always has a moody look about him, whether it is a way of acting cool or a genuine chip on his shoulder no one really knows. His mother originally from London, his father from Nigeria, he'd come to live in Carraigbrin when he was five. His dark looks, making him very popular with the opposite sex.

'Thanks Jackson, Brian is good to me, I'm a lucky woman.' Her reply, clearly emphasising she is grateful to Brian for the new clothes. Not wanting anyone relaying the conversation back to him in any other way. 'Are you and Colette coming to Danny's party on Saturday? Brian is getting him a bouncy castle and magician. He's dead excited.' She purposefully asks, eyeing the petite blonde sitting next to him.

'Yeah...sounds deadly, though I won't be bringing Colette, ya know how it is.' Jackson replies suggestively raising of his brows and winking. Jackson nor his new girlfriend seeming perturbed by her comment. Evelyn knows this will suit him, because as soon as a woman becomes serious or hints at permanent relationship status Jackson moves on with speed. This girl is obviously aware of his track record accepting being with him while she can, no doubt making all her friends jealous in the interim.

'Don't be invitin him over.' Jimmy hisses, when Jackson is safely out of earshot.

'Why not?' Evelyn questions confused, Jackson practically as regular a visitor, as Jimmy is. With Evelyn working long shifts to pay the bills it sometimes feels as though they spend more time in her house than she does.

'Brian doesn't want him comin round the house since he made a comment about yer arse being tight.' Jimmy informs her. 'Have ya not noticed the way he ogles ya? Stay clear or ya be askin for trouble there.' Issuing a friendly warning. 'Surprised Brian hasn't landed him one, I'd say it's to do with him being a good contact at the mo.'

'I didn't know.' She is grateful for the heads-up, liking Jimmy as a friend. Having always felt he has her back even though he is technically, Brian's best friend. Most people find Jimmy irritating, referring to him as being a sandwich short of a picnic, Evelyn on the other hand sees him differently, rather that he pretends to be dumb, an expert at watching everything around him from a sideline perspective and is very switched on under his false veil of stupidity. His behaviour tonight seems a little uncharacteristic in the way he is being watchful of her, she soon learns why.

'Heard anything from Dessie?' To those who are unaware of the history, it might seem like a casual enquiry about a friend. In its context, it causes Evelyn concern.

'No, why would I?' She tries to sound blasé, resulting in sounding like a strangled cat. If there was any gin left in the glass she would drain it, throat constricting due to being guilt-ridden over having thoughts about Des, in recent days.

'He's out of prison, another reason why Brian is watchful.' Jimmy informs her.

'Brian never said...I thought...since when?' Evelyn blusters, conscious Jimmy is gauging her reaction to this news. She'd always been aware this day would come, just not this soon. The thought of Desmond being free, of being within close proximity filling her with dread.

'Brian isn't likely to share that bit of news now is he?' Jimmy raises a brow. 'I met Des yesterday in Donegal, he's out on parole.' Making light of the revelation, he adds 'Guess what?' Evelyn shakes her head, still grasping the fact Desmond is back. 'He's livin with his Ma.'

'Who is livin with his Ma?' Brian questions. They had not noticed his return, resulting in Jimmy's expression changing to one of apprehension, he won't lie, not when it comes to Brian. Evelyn is aware of what the consequences will be. Yet, she cannot stop thinking about Desmond being home from prison.

Chapter 5

Sarah is standing staring out of the kitchen window, watching tiny droplets of rain land on the pane. First just one or two, before they become more rapid and urgent until everything outside becomes a blur, matching the events of the past forty-eight hours of her life. The pressure having inevitably taken its toll.

Immediately after leaving the hospital, Tommy phoned their brother Martin in Galway and sister Aine in New York, to break the news. Martin arrived with his wife Grainne and their three teenage children, late that same night. In true Connolly family form, the two couples worked alongside Sarah making the necessary funeral arrangements. Lily took charge of organising beds and food while, Grainne and Sarah organised the flower arrangements for the funeral. Tommy and Martin spoke with the undertakers, making the decisions of whether their father would have liked a light oak veneer coffin rather than mahogany. It had gone with precise clockwork, a way for them all to pull together and keep their minds off Paddy's absence, and the void it has left in their lives. The atmosphere changed when, Aine the eldest sibling arrived on the Tuesday evening. Her presence bringing more gloom to an already sombre circumstance, primarily due to disagreeing with the funeral arrangements already made. This disruption causing a whirlwind of unhappiness among the family, disgruntling Tommy in particular.

'Daddy would have hated that, Tom.' She sneered at the coffin they had picked. Paddy being laid out in the front room in the oak coffin, Tommy ordered. Having been brought from the morgue the previous day by the undertaker, to spend his last night at the farm. The home, he inherited from his father before him, and had carried his new bride over the threshold of. Locals had poured in throughout the evening to pay their respects to Paddy, and commiserate with his children and grandchildren.

'What the hell would you know about what our Da, wanted?' Tommy had retorted angrily, surprising Lily and Sarah as he is the mildest mannered, kindly person on the planet. 'Ya haven't been home in years. Didn't even have the decency to come home for our, Jack's funeral.' There it was laid bare, what they had all been thinking but never said. It didn't put a stop to Aine and her spiteful ways, especially when it comes to matters involving Sarah.

'I couldn't just drop everything and run home, I run a magazine. You lot know nothing of my life and wouldn't understand the responsibility. Besides the past is the past, we are talking about the here and now, so in going forward we are discussing Dad.' Aine replied indignant. They knew about her life, her divorced live in lover of twelve years, their glamourous busy social life and the luxurious loft in Tribeca, Lower Manhattan. When she Skyped Paddy, about once a month if he was lucky, she made sure to drop into the conversation having neighbours such as, Taylor Swift, Jay Z and Beyoncé. 'Really! Sarah, how Daddy survived in this place for so long, surpasses me. You could have at least spruced the place up for people coming from the village to pay their respects.' Aine berated, flicking a finger across a bookcase drawing a thin line in the dust.

'Sarah looked after Da, very well while running the shop with Lily to keep the farm afloat.' Tommy immediately threw back, coming to his younger sister's defence.

'Well there you have it, running a little country shop is hardly rocket science now is it. It certainly doesn't need the two of them all the time. Remind me, is the shop part of the farm?' Aine threw the question in casually but Tommy walked away without answering. It was the look of pain on Tommy's face, which got to Sarah.

'Can't you be civil for once, can't you see he is upset.'

'Ah...poor little Sarah.' Aine reverted to her native accent. 'Had Da and the boys wrapped around her little finger, cause everyone felt sorry for her. She was so young when her Ma died,' she continued to bait. 'Well, Da isn't around to protect you now. It's about time you got your come-up-pence.' She stormed from the room leaving Sarah aghast. Aine's reasoning behind this attitude towards her younger sister, Sarah cannot fathom. It had always been there as they grew up, possibly stemming from the eight year age gap or Sarah's arrival into the family taking Aine's position as only daughter away. Whatever it was, it became obvious to Sarah as they grew older, Aine would never change. If anything, the resentment appeared too become magnified. It had been a relief when Aine went to Galway University, and then on graduating with a Master's in business, she immigrated to America.

'Sarah, there is no hot water left.' Aine breaks into her thoughts with her whiney tones of mixed accents. Sarah swings round acknowledging her older sister standing in their kitchen wearing a black silk robe, large curlers in her hair and green goo covering her face. Stifling the urge to laugh, Sarah informs her turning on the immersion usually helps. This does not please, Aine one bit. 'How long will it take to heat?' She bristles, causing cracks to appear in the drying goo.

'Usually about half an hour or so.'

'Oh for crying out loud.' Aine retorts reverting back into full American twang. 'Let's hope I can get into the bathroom when it does heat up. First Grainne was in there for over an hour, then the girls. Matt was banging on the door like mad. I thought the girls were staying over at Tommy's, the house is overcrowded. One bathroom in a house is ridiculous anyway in this day and age. Of course that will all change.' Aine swoops from the kitchen leaving Sarah feeling so deflated, she does not pick up on the parting comment.

Annoyance sitting tightly across her shoulders, Sarah decides there is only one way to banish this resentment. Drying her hands in a towel and leaving the remainder of the dishes for someone else to finish, she slips outside to the shed and grabs her surfboard from the rack. With a glance over her shoulder to make sure no one's spied her departure, she walks down the narrow pathway towards her most beloved spot on this earth, surfer's cove. She makes her way to the water's edge slipping off her dress, allowing it drop to the ground she steps out into the inviting water. Soft droplets of rain begin to fall, wetting her face mingling with tears she finally allows to flow freely. It is moments like this she wishes she could be with Him, could pick up her mobile and He would be at her side, comforting her the way he had the night of Jack's funeral. Paddling out the water is calm, even the sea is letting her down today, not a ripple in sight. Lying on the board, she listens to the sound of the water lapping against its sides. Soothing her from the resentment she has been feeling over Desmond's early release. Bringing Sarah to another realm where she can pretend her life has not been cruelly changed once again. Trying not to think of the day's events which lay ahead, a day Paddy Connolly will be put to rest with his wife, alongside their grandson. Fate has taken everyone she loved, one by one. It had started when she was four, her mother lost a long tiring battle to cancer, and if it weren't for the stories her father and brothers provided her with, she would not know anything about the woman who had given birth to her. A quiver runs down her spine as she paddles back to shore, it is time to face reality.

'Hey Auntie Sarah, cool way to start the day.' Matt says, walking towards her wearing a cheeky grin. Eerily similar to Jack, with a flop of dark curly hair. The only distinguishing difference being, Matt has inherited his mother's steely grey eyes, rather than the Connolly's blue.

'Best way to wash away your worries and start the day with a fresh outlook. So how is Uni, are you enjoying the course?' Matt is in his second year studying Biomedical Science.

'The course is great.' He averts his gaze, indicating something playing on his mind. His mannerisms also very like Jack, meaning she can read him like a book.

'You alright?' Sarah asks. Matt at nineteen would be two years younger than Jack, they had been very close when they were young. It didn't go unnoticed Matt stopped visiting and staying during school holidays, like he would have done before Jack's death. As though reading her thoughts, he says.

'I feel guilty, in recent years I haven't spent as much time with grandpa.'

'He knew you still loved him, understood you are all growing up and have busy lives.'

'It wasn't that...I don't want to upset you by saying...'

'What is it Matt?'

'I found it hard coming here without Jack...it didn't feel right anymore.'

'No, you're right it doesn't...it will be worse without Da now too.'

'Sarah, can I ask you something?'

'Sure go ahead.'

'I'm thinking of doing the Dublin marathon in October...well...I admired Jack, his talent and all. I thought it might be nice to run in his honour, would you mind if I got t-shirts printed and did that?' His gesture catching her unaware, fresh tears sting her eyes.

'Matt that is a beautiful thing to do...I don't know what to say.'

'I was hoping you might say you'd join me and do the marathon too.' He throws her a wistful grin.

'Me running!' She replies shocked, flattered he should think her fit enough to do a marathon.

'Yeah, why not?' Matt sounds genuinely surprised by her response. He is right, running the marathon in Jack's honour makes sense. The timing perfect to bring attention to the injustice of Desmond's prison term for her son's life. 'You'd be able for it, you have the fitness. Not like me mam, sitting around always on her phone or laptop addicted to social media. If I ask her to join me for a run, she claims she is tired after working all day. She sits down for the best part of that, how can she be so tired.' He quips, turning pink after his revelation.

'Okay, I'll do the marathon with you.' She replies with renewed ferocity. Ignoring Matt's comments about his mother, she adds, 'come on we better get back before they send out a search party.'

When they arrive back to the house, the kitchen is a hive of activity. Lily is standing at the sink finishing the dishes Sarah had left, looking elegant in a black shift dress, her hair pinned in a neat bun. Lily doesn't go for the latest fashion, but her slim figure meaning she always looks great whatever she wears. Grainne is sitting at the table with a coffee in one hand and her mobile in the other. Sarah grimaces before picking up a dish towel to dry the pans, Lily has placed on the drainer.

'Leave them, you should go get showered and ready.' Lily says. 'Matt will help me, won't you Matt it'll give us a chance to catch up.'

'Eh.' Matt is clearly horrified at the notion of doing something menial as drying dishes.

'You know me, I don't need long to get ready.' Sarah replies winking at Matt. Preceding to watch Grainne, as she helps herself to coffee from the cafetiêre before sitting back at the table.

'I can't get any internet connection.' Grainne complains, lifting her phone high above her head moving it about. Sarah wonders why people always do that, wave their mobiles like magic wands, expecting it to make a difference getting a signal.

'It's a nightmare, you have to go outside sometimes to get coverage.' Lily informs her. 'I think it's these old stone walls.'

'Have you checked the connection Sarah?' Grainne furrows her brow. 'Who is your network provider? We just signed up with Digi connect, they're a new company but OMG faster and more megabytes.'

'It could be something to do with all the building for the campsite and rewiring, I'll ring them tomorrow.' Sarah pacifies, not particularly concerned as she has other more pressing things on her mind.

'I better try outside so, I'm expecting a message.' Grainne announces, before disappearing out the door.

'It's nice having everyone around, especially the kids. Though they are far from kids now.' Lily says. 'Everyone apart from you know who upstairs, she's worse than I remember. Grainne told me, Aine had torn strips off her for being in the bathroom too long.' Lily throws her eyes to heaven. Gauging Sarah's silence, she places a soapy wet hand on Sarah's. 'You okay Kid? I'm sure this has been particularly tough on you.'

'I think he needed to be with Jack.' Before Lily gets a chance to reply and give Sarah the comfort she desperately needs. Aine appears at the threshold of the door once again. This time her hair pinned up with loose curls sweeping dramatically down one side, the rollers long discarded. Replacing the robe is an Armani black wrap effect midi-skirt and a pair of Jimmy Choo, Roz 85 heels. A Gucci black printed silky blouse clinging to her too slim body. The sharp features of Aine's face a reflection of her entire body structure, everything from her skeletal arms to paper thin waist, screaming unnatural skinniness. The two sisters' should be similar in looks, both having inherited their mothers colouring, but Aine prefers to think she is the epiphany of style and sophistication. Her job as editor of "Elégance," magazine in New York, meaning she has a persona to withhold, to look her best at all times and wear the latest fashions. Aine fixes a steady gaze, shrieking instructions in the same way as she would her staff on the magazine.

'Sarah, instead of standing around could you go and get Martin, I believe he went down the garden to have a cigarette. Oh...my...lord!' She gasps dramatically in the American accent again. 'The state of your hair, surely you are not going like that.' Sounding Irish again. 'The hearse will be here in less than twenty minutes, I can't believe how dispassionate you all are.' Sounding posher, with no particular accent. 'No respect at all for our daddy.' The dismissing comments, causing Lily to throw a sharp glare in her direction. Sarah slams down the pot she is drying and is about to walk out the door, when Aine dishes a blow which practically floors Sarah. 'FYI, I've spoken to dad's solicitor, Adam is that his name. One of the Sullivan's, the one with the bad dandruff problem.'

'Alan?' Lily corrects, irritation evident in her voice. Aine having the ability to rile even the mildest of souls, which she has already proven with Tommy.

'Which...eV...err.' Aine drags the word purposefully throwing Lily a dismissive glance. 'I want to look over your plans, I believe you have been building on our land. This campsite you're setting up and planning permission in the pipeline for other projects, my accountant will need to look over the figures. I will be heading to Dublin right after the service, as I have a meeting scheduled for my new job over here, before I return to New York.' Aine adds, in a tone which implements an air of self-importance. 'I don't see the need to go a pub, it's just a feeble excuse to get drunk in my opinion.' Sarah and Lily are dumbfounded by what they are hearing, apart from the suggestion of them all using the funeral as an excuse to get drunk, rather than honour their father's memory it is also the mention of their family solicitor. Rather than further engage with Aine, Sarah opens the door,

'I better get Martin, will you see if Grainne is ready?' Sarah says as a welcoming gust of air enters the room but fails to quash the stifling atmosphere.

'There isn't room in the cortège car for everyone, only immediate family.' Aine rebuffs, stopping Sarah in her tracks. 'Lily, you'll have to drive your car behind with Grainne and both your broods.' Words purposefully suggesting Lily, Grainne and Paddy's grandchildren are insignificant. Sarah levels her sister a glare, unable to hold her tongue any longer.

'How dare-' her protest cut off by Aine raising her hand, waving dismissively and leaving the kitchen quicker than she had appeared. The only evidence Aine had been present in the first place, is the heady scent of Faubourg perfume left in her wake, along with an unpleasant atmosphere. 'She had no right.' Sarah says, as she and Lily walk outside.

'Aine is Aine, nothing will change that fact unfortunately. Today, let us bury Paddy with the dignity he deserves. Your sister will be gone by the end of the day, so there is no point in rising to her.' Lily points out, ever the mediator. 'Though in hindsight, we've been more than patient since her arrival. Paddy's death is raw for us all and I don't want to worry Tommy. Go get Martin, and not a word to either him or Tommy, they have enough to contend with. I'll ring Alan now and make sure Aine does not receive any documents in connection to Oceanic Temptations and our future plans, it is no concern of hers.' Lily gives Sarah's hand a reassuring squeeze before heading towards her own dormer bungalow, next door.

Chapter 6

'Hey you.' Martin greets Sarah, on her approach. The fact his smile does not quite reach his eyes, giving away deep unhappiness. He is sitting on a wooden bench under the eucalyptus tree where Paddy would often position himself, his mind evidently elsewhere, by the faraway glaze in his eyes. It pains Sarah to see her brother looking so forlorn, as she has always been close to both her brothers.

'You'd do anything to escape herself.' Sarah says grimacing. 'I've been ordered to get you, the hearse arrives in twenty minutes.' Still dressed in a light summer dress and flip flops, she adds. 'I should get changed.'

'We've no rush so.' Martin replies throwing her a roguish grin. 'Dad would want you to be yourself, you look fine to me.' He takes a drag of the cigarette grasped between his forefinger and thumb. 'Either my memory is bad or she has gotten worse since going to America, and don't get me started about that bloody accent. Here sit down, chill.' He instructs moving across to make room for her. 'I was just thinking about the time Dad brought us all to Tramore for a few days after mam's months mind. It was the most impulsive thing the aul man ever did, but it had been magical. You probably don't remember, you'd have only been barely four at the time.'

'No, I can't say I do.' She replies, her own eyes taking on a glassy look. 'Sadly, I have no physical memory of mum either. He was an amazing man our Da, bringing up four children on his own, then being there for me with Jack.' Sarah enviously watches her brother take another long drag of the cigarette. She cannot hold back any longer, the longing becoming too much. Whipping the cigarette from between his fingers she sucks deep into her lungs, allowing its toxic poison engulf her before rounding her lips and blowing the smoke back out. How can something so wrong feel so good, even if it's only for a few seconds?

'I thought you had given up years ago.' Martin comments as he surveys her, his lips twitching into a bemused smile.

'Mm...so had I, but its times like this and believe me there are plenty of those, I falter a little.'

'Ditto.... I falter a lot, which makes it harder to hide.' His admission causing Sarah to stare at him wide eyed. Her brother's expression unreadable as he adverts his gaze to study the ground.

'I didn't think you and Grainne, kept secrets from each other.' Her initial worry increased by the despondency in his expression.

'Ah...only the ones that I need to keep me sane.' He throws her a lifeline, she finds unconvincing.

'She doesn't approve so.' Sarah surmises, surprised there are secrets within her brother's marriage. Then again, she is no expert on relationships herself and should be last person to issue judgement.

'Got it in one.' Martin admits, tapping the side of his nose.

'Can I ask is everything alright?'

'Ah...we're grand...though, sometimes I think we've bitten off more than we can chew. You know the bigger house, new cars, it's all materialistic but Grainne seems to be carried away on the necessity of having it all, as they say. I envy you and Tommy, you had the right idea staying here, living life as it should be lived.' His admission completely out of the blue, since Sarah always perceived him to be happy with his life, had thought he'd been delighted to gain the promotion eighteen months ago, with a significant increase in his wage. Remembering, how excited he and Grainne had been when she'd gone to visit, as they showed her around the large five bedroomed house they'd bought with two reception rooms, a generous sized sunroom and garden and five bathrooms. The kitchen a sleek modern design with every gadget invented, including the massive American fridge with its drinks dispenser. 'Don't mind me...we are lucky, I should be grateful for all we have instead of moaning. Can't have it all can we, ya either enjoy the fast pace of city life or the peace of the country. Grainne ain't a country gal like you and Lil....You've done some job with expanding the shop, I'll give ye that.'

'Pure luck with being perfectly situated on the Wild Atlantic Way, on route to Kilmer Cove lighthouse, with it being a popular place with the tourists these days. Though, I had my own notions too remember and poor dad paid out a fortune in fees for Trinity, only for me to end up pregnant after only a year of study behind me.' She leans back on the bench, becoming far more relaxed than she should be feeling. 'I don't regret it though.'

'How could you? Jack was a gift from Mam, I'd say she wanted you here with Da. He missed you that year, never seen the old man so unhappy...It was like the first months after Mam's death all over again.' These words causing Sarah to sit up again, eyes widening with interest. 'It's weird being here without him around, something I could never imagine. When Mam died, she had been ill so long, I think it was expected. Dad though, I foolishly thought he would always be here. It'll be tough for you especially.'

'I'm dreading you all going back to your lives and being on my own.' Sarah said, handing him back his cigarette. Backtracking adds. 'Except Aine of course.'

'I know...she is my sister too, but...ah...Aine changed after Mam died.' Martin stares at the ground, causing Sarah to wonder if there is more he wants to say, but can't bring himself too.

'Death and loss changes people, I should know. Was she and mam very close?' She asks, hoping to find some understanding for her sister's resentment.

'Yeah, Mam was the type of woman who spent a lot of time with us as kids. Baking with Aine, teaching her how to knit and sew, all that kind of stuff. They were always side by side, apart from when Aine had her head stuck in a magazine. She was obsessed with fashion magazines from a very young age. Da would have to give her money every Friday to go and buy the latest one from Molloy's. I suppose she has accomplished her dream, but it sure as hell hasn't made her a happy person.' He says, causing her to glance at him skeptically.

'There you are.' Aine's shrill tone cuts through the peaceful rustle of the eucalyptus trees, as though on cue. 'The undertaker is waiting, have you no respect for Daddy.' She doesn't wait for them to reply. Turning on her heels to walk back to the house, muttering under her breath. Her emphasised footsteps displaying a hate of having to trudge through wet grass in Jimmy Choo heels.

'See what I mean, too much anger in her bones. Right so, let's give dad the send-off he deserves.' Martin says, crushing the end of the cigarette on the ground with his foot. 'Here, have these finish the packet, it's about time I gave them up.' He thrusts a packet of cigarettes into Sarah's hand. Throwing her a cheeky wink, he wraps an arm around her shoulder as he guides her towards the house.

Less than half an hour later, Sarah walks into the church alongside her family. Having quickly changed into a loose fitting black dress and low heeled court shoes, hastily sweeping a brush through her shoulder length hair. No fuss or curlers needed. A silhouette of her former self, pale face wearing dark shadows under the eye area, depicting the strain of the past few days. Friends and neighbours fill the small church, wanting to pay their respects to one of the oldest and much respected members of the community. A man who would have given his last cent to anyone in need. Had listened to their woes and helped where he could, while respecting the need for discretion.

The angelic voice of Lauren, Tommy and Lily's daughter, Paddy's eldest grandchild, fills the small country church, singing, "Somewhere over the Rainbow." The only other sound in the church to be heard, is intermittent sobbing. Father Kennelly opens the mass by addressing his congregation, and offering his sorrow and sympathy to the Connolly family, proceeding to bless the coffin with holy water, intoning deeply. The smell of incense making Sarah feel nauseous, as she plays with the delicate gold chain around her neck. A locket, Paddy had given her for her twenty-first birthday which had been her mother's. Inside placed on either side of the heart, a picture of her mother and one of her son. It had been the best present she'd ever received, she would miss the old man. Life without his dirty wellies discarded at the back door, will seem too empty and cold.

'You okay?' Lily whispers slipping an arm around her shoulder. Wet tears stinging Sarah's face, having not realised she had been crying until asked.

'I can't believe both Mammy and Daddy are gone.' Aine says, dabbing her eyes with a scented tissue. Unthinking, Sarah reaches out to squeeze her hand in a gesture of comfort. Aine quickly pulling away, making Sarah wonder why her sister continues to maintain such a cold distance. Trying not to let it cloud her mind too much, Sarah listens to the beautiful eulogy Martin is giving, speaking about the dad they loved.

The service ends, prompting the organist to spring into life and the congregation to their feet. Paddy's coffin is carried by Martin, Tommy, Conor, and the pallbearers to his final resting place. Sarah following with Aine, Lily, Grainne and his grandchildren. As Sarah steps outside into the blinding sunlight, she catches a glimpse of Him standing next to his wife. Sending a bolt of loneliness for his comforting arms around her, followed by guilt. She should not be thinking like this as her father is about to be laid to rest. Aine grabs hold of Sarah's arm, pulling her hastily aside.

'I can't bear to watch Dad being put in the ground, so I'll go now. My lawyer will be in touch regarding legalities.' Aine whispers in her low American twang, before slipping away. Sarah is speechless, over the cold and uncaring way Aine has walked away, without having the decency to lay their father to rest.

'I know it's hard but don't let her rile you.' Lily slips an arm around Sarah's shoulder, directing her to re-join the funeral procession. 'I spoke with Alan, he assured me everything will be alright. I'm only sorry and annoyed, we have to be discussing this as we bring him to rest. I think that woman brings out the worst in us all.' Lily says, her face having lost its normal serenity.

Kilmer Cove Graveyard is set on a hill above the church, with one of the most picturesque views of the bay, taking in the town and harbour. An idyllic garden of rest, with manicured flowerbeds and cherry blossoms separating rows of gravestones. Patrick Connolly is lowered to the strains of "Footprints in the Sand," and muffled sobs. Sarah gritting her teeth, in an attempt to suppress the rage that is beginning to boil over from the resentment she has been feeling, since learning of Desmond Shanahan's early release from prison. A bitter taste filling her mouth at justice having not been served fairly, making it hard knowing he is allowed to get on with his life, while she buries her father next to her son.

'They are together and at peace.' Lily whispers as though reading her mind, giving her hand a squeeze in a gesture of comfort.

'They've left me behind.' A sharp gust of wind comes from nowhere on an otherwise still day, whisking around the gravestones carrying her words with it. If spoken in jest along with tears and emotion, it would not have as much of an impact. It is the sadness, the hollow nothingness projected from Sarah's eyes giving cause for concern, which only those who truly care and have been there before to catch her fall, can see. That's when she catches His eye, the electricity passing between them almost giving their secret away, leaving her with a desperation to be cocooned in his arms.

'C'mon, I'll drive you over.' Lily places a protective arm around her shoulders, steering Sarah gently away from the graveside, knowing she is dousing a fire, which could all too easily become an inferno. 'Kitty is putting on a spread and I could do with a coffee, my head is beginning to pound from the tension.' She adds, as they stroll towards Tommy, Martin and the others. 'You're shaking, I'm guessing you skipped breakfast this morning.' Lily exclaims, matter-of-fact, before stopping next to her husband. 'You ready to head love?'

'Shouldn't we offer Aine a lift?' Tommy asks, glancing behind them, a frown forming on his weather-beaten face, everyone else having dispersed heading to their cars or making their way to The Nook on foot.

'She's gone.' Lily's curt tone, cutting sharply around the gravestones, almost as sharp as the wind that picked up a few moments ago, revealing how clearly perturbed she has become. Her lips narrowing into a tight thin line, twinned with an inability to meet her husband's pleading stare, also showing her frustration. Gentle Lily, always calm even in a crisis, the backbone of the family through good times and bad, especially the bad. 'Gone to Dublin, the country air was suffocating I'd imagine.' Lily adds, linking her arm in Sarah's guiding her down the hill, leaving Tommy confused. In all their years together, he had never heard his wife sound so vexed. Lily would not be defeated easily, not when it comes to her family, like a lioness she will protect, reluctant to allow Aine come in and bulldoze her family, not when they have already been through so much. A meeting having already been set up for Tommy and Sarah to meet with the family solicitor. Alan assuring Lily, the farm is in Tommy's name and the business in hers and Sarah's. Paddy Connolly had been a man to keep his affairs in order, underneath the mild mannered country farmer and father, lay a very clever minded business man.

Chapter 7

The Nook public house, is situated at one end of Kilmer Cove Main Street. A Street with the unique advantage of having only buildings running along one side of the road, facing a full view out over the Atlantic. The pub hosts a generous sized beer garden, boasting spectacular views over the bay. Making it a perfect stop for both locals and tourists alike, on a sunny summer afternoon. Adjacent to The Nook's car park is a small pier with, sailing boats neatly lined along one side and fishing boats on the other. A footpath with a low wall, curves its way along the remainder of this side of the street, giving the private residences and businesses, a perfect view of the surrounding landscape and vegetation. One of the finest views in Ireland.

The Connolly family enter the pub, which is already filled with locals wanting to toast Paddy's final send off. A man who was very much respected in the small town of barely over four hundred residents, attended mass every Sunday morning with his only vice in life a visit to The Nook public house on Friday and Sunday evenings, for his two pints of Guinness and whiskey for the road. Sarah squints, adjusting to the dim light of the pub after the contrasting bright sunlight outside. Kitty the owner, rushes from behind the bar giving a warm welcome. Her husband Dini, appearing from nowhere as though by magic, his small thin frame overpowered as always by his wife's large presence, both in her personality and bulk. Dini may be slight in frame, but is a very athletic man, had been a physical education teacher in Carraigbrin secondary, until retirement. Along with volunteering as an athletic coach in Kilmer Cove, a position he still holds. Dini had seen potential in Jack and spent every spare moment possible, bringing him to Olympic standard. He had been heartbroken over Jack's death, giving pride of place behind the bar to a picture taken of Jack holding up his first gold medal, as all Ireland champion long distance runner.

'Come, I've a table reserved here for ye,' Kitty says. 'Wasn't it a beautiful service, your Da would have been proud.' She instructs her husband. 'Bring over that tray of whiskey's Dini, and we will have a drink to Patrick Connolly, god rest his soul.' Dini as usual does as he is told. Lily protesting in vain, she would prefer a cup of coffee being designated driver.

'One drink won't hurt ye girl, warm the insides, t'was Paddy's tipple at the end of a Sunday night before he walked up the road, no matter what the weather brought. He was a great man.' Dini passes round the whiskeys.

'Slainté.' Kitty and Dini shout in unison, as they raise their glasses. 'To Paddy, may he rest in peace.' Everyone reciprocates in the toast, Tommy, Martin and Grainne downing the whiskey easily, Lily less enthusiastically. Sarah stares at the glass of honey coloured liquid clasped in her hand, the potent smell enough to make her feel queasy, not normally a spirit drinker.

'Go on it'll do you good.' Kitty encourages, leaving Sarah with little choice. 'I've made a buffet, so ye help yourselves and if there is anything myself and Dini can do, don't ye hesitate to ask.'

'That's very kind of you.' Tommy says.

'Yes, Paddy would be overwhelmed by your generosity.' Lily adds, the whiskey having a relaxing effect, bringing her back to her normal persona.

'Da would have been blown away by your kindness.' Martin lifts up his empty glass, making a beeline for the bar. Due to it being the first time he'd relaxed and had a proper drink in months. Technically, having a glass of wine or two at night after work to wind down, could not be classed as having a proper drink.

'He'd have done the same, sur didn't he often help us out in bad times.' Dini says, referring to a time before the Wild Atlantic way and Kilmer Cove lighthouse, brought hordes of tourists to the town. 'He was a true gentlemen and that's why as we speak, I've sent our Sean up to the farm to help Eamon and his lad fix that fence of yours.'

'Aye, and don't be worrying about the shop either. My sister Denise will be along tomorrow to help Olive and Lena open up for the tour buses.' Kitty's gesture receiving a further response of gratitude from all the Connolly's. Sarah touched by emotion, thankful for the wonderful support from their neighbours, it does not surprise her as they had been down the same road before. 'Ye needn't worry, bout that Shanahan fellow, he'll find it hard to grace any shop or business in this town, you mark my words.' Kitty whispers to Sarah, giving her hand a squeeze. Eyes searching the bar, she adds 'Your Aine not joining us?' A frown forming on her deeply lined face, as she speaks.

'No, she's already on her way to Dublin.'

'Oh.' Kitty raises a perfectly pencilled eyebrow.

'Mm....' Lily adds grimacing, the whiskey brutally losing its warm effect. Kitty refrains from querying further, not the type of woman to dive into someone else's business, loose tongues after a few drinks and they did that for themselves. She never repeated a single word told, not even if her life depended on it. However, she did often put the information to use by helping out whenever possible. The expressions on Sarah and Lily's faces, indicating they may need support in the near future. Kitty had never taken to Aine, not because she is a judgmental woman, but Aine had always been a sly one with a sharp tongue, especially over the years when it came to Sarah.

Climbing onto a stool at the end of the bar, where her father had often positioned himself, Sarah surmises how Paddy must have looked forward slipping into the Nook on occasion when they were all young, grateful for adult company and conversation. Running a farm while looking after four children, can't have been an easy task for a man on his own.

'How are you holding out?' Dini asks, leaning on the bar. 'Paddy will be missed around here, a true character with a heart of gold. Kilmer Cove and certainly The Nook won't be the same without his presence sittin here.'

'I can't believe he is gone, what will I do without him Dini?' Sarah asks, staring at the picture of Jack, hair stuck to his forehead from sweat, face flushed, smile wide full of pride.

'Don't you dare cave in on me, ye've survived worse and we both know it.' Dini frowns following her gaze towards the picture. 'He was delighted with himself that day.' Dini shakes his head. 'He was a natural, a true out and out athlete destined for success.'

'Thanks to your dedication.'

'And to his, I used to be bringing up barrels early of a mornin, long before the cock crow and Jack would glide passed with a cheery greetin. For a long...long...time, I couldn't get used to him not passin me door. We're here for ya Sarah, me an Kitty... we'll always be here for ya pet.'

'Thanks,' she swallows back the lump which has formed in her throat, as she slips off the stool. 'Oh, guess what, Matt has signed up for the Dublin Marathon to run in Jack's honour. He's roped in yours truly here, might do me good taking up running, pound away my inner anger.'

'Don't pound too hard, you'll end up injured.' He warns. 'Make sure you stretch to warm up the muscles beforehand and again afterward to cool down again, very important you know.' Dini turns coach entering his comfort zone. Sarah eyes him boldly, with a wry smile. 'I'm away next week for trials, but I'll give you a ring when I get back. You can do a few laps of the track so I can take a look at your running style. I'll do up a programme, keep a constant training routine with a rest day.' Dini's professionalism taking over as he speaks about his true passion in life. 'I'll talk ta young Matt too before he goes today, see what trainin he's been doin, whether he has a coach or not. I can easily do him up a programme an keep in contact via video call, check his progress and maybe get him up here on the track one day if he can spare the time.'

'Thanks, I appreciate it.'

'Anything to help.' He winks before turning to serve a customer, having left Kitty to tend solely to the bar. She is not the type of woman to complain or interrupt, knowing Sarah would benefit from having Dini to talk to. Besides, the bar is her passion, loving chatting with familiar locals as well as meeting tourists with interesting stories to tell.

Sarah joins the rest of her family seated at a nearby table, where they are either chatting amongst themselves or talking to old friends, who've dropped by to give their sympathies. Most of the businesses in Kilmer Cove have shut for the day, their proprietor's wanting to see off Paddy with a proper wake and give their commiserations to the family. Maggie and her husband Finn, join the Connolly's at their table. Finn is a self-employed architect, working from an office set up in their house. When their two daughters were young, it had been a perfect set up with Maggie initially away doing her training and then working awkward shifts. Finn's dark looks, next to Maggie's flowing red locks make them a stunning looking couple.

'Could I get a cuppa tea?' Maggie enquires, receiving a displeasing look from Kitty in return.

'Not another wan….Ye do realise this is a pub, not a café?'

'I'm on duty later and sur it's not even lunchtime yet, bit early to be knockin back drink.'

'Tell yer husband that,' Kitty quips. 'G'wan sit down, I'll get yer tea….I'm only doin this today tho.'

'Thanks Kitty,' Maggie replies sitting next to Sarah. Normally, vying to be the centre of attention and full of chat, Maggie is unusually quiet keeping her gaze permanently fixed in the direction of her husband. Sarah decides to break the silence.

'You know I don't blame you.' Sarah whispers. 'I do blame Desmond bloody Shanahan though.'

'I know that don't mind me, I'm edgy.' Maggie replies, her gaze remaining firmly fixed on Finn. 'There's no justice, he better keep his head low or I'll have him back in Castlerea so quick, he's feet won't touch the ground.' Maggie adds, with conviction in her voice. If Sarah didn't know otherwise, she would think Maggie was talking about Finn by the way she is glowering at her husband.

'Is everything alright?'

'Yes…yes of course, been busy at work that's all.' Maggie retorts, a little too sharply.

'In Kilmer Cove station. No offence, but we are not exactly a crime filled town.' Sarah tries to lighten to mood with a weak joke, catching Finn watching them.

'You'd be surprised, I tell you.' Maggie gives her a wry smile. 'Kev is off at the moment on leave, his wife had another baby. Then there is this problem with damage to farmland recently, Ted O'Neill is on the phone constantly giving out.'

'Can't blame him there, we've had a few problems ourselves. I told Da we couldn't be botherin the Garda with it, but if it's getting out of hand.' Sarah is reminded of him arriving in late, upset over the fences being damaged and all she could focus on, was the mud all over the floor from his dirty wellies. She'd give anything to go home and find the floor muddy and his craggy face sitting at the kitchen table.

'We'll keep an eye out for ye so, it's all we can do really.'

'What? Oh ya...thanks Mags.' Sarah pats her hand in gratitude, while intently glancing around the table taking in family and friends surrounding her. Her gaze rests on Martin, the normally laid back one of the family knocking back pints followed by a whiskey chaser, quickly becoming drunk while holding animated conversation with Finn. Both of them laughing loudly at each other's stories, only Martin's laugh is forced rather than hearty, worrying Sarah.

'Bloody internet around here.' Grainne says loudly, clasping her mobile above her head, an activity she's taken to since her arrival. She jumps up and in her haste to leave, collides with Conor O'Dowd.

'Sorry for your loss again lads,' he shakes hands with Martin and Tommy, before grabbing a stool and squeezing into a space next to Sarah. This move receiving knowing stares from around the table.

'Sorry about your Da.' He says, notably not meeting Sarah's gaze as he speaks. 'He was a good man Paddy.'

'Thanks for carrying the coffin with the lads, it's what Da would have wanted and I appreciate you closing the factory today out of respect too, Kilmer Cove must appear to be a ghost town to any tourists coming into the place today.'

'He was good to me, better than my own Da, it's the least I could do.' Conor replies in a shaky tone, his face turning crimson. The normally poised handsome Conor is acting strangely uncomfortable in her presence. Before Sarah can question if everything is alright, Finn shouts across to him.

'Here...Conor settle a dispute between me and Martin.'

'Come ov...er here O'Dow...d....' Martin slurs his words. 'Settle th...ish.'

'I better get to work.' Maggie suddenly stands up appearing far from happy, she whispers to Kitty. 'Would you mind keeping an eye on him, don't let him drink too much more an maybe stick him in a taxi when he is going. I want to be sure he gets home in once piece?' Maggie nods in the direction of her husband. 'I'll see ye later.' Maggie's words prompting Sarah to glance in Finn's direction, then quickly turn away as he catches her stare. Instead locking eyes with Conor, who seems to be watching the interaction intently. Something inside Sarah shifts, Conor's steely eyes mesmerizingly sexy, having a smile which would melt even the coldest of hearts. Yet, Sarah could never ignite a spark when it came to Conor, seeing him only as an extension of her brothers. If only she could find the kind of love Lily and Tommy share, even after twenty-five years of marriage and two children. The automatic brush of a hand or locking of eyes, as though sharing silent words, a secret no one else could decipher. It would seem, every time she has considered allowing Conor into her affections, something comes between them putting up a barrier, higher than the one she'd begun to take down. She has always been an independent person, mainly content with being single. Over the years, Maggie has not so discretely or successfully tried to set up dates with male friends or work colleagues, Sarah having no interest, as her only focus in life had been to be a good mother to Jack. Since his death nothing matters apart from Jack's father, the only man she cannot give up, but cannot have either.

'I'm happy to stay here with you, if you'd like?' Conor says breaking into her thoughts, seeming to be always on the sidelines waiting patiently.

'No you better go over there and join the musketeers' they're odd as a drunken twosome.' She replies deciding she is happier being alone.

'You sure?'

'Couldn't be better.' Whether it was the context of her words in light of the day that is in it. Conor throws her a concerned look, before giving her hand a comforting squeeze then he quickly joins Martin and Finn on the other side of the table.

The hum of chatter reaches a high, as all around her family and friends become intoxicated, apart from Lily who is keeping a watchful eye on how much alcohol her daughters' are consuming. They might be of age and at their grandfather's wake, but it does not mean they can get drunk like their father seems to be doing. Something Tommy would not normally do, proving grief has a strange way of affecting even the most poised and sensible of people.

Weary from emotion, Sarah slips quietly out the side door of The Nook hoping no one notices her escape due to desperately wanting to be alone with her thoughts.

Outside, Grainne is sitting on the wall her mobile poised in her hand, face contorted, obviously not happy with whatever she is being told. Sarah walks around the back of the pub and wanders across to the playpark, lighting a cigarette from the packet Martin had given her earlier, cursing him for introducing her back to intoxicating her body.

Chapter 8

The play area is deserted, allowing the luxury of being able to sit on one of the brightly painted benches staring aimlessly at the swings, her thoughts reverting back to a time when Jack was a little boy. Clasping his chubby little hand in hers they would walk to the park after playschool, taking time to have a play before heading up to the farm to make lunch. He would always head straight for the swings first, demanding to be pushed higher, yellow wellies swinging through the air, head thrown back laughing heartily. He loved wearing wellies, a phase which lasted so long Sarah had to replace them each time his feet grew too big. Squealing with delight, he would make his way up the climbing frame, Sarah standing rigidly close by in case he fell. Always waiting in the side lines, ready to catch him and be there no matter what. When he reached adolescence expecting battle lines to be drawn, they never came. Jack never stopped being free with his smiles and generous with hugs, an ambitious boy stealthily growing into a talented young man. Her battle in life began, when the joy had been swiped away. Being a good mother had been the only focus in her life, his happiness and safety her priority, his loss leaving her with little focus and an emptiness only anger can fulfill.

Sucking on the cigarette Sarah glances upward, soft white billowing clouds lazily drift across the deep blue sky. Today the loneliness is beginning to creep in, bringing with it a darkness inside, a feeling she hates as it consumes her, leaving her feeling out of control. How dare the sun shine brightly, how dare life move on while she does not want it to. Her father and Jack out there somewhere back together again leaving her alone missing them both, the magnitude almost too hard to comprehend.

'I didn't know you smoked.' His familiar voice, husky and low as he joins her on the bench. 'I hope you don't mind. You look peaceful sitting here, I almost feel guilty for disturbing you.'

'Almost! Are you stalking me Conor O'Dowd?' The question is said in jest, though she does wonder why he has managed to seek her out.

'Something like that.' Conor replies, giving her one of his smiles. She catches a whiff of his aftershave, fresh and masculine. Sarah has always felt safe in his company, like putting on a comfortable pair of shoes. That is the very essence of Conor and also his downfall.

'So did you settle their childish dispute?'

'Don't I always? Good ole safe dependable Conor. I think they only used to let me hang with them, because of you when we were younger.' He replies almost reading her thoughts. For a couple who never made it far together, they gel more than Sarah would ever admit to herself.

'That's not true and you know it, Martin and you were...are,' correcting herself, 'good friends.' Detecting a certain sadness in his eyes, making her feel guilty for treating him so badly over the years.

'Mm...and Finn used to take the piss.'

'He did that to everyone.' Her mind drifts. 'Shit,' she'd burnt a hole in her dress, not paying attention to the cigarette smouldering in her hand. Throwing it to the ground, Sarah crushes it under her foot like stamping out resentment.

'Not like you to swear, I'll put it down to the day that's in it.' Conor says matter-of-fact, eyeing her with interest. 'Are you alright, you didn't burn yourself?'

'No...I'm full of awful vices the last few days, including these.' She crushes the reminder of the packet, placing it into a nearby bin. Hating the vile taste smoking has left in her mouth. 'I feel like my world has been turned upside down all over again.'

'I'm really sorry bout, your Da.' He stares at the ground, unable to look her in the eye. Having never received affection from own his parents, has left Conor unable to express feelings properly, making him come across as cold and standoffish.

'I know, you said.' She replies, detecting a nervous quiver in his voice similar to the night he had proposed, making it clear there is something playing on his mind.

'He was a good man Paddy....taught me how to drive, do you remember?' Conor says bringing them both back to their younger days, a time when life had been less complicated.

'Mm...' Sarah smiles, remembering fondly. 'How could I ever forget? You got his auld jeep bogged down in the back field, and Martin had to pull it out with the tractor before Aine came home from the shops and killed us all.'

'Not one of my proudest moments that's for sure.' A wisp of perfectly combed hair escapes, blowing down over his eyes. He quickly brushes it back, with a smooth flick of his fingers, sadness creeping in clouded by a past he would never let go. Sarah does not seem to notice his change in demeanour as she carries on talking, having been fully relaxed by the happy memories.

'Chalk it down, you must be the first man in history to bog down a four wheel jeep.'

'And you were always one to over exaggerate, Sarah Connolly.' Conor keeps his tone even, yet exceptionally cool. His body stiffening, aware the cracks which had been formed between them previously, would be forced wide open once he reveals the reason he had specifically sought her out.

'If that's how you see it.' Her reply sharp and defensive causing a stilted silence, knowing deep down he has never let go of something which had never really been there in the first place. It does not quash the underlying resentment, remaining uncomfortable between them, no amount of pretence could disguise it. In truth, they have been hovering on the edge of a frail friendship for years and unknown to Sarah, the tipping point is about to come.

'Sarah...I need to tell you something.' He glances away, unable to meet her gaze. She has a habit of making him relent with one look, knowing he still has a soft spot for her. 'I know today is not an appropriate time, but I was worried...and its better you hear it from me rather than someone else. I'd like to think you won't hate me...it's not as simple as it may seem.' He hesitates for far too long, clearly unable find the right words, causing Sarah to become agitated by his dithering.

'Jesus, Conor spit it out will you....and you say, I'm the dramatic one.'

'It's Desmond Shanahan.' The mention of the name making Sarah's blood run cold, the stilted expression on her face reflecting her horror.

'What about...him?'

'His parole officer came to see me...well as a town councillor and local businessman...I couldn't be seen to appear...prejudiced, is that the word I'm searching for? I'm not sure what it is....look the bottom line is, I couldn't turn my back on my responsibility.' His words come tumbling out. Sarah watches the normally poised and self-confident man before her, become uncharacteristically tongue tied. His face ashen as he clenches his teeth, while searching her face for some sort of understanding considering the difficult position he has been put in.

'What are you trying to say?' She asks, urging him to explain. Panic rising in her chest causing the nasty feeling of suffocation to return, making it hard to breathe. Every indication spells out where this is leading, and yet she chose to ignore the warning signs, because as far as she is concerned Conor would never betray her, even if she had once betrayed him.

'Christ Sarah, this has no bearing on our friendship, I need you to understand. I've always lov...liked you, even after... Look, just promise me you won't take this the wrong way.' He pleads, forcing him to beg her in a way he never thought he would. Having walked away with as much dignity as he could hold on to, when she fell pregnant for another man.

'I can't promise you, till I know what you are talking about.' Sarah replies, matter-of-fact. She could never in her wildest dreams expect to hear his next words. Having clearly underestimated him, changing the dynamics of their friendship, as there will be no going back from this point in time.

'Desmond will be starting work in the factory on Monday.' A high-pitched laugh escapes her lips, resonating around the empty playground. It isn't until she has sobered and gauges the cold expression on Conor's face, does she realise he had been serious. Conor one of her oldest friends, her ex-fiancée would be giving Desmond Shanahan, the man who murdered her son a job. The second blow comes as though you might almost expect it, but really nothing prepares you for the shock, for the unfairness of it all, and deep down you are filled with resentment. That dark ugly feeling of, haven't I already had more than my fair share of heartache, so why me. When the brain engages it really is happening, then you wonder, how will I ever get through this? Will I ever find a way out of the darkness?

'You can't be serious.' She finally manages to say, voice laced with contempt. 'Conor...please tell me you are not going to betray our friendship in this way.'

'Sarah you have to understand the difficult position I am in. I'm a representative of the community and can't be seen to turn my back on a man who has served a jail sentence and paid for his mistake.' A poor choice of words making a bad situation unrecoverable, spiralling Sarah into further discontentment.

'Mistake....mistake.' She shrieks, jumping up from the bench. 'Are you suggesting my son's murder was an unfortunate mistake? Have you forgotten what that man did? He was on drugs while driving a car, he killed another human being? It was no mistake, he purposely got into that car and used it as a weapon. Where is your loyalty to the honest citizens' of Kilmer Cove who want to feel safe walking through the streets? What about turning your back on Jack's memory? He adored you, looked up to you as a....Jesus, Conor, I can't believe what you are saying.'

'Maybe I could have chosen better words, but you really are getting this out of proportion. Desmond won't be driving, he is banned and the man has paid for what he did. You cannot expect him to spend the rest of his life locked away, he has to work and make a living. Besides isn't it time to move on with your own life, instead of making your son's death define you.' Conor's lack of understanding does not surprise Sarah in the least. How could a single man, with no children ever understand the devastation losing a child brings. There is no time limit for grieving, nothing abates the immense hole left due to their absence. There was a time she thought he knew exactly how she felt, knew the depth of her pain. Now she is unsure, making it hard to digest the revelation he has just landed on her.

'I can't believe you are saying this to me.....You of all people, my god you are a backstabbing traitor.' Unleashing her disappointment in his actions, anger seeping through every pore, her body trembling. His words hurt but she would not cry in his presence, having more dignity than to allow him witness her crumble. Nothing could prepare her for the backlash, for his unexpected response to her protest.

'That is rich, coming from the woman who broke my heart in pieces when she fell pregnant for another man. I had planned to marry you, spend my life with you and have children. I loved you for Christ sake and you threw my dreams back in my face when you cheated on me.' His face turns deep red, the vein in his right temple pulsating indicating the depth of his annoyance. Years of pent up resentment coming flooding to the fore.

'Are you seriously throwing this at me now, I can't believe you are still bitter and holding a ridiculous grudge. I met someone at university, it happens in life, people grow up and move on.' She spits back equally furious, disbelieving they are revisiting this argument after all these years.

'Ha...Oh Sarah, you had me. For years I have been an idiot while you have laughed behind my back. Stop hiding behind a guy who doesn't exist, I know who Jack's father is, have done for some time. I didn't want to believe it at first but there you go, I always thought the best of you and held on to a stupid hope one day-'

'What did you say?' She asks, a catch in her voice, every nerve in her body freezing causing the soft hairs on the back of her neck to stand on end, as a cold shiver runs down her spine.

'You heard, I know who Jack's father is, you're a hypocrite Sarah and a liar.' His contorted expression making him barely recognisable to her. Sarah however, is not about to back down, who Jack's father is does not excuse his behaviour.

'How dare you, who Jack's father is doesn't change the fact you have betrayed us. Christ Conor, it was twenty-two years ago we were teenagers, it was different back then. Hormones and confused feelings, can you honestly tell me you stayed faithful when you were in Europe?'

'I can't believe you are asking me that. Is your memory so bad, I still wanted to marry you, would have raised Jack as my own. I accept people make mistakes, like you said we were young but you still lied to me. Told me it was some guy in Trinity when it was one of our friends right here in this town, how could you?' It becomes clear, he had not been bluffing. Throwing it out in the open like gutting a fish, its insides spilling out for everyone to see. Sarah's precious secret is out. She had only ever confided the truth to her father, Lily and Tommy, if Conor is not willing to keep it to himself, there would be so many people hurt by her betrayal. Those immediately involved, as it affects their lives, and those she has chosen not to tell, because she thought it better they didn't know the truth. As those peoples' faces fill her head a sadness ebbs with it, like a horrible sea mist. She cannot bear to be hated by those she loves the most. Conor's hurt is understandable, she had treated him badly, should have been honest knowing his feelings reached far deeper than hers. Their relationship had been one sided, she saw him as nothing more than someone who had always been there. A best friend, a comfort blanket, no spark no heart thumping like they said in magazines, no missing him when they were apart.

'How do you know?' Sarah manages to ask, wondering how this would play out. What the question should have been. How much does he know?

'Does it really matter in the scheme of things? The point is you should have told me the truth instead of making up some story about a drunken one night stand. What I don't get is why all the lies....we could have made things work, you and me.' Conor, roughly shoves a hand, through his perfectly layered wheaten hair, giving him an unusually dishevelled appearance.

'Why did you never say anything?'

'I don't know...when you broke off our engagement, I was in a bad place and as much as I hated what you did, I still loved you. The ole thin line, I could see how awkward it was for you when he returned to Kilmer Cove that Christmas, with a pregnant wife on his arm. It surprised us all. How he treated you was unforgivable, a fictional father for Jack had been the right thing to do. I guess, I never understood why you never told me, I would have still married you if you were willing to let me bring, Jack up as my own. I would have loved him, Sarah. For Christ's sake, I did love him....loved you.'

'You were the closest thing to a father for Jack, he adored you......I can't explain why, I acted the way I did. I had no knowledge of a girlfriend back in Galway.....I guess there was always a little part of me that secretly hoped, he might wake up one day and realise he loved me and Jack and wanted to be with us.' Sarah replies, finally admitting the truth to herself as much as Conor.

'Funny that was my thinking about us, I always lived with that hope. Nothing changes how much you hurt me and there are times I wonder, if I really ever knew you at all.' His words hit a deep nerve. 'I need you to know, I haven't employed Desmond out of spite.'

'Maybe not but it doesn't make it any more forgivable....I think, I'm the one who underestimated you.' She walks away a bitter taste in her mouth, as far as Sarah is concerned, there is nothing more to be said. She would never have intentionally set out to hurt anyone, in her eyes by employing Desmond Shanahan, Conor has intentionally betrayed their friendship, hurting deeply.

Chapter 9

Desmond makes his way down towards the pier, having come through a narrow pathway behind the adventure centre. He had overheard Sarah Connolly's heated conversation with Conor, bringing to mind painful memories of a time he would rather erase from his life. Aware of how much Sarah hates him, sees him as some kind of monster, having endured a barrage of abuse before she had been eventually removed from the courtroom, during his sentencing.

The smell of frying chips wafts through the air filling his senses, bringing a longing for Quilty's, fresh fish and chips. His stomach rumbles in protest, having not eaten much over the past few days since being home. There is nothing wrong with Agnes's cooking, his mother a dab hand in the kitchen. He simply cannot get used to sitting at the kitchen table pretending to be a happy family, while acrimony sits like an ugly silent demon across the table.

Fran Quilty is serving behind the counter when he walks in. She lifts her head, uttering a greeting while her cheeks turn pink reminding, Des of the crush she'd had on him when they were younger. She used to make excuses to walk past, any time Des was at their house working in the garage with her brother Paul on his Celica. Fran is still as pretty as she was back then, overly shy and still evidently so, by the way she is unable to meet his gaze. It wouldn't have mattered either way, at that time, Des had been besotted with his fiancée Evelyn. Back when he'd lived with Evie, a supermodel could have passed by and he would not have paid attention.

'Hi Fran, Fish and chip please....How's your brother Paul is he still driving the Celica?'

'He had to-' before she gets to finish the sentence, the gravelly voice of her father Ross Quilty comes bellowing from behind Desmond.

'We're closing, the fryers are turned off.' He is dressed in his best suit, having dropped over from the wake to check on Fran. Just as well he did, it would seem.

'I'll just take one of these so, be a shame to waste when a customer could buy one.' Des points to three golden coated pieces of cod sitting in the warmer, missing the point of Ross's comment.

'They are already taken for an order.' Ross barks back, causing Fran's face to flush a deep red, her eyes dart nervously between her father and Des, knowing her father had literally told her to turn the fryers on in preparation for people piling out of the Nook wanting their supper. Ross's nostrils flare, his stout belly and wispy tufts of hair giving him a pig like appearance. If there is one thing he does not like, it is to be confronted, especially by the likes of Desmond Shanahan.

Grasping the situation, Des smirks indicating he will not be fooled easily. A stand-down ensues, fast becoming a battle of wills between two very stubborn men.

'If you are closing,' Des glances at the clock behind the counter, grasping it's still very early, 'they haven't picked them up, so the fish will go to waste. Think of the profit you are losing by not selling.' Des rests his gaze on Ross, clearly challenging the older man. 'Fran, can I have a fish and chip please.' He repeats his order, keeping his voice low and calm.

'I said, the fryers are turned off.' Ross retorts, placing his hands on his hips for effect. Desmond, is not about to back down and allow Ross get the better of him. While awaiting trial he had become introvert and suffered with panic attacks, it had been a long hard road, a journey in which he has survived. What people like Ross Quilty fail to realise, Desmond is prepared for rejection after his visit to Charlie, now fully aware the accident will follow him around like a permanent shadow.

'I will take the fish then, don't worry about any chips.' He raises his voice showing conviction. Having endured his father all his life, a harder man to battle against than Ross Quilty. Adding to the rejection from his fiancée, having hardened his soul as well as his heart. He will not allow anyone to make a fool of him ever again.

'Get out...I ain't serving the likes of you. You have no business coming in here.' The older man snarls, equally unwilling to back down.

'I'll take two portions of fish and chips please Fran.' No one had heard Conor O'Dowd, walk into the chipper. Feeling defeated Des turns to leave, the last thing he needs is for Conor to think of him as a thug. If he lost this opportunity of a job, Gary would need to know why. As easy going as the kind-hearted parole officer is, he would not be able to overlook something like this and Des would be back inside so quick, he would not have time to pack a toothbrush. 'Hang on a second Desmond, I need a word.' Conor says, stopping Desmond in his tracks. He closes his eyes, inhaling deeply before turning around, heart pounding in his chest, wondering if it is too late, had Conor overheard the whole thing. Fran turns her back on the scene busying herself putting chips into the hot fat, while Ross remains poised like a soldier on guard beside his daughter. Arms crossed, his chest puffed out.

'Sad day having to bury poor, Paddy Connolly.' Ross breaks the silence, receiving no reply to his comment. Instead, Conor makes a move which undermines him detrimentally.

'Will you have salt and vinegar on yours, Des?' Conor asks, surprising Des and obviously Ross too, his jaw visibly clenches as does his fists.

'Tis a sad day alright.' Ross points out. 'When those show no loyalty in this town, an you a so called friend of young Sarah and practically brought up by Paddy an all.' Ross is firing on all cylinders, there no holding back as polite words have long surpassed him. 'What that poor girl has been through, you'd expect a bit of empathy.' Ross shakes his head showing his frustration. 'I'll get one of the boys to come and help ye Fran.' He blusters as he leaves his own shop, disgusted.

Ross will take immense pleasure in telling everyone in The Nook. Kitty and Dini would then be straight on the phone to, Conor's parents in Spain telling them how disloyal their son has been. For over forty years, Quentin and Gloria O'Dowd have had no interest in their son, so it isn't likely to change now. Besides, it ceases to bother Conor, nothing does anymore, not since Sarah broke his heart, crushing it into tiny pieces. The sad truth being, she has been used like every other woman who has fallen for the infamous charms of Jack's father. It doesn't change the fact, Conor handled the whole situation with Desmond wrong, had attacked her turning his guilt into her shame. It had been cruel and unjust, because deep down he is fully aware of what his friend is like, had always been promiscuous, marriage having not stopped him. After all, Sarah isn't the only Connolly female to have been bedded and left heartbroken.

'Thanks Fran, sorry for getting you stuck in the middle of that.' Des apologises, when Fran hands them the order. Her shy smile in response making him feel guilty. 'Thanks for that.' Des says, as he and Conor walk amiably along Main Street. 'Aren't you worried they will be pissed off with you?'

'I learned to stop worrying about what other people think of me a long time ago.' The street is deserted, apart from the chipper all the other establishments are closed out of respect for Paddy. Kilmer Cove Main Street, whether busy or quiet with its old stone whitewashed buildings looks like something out of a picture postcard. Brightly painted windows and doors of various colours, with flower boxes gracing every windowsill spilling over with brightly coloured annuals. The only sounds which can be heard, as the two men walk slowly along the path overlooking the Atlantic, are the clanging of masts on nearby sail boats anchored in the bay and the distant hum of chatter coming from outside The Nook.

'I suppose, it's easier when you're rich and successful.' Des says displaying naivety, making him sound immature for his age.

'I wouldn't go that far, more to do with being bitten once too many.' Conor replies absently. Aware, Des is most likely knowledgeable of his involvement with Sarah, and possibly curious as to why he would employ him. Conor admires the younger man's restraint for not asking.

'Aren't you worried they will shun you for employing me though?' Des persists.

'They'll get over it...Like I said Desmond, I answer to no one....just do me one favour, if you get any trouble in the factory, come and tell me.'

'Don't' get me wrong, I appreciate your gesture but I served nearly four years in prison. The first thing you learn as part of survival, is to never become a snitch.'

'It's different when I'm the boss, don't let the small minded bastards in this town get the better of you.....Did you find it tough in prison? Sorry, I don't mean to pry...you were young and I remember you as being very quiet and shy.'

'It wasn't that bad, my cell mate became quite a saviour. A kind of father figure if you like, I count myself lucky. I realise now my parents had it tougher than I did, mum especially.' Desmond lets out a nervous chortle. 'You are the first person to ask me about prison. Mum is too frightened, I think. I'm sure she's imagined large muscular, tattooed brutes lurking in the showers waiting to rape me. As for my father, he's blanked it out ashamed. He never visited the whole time I was in, not even once.' This revelation is no surprise to Conor, though it is pleasing that Des is confident enough to confide easily, it's as though the two men share an unspoken understanding.

'I'm sure it's not you, he's ashamed of. People in this town...they can be judgemental. It's a small place where everyone knows everyone's business, not always a good thing. Ger is possibly finding it all very hard to deal with, he's a quiet private sort of man.' Conor replies, hoping to give Des hope of salvaging their relationship. If they are confined under the same roof things will be difficult enough.

'Thanks for the kind words, but believe me my father was never...' Des pauses, realising he has gone too far, so abruptly changes the subject. 'I've known the Quilty's all my life, used to service Paul's car for free. I've never had a falling out with anyone round here before, I can't believe Ross's bloody minded attitude considering I never intentionally set out to kill that boy, so you'd think they would know I never meant to....it was an accident.' His tongue rolling freely again without thought.

'You have to understand, and please don't think I am judging you. I'm only pointing out why they are being so negative towards you. The fact you had taken drugs and driven your car, you weren't in control.'

'I wish...I could remember what happened...all I know is I'd been working all night, a second job to help cover the expense of our wedding....the last thing I remember was finishing the shift and going home, or at least I'm sure that's where I should have gone. What made me drive over here at that early hour is a mystery and I'd never have taken drugs or any sort of pills, I swear. I wouldn't even have a drink if I was driving, my car was everything, my passion you know what I'm sayin.' Conor doesn't answer. Des finishes his chips putting the paper in a nearby bin. 'Look

I better get back, Ma will be worried.' He lets out a nervous chuckle. 'Jesus, I sound like a kid with a curfew.'

'You take care Desmond...it will get better, just give people time to learn to trust you again. I'll see you Monday for work and remember what I said.' Conor crosses the street, getting into his Toyota Landcruiser. He sits for a moment watching Desmond walk up the hill, wondering has he made the right choice. By giving this man a chance, he has risked any miniscule possibility of a reconciliation with Sarah. When all is said and done, if there is one thing about Sarah, it was her devotion to Jack. Conor admires that quality in her, wishing things could have been different. That they could have filled Atlantic View with a family, making it a home rather than the lonely mausoleum it has become, devoid of laughter and even tears. If only Sarah realised he had built that house for her and Jack, always living with a small hope.

◆◆◆

When Desmond arrives home Agnes and Ger are sitting in the lounge, Ger in his usual chair watching some documentary on the television. Agnes is staring at her phone, lips twitching. Des notices tears glistening on her cheeks, causing his heart to plummet.

'What's up Ma?' Des asks frowning.

'Oh...I'm being silly...don't mind me.' Agnes wipes the tears away with the back of her hand. 'Tears of joy would you believe.' She feigns a weak smile, gaze still transfixed on the screen of her phone. 'You are an uncle, come...have a look at the pictures your brother sent. She's just a little dote, they called her Amelia...Amelia Rose, isn't she just the finest.'

'She is Ma...a little princess.' Des sits on the couch alongside his mother, peering at the tiny person wrapped in a pink blanket while Agnes scrolls through various shots.

'Seven pound three ounces...same as you in fact, Phil was seven pound six. She has his nose don't you think?'

'Yeah, she has.' He gasps in awe of the similarity between the baby and his brother, like a miniature version. Phil two years older than Des, had always been the more studious of the two growing up. He went into banking, getting a good job in Donegal with solid prospects for a secure future. After the accident, Phil claimed his reputation was put at stake wanting to move away, so applied for a job in Edinburgh. The two brothers had never been particularly close, but Phil's lack of support put an invisible barrier between them. He moved away long before the trial, only ever making contact with their parents and never asking about Des or commenting on the fact he'd gone to jail. Close or not, they were still brothers and his rejection hurt Des to the core. It doesn't not stop him from being happy for his brother, securing a job as a branch manager, meeting his wife Gina and now the icing on the cake for Phil, a beautiful daughter.

'You've only just missed his call on Skype, he was holding Amelia and she opened her eyes. Ah...it was as though she was looking at me and I felt, I could almost reach out an touch her.'

'It'll be the closest we'll get ta see her, because Phil refuses to bring Gina and the baby over here. Doesn't want the embarrassment of them being shunned by locals...can't say I blame him.' Ger chides, having remained quiet until this point. He rises from his chair, leaving the room before anyone can furnish him with a response.

'Ignore him.' Agnes protests. The jibe had already succeeded in its cause, making Des wish he was far from here too. Envying his brother in a way he never thought possible, a feeling which is alien to him. One look at his mother's distraught face enough to enlighten him to the reality of her pain. For as long as Des can remember, Agnes has tried her best to build a loving home and make their family unit a happy and loving one, but Ger never partook. He never came to watch either of his sons' play a football match. Had never praised either, Phillip or Desmond when they did well in their exams or won a trophy for something. If truth be told, Desmond can never recall receiving a single hug from his father. Ger might blame Desmond for wrecking their lives and causing a breakdown in their family, but in truth it had never been there in the first place.

'Would you not go over an visit them yourselves.' Des suggests, seeing the longing in his mother's eyes.

'We wouldn't have that kind of money spare.' She replies, flippantly. Putting her mobile away, she adds, 'will I make us a cup of tea?' Making Des aware the subject is closed. It does not mask the fact, he knows she is trying to play it down. That having helped him in the past with solicitor fees has drained any little savings they might have had. 'Don't mind my fanciful ideas, I'm a silly woman at times. It's...only, I always imagined having grandchildren popping in here, an spending time with them... ' Amelia Jade would probably never see the beauty of Kilmer Cove. Would never walk hand in hand with her grandmother, along its golden sandy beaches or eat ice cream sitting on the pier. 'Will we have a bit of cake with the tea, are you hungry?'

'Sure Ma, a bit of cake with the tea would be lovely.' Des follows her to the kitchen, his heart as heavy as stone.

Chapter 10

'Mam, do you still have my old sewing machine.' Evelyn calls out, as she rushes into her mother's house with a parcel of material under her arm. Having successfully retrieved it from the boot of the car, without raising suspicion from Brian. His mood in general these past few days good, so she has no intention of infuriating him in any way. Her only snippet of discontent coming from Jimmy's announcement, Des is working alongside him in the fish factory. A revelation which worries Evelyn, as Jimmy is liable to let his tongue run away with him, bringing repercussions for her.

For now, Evelyn must brush any thoughts of Des aside, happy life has finally picked up at home and also her regained passion for designing and making clothes.

'Course love, sur all your stuff is still upstairs in your bedroom.' Gillian shouts from the kitchen, unable to come out to the hallway as her hands are covered in flour. The smell of home baking wafting out into the hall makes Evelyn's mouth water.

'Great, can I set it up and work on something over here from time to time?' She asks quashing the urge to join her mother in the kitchen, not wanting to waste time in getting started on making the dress.

'Of course you can.' A smile spreads across Gillian's normally pinched face. An expression she has adapted since the death of her husband nearly six years ago. 'You head up, I'll bring you a mug of tea and a bit of this pie once it's cooked.' Words to Evelyn's ears, delighted at the prospect of being able to savour her mother's cooking. No wonder Danny loves coming here, she surmises.

'Thanks, mam.' Evelyn bounds upstairs to her old bedroom with the bag she had been carrying. Delighted with having a rare day off work during the week, she has decided to take advantage of the free time having just dropped Danny to school. With Brian and Jimmy busily painting the house, it's the last place she wants to be, so she told him she had some last minute shopping to do for Danny's party. The announcement prompting him to hand her yet another large wad of notes.

'Buy whatever ya need.' Brian had said, before kissing her. 'G'wan before ya have me turned on.' Her body tingling at the thought, wishing Jimmy hadn't been there as Brian would not have let her go so easily.

Once inside the room which her mother has kept pristine, she uncovers her sewing machine plugging it in. Opening her portfolio, she retrieves the design she'd created nearly six years ago, the dress she'd planned to marry Des in. A slim bodice, flaring out just above the knee with a neat trail at the back, while scooping down at the neckline to show cleavage at the front. Gems hand sewn in a unique design she would wear on her wedding day, having often imagined it on so many times in the past. She has to question, when did it all change and the dream become a nightmare? Was it the loneliness that made her fall into Brian's arms so easily the night he'd called round?

Des had rang to say he would be late home, as he was collecting a car in Galway with Charlie and she'd been bitterly disappointed as they were meant to go out. Evelyn having showered and dressed in a new top and mini skirt with knee high boots, a vain attempt in getting Des to notice her. Since living together, they had slipped into being a cosy couple too easily. The knock at the door came just as she'd literally hung up from the call. It was the look in Brian's eyes when she'd opened the door to him, could tell by the expression on his strikingly chiselled face, he was drinking her in with an admiration she craved. Before she knew what was happening they were having sex on the couch in the lounge. The way he'd stimulated her, leading to a frenzied climax she had never experienced before. From then on he'd become her necessity, even when they weren't together her body contracted rippling at the thought of his touch. Couldn't wait for Des to go to work, so Brian could call over and bring her to orgasmic heights she had never thought possible. Her lips twitch smiling at the memory, in the past few days he has been showing her the same affection, yet she still feels an uncertain need to keep her guard up. To keep her renewed passion for making her own designs a secret, like her second mobile.

Carefully unwrapping the silk material soft to touch and as beautiful as she remembers, Evelyn wonders will she ever wear it for her own wedding day. Brian had never broached the subject and she has never questioned him. Their relationship being a constant rollercoaster ride, always with the feeling of spiralling dangerously downwards.

It doesn't take long for her to get stuck in to her old passion, bringing her back to a time when she would do this with regularity. Spreading the pattern out on the floor, she places the material on top carefully cutting it out. She had done all the measurements for the pattern six years ago, now hoping she has not gained too much pre-natal weight after having Danny. Sadly, Evelyn doesn't realise, she is more likely in need of taking the dress in as she has unhealthily lost, rather than gained weight.

'Wow....That must have cost a fair packet.' Gillian says as she enters the room, carrying a tray laden with cups and plates of home baked apple pie, each generously dolloped with fresh whipped cream melting on the hot pastry. I can see why you'd be hiding over here. What are you making?' She asks, placing the tray on the bed and lifting a piece of the silk, caressing it in her hands. 'Is that the dress?' She eye's the sketched picture Evelyn has spread out beside the sewing machine.

'Yes Mam and you can relax, I'm not marrying Brian.' Evelyn retorts, becoming immediately defensive. 'I happened to pass the haberdashery the other day and was drawn in. I never got to...anyway, I thought it would be nice to keep me hand in before I forget how to sew.' Evelyn blushes due to her unnecessary lie and need to explain her actions to her mother. If Brian did ask her to marry him, Gillian would have to accept the fact whether she approved or not.

'Right, of course.' Gillian replies handing Evelyn a plate, refraining from pushing the subject any further. 'Are you all set for Saturday, do you need me to make sandwiches?'

'Ah no, it's grand Mam thanks, Danny wants pizza delivered from Max's, it's all been organised.'

'I have those curtains ready for whenever you want to take them away. If they are too long, you could take them up and make a few scatter cushions with the leftover material. In fairness, Brian and Jimmy are doing some job on the house.'

'Yeah they are...though, I think Jimmy pulled a sickie from work today so they could get it finished, I'd hate him to be getting into trouble. You know Jimmy, he goes along with whatever Brian tells him and it's not always a good thing.'

'Jimmy Duggan is well able to look after himself.' Gillian scolds. Evelyn aware, her mother has never liked Jimmy, claiming he cannot be fully trusted, whatever she means by that Evelyn is not quite sure and she has never bothered to ask.

'Shit...is that the time?' Evelyn exclaims glancing at her watch, having not realised how long she's been there. 'I better go pick Danny up.'

'I'll go pick him up if you want more time here.' Gillian suggests seeing how relaxed her daughter looks, for the first time she can truly remember.

'No it's grand...can I leave it all like this, you don't use this room do you?'

'No, sure it's your room, feel free to pop round anytime you want to work away on it, you have your own key. It's not as airy as the studio you had in the flat, but we could move the bed and set up a table if you need more space for cutting.'

'Thanks mam....and for the lovely pie...it's been nice being here...would you mind if we didn't mention any of this,' she waves a hand in the direction of the sewing machine, 'to Brian.'

'Of course not, your secret is safe with me.' Gillian taps an index finger on the side of her nose. Evelyn opens her mouth to defend Brian, then thinks the better of it. He probably would be pleased for her, she just needs to find the right time to broach the idea of fulfilling the dreams she had before becoming pregnant. She slips, half the money Brian gave her into the bag of surplus material though doesn't know why.

When Evelyn arrives at the school ten minutes later, the playground is full of mother's waiting, some standing in pairs chatting, others in collective groups.

'Hey how are you?' Mia, one of the mother's from Danny's class, sidles up beside her. She is a big girl, not fat rather tall and stocky built with platinum blonde hair tied up in a trademark pony tail. 'Haven't seen you in ages. Y our mother normally picks Danny up doesn't she?' Mia doesn't wait for Evelyn to answer. 'Thanks for the invite to Danny's party on Saturday, Sheldon is really excited about going. Sounds like you are having a big do an invited practically the whole class. Sheldon mentioned there'd be a bouncy castle and magician.'

'Yeah, Brian's idea to spoil him.' Evelyn tries to sound blasé about the whole thing, aware Mia would be interested to know how they could afford such a lavish do. When in truth, Evelyn herself does not know where the money has come from.

'I see he's doing a bit of work on the house.' Mia probes. 'I wish my fella'd get off his lazy arse an do something.' The comment may have sounded flippant, but Evelyn knows Mia's game. In response, she tries to turn the conversation around.

'Your Ben works long shifts though, must be tiring. I know, I'm fit to collapse after being on me feet in Roaster's.' Evelyn replies, refraining from pointing out to Mia, she should appreciate what she's got. Ben is a builder by trade and even with the downfall takes on any work he can, working long hours. Also holding down a position in Roaster's often doing double shifts like, Evelyn has to. Mia has never had to work a day in her life because Ben has allowed her the privilege of being a full time mum.

'I have it harder trying to look after Sheldon and keep the house.' Mia replies, pleasing Evelyn that the heat seems to be taken off Brian and his sudden abundance of money. 'If anyone deserves a break, I do.' The reprieve short and sweet, Mia soon throws the heat back on Evelyn. 'Anyway, ye must be flush at the moment, all the new gear going into your place and the flash new car in the driveway.' What car! Evelyn wonders, suspecting Mia may have gauged her surprise at this revelation. Trying to sound nonchalant she says.

'Thankfully Brian has a bit of work at the moment.' Evelyn can feel her cheeks burn, finger going straight to her mouth she crunches on a nail.

'Is that what he calls it?' Mia raises her voice, feigning shock while shaking her head dramatically, spiralling her pony tail to flap about behind her head, she adds. 'Look I'm not one to gossip or get involved in anyone's business. I know a lot of the other mothers on the estate think yer a little stuck up...well...I like ya. So I'm going to give ya, a bit of advice. Watch yer back, there's talk about your Brian trying to push in on the Murphy's business an they don't like it.'

'Mammy, mammy, look what I did in school.' Danny's enthusiastic appearance a welcome interruption, arriving at her side he hands Evelyn a picture. 'Nathan told me, he can't wait to come to my party an see the magician.' Danny jumps up and down excitedly.

'Don't say I didn't warn ya.' Mia raises an over pencilled brow before striding away, her pony tail swinging from side to side.

Evelyn quickly manoeuvres Danny towards the gate, wanting to make a swift exit from the playground. In her pathway, stands a group of women where, Janine Murphy has taken court. Every pair of eyes bore into her like lasers, making her suddenly nauseous, in return Evelyn throws them a bright smile along with a friendly hello, as she passes by. One thing Evelyn won't do, is let this lot think she is scared of them. She has chosen not to question where, Brian is getting the money from, knowing its source will be far from genuine, fooling herself there would be no repercussions if she didn't know. Going up against the Murphy's is the last thing she would have expected Brian to be stupid enough to do, or is it she, who is the stupid one?

Chapter 11

Hating herself for faltering again, Sarah allows the intoxication to travel deep into her lungs, before blowing out. Making a silent promise it will be the last cigarette she will smoke. Muttering under her breath, she flings the packet with the last two still inside into the bin. Conor's betrayal is still sitting uneasy, though not as worrying as his revelation. So much had gone unsaid, but she cannot bring herself to face him and obviously he is doing the same, as his cousin Alice has been collecting his bread the past two days on her way to the factory. Sarah doesn't know whether to be relieved or annoyed at him, for purposefully avoiding her.

'Damned men, now I know why I stayed single.' She mutters, kicking the side of an empty box.

'They say talking to yourself is a sign of madness.' Lily says, coming out to join her. 'My feet hurt, that was one hell of a rush this morning. Six buses within the space of two hours, I thought we were going to run out of food at one stage.' She sits onto some neatly stacked, empty wooden crates.

'Mm...though, I did appreciate being busy. The house is empty with Martin and Grainne gone back to Galway.' Sarah replies, moving down beside her to sit on a lower crate.

'It's tough trying to return to normal, everything feels too off balance. Tommy looked lost this morning feeding the animals on his own.'

'Used to dad bossing him around, I'd say.' They both laugh at this breaking the gloom from taking over.

'Possibly, how are you progressing with the training? I saw you head out early in the car again this morning?' Lily asks.

'Ah...ya...Dini is taking a look at my running style next week when he is back, so I've been heading over to the track to practice.' Sarah hates lying, an ironic metaphor in the scheme of her life, but not to Lily. How could she explain parking outside the Shanahan's every morning? Watching Desmond leave for work and continue his life as though nothing matters, filling her with bitterness. Fortunately, Lily hasn't noticed Sarah's sudden lack of eye contact. Maybe she has, but instead has chosen not to pry.

'He's some man, dedicated to the last Dini.' She sighs. 'Everyone has been wonderful, Eamon wouldn't take any money for the wood or fixing the fence. Ted O'Neil has been helping with the milking. As for the food being dropped over, neither of us will have to cook for at least a month. We are fortunate to have wonderful neighbours don't you think?'

'Everyone had great respect for him, Kitty claims the village won't be the same.'

'Lol, she had a soft spot for your Da and will miss eyeing him up at the end of the bar every Friday and Sunday night.' Lily giggles. Sarah shakes her head in bemusement. Her sister-in-law is getting carried away with trying to keep in line with the younger generation. It does not suit her otherwise motherly nature, it is only fair to let her know.

'You really are spending too much time checking your daughters' Facebook pages.' Sarah points out, hoping a polite hint might do the trick. It doesn't.

'Oh girl, you are way behind the times. Mind you, I'm finding it hard to check anything, between snap chat, Instagram and what its name...is, oh whatever else they seem to be on.' Lily grimaces finally showing defeat, causing Sarah to feel sorry for her. Why can't she see they all love her, for being Lily, without the spiel?

'Come on, we better go back inside or Olive will be handing in her notice, the poor woman has been a gem with all the hours she's putting in.' Sarah jumps down from the box she is sitting on. It has been nice sitting in the sunshine, allowing her worries float briefly away.

'She has been doing a great job, Lena too, but we should be looking at our staff situation. Tommy will need help with the first phase of the campsite almost ready, we have bookings for next week.' Lily says slipping off the boxes, her face creased with worry. Due to the success of the shop and café, they have decided to erect a campsite with the increased tourism in the area. The farm itself proving to be not sufficient enough in recent years.

'I guess we should all sit down tonight and make a plan, I suppose. Hard to think of making decisions without Da here to boss us all. I've been aware we should be sorting it all out, somehow it didn't seem right over the last few days. Making plans without Dad and moving life on as though he doesn't matter.'

'Yes, I know what you mean but Paddy would not want to see all his hard work crumble either. You're right we should start looking at taking on a bit of help.'

'Maybe I'm jumping the gun a bit, after all, Tommy and I have our appointment with Alan this afternoon, it could change everything you know.'

'Don't say that, I'm sure Aine was full of empty threats.' Lily pauses, looking thoughtful. 'I didn't mention anything to Tommy...you know, what Aine was saying, he's had enough on his plate as it is.' Lily looks at her pleadingly, prompting Sarah to tap the side of her nose with an index finger.

'Mum's the word, I didn't say anything to Martin either. He and Grainne seemed...I don't know on edge. Maybe it was all the upset and I'm over analysing.'

'I wouldn't be too sure about that.' Lily replies opening the back door to the shop, waving her hand for Sarah to walk in first. 'Don't let on, I said anything as I don't want to pry into their business but Grainne mentioned he is under serious pressure, working long hours too. The bigger mortgage has put a strain on them financially.'

'He hinted something was amiss the morning of Dad's funeral. Maybe I should have taken it more seriously, would explain why he was smoking heavily and not his usual self. Led me astray with the fags again.' Sarah replies, hating the thought of Martin being under duress.

'Dirty bloody habit, smoking.' Lily points out in mock exasperation. 'What about your marathon, poisoning your body when you should be caring for it, rest assured I'll be keeping my eye on you.'

'I hoped you would say that.' Sarah replies with a wry smile.

Two hours later, at ten to four Tommy parks outside oceanic temptations, the name Sarah had given the business. Sarah's feet are aching, as four further busloads of tourists had stopped in throughout the afternoon. All she really wants to do, is to go home collect her surfboard and head down to Surfers Cove.

'Good luck.' Lily whispers, as Sarah hangs her apron up and grabs her bag.

'It's only reading the Will and tying up loose ends, right.' Sarah tries to convince herself more than Lily, her stomach churning like a washing machine on a rinse cycle. Trying to shake off any fears as she jumps into the passenger side of Tommy's old 4X4 old jeep.

'Martin should have stayed on to be with us for this.' Tommy says as he drives out of the carpark onto the main road.

'He was worried about being off work. Being our own bosses here, I guess we don't know what it is like working for a firm. It's a different world.'

'You maudlin? I didn't think you ever regretted not finishing your law studies.' Tommy stares straight ahead as he drives.

'Jesus no, I just meant we don't know what it's like for Martin.' Sarah replies with sincerity. Horrified he had thought otherwise, as she could never imagine living anywhere but Kilmer Cove. It had been a mad teenage notion due to everyone else going away to college and University, along with becoming enthralled in Ally McBeal on the television. A woman with a career, self-confidence and beautiful clothes, Sarah had been drawn in by the glamour of it all. In hindsight, it was not a life she would have been comfortable living. Sarah turns to look out of the passenger window, cringing at the thought. In a way it had been a need to break ties with Conor already unsure about marrying him so young, an excuse she convinced herself of. She decides to change the subject. 'Lily and I, were discussing having to take on more staff with the expansion and maybe even someone to help you on the farm.' Expecting a negative reaction to the latter suggestion. Tommy only ever used to working with Paddy might find it hard taking in someone as his replacement.

'I think that's a good idea, anyone in mind?' His reply surprising, yet pleasing.

'I might have.' She smiles inwardly as they pull up outside, Alan Sullivan's office, situated on Kilmer Cove Main Street next door to, Quilty's Chipper. 'Just the man we need to talk too.' Sarah adds with a knowing smile.

'What Ross?' Tommy questions as Sarah jumps out of the Jeep to greet the stout chipper owner.

'Evening Ross, thank you so much for the fish and chips you sent up to the house the other night. The local support has been overwhelming, once again.'

'Aye, very kind of you Ross.' Tommy adds, coming round to join them. 'Like Sarah said, everyone has been very kind and supportive and it's not the first time. Makes me proud to be part of this community.'

'My pleasure, Paddy will be missed around here. A great man, he'd do anything for anyone he would.' Ross replies crossing his arms over his generous stomach. 'Though sadly not everyone is as loyal.' This comment receives wide eyed stares from both Sarah and her brother. 'Aye, I believe Conor has given that Shanahan fellow a job in the fish factory. Patrick Connolly would turn in his grave, to think Conor practically lived in your place as a teenager.' Ross tuts, shaking his head. 'Ungrateful sod, where would he have been only for your Da. His own parents too busy travelling to care.' He tuts again for effect. 'Aye, no accounting for loyalty.'

Sarah cannot bear the older man's pitying stare any longer, averting the conversation. Asking Ross, the intended subject when they first pulled up.

'What is your Paul at these days?'

'Ah, don't talk to me about that fellow. Sometimes I wonder if he's one of mine, possibly he was swapped in the hospital.' His reply resulting in Sarah having to stifle an urge to laugh.

'Is he not still at college then?' Tommy asks, also wearing a bemused expression. 'Ph....he gave up, says he's not academic.' Ross re-crosses his arms over his stomach, resting them on top. 'Mel is heartbroken and wants him out from under her feet, he's twenty-six next month for feck sake. Though there ain't much work around here. I have Fran with me already, I can't provide work for all me kids or I'd have nothing left to run the business on. Would have asked Conor about getting him in the factory only I don't need, Paul getting mixed up with the likes of that Shanahan fellow. Paul would be too easily influenced, you know.'

'Would he come and work on the farm?' Sarah shoots the words out, concerned Tommy might walk away before she seizes a chance.

'It'd be early starts and hard graft.' Tommy adds, brow furrowing as he eye's his sister, showing his confusion over Sarah's suggestion.

'I'll have him up to ye at five in the morning and he won't let you down, you have my word.'

'Six is fine.' Tommy winks turning to go. 'Come on, we're late.' He grimaces at Sarah. She knows what he is thinking but he will thank her soon enough of that, she is confident. Paul used to help out at the adventure centre when, Sarah worked there as an instructor and proved to be one hell of a hard worker. There were times when she had to force him to sit and have a break. Smiling, she turns to join Tommy, who is already at the threshold of the solicitors quaint offices.

'Didn't think you would approve of Paul, isn't he the one who drives around in the sports car?' Tommy whispers as he pulls open the door, allowing her to walk ahead.

'I'm surprised at you, Thomas Connolly not every young man who drives a particular type of car is a danger to society. I'm not judgemental where I'd tar everyone with the same brush.' Sarah breezes past, acting blasé about it all. 'Trust me, Paul will be a perfect choice.'

Inside the solicitor's office, Tommy and Sarah are warmly greeted by Grace, Alan's receptionist. A petite woman in her late fifties, immaculately dressed and very efficient. Managing the files and clients of both Alan and his brother Padraig, the local accountant.

'Hi, you can go straight through, Alan is waiting for you.' Grace says with a warm welcoming smile. Sarah and Tommy thank her. Sarah grateful they do not have to climb the narrow creaky stairs where, Alan usually situates himself, due to the magnificent view of the ocean outside. The small room they enter into, would once have been a kitchen when the building was a residential cottage. The old range has been removed and reinstalled in, Alan's modern bungalow.

Although considerably changed for its new use, the room still exhibits some original features such as low oak beams where, a laundry airer once hung. The stone heart, where pots once boiled water for food and washing. The flagstone floor still visible making an enchanting feel. Sarah could almost imagine a family living here, the room like the farmhouse kitchen projecting the heart of the Irish home.

Alan stands up as they enter shaking both their hands, bringing her back to the reality of why they are here. Reaching his full six foot-two, he has to bow slightly because of the beams and low ceiling, probably why he never usually uses this room as his office.

'Sorry for your loss again, I'm still stunned myself. Paddy was as strong as an ox. I don't think, I remember him being sick a day in his life.' Alan hovers between being a professional and neighbourly. Alan sits gesturing for them to do the same. Older than Sarah at school possibly more Tommy's age or even Aine's, she had never paid much attention to him before. Aine had been right, he does have a dandruff problem, how the hell had her sister remembered such a petty detail!

Sarah clutches her bag tightly, suddenly feeling quite tense as she sits on one of the large old leather chairs. Her stomach beginning to churn, along with the same unsettled feeling she got the day Desmond was released from prison, causing her father's heart attack.

'Lads, I appreciate you coming in when...well it's so soon and your pain is still raw as they say. I wouldn't have bothered you only...god, I don't know where to start or how to put it.' Alan shuffles a file, averting his gaze while Sarah and Tommy sit rigidly staring at him. Waiting. When he doesn't speak immediately, Sarah can feel bile rise from the pit of her stomach to her throat. What can only be seconds, feel as though they have been sitting there for hours. She can hear a clock behind her somewhere ticking. Tick, ticking. Grinding in her ears while she suppresses the urge to scream at Alan to tell them what Aine is up to, because this can only be her doing. 'As you know, Paddy signed over the farm land and livestock to you, Tommy a couple of years back. He also signed over land and the old stables to you, Sarah which houses the business with Lily so everything from that respect is in order. Now the farmhouse itself remained in Paddy's name, however, he did entrust the title deeds to myself for safe keeping. In retrospect he made a Will instructing the house go to Sarah, if she's still living there on his death. If she had married,' he coughs, causing Sarah to flush though unsure why, 'or moved away for any other reason, the house was to be passed on to whichever family member would live in it. He was explicit for the house not to be sold, or the farm split in any form outside of the family unit. His wishes were for it to stay within the family, handed down through generations. Now, in retrospect of Sarah staying in the house, he left a generous inheritance from an insurance policy to Martin and Aine totaling a sum of one hundred and fifty thousand euro each, along with stating they be allowed build should they wish to move home and the main house be occupied by Sarah. Lastly, a healthy contingency fund for the farm and business has also been put aside. Paddy felt it was only fair the assets be split in this way, reckoning it would suit all his children's needs.' Alan hesitates and Sarah realises there has to be a hitch. By now she wants to grab him by the shoulders and shake him, he is stalling so much. 'Your sister Aine, as the eldest is contesting the Will. She feels, she should inherit the farmhouse and a portion of the land surrounding it, which she has also stated was unfairly signed over prematurely.'

Sarah attempts to speak, but her lips are glued together, she glances across at Tommy, willing him to say something but he remains silent beside her, his eyes fixated on Alan. Finally he asks the question which Sarah cannot.

'What does this mean exactly?'

'Her solicitor, a man named Fintan Power in Dublin, has requested all assets be frozen until the matter is resolved.' Alan replies. Sarah watches a flutter of dandruff fall on his shoulders. Clearly, Alan is not confident about anything and the possibility of losing her home is fast becoming a reality.

'Again, Alan what does this mean exactly?' Tommy persists, confusion etched across his face. To anyone who didn't know the man the repeated question perceives him as stupid, but this is further from the truth. Sarah stifles the urge to release a nervous laugh, the negative energy in the room fast becoming suffocating.

'She has also requested the accounts from the shop and the plans, which were passed for the campsite. I can assure you neither myself, nor Padraig as your family accountant have parted with any such documents and have informed Mr. Power, he will have to take us to court if he wants them.'

'And?' Sarah dares to ask.

'He will see us in court....Look.' Alan leans on the desk, causing another flutter of dandruff to fall on his shoulders. 'The business was built by you and Lily, on land which legally is already yours, however it is the house which concerns me. Although, I can't see how when Paddy's instructions were specific, added to the fact Aine has not lived there for, how many years?'

'Twenty-three, I think.' Sarah replies. 'It depends whether you count from when she went to Uni or went to America.'

'This freezing of assets though.' Tommy intervenes. 'Surely we can't stop running the farm and shop, it's ridiculous. Especially at this time of year, when it's the only time we can make a proper living wage. The campsite is due to be opened in two weeks, we have a lot at stake here Alan and if our Da left a Will stating Sarah stay in her home, how can his wishes be questioned. Where does Aine expect Sarah to live anyway?'

'The farm and café can run as normal, however the expansion has to be put on hold while we sort this out, either in court or by coming to a reasonable agreement with Aine. I have to say she is shooting herself in the foot a little, she and Martin will not receive their inheritance money until this is resolved.' Alan taps his pen on the desk as he speaks, adding to the already stifling tension in the room.

'This is a joke, she can't seriously expect Sarah to give up her home and for us to hand over half the farm. I know she can be a bitch but this has to be the lowest.' Tommy's face glowers the vein in his temple pulsating. Sarah hardly recognising the man sitting next to her and neither does, Alan given the shocked expression on his face, along with another flutter of dandruff.

'Sorry I'm a little confused.' Sarah looks for confirmation. 'If our father has left a Will which you say, states I am to inherit the house unless I choose to live elsewhere and my brother already owns the farm, how can she....?'

'I imagine as the eldest, Aine assumed she would and should inherit the house and some of the farm. I am only guessing you understand, what makes it so awkward is the stipulations in the Will. You didn't inherit outright, he requested you live there or a family member. His explicit instruction was for the house not to be sold, to be kept in the family. It leaves the ownership of the house questionable so to speak, as technically you all own it.'

'She had no interest before, she has a life in New York, a fancy apartment and great job why would she want the house here, when we have lived here all our lives?' Sarah replies, realising why she had never struck up a friendship with Alan at school, it had nothing to do with an age gap. Like his younger brother Padraig, the local accountant, he has a tendency to make a person feel as though they are beneath him. The Sullivan's, like the O'Dowd's, moved to Kilmer Cove buying big houses on money they had inherited preferring to think, how would her father have put it? "They are a cut above the locals."

'I wish I could answer your question Sarah, I can only promise to fight your corner-'

'Why did you not point this out as a potential problem to Da, when he was makin the will? Surely as his solicitor it was your duty to advise him properly and point out any possible pitfalls.' Tommy abruptly interrupts, showing clear annoyance. Deemed speechless, Alan's face turns deep crimson, failing to meet Tommy's angry glare. 'Tell this Fintan Power, he has a fight on his hands.' Tommy hastily stands up to leave, 'c'mon Sarah.'

Chapter 12

An hour later they are in the kitchen of Tommy's bungalow, nursing mugs of coffee while Lily bustles around preparing dinner. The room is decorated in a bright retro style, giving a unique and more modern feel than the farmhouse kitchen, yet equally inviting and homely. Sarah is still in shock from their meeting with Alan, unsure how to digest the information he had revealed. The short journey home had seemed unnaturally long, the silence in the rickety old jeep almost deafening. Neither of them had been able to utter a single word, scared voicing their fears would make their worst nightmare a reality.

'So what you are telling me is we could be in deep trouble. Why does it not surprise me, Aine having practically spelt it out when she was here.' Lily says as she opens the door of the Aga to check the chicken, she had put in earlier to roast. Even the smell of her sister-in-law's wonderful home cooking does nothing to wet Sarah's appetite. It dawns on her, if Aine won her case and inherited the house she would change everything in their home, including ripping Jack's bedroom apart. A room which has not been touched apart from, Sarah going in to dust and vacuum once a week since the day he died.

'Did you know that Aine was contesting the Will?' Tommy asks throwing his hands in the air, showing confusion over his wife's statement.

'Not exactly, I worked out she was up to something from what she said to, Sarah and me the morning of your dad's funeral.' Lily carries on draining pots of vegetables. Sarah watches their interaction as though following the plot of a television programme. Unable to join in or participate in the conversation, because her body will not allow her to move. Tommy glances from his wife to his sister and back, fine lines on either side of his eyes prominent showing the strain he has been under recently, ageing him prematurely.

'Jesus, Lil you could have warned me. If she goes ahead with taking us to court this mess could drag out for months and that's only if we are lucky. The farm will not survive, we need the campsite up and running, what about the bookings already made? If we turn people away now it will ruin us.'

'Oh, love it won't come to that, I think you are getting it all out of proportion. Paddy left a Will, how can a man's distinct wishes be over ruled in a court. Now sit down dinner is ready.' She places plates of food on the table.

'Rach...dinner,' she calls out to their daughter. 'Lauren's gone to the pictures with Daryl they'll probably eat out though, I might keep them something to be certain. It's lovely having her home, even if it's only for a few more days.' Lily explicitly directing her words to Sarah. Sarah admiring the way, Lily even in the face of difficult time's concentrates her energy on nurturing them all, Sarah included, and loving her for it. Far more than she will ever care for her blood sister. Lily had been, Sarah's rock throughout her pregnancy and Jack's birth, even with a young child of her own to look after. 'With a bit of luck, we might see a wedding before the year is out, this family could certainly do with something to smile about.' Lily continues, clearly fighting back unshed tears as her inner angst starts to reveal itself. Lily generally going into overdrive and talking too much when distressed. Sarah purses her lips managing a weak smile, wishing she could think of something comforting to say to the woman who always knows how to cheer everyone else up.

'Sarah, you've gone very quiet what do you think? It's your home after all.' Tommy asks, prompting Sarah to bury her head in her hands, unable to make sense of why Aine would want the house when she has an established life in New York with her live-in lover. A man, Sarah has never met but has endured listening to her sister boast about. The wonderfully handsome Chad, in Aine's opinion with his bleached white teeth and all American smile. The fact, he owns his own fashion label amongst other businesses is something Aine never fails to point out, along with the apartment in the city, a house in the Hampdens and another in Portugal. Obviously, they want to add a quaint farmhouse in Ireland to their current portfolio. It dawns on Sarah, although her visit had been abruptly short, Aine never once mentioned Chad the whole time.

'Does she really hate me that much? Tell me honestly Tom, it's not my imagination Aine has always resented me, why?' She didn't intend to bring it up so bluntly but the situation has presented itself.

'Honey, she doesn't hate you.' Lily says, placing a hand on Sarah's shoulder. 'Aine is simply a bitch.' The unexpected comment coming from Lily's lips, cuts through the room. No one has ever heard Lily swear before and are clearly unsure how to react. Rachel, who had literally entered the kitchen, freezes at the threshold of the door her eyes wide like saucers. Tommy sits open mouthed, fork poised in the air. Sarah simply stares at her sister-in-law in dismay. Eventually, Tommy slams his fork down announcing.

'I'll ring Martin after tea get his input. We have to put a stop to all this nonsense.'

'That still doesn't answer my question.' Sarah ventures, knowing she is pushing her brother to say something he is reluctant to reveal, causing concern.

'Oh, I don't know.' Rachel says, finally come down from her shock and joining them at the dinner table. 'I think Mum has put it into perspective.' This however, leaves Sarah feeling annoyed. As it is obvious, Aine does have an underlying resentment towards her which has festered over the years. Everyone knowing what has caused it apart from Sarah herself. When their father was alive, Aine would not have been allowed to act upon her grievance, now he is gone. Sarah, once again silently blames Desmond Shanahan for inflicting his death and making her life one big dark cloud. Only this time it has a domino effect, dragging Tommy and Lily down too and it isn't fair. Claiming she is feeling jaded, Sarah rises from the table having barely eaten any dinner.

Outside the night is still, an inky dusk setting in early for the time of year. Usually this is a sign of a thunderstorm or rain at least, she bows her head as she walks across the yard. Entering the empty farmhouse with nothing but silence is eerie. Fortunately, Lily is right behind her bringing a much needed sympathetic ear.

'Thought you might need someone to talk to.' She says, in a tone which implies she is not fooled and points this fact out. 'I can tell when you are holding back. My guess is it's nothing to do with this situation your sister has created. Is it because of Conor taking on that Shanahan fellow? I have to say, it has come as a bit of a surprise. Ta think he carried Paddy's coffin with the boys and had spent more time in this house than his own as a youngster...makes my blood boil....I'm tempted to go and give him a piece of my mind.'

'Conor knows I lied to him about Jack's father being someone I met in Trinity, he thinks I'm some harlot.' Sarah blurts out, finally able to reveal her worries. When Sarah realised she would be bringing up her unborn baby without any input from his father, she decided to pretend she'd gotten pregnant by someone she met at Trinity, too honest to trap Conor. It had seemed the best thing to do at the time.

'It doesn't excuse what he has done, it's in the past. You were honest with him at the time. Who it was, is irrelevant in the scheme of things after all these years.' Lily points out, screwing up her nose as though she's inhaled a bad smell.

'It obviously isn't sitting right with him, to bring it up now. He never really forgave me. On paper Conor is perfect, handsome, rich, even worshipped the ground I walked on, but I didn't love him and couldn't live a life steeped in lies allowing him to think Jack was his son, or that I loved him for that matter. He'd been too much like a third brother, when we were growing up.' Sarah stares out of the kitchen window, her thoughts drifting far from the room they are in. 'Ironic since I made Jack's whole existence one big lie, a lie I have to face every day.'

'You fell in love there is no shame in that.' Lily offers a much needed comforting hug. Sighing heavily she adds, 'I'd be very surprised if Conor will say anything. He would have done so long before now if he really wanted too.' Lily continues. 'He wanted to get at you and it worked.' If she had the luxury she would pull, Oceanic Temptations regular salmon order from his factory. 'He wouldn't wreck a marriage in spite of his own feelings. No matter what, we agreed at the time, you would never have changed having Jack, remember. You could have easily duped Conor into bringing up Jack as his Sarah, it is no one's business and no one ever got hurt over a white lie.' Lily points out, matter-of-fact.

'I deceived Jack though, and have lived with that guilt ever since his death. Especially now....all along he was right here in this town, practically saw his father every day and didn't know. What sort of person am I to do that?'

'You were a good mother protecting your son.' Lily points out matter-of-fact. 'Do you think Conor knows you are still seeing...I mean it does make things...I'm not judging, I understand you love him and I promise not to give the speech about him being a philanderer...I'm worried about *you* in all this, cause you'll be the one to come out the worst, an get hurt all over again.'

'I know....you'd think at my age I'd have more sense, believe me I've tried to end it so many times....it's pathetic to keep convincing myself he loves me...I'd never in a million years expect him to leave her for me, wouldn't want to hurt her like that. I'm a bloody hypocrite Lily, cause I can't live without him either.' Ashamed to have allowed him back into her affections again since Jack's death, rekindling their affair after being sucked in by his attentiveness. She is aware her actions are deceitful, it doesn't stop the need, like a drug she cannot give him up. It's as though being with him holds onto a part of Jack, she cannot let go of.

'Oh pet, I wish, there was some way of making all this easier for you.'

'You've all been so good, I don't deserve......' Sarah's mobile comes to life with its cheery ringtone interrupting them. She picks it up checking the caller ID. 'It's Maggie.'

'We will stay strong and fight past this.' Lily gives her another hug to eradicate she doesn't have to go through all this alone.

'What happens when you get tired of fighting all the time and the fight has left you, what then.' Coming from a woman, who has lost a child and is now grieving for a parent, these are not the words those who care about her want to hear.

'You will always have me and Tommy at your side, we won't allow you to give up. I'll leave you to your call.' Lily says with a noticeable quiver in her voice.

'Hey is everything okay?' Sarah asks, not knowing why.

'Sure, I'm stuck here in the barracks and it's a quiet one, thought I'd check on ya.' Maggie says.

'What would I do without you?' Sarah replies, hoping Maggie cannot detect the quiver in her voice.

'By the sounds of things you need someone on your side, I heard about Conor.'

'You did.' Sarah coughs. 'Sorry, catch in my throat.' She grabs a glass, turning on the tap and soaking her top in her haste. 'So...am what have you heard?'

'About him hiring that Shanahan fellow.' Maggie replies in a tone which implies what else could it be. 'Jesus what was he thinking? I mean, I know you and he are not together anymore...unless of course I'm wrong, either way, you have history...is he out of his tiny mind? Hang on a sec.' There is a shuffling sound, voices, then Maggie speaks again. 'Sorry about that, some eejit has robbed the sign from outside Fahey's butchers. It'd make ya wonder about people it really would. Look I'm off tomorrow night, how about I call round with a bottle of wine and takeaway.'

'That sounds wonderful, just what I need. The house is eerily empty every night without Da here, I'd appreciate the company.' Sarah replies, filled with genuine gratitude.

'It won't be the same walkin into the place without Paddy siting in the kitchen, shouting above the blare of the television....ah what now...would you believe it was quiet until I phoned you. Apparently there is a disturbance outside the Nook, I better get across there and see what's going on. It's Kilmer Cove, not Carraigbrin, I don't know what's wrong with people....we're getting nothing but trouble recently. I'll be over round seven tomorrow so, see ya then.' She is gone before Sarah can reply.

The following morning Sarah reluctantly pulls herself out of bed, legs as heavy as her heart having barely slept. Her life spiralling out of control giving the feeling, a heavy avalanche has fallen on top of her and she is unable to bear the weight of it all.

By the time she creeps out onto the landing, averting her gaze from the door of Jack's empty bedroom to creep downstairs, realisation kicks in that there is no need to be quiet, she is the only person now living in the house. A harsh reality, making her feel suffocated by the intensity of loneliness. To quash the urge of simply jumping into her car and arriving outside the Shanahan's house, as she has done over the previous few days, Sarah decides to take her training seriously and go for a run.

Closing the front door firmly, Sarah steps out into the warm morning air. The sun having already risen in the sky, she lifts her head basking in its rays. Her senses met with the sweet scent of her father's climbing roses, framing the front door. Although her body has still not engaged in the concept to loosen her leg muscles, Sarah begins her training with some light stretches and jogging on the spot. Jack had been very particular about stretching properly. "If muscles aren't loosened properly first, they will stretch like an elastic band, and that's how you end up with a hamstring injury or worse." Her son's words resonating in her ears, explaining the importance of stretching properly at the beginning of a training session, and again at the end to cool the muscles down.

Sarah begins with a slow jog down the drive, before easing out onto the open road picking up a nice steady stride. Gliding along the pavement her feet hitting the concrete hard giving a sense of freedom, reaching out with each stride imagining Jack is running alongside. His tall frame and broad shoulders moving easily along, without any effort. No matter how far he ran or how hard he trained, he never appeared out of breath. She can feel him now pulling her along, her feet becoming lighter along with her heart. Freedom of being able to forget reality, wipe all worries from her mind. Afterwards, she would head down to the Cove for a swim and allow the watery embrace wash away all her fears, allowing her to escape the full weight of her problems. It's as free as she will ever be, a time when she can truly submerge in herself and pretend the past five and a half years never happened.

Cutting down through the village, she swoops along Main Street with the freedom of a bird. A soft breeze cooling her face which is a godsend, as she's forgotten to bring a water bottle. It does not perturb her, as she turns towards the coast road in the direction of Carraigbrin. Passing by the GAA pitch across from Seaview, Sarah willing herself not to glance in the direction of the Shanahan's house, causing her to practically collide with a man walking his dog.

'You have to stop doing this.' His red face creases revealing anger. Something inside Sarah snaps, all resolve abolished by this chance meeting.

'What running?' she retorts in a questioning tone. Sarah doesn't allow him to answer before unleashing all the pent up animosity, she has been harbouring. 'I suppose, my son shouldn't have been out running early in the morning either.' Sarah adds, sounding a lot braver than she is feeling inside. Barely recognising her own voice as she speaks, having become aggressive and detached from her normal persona.

'You know bloody well what I am talking about.' He stretches to his full five foot, five. Chest puffed, Ger is not a man to take criticism lightly. 'Hanging around outside our home, harassment that is what it is, you know. We are entitled to live our lives, so you bloody get over your resentment and leave us be, do you hear me?' Little does he know, he has just met his match in a woman who's long given up being passive, especially when it comes to the subject of her son.

'How dare you, I am entitled to walk or run wherever I want. Something my son can no longer do. Tell me this, if it was one of your sons' do you think you could forgive his killer?' The question accomplishing its purpose, Ger's steely cold stare quickly drops to the pavement. 'No, I didn't think so.' She turns to walk away, then decides she is not finished. 'My son, was a sixteen-year-old boy with his whole life ahead of him, and your son took that away from him. I will not apologise for my grief and you should not expect me to.' Fists clenched, she swiftly moves away on shaking legs. By the time Sarah reaches the farmhouse, her head is pounding. A morning, in which she had battled to start with positive resolve has ended with her feeling worse than ever. The Shanahan family are beginning to feel like a bad curse.

Chapter 13

'Pay day, the only day worth comin in for.' Jimmy grins as he guts a fish without watching what he is doing. An ironic comment, considering he'd rung in sick the past couple of days 'Fancy headin into Carraigbrin tonight. There's this new club, Crystal. It's hoppin man, plenty of hot birds for the takin too.'

'Ya sur why not sounds like a plan.' Des replies relieved to have clocked up a week working in the factory, only roughly eleven more to go. His intention to give his mother some of his wages, then save the rest. Planning, by the end of his parole period to have a substantial sum put away to make a fresh start somewhere else. Somewhere far from Kilmer Cove. Life outside prison, has not been any less daunting than being behind bars. Each morning as he leaves the house having to endure passing Sarah Connolly, sitting in her car eyes following him with each stride, each step he takes. Rounding the corner out of sight allowing a sigh to escape, yet still conscious of the weight of her stare. Working in the factory is as boring and repetitive as he had predicted, there is little enjoyment in gutting fish, their eyes staring eerily as he slits each one open. Ominously, bringing to the forefront of his mind the nightmare he has tried to banish. Although he is grateful to Conor O'Dowd, for an opportunity no other person would be kind enough to give, it doesn't quash the fact of his home town having become a desolate place, when you are cast out in the cold. Generally, he has managed to get through each day easily on the line he works, it is going to and from his locker which poses a challenge, along with going to the canteen at lunchtime. Jimmy seems to always sneak off somewhere during lunch, leaving Desmond with icy stares, whispered conversations and stilted silences. On a whole he has managed to let it go over his head, but there are moments he has had the urge to react. Reminding himself there would be no satisfaction only regret on his behalf, taking to eating lunch outside on his own for the sake of his sanity.

'Desmond Shanahan……Desmond Shanahan?' A female voice calls out.

'Yeah.' Des glances up to see the most beautiful girl, he has ever set eyes on smiling at him from the doorway. Her lips glossy cherry red, her pale skin flawless with a sprinkling of blusher perfectly placed on her cheeks, giving a rosy flushed effect. His heart flutters in a way it hasn't since he was sixteen, waiting in anticipation for her to speak again. Aware, he must appear gormless standing with his mouth open, eyes fixated on her.

'Mr. O'Dowd would like to see you in his office right away, if you'll follow me please, Desmond.' She says in the sweetest voice, the way she pronounced his name causing him to flush. This does not go unnoticed by Jimmy and true to form he teases Desmond, alerting every pair of eyes along the line to look up, as Des passes by. He doesn't care, drawn to the paragon of beauty, mesmerised by this angelic figure he is approaching. Only stopping briefly by the sink to discard his gloves in the bin and wash his hands, before following her down the hallway. His eyes drawn to the short skirt and low cut blouse, sexy though tasteful, revealing an acceptable amount of cleavage. Enough to entice imagination, but not too much to be classed as slutty.

She walks quickly in her kitten heels, resulting in Desmond having to increase his stride to keep up. As they reach the other end of the corridor which separates the factory floor from the offices, she turns to face him before pulling open the door. A girlish giggle escaping from her moist lips.

'Oh you better take that off before you go in, don't want to look silly do we.' Her smile melting, making him flush deep red from the neck up. He quickly pulls off the hairnet, slipping it in his overall pocket. 'That's better, you look a lot sexier without it.' She breezes through the door as though it is the most natural thing in the world to say, without realising the effect she's having on a young man in his prime who has not had any affection, not to mention lacking sexual relations in over five years.

'Do you know what Mr. O'Dowd wants to see me about?' Desmond manages to ask, desperately trying to sound confident and not the spluttering idiot he fears, he is perceiving to be.

'Relax, don't look so tense.' She raises her perfectly shaped brows, obviously picking up on his unease. 'Conor is very happy with you, he only wants to make sure you are happy working here.'

'Better now.' The words slip from his tongue without thinking.

'Good.' She beams. 'But if there are any problems, don't be afraid to say.' Her look projecting more than words, she still makes a point by saying. 'Mossy can be a bit of a shit, don't pay any attention to him.' She crinkles her nose, causing her face to crease. He has never met anyone so animated each time she speaks, her face open and honest. He'd always thought love at first sight to be a cliché, not anymore.

All too soon they are standing in Conor's office, ending the magic.

'Desmond, come in, have a seat.' Conor stands up from behind a large sleek black desk, gesturing for Des to sit. 'Would you like a coffee or maybe a cold drink?'

'No, I'm fine thank you.' Des finds himself comparing the large airy, sparsely but tastefully decorated room, to Gary's dull grey office. A highly polished desk, leather chairs and large wooden carved wall unit containing trophies, rather than filing cabinets. The window behind the desk in this office overlooks the harbour below, giving it a spectacular perspective. An ever-changing view due to the bustle of the fishing boats, but also giving a sense of tranquility, due to the beauty of the sea and the greenery of its surrounding coastline. Alice throws Des a nonchalant smile, as she leaves the room.

'Don't look so tense Des, I only want to check how you're getting on?'
'Good.'
'Stop being polite, it's a boring mind numbing job but unfortunately important for my business. I had a chat with Gary, he phoned this morning, asking how you were doing. How are you finding your peers, no trouble I hope?' Conor catching Des' look. 'You wouldn't tell me if there was, I get it.' He leans back on the soft leather chair.

'I'm getting on very well with everyone.' He throws the other man a lifeline, not wanting to come across as ungrateful. The statement not quite true, not a complete lie either. The upside being, working alongside Jimmy and a Polish man, named Malik, enjoying easy banter as they work. The rest of the workers on the line abstaining from joining in, not that this phases Des in the least. There would be no advantage in pointing this fact out, or the difficulties he faces with the lads in the packing department. Des does however consider mentioning the need to leave early on Tuesday's to sign at the Garda station but then refrains from mentioning it. Having been fortunate this week, arriving at ten past five, worried Red would be there. A young Garda was at the front desk in her place much to his relief. He had no problem when, Des explained about working until five and apologised for being late. It was a lucky escape, Des would not be so lucky next time round.

'Good, I'm delighted.' Conor replies with a warm smile. Looking less than convinced due to his concern lying with, Mossy the line supervisor flagging, Desmond's friendship with Jimmy Duggan. On the outside, Desmond presents as confident and worldly, inside lies a naïve and immature for his age young man. 'You know where my office is and you have my number if you want discretion. I know what you said about not being a snitch, but there is a limit when it comes to putting up with bullying. I, for one won't tolerate it and I'm very aware of the difficulties your family has faced around the town.'

'I appreciate all you are doing for me.' Is all Des can think of saying, still unsure of why Conor would go to such lengths to help him.

'Enjoy the weekend.' Conor stands indicating the chat is over.

Back on the factory floor, Desmond re-joins the line ignoring inquisitive stares from his peers. Picking up his knife and continuing to work, as though having never been absent. Jimmy, however, is itching to know what Conor had wanted to see Des about, as well as tease him about Alice.

'She is well out of your league, lad.' Jimmy proclaims. 'Ya'd want a degree and bank load a dosh to impress that one. She'd be high maintenance.'

'What is your meaning?' Malik asks when Des does not offer a reply of his own. 'This girl, she is a nice person, why would she not like Desmond for his self.'

'Nah...Mal...girls like that, don't go for fellas like us.'

'I do not understand, Desmond is a handsome man no. Why would a pretty girl not like him?' The other man clearly not following Jimmy's meaning.

'You think his ugly mug is handsome.' Jimmy continues, now teasing both men. 'Fancy him yourself do ya Mal?'

'No, I simply make an observation.' Irritation evident in Malik's voice. 'I am not how you say....I am a married man, but I do not understand why this pretty girl would not like Desmond.' Malik points out, shaking his head to reiterate his annoyance. 'Don't you agree Desmond?' Des doesn't get a chance to reply, Mossy the line manager appears at their side.

'The shift hasn't ended yet Duggan, and considering you've hardly been here this week, I suggest less talk....get your work done.' Mossy says with an air of disapproval. 'Since when is it against the rules to talk. I don't see ya tellin anyone else to be quiet.' Jimmy retaliates, throwing his hands in the air for effect.

'Maybe, it's your attitude that gets you in trouble or the company you keep.' Mossy quips back shaking his head in dismay. Desmond sees this as a personal jibe, wondering is it a way of indirectly getting at him.

When the bell sounds indicating the end of the shift, Des swiftly walks to the locker room. Grabbing his knapsack and clocking out, he rushes outside for some desperately needed fresh air, unable to cope with the smell of fish any longer.

'Hey wait up,' Jimmy shouts, catching up on Desmond. 'What time d'ya want ta head into Carraigbrin?'

'I don't know, as soon as I've showered and changed.' Des replies, still undecided whether to go out. On the other hand, staying in isn't an option either and at least in Carraigbrin, he would be away from the small mindedness of Kilmer Cove.

'Right an hour top so. I'll blow the horn, cause I ain't comin in to be givin out to by yer Da. Unless he's out and yer Ma has made some of that nice cake.'

'He'll be there...unless by some miracle he's been abducted by aliens, I'll run out as soon as you pull up.'

'Ha good 'un.' Jimmy chuckles giving full belly laugh, before getting into his car and speeding off.

Precisely and hour later, he pulls up outside Desmond's and they are on the road. Des intending to enjoy the night ahead, his first time out socialising since before the accident.

While awaiting a trial date, he had become introvert, locking himself away in the flat. After he had been charged and appeared at Donegal district court, Des was released on bail. The bond set at €4000 taking all his savings with a condition to sign in everyday at Carraigbrin Garda Station, thankfully he lived there at the time. When Des arrived back to the flat, Evie had hastily packed her belongings and gone back to her mother's. He could understand her being distraught over what had happened, annoyed even over him having to use all their savings for the wedding. He thought she would have at least stood by him that their relationship was worth more. After several attempts to make contact, he gave up baffled by her rejection. Though she hadn't been the only one, his so called friends deserted him too. Before the gavel went down on his sentencing, Evie had moved from her mother's into Brian Lennon's arms, the deception had been hurtful. He knew, Brian had a reputation with women had been a chick magnet but never imagined, Evelyn to be fool enough to fall for his spiel. Especially, after the way he had treated one of her friends.

'I need to stop off an fill up on petrol. We could grab some food at Roaster's, I'm famished. Me, Ma was cooking fish for tea, feckin fish, can ya believe it? Last thing I want ta see on a Friday evenin. I keep sayin I'm going to move into a place of me own but in fairness she does all me washin, an doesn't ask for rent.' Jimmy says, as they speed along the coast road towards Carraigbrin. Des switches off, disinterested in Jimmy's chatter, instead thinking about the mouth-watering chicken from Roaster's Flaming Grill. Surprised he'd forgotten how tasty, their spicy wings and chargrilled chicken breasts were.

'Now you are talking.' He replies, oblivious to Jimmy's underlying ulterior motive for stopping there.

Roaster's is packed when they arrive, seeming everyone in the town has opted for fast food rather than home cooking at the end of their working week. Jimmy insists, Des go in and queue to save too much delay, while he fills the car with petrol and finds a parking space. There are four tills open all with long queues so, Des slots into the one closest behind a group of teenagers, overhearing their discussion about exams and Shakespeare. Des had not been academic when at school, even then he knew what he wanted to do in life and it wasn't to be found in any text book or literary works.

The aromas and bustle lift his spirits, giving him an appreciation of life outside prison for the first time since his release, mindful that adjusting to normal life will inevitably feel strange. Being in Roaster's bringing back memories of happier times, this happiness short-lived, shot down in flames as he reaches the top of the queue.

'I'll have the chicken wings with barbecue sauce.' Des obliviously gazes up at the menu board, indecisive of what to have.

'Des?' The familiar voice questions.

'Evelyn!' He almost screeches in surprise, taking in the waif like appearance behind the counter. 'I didn't know you worked here.' He blurts, unsure of what else to say. It crosses his mind, Jimmy would have known and should have warned him. It is the last place he would expect to see his, ex-fiancée working. Evelyn had worked in a wedding boutique when they were together, had been interested in fashion and design. They had discussed the idea of her going to college, since Des had already secured a second job to finance their wedding and deposit for a house. He would have happily continued to keep it after the wedding, to finance her tuition and manage the domestic bills without her wage. She'd been a talented seamstress with a flair for creating unique designs of her own.

'Needs must.' Her frosty reply like a punch in the stomach, Desmond struck with disappointment from her rebuff. 'The chicken wings, do you want the bucket special it comes with a drink and chips?' She asks in a monotone way, as though speaking to a stranger rather than the man she had once planned a future with.

'Ah...ya...I guess so.' Des replies, confused by her change of demeanour. 'I'll take two of the fillet breast burgers and a second drink.' He adds, eyes never leaving her, watching for flicker of something in her eyes only to find them empty and lifeless. Was she wondering who the second person might be or is he only fooling himself she might care? Becoming dispirited by her aloof manner, the fact her gaze is firmly fixed on the till clearly avoiding his, Des swallows back bitter disappointment.

'Salad and mayo on the breast burgers?'

'Am...ya.' His tone one of defeat, she hasn't asked how he is or acknowledged his early release. Then again, why would she, having obviously moved on in life. He genuinely hopes she is happy, though if working in Roaster's, he very much doubts it. 'How are you?' The words slip out, a natural thing to ask. She finally looks up acknowledging him and for a moment their eyes lock, causing something inside Des to shift.

'What drinks do you want?' Her cool tone snapping him back to reality with a jolt, a reminder they are no longer a couple. How could two people share what they did to end up this distant, almost as though they are strangers?

'Coke is fine.' Des replies, having lost his appetite entirely. Evelyn turns her back to prepare the order, giving Des the opportunity to run away somewhere far from this crowded place, with its bustle and noise, from the suffocation of the harsh reality revealed in this fast food establishment, a reminder of what he has lost.

Evelyn slaps a tray down on the counter causing, Des to judder back to the present. Seemingly unaware of his discomfort, she loads it with napkins and sachets of various sauces.

'Enjoy your meal.' She says, her gaze already shifted over his shoulder to the person behind. 'Hi can I take your order?' Annoyance sitting uneasy across his shoulders, Desmond picks up the tray and grabs a seat that a couple has literally vacated next to the window. From here he can peer out across the car park while trying to make sense of how Evelyn had ended up working in this place. It is not a form snobbery on his behalf, it is the fact he knows or at least thought he knew Evelyn, a person whom held high hopes of a career in fashion design. He spots Jimmy, talking to Brian one of his so called friends, wondering if he and Evelyn are still together. Though in hindsight, he had only got to know Brian when he started dating one of Evelyn's friends, regularly going out as a small group with other friends and Evelyn's brother Frank, before he immigrated to Canada. Jimmy and Brian, appear to be deep in conversation, then they bump fists before Jimmy strides across the car park. Des finds himself questioning whether he should trust Jimmy.

Chapter 14

'You could have warned me, Evie works in Roaster's.' Des unleashes pent up anger as they enter, Crystal Night Club. Having not trusted himself to speak sooner, the underlying annoyance sitting through eating their food sticking it in his throat. Twinned with Evelyn's constant nervous glances in their direction after, Jimmy had joined him at the table.

'What difference does it make?' Jimmy replies, screwing up his nose. 'You're not with her anymore.' He nods at the doorman. 'Well Vic.' He reverts his attention to Des again, once inside. 'You're not still hung up on her are you?' He asks in a way which suggests Des shouldn't be. Des doesn't reply to this, torn between personal embarrassment and regretting starting this conversation with someone like Jimmy. Too late, Jimmy makes his own assumption. 'Jesus, lad, why would you bother with her, when she cheated on you.' His words connecting like a hard slap in the face. As much as he wants to know what Jimmy meant by this statement, he can't ask. As far as he knew, Evelyn started seeing Brian after the accident, Jimmy must be referring to how quickly they had gotten together. 'Anyway she has a kid, who'd want baggage like that.' Jimmy's tongue continues to roll, turning the slap into a punch.

'A kid?' Desmond shouts, trying to fully comprehend this piece of information. Desmond grabs Jimmy by the shoulder. 'Evelyn has a child like?' The repeated question making him sound dumb.

'Yeah, thought you knew.' Jimmy replies nonchalantly.

'No...no...I didn't.' Des swallows back bile, his mind racing. 'How old?'

'Wha?' They begin pushing their way through the crowded club, towards the bar. Des feeling as though he is being pulled into a hollow, entrapment and suffocation filling him with desperation to escape, his body unable to correspond properly with his mind.

'Evie's kid, how old?' Des shouts louder, battling to be heard against the beat of the music. They reach the bar enabling them to stand face to face again.

'He's five tomorrow, they're havin a big party load a fuss bouncy castle, magician all that shit. That's why I had to pull a sickie, help Brian paint the house...Jesus, Dessie, ya wouldn't tell O'Dowd or Mossy on me, will ya.' The later part of Jimmy's statement landing on deaf ears, Des transfixed on the age of the child.

'Definitely five and not four...are you sure?'

'Jesus, Des what does it matter...we are on a night out? Two single men havin a crack, lighten up or we won't pull.' Jimmy averts his attention to the barman. 'Two bottles of snake larger, cheers.' Jimmy pays, handing a bottle to Des. 'Here, get that down your neck, an chill out. You're beginning to be a killjoy, it's like being on a night out with me, mother you talk too much.' Jimmy swaggers towards the dancefloor, leaving Desmond wide-eyed shaking his head in dismay.

Jimmy works his way onto the crowded dancefloor, disappearing among the throng. Every so often, Desmond catches a glimpse of his head bobbing up and down, arms flailing in all directions. He is soon joined by a petite dyed blonde and it isn't long before he is inspecting her tonsils. Eventually, they move off the floor and out of Desmond's sight. Des remains on the edge of the dancefloor looking as uncomfortable as he feels, clubbing never really having been his scene, preferring to be under the bonnet of a car. Though, he used to sometimes go along in the past to please Evelyn. Trying to banish her from his mind, he sips the beer which is warm and vile tasting. For the first time in his life he wishes, he was drunk allowing him to blank everything out to be some place far from the club and Jimmy's revelations. Seeing Evelyn earlier, had been surreal having often wondered how he would feel when the day came to meeting her again, surprised to have felt nothing back in Roaster's apart from uncomfortable. She had lost weight, looked unnaturally thin with deep dark shadows shrouding her once sparkling eyes. He tries to imagine her having a child, what he or she looks like and wonders is it possible?

'Hey, I barely recognised you in your clothes.' A nervous giggle. 'Oops, that came out wrong.' Des turns round to find Alice standing next to him, her naturally blonde curls falling softly over her bare shoulders. Wearing a short strapless dress with knee high boots, this vision whom could have any man in the room is by his side, waiting for a response. He is completely lost for words, eyes transfixed willing her to not take his silence as a rebuff. 'I haven't seen you in here before.' She shouts above the music, seemingly having not noticed.

'No, I've been away.' It's all he can manage to say, their eyes lock drawn to each other like a magnet.

'I know.' She replies casually. 'Want to get out of here and go for a drink somewhere we can have a proper conversation.'

'Sounds great.' Des let's out a sigh of relief, from the corner of his eye, he catches a glimpse of Jimmy, having returned to the dancefloor with the dyed blonde. Jumping around like he is on something, it is unlikely he will notice Des' departure, allowing him to eagerly follow Alice as she pushes her way through the densely crowded room.

The air outside is cool and refreshing after the intoxicating dead heat of the club, the late evening light and bright sky giving a picturesque hue of colour. Des catches the aroma of her perfume, when she turns to ask him where he would like to go.

'I was about to ask you the same thing.'

'Great minds.'

'Mm.' He smiles feeling relaxed in her company. 'What do you like to do in your free time, apart from noisy overcrowded clubs?'

'Well when I'm not pleasing my friend going to clubs, I hate by the way. Oh, I haven't dumped her in case you are worried,' her soft laugh, endearing to him. 'She hooked up with the guy she was hoping to meet...I love to watch old black and white movies, visit art galleries, travel and discover new and interesting places. When I'm home not doing any of the above, I like to spend time with family and swim. What about you?'

'You do know what I've done, where I've been.' He ventures onto unspoken ground unable to look her in the eye. A subject he has purposefully avoided before this point.

'Desmond, I'm blonde not dumb.' Her words catching him by surprise, he glances up to see her eyes dancing in the dusky evening light. Her dazzling smile causing his heart to skip a beat, she has him smitten no matter how hard he tries to fight it, he will fail miserably. Unable to hold back a smile escapes his own lips. 'You have a great smile, better than the pout you were wearing a few minutes ago.' She adds matter-of-fact. It makes him wonder who this girl is, a breath of fresh air in a stifling world where he had begun to slowly suffocate, she has revived him. He has to ask the question, which has been simmering since she'd called him into Conor's office. Is it possible, he literally met this girl roughly five hours previously, yet already she has managed to cast a lasting spell on him?

'What is a girl like you doing in Kilmer Cove? How come I never met you before now?' They both burst into laughter due to how corny the question sounded, when Alice finally sobers she replies.

'Well to answer your first question, I was brought up in Ashbrook on the other side of Carraigbrin. Maybe that answers both questions, now I think of it. When I left school, I went to Limerick Institute to do a BA in graphic and digital design.' She laughs, gauging his confusion. 'I may as well be talking in a foreign language, am I right?'

'Ah...yeah.' Des admits sheepishly.

'Well...I'm not in any hurry to go home, unless you are.'

'No, I've got all night, fancy popping in here for a drink?' Des magically looks up to see they were standing outside a quaint bar. Somewhere with real beer, comfortable seats and you don't have to shout to hold a conversation.

'Perfect.'

'So what? You're working in the factory for the summer then.' Des asks as he places a gin and tonic on the table, before sitting down next to her, and taking a sip of his pint. It is cool and refreshing compared to the warm bottle of beer, Jimmy had bought in the club. For a split second, he feels guilty for not telling Jimmy he was leaving, the thought soon diminishes when Alice speaks.

'Something like that, Conor is my cousin so when his secretary Miriam went on maternity leave, I stepped in to help out for the summer. He will have to find someone by September, Miriam has decided to take extended leave until the end of the year. Fancy a change from the factory floor, I'd say you're handy with numbers. I have to go back to Limerick to finish the last year of my degree.'

'Not my thing being stuck in an office.' He refrains from adding, neither is being stuck working on the factory floor, but doesn't want to sound ungrateful for the opportunity Conor has offered. Especially, having learned he and Alice are related. Still, he has met Alice, a definite plus. 'No offence to you.' He adds, wondering if he has caused offence when she doesn't reply immediately.

'It's okay I get it. What did you do before?'

'I worked in Charlie's Classic Auto's in Donegal, restoring classic cars, panel beating and mechanical work. Did a bit of general servicing on other cars too.'

'Cars are obviously your passion, I can see by the way your face lit up as you spoke. So how come you haven't gone back to doing it?'

'Not everyone is as kind as your cousin and willing to give me a second chance.'

'I'm sorry to hear that...tell me what the attraction is?' She takes a sip of her drink. 'In cars...I mean, to me it's a way of getting around, sorry for my ignorance.'

'You're not ignorant most people see cars that way. I was fascinated by them from a young age. How they work, you know that sort of thing. It's not about driving a car fast but respecting the vehicle. Knowing it inside and out, distinguishing a car by the exhaust note made by its engine...a real classic car, not modern cars I mean. The hum of the engine, its heartbeat...sorry, I'm boring you. I can see your eyes glaze over.'

'Not at all, it gives me an understanding of you, I'm impressed honestly.' Her words sound sincere, though it makes him wonder what is meant by an understanding of him. Whether it is to do with the accident.

'I don't do drugs, swear I never have.' He offers, wanting to make it clear while hoping it was the right thing to do.

'Des, I believe you.' She replies without meeting his expectant gaze. This sits a little uncomfortable with him. 'I collect Conor's bread from oceanic temptations, every day. He's too chicken to face Sarah, since he employed you....' She hesitates, her expression changing to one of embarrassment. 'Sorry...that came out a little...Conor was engaged to Sarah. I don't know the ins and outs of the situation, only she broke his heart by getting pregnant for someone else and calling off their wedding.' She takes a sip of her drink. 'I think she looks very sad...Sarah. It can't be easy losing a child so tragically. Have you ever tried to talk to her, yourself? Sorry it's none of my business.' Her cheeks turn pink and she glances away, Des doesn't respond unsure of what to say. He stares aimlessly at beer stains on the carpet, wondering is this why Sarah sits outside his house. Does she want to know what happened and why? Would she listen if he tried to explain? Nagging doubt suggests she wouldn't even listen. 'Have you thought about, going back to college or university as a mature student? You can't tell me, working for my cousin here is something you would be happy doing for the rest of your life.' Alice cuts into his thoughts. 'Not when cars are clearly your passion. It might be a good way of getting back into something you enjoy.'

'I never thought of that, it's a good idea.' He replies, relieved the subject has returned to safer ground, also impressed by the interest shown. Having only spent roughly an hour in this girls company, yet it feels like she understands him better than Evelyn had in the six years they had been together.

'You should look into it. I'll help you if you like.' She throws him an alluring smile sending his heart soaring. The suggestion confirming, she would be happy to meet up with him again.

Chapter 15

Evelyn forces her eyes open, head pounding from too much alcohol the previous night. Brian is still fast asleep snoring gently, allowing her to slip out of bed and quietly creep from the room. She pauses on the landing peering into Danny's empty bedroom, regretting having agreed to leave him with her mother overnight when Brian suggested going to Chrystal after her shift in Roasters. It's not that she resents her mother having him, in fact grateful to Gillian for being a keen hands on grandmother. Today being Danny's fifth birthday, he should be here waking up at home with his parents, excited at the prospect of his party while happily opening the kiddie workbench and tool set, she'd bought him.

On entering the lounge she is met by the smell of stale cigarettes and alcohol, making her stomach heave. With a heavy sigh, she clears away the debris, another mistake, allowing their friends to come back to the house for more drink after the club. Especially since Brian and Jimmy had done a fabulous job of decorating, albeit the new flat screen television taking up practically a whole wall. The walls look fresh and clean along with the new black leather suite, a big improvement on the shabby old second-hand one they had bought when moving in, five years previously. Danny had shrieked with delight when Brian had shown him how to sit in and pull the lever on the reclining armchairs'. Declaring it's like being in a space ship, this week's obsession, making her wonder has she done the right thing in getting a racing car shaped cake made? The curtains her mother put up with the matching cushions she made finishing off the room. Giving an air of luxury like something out of an interior design magazine. Evelyn loved it all.

The kitchen, also newly painted with Brian's pride and joy, a gleaming silver coffee machine sitting proudly on one of the counters. It had only taken himself and Jimmy a couple of days once they had got started. A home she could proudly entertain Danny's friends and their parents in, in a few hours' time. It doesn't stop her from feeling a gloom is rising inside. Unsure why, possibly due to seeing Desmond last night, bringing back painful memories. Uncomfortable with him seeing her wearing the dull brown Roaster's uniform, stuck behind the counter of a fast food restaurant, when they had made so many plans for a future together.

Bringing to the fore painful memories of what she has done. Then seeing him again later on, leaving Chrystal with the stunning blonde. He hadn't noticed Evelyn walking in, his eyes transfixed on the other girl. The adoring way in which he looked at her, once reserved for Evelyn. It stung in a way she had never expected it to, but she couldn't blame him, it hadn't been enough for Evelyn when they were together. Safe dependable Desmond, always willing to please her. Overly reliable and lacking in passion, causing her to fall for Brian's magnetism.

She sinks onto one of the kitchen chairs, wondering if nearly five and a half years on would she still make the same choice? Would she still choose Brian making her world a rollercoaster ride, or opt to keep her feet firmly on the ground with Desmond? She shouldn't give Brian a hard time, in recent days he has been in good form spoiling her and Danny with extravagant gifts. Like the chain she is wearing around her neck, she fidgets with it deep in thought. All well and good, but what if the money dries up as her mother has so cynically pointed out. Would things go back to the way they were? Struggling to make ends meet, while enduring Brian's mood swings.

Evelyn glances up, spotting a man peering through the kitchen window. She gets up and opens the back door without giving it a second thought.

'Sorry missus, I did knock on the door there an rang yer bell at the front. I'm here to set up the bouncy castle.' The man flushes while, struggling to avert his gaze from her chest where the dressing gown is gaping open. Unaware of this fact, Evelyn is about to answer when.

'Evie, what the fuck.' Brian bellows from behind, his face contorted as he strides across the kitchen towards her.

'Sorry, sir.' The man's face crimson from the neck up, beads of perspiration form on his forehead unlikely to have been caused from excessive heat. 'I was just telling yer missus, I have the bouncy castle where do ya want it set up?'

'Jesus, it's too early for this shite.' Brian barks back, grabbing Evelyn roughly by the arm and coaxing her inside. 'I don't know stick it anywhere in the back garden there.' He adds. Evelyn manages to squeeze out a weak smile as she backs away. 'What the fuck do you think, you're doing? Go cover yourself up.' Brian shouts as he slams the door shut, face red with fury he raises a hand. The sharp connection shocking him more than her, as she's grown used to his invidious behaviour. The only difference this time, she believes there is a glimmer of remorse in his eyes. Unwilling to allow him the pleasure of her tears, she rushes upstairs closing the bedroom door firmly behind her, whereupon allowing them flow freely. Catching sight of her reflection in the mirror, unable to recognise the young woman peering back with a hollow emptiness in her eyes. Missing the girl she had been before, the one who had been ambitious and determined.

The bedroom door opens; she knows this from the tiny creaking sound it makes. Evelyn steels herself from looking up and watching his approach through the reflection in the mirror. Seconds later, can feel the heat of his body indicating his close proximity. Her body stiffening from the apprehension of where this will go, until his hand slides gently working its way inside her robe cupping her pert, perfectly rounded breast. Her body simultaneously relaxing in response to his touch, she closes her eyes allowing indulgence of the tantalising sensation as his fingers caress her nipple, making it hard and erect.

'I'm sorry, I don't know what comes over me.' His breathing becoming heavier with each word. 'I don't mean anything by it. I love you, you do know that.' He declares, as his hand moves further down expertly undoing the belt of her robe. It slitters off her shoulders falling to the ground like a pool around the stool. Their eyes lock in the reflection of the mirror, Evelyn tilts her head pressing against his broad muscular chest gauging his longing, parting her legs to entice his hand to move lower. His hot breath on her neck electrifying, as he plants soft kisses knowing any resistance she might have had will immediately crumble. As usual, Evelyn relents arching her back in anticipation of a pleasurable climax, while reveling in his touch. She moans, letting out a gasp of disappointment when he hastily pulls away, unsure whether he is teasing or wanting to prolong the enjoyment. She will not beg, willing to allow him control the pace, she rises following him to the bed where under a spell of desire, they fall together locked in the magnetism of their passion. Kissing with a raw intensity, his erection throbbing against her thigh desperate to be inside of her. Whimpers of anticipation escape from her lips unable to hold out any longer, she begs him to enter her. All is forgotten lost in their heady lust for each other, pain turning to pleasure and the illusion of being loved.

In his own deluded way, Brian possibly does love Evelyn, his method of expression far from orthodox. An abusive upbringing, lacking in emotional stability sadly being transferred. So far Danny has been spared from witnessing or enduring his short temper, a minor sacrifice in Evelyn's eyes unable to deny her son, his father.

Fortunately, when Gillian arrives on the doorstep with Danny half an hour later, they are dressed and ready to greet them, albeit slightly dishevelled looking. Evelyn glowing like a beacon, her wide smile practically advertising the fact they'd just had sex. Gillian doesn't say anything, she doesn't have to the look she delivers to both, Evelyn and Brian is enough. However, Gillian Priestly is no fool, she can see the red mark on the side of her daughter's face, but she will hold her tongue for the sake of her grandson. Knowing, men like Brian Lennon it pains her having no control, unable to intervene for fear it would only push her daughter away.

'Mammy, mammy. Look what nanna got me, for me birthday.' Danny says, waving a new car in his hand, clearly excited as he bounds into the kitchen, Evelyn whisks him up in her arms.

'Wow that is cool, happy birthday my precious little boy.' She twirls him around delighted to be with him, lavishing in his baby smell.

'Come and see what yer, Da has organised for yer party.' Brian cuts in grabbing his hand and sweeping him out to the back garden.

The party turns out to be a huge success, all the children turning up including Nathan. His mother Janine particularly watchful on her arrival. Eyeing the flat screen television and coffee machine, when she dropped her son off.

'Be good now Nate, an ya have yer mobile if ya want me ta come an pick ya up, love.' Janine had said, eyeing Brian with contempt. 'Classy machine that and the new car outside, yer missus must be working extra shifts at the takeaway.' The jibe directed at Brian, clearly intended for Evelyn's ears. The last thing Evelyn needs is for Mia to have been right about Brian coming up against the Murphy's. The previous person who'd crossed them disappeared during the night, eighteen months ago and hasn't been seen since.

Apart from the initial awkwardness, which dispersed once Janine left taking her bad vibe along with her. The children get on well thrilling in the bouncy castle, only stopping for the magician before clambering back on. The beautiful summer sunshine reflecting a perfect day. Evelyn watches her son, his head thrown back laughing freely, banishing any regrets and worries from her mind.

Leaving the heart of the party, Evelyn slips into the kitchen to organise the party bags for when the children would be going home.

'Now ya can't say I didn't do me godson proud.' Jimmy quips getting up from the table, where he'd been sitting. Evidently hung over, he grabs a bottle of beer from the fridge. 'Hair of da dog.'

'D'ya hear him...the lazy bollix.' Brian's sudden entrance making Evelyn jump. 'Stood an watched while I did most of the work.' Brian playfully shoves Jimmy aside, grabbing a beer for himself. 'Tho the place looks great, an Danny is dead chuffed. They are havin a ball out there.'

'He's not a baby anymore, ye'd want to be thinkin of havin another one.' Jimmy suggests winking at Evelyn, giving her one of his trademark goofy grins before taking a swig from the bottle in his hand. Evelyn flicks him a look of repulsion in return, wishing Jimmy would learn keep his mouth shut at times.

'What d'ya think Evie, not a bad idea.' Brian immediately jumps on the bandwagon. 'Danny would love a little brother or sister, an the council'd give us a bigger house. One of them new three beds they are building over on Furan Drive.'

Her mother's interruption coming as a rare godsend, even if her disapproval is unwelcome by Brian. It prevents Evelyn from having to voice her own thoughts on the subject.

'That's no reason to go having a wain.' Gillian scolds from the threshold of the doorway, almost dropping the plates of discarded food she had been bringing in. 'An where would you be all the way over in Furan Drive.' She put the plates down on the counter, before scraping crushed bits of cake into the bin. Two dimples of red on her cheeks indicating her anguish. 'Ya wouldn't be able to pop round the corner to your convenient babysitter if ye lived over there.'

'You like having Danny.' Evelyn cuts in. 'Aren't ya always saying drop him over. Why are ya making out I dump him on you?' Her face creasing, showing annoyance.

'I'm not. What I'm saying is, trying to get a house in Furan would be too far away.'

'They've a nice view of Carraigbrin bay, Gillian.' Jimmy points out, clearly missing her point. Though his input, does tame the discussion slightly, until adding. 'An they're building a new school an shops there too. Be a feckin deadly place ta live. I might find a lack meself and get her up the duff.'

'Shut up Jimmy.' Gillian spits, throwing him a filthy glare. 'Danny is settled here, he doesn't need to go to another school and be separated from his friends.'

'More like you don't want to be separated from Danny.' Brian cuts in, sneering and throwing his eyes to heaven. 'He's our son, Gillian sometimes I think you forget that.' Brian points out. 'I'm going back outside it's after becoming fecking stiflin in here.' He grabs another bottle of beer from the fridge. 'Evie, are ya bringing out that cake for Danny to blow his candles, before his friends all leave.' He shouts, over his shoulder as he departs.

'One minute, I'm just sortin the party bags and I'll follow you.' She says without looking up, glad the subject of moving house and having more babies, has ended. Though, unhappy her mother has unnecessarily riled Brian. 'What ya have to go sayin that to him Ma?' She hisses as Jimmy passes by, loyally following Brian outside.

'It's not just about Danny love, I've held back too long. I saw the red mark on your cheek when I arrived with Danny, I'm no fool. He only wants another child, cause he wants to trap you more than you already are. I'm guessing it's got something to do with Des being released from prison. How many times did he question about Danny? And have you forgotten what happened, you could have lost Danny and died yerself cause of him. I didn't buy the bullshit story he gave about you fallin, my only regret is keeping quiet this long.'

'Mam, please not today.' Evelyn pleads, bile rising in her throat.

'I'm sorry love, I can't stand back anymore. Please say you won't give in to another child, for now at least.' Gillian begs as Evelyn lifts the cake from its box, strategically placing five candles along the top. 'I hope you know what you're doing?' Gillian adds eyeing the cake, a perfect replica of a formula one racing car.

'Mam please,' Evelyn retorts impatiently, becoming irritated by her mother's constant interference. 'Don't spoil Danny's day.'

'I'm not trying to pet, I'm worried about ya that's all.'

'Don't be, I'm a big girl I can take care of myself.' Evelyn's hands are shaking as she lights the candles. 'I know what I want and it's not more babies.' Words surprising herself as much as her mother, not usually so free with her inner thoughts. 'Not yet anyway.' She adds without knowing why.

'Have you spoken to him at all since his release?' Gillian probes digging the knife deeper, sending a bolt of emotion through Evelyn. Having tried for over five years to banish Desmond from her mind. Guilt ridden by the memory of his downcast expression the previous evening, when she had brushed him off.

'Desmond has nothing to do with it, he's in the past.' She retorts a little too harshly. 'I told you, I got the car made cause Danny likes that racin car on the telly.'

'I hope you're right, because he is bound to have questions wanting the truth.' Gillian pushes her unwanted opinion too far. Unaware of the depth of her daughter's deception towards Desmond. 'And that fella you've landed yourself with out there.' She nods in the direction of the garden. 'Will only give ya grief and a black eye for good measure. I often thought it would have been better if Danny was –'

'Leave it Mam, now is not the time.' Evelyn cuts her off with a warning glare, as she lifts the cake to carry outside. 'I'll cross that bridge, if I have to.'

Stepping out into the garden where the glare of the afternoon sunshine, low in the sky almost blinds her. All resolve having left her, if Desmond ever found out the truth, it would have a damaging effect on Danny and she could not allow that. Brushing aside the seed of doubt her mother has just set, Evelyn pastes a smile on her face.

'Happy birthday to you...' She begins singing, instantly everyone joins it.

'Wow cool...a racing car.' Danny screeches with delight. Brian's smile fades, his face darkening as his eyes rest on the cake. Evelyn's heart sinks to the bottom of her toes and back, knowing the trouble she would be in once everyone has gone home. If only she could explain, tell him it was bad judgement on her behalf. Her only saving grace at this moment being, Brian would not cause a scene while their friends and neighbours are still present. He is too clever for that.

Evelyn closes the door firmly behind her mother, the last guest to leave. Brian had gone into the lounge and turned the television on full volume, while they cleaned up.

'Mammy I had the best day, thank you.' Danny throws his arms around her waist giving a much needed hug and bringing tears to her eyes.

'I'm glad Danny bear, Mummy loves you with all her heart, you know that don't you.' He simply nods an acknowledgement of her statement. 'Come let's get you bathed and into bed, you must be tired after all that jumping around.' She takes him by the hand, leading him upstairs. Evelyn runs a bubble bath for Danny allowing him play for as long as he wants, stalling the moment she would have to face Brian's contempt over the cake, an empty jealousy Brian would not be reasoned by.

Tucking Danny into bed she suggests a story, getting no further than halfway down the second page before he is sound asleep. Her beautiful, innocent little boy with his shock of sandy blonde hair, deep hazel eyes and thick eyelashes, a mirror of his father. With a heavy sigh, she reluctantly places the book back on the shelf.

Glancing around the bedroom gives the impression of a normal family life, the walls are painted blue with motifs of trains and trucks, the usual décor of a little boy's bedroom. Right now her life feel's far from normal, having been brought up by parents who adored each other. Christie Priestly, a gentle caring man doting on his family. Stalling on the landing, Evelyn wishes she could slip over to her mother's house and lock herself in the bedroom, where she could finish off the dress now looking spectacular draped on the tailors dummy. Tonight, she cannot even risk going on Instagram in case Brian came upstairs discovering her second secret mobile. Her second secret self, the person she dreams of being.

Slipping quietly downstairs bypassing the door to the lounge, she walks into the kitchen. Realising she hasn't eaten much all day, she decides to make a sandwich. Grabbing some leftover chicken from the fridge, generously spreading butter over two slices of bread. Her mind somewhere far from the room, dreaming about the penthouse she'd own as a fashion designer, swimming in the heated pool after a day of creating a new range of elegant lingerie. Her head connects with the eyelevel wall press with force, meeting sharply with the corner. The pain so numbing, she doesn't immediately comprehend what has happened, until a trickle of blood drips down her forehead onto the white bread. Her whole body freezes, dazed and numbed by the impact and subsequent pain.

'Do I look like a fucking fool?' He yells in her ear, jerking her head back by pulling her hair. 'D'ya think it was amusing having a fucking cake shaped as a racin car, d'ya? You are mine, d'ya hear...answer me bitch.' Brian snarls, face scrunched up in anger.

'I don't want anyone but you Bri....Danny watches the car racin...there was nothing in it, I swear.' Evelyn pleads, trying not to cry even though her head is throbbing, blood now pouring down her forehead almost blinding her.

'Yeah...well as long as ya know yer mine, cause he doesn't give a shit about ya. He was with that sexy bird related to O'Dowd...all over her last night he was. Doesn't give a fuck about you...an why would he...she's easy on the eye...tight arse, wouldn't mind givin her one meself...a bit of posh would be a nice change from the skank I put up with, gone up in the world our Dessie.' His words deliberate to make her feel small. He yanks up her skirt using his body to trap her against the counter, one hand still clasped on her hair pinching the back of her head. With her back to him, it is impossible to gauge his next move. She doesn't have to wait long, his rough hands invade her body grabbing her knickers and ripping them as he forces them down. Evelyn is paralysed with fear, disbelieving of what is happening. He had never done anything like this before. A slap, a punch followed by remorse and makeup sex, never forced always gentle and loving, always with her a willing participant. She can feel his fingers digging into her skin and wonders does it make him feel better, thinking he has control. 'Better get you knocked up, so ya know yer place.' He hisses as though reading her mind.

It becomes clear he is scared of losing control, of losing her. She can feel his breath hot on her face, his breathing becoming heavier. Keeping her eyes focused on the knife in her hand she wonders, could it be counted as rape if it's with someone you had made love to only hours previously. If she tries to struggle, he would counter act, a move which might disturb Danny sleeping upstairs. The thought of her innocent child coming down and seeing her like this. His own father treating her like a piece of meat, determining her decision to surrender.

'You like it rough don't ya.' He hisses as he enters her, crushing her already wedged body against the press with force, resulting in a handle digging into her bare stomach. As his pleasure increases, so does his grip forcing her head down onto the counter, pinning it by wedging the palm of his hand against her face. She closes her eyes, fearing he is getting satisfaction from knowingly causing her pain. He groans loudly, pumping harder. Tears stream down Evelyn's cheeks mingling with the blood from her forehead. 'You're mine....No one else would have ya.' He twists her head round pressing his lips roughly over hers, while letting out a moan of pleasure as he ejaculates. The smell of alcohol mixed with cigarettes pungent as it reaches her nostrils, making her feel sick. A smell, which will forever remind her of this moment. The moment when he crossed the line from being her boyfriend to her attacker. An occurrence they will never go back from.

Chapter 16

'You okay kid? You've been quiet all day.' Lily asks Sarah, as they close up the café after doing a late stock take. 'Don't let this thing with Aine get to you, we'll sort it.'

'Why is she doing this, how can she think she can bulldoze her way in and it not affect us? This is our home, our livelihood everything we love. Hasn't she a great job and apartment in New York. What does she want the house for? A holiday home in Ireland, so she can boast to her friends over cocktails.'

'She's moving home apparently.' Lily's words cut through the late warm summer evening, like a cold gust of wind whipping through the air. 'Tommy phoned her, he was so annoyed and couldn't let it lie. She has split with Chad caught him in bed with her assistant would you believe. That's why there is all this talk of a job in Dublin. Why she can't just buy a place there is still a mystery.'

'Did you say her assistant, as in...oh sweet Jesus.'

'Apparently they have been having a relationship behind her back for the best part of a year. I haven't much time for Aine, but catching them together must have been one hell of a shock.' Lily eyes glaze over. 'I wish Aine felt she could come to us, it would have saved a lot of bad feeling.'

'I agree, she could easily share the house with me as long as she doesn't bulldoze walls. It wouldn't be that hard to avoid each other or would it? On second thoughts she is welcome to build a modern dream home, there is enough land.' Sarah is thoughtful. 'I guess, I always assumed this life didn't suit her and she preferred city life.' They pause where the road splits in two. 'I never understood her hostility towards me. I always wished Aine and I could have been closer, thought maybe the six year age gap had some part to play.' She leans against the low stone wall separating the farmhouse from the driveway. 'It must be a serious kick in the guts what Chad did, they'd been together for years. Did you say she'd caught them in the act?'

'Doesn't bare thinking about does it? Another woman would be bad enough but....sometimes you think you know someone.' Lily sighs heavily. 'Oh, I meant to say. Thanks for getting Paul, he's some hard worker and a nice guy too. He and Tommy are getting on really well, it's taken a massive amount of strain away...as long as we can afford to keep him on. '

'We'll make sure we can get through this together, we're a team remember. You have always been there for me, Lil and I appreciate the fact you've been a mother and sister rolled into one, since you married Tommy.'

'Stop you'll have me bawling in a minute...but thanks kid, I needed to hear that. I have wondered recently could I be doing more, especially with Tommy.' She brushes a stray hair which has fallen from her roughly pulled back pony tail. 'Are you stopping in for a bite to eat?'

'Thanks but no, I've a few things to do like wanting to call Roz, before Maggie arrives. We're having takeaway, wine and a good ole chinwag.'

'Sounds lovely, better than bacon, cabbage and spuds.'

'Join us, I'm sure knowing Maggie there'll be plenty.'

'Not at all, kid. You relax and catch up with Maggie, I'll see you in the morning.'

'Don't forget I'm meeting Dini, so won't be in til around eleven.'

'Why don't you take the morning off there are no buses scheduled for tomorrow.'

'It's fine, besides I like being busy. The fruit will be picked and ready, I'll leave it in the kitchen.' Sarah waves as they part. Sarah veering left, while Lily turns right opening the little gate of the picket fence, which separates her house from the road into the farmhouse.

The kitchen is eerily silent when Sarah enters, sending a shiver down her spine. Her father would normally be sitting in his chair next to the Aga with the evening news on full volume, blasting out of the television. Sarah had it installed a few years back fixing an arm to the wall, making it easy to turn and face wherever they had decided to sit. Be it, at the table or in his arm chair, Paddy loved documentaries and quiz programmes. The television made sense as they spent all their time in the homely kitchen, only ever using the big front lounge at Christmas or other milestone events. She hasn't gone in there since the funeral, had closed the door not wanting to see the empty space where his coffin had lain. Everything about the house echoes memories of her father, of Jack and even her mother.

Though Sarah had hardly known Moira, there are pictures and trinkets, treasures her mother had adored, placed lovingly in the house she made into a home to bring her family up in, only fate had other ideas. Paddy would not allow anything to be changed or moved over the years. Even the rocking chair on the opposite side of the Aga facing her father's chair, no one but little Jack was allowed to sit in it. Although Sarah had caught her father sitting in it a couple of times his eyes glazed over, his mind somewhere far beyond the room.

Sarah flicks the switch on the kettle, along with the television to create noise. She fires up her laptop and quickly types a post in the Justice for Road

Victims' Facebook page to highlight, the injustice of a victim not having a second chance when people like Desmond Shanahan, are released without serving their full sentence. Allowed to move on with life as though nothing had ever happened. She connects to skype and immediately her friend Roz, the other administrator of the group, springs into view. She is also sitting at her kitchen table, Sarah can see rows of freshly baked cupcakes cooling in the background. Roz's daughter had been struck by a hit and run driver, when he ran a red light as she was crossing the road. Luckily, a witness took the registration number of the car and phoned for an ambulance. Natasha, later died of her injuries, the driver showed no remorse stating he was late for church. He received an eighteen month suspended sentence, due to his clean record and high standing in the community. The note of apology clearly written on instruction from his defence counsel, Roz and her family received, had also played a part in the leniency the judge showed. It was little consolation to Roz, her heart ripped to shreds by her loss. Natasha had been thirteen years old, when her life was taken. Roz had shown Sarah, photograph's of Natasha, when they first met up. A beautiful girl with long golden hair, an elegant and talented Irish dancer, she was the youngest child in the family, Roz and her husband Ray were heartbroken.

Unfortunately, their grief took its toll on their marriage each pulling in different directions, coping with the loss in their own way. Roz focusing her pain and anger in seeking out other parents sharing similar experiences, wanting the government to change laws for harsher penalties for the perpetrators. She's been a lifeline for Sarah, someone who truly understands what she is going through. They set up a page on Facebook, along with a website and regular blog. Social media their initial ticket to getting their campaign noticed, when more and more members joined they began to arrange a few small peaceful protests.

'I'm sitting here contemplating life and like a guardian angel you appear. How are you holding up girl?' Roz says using the comforting tone she often does when speaking to other parents of victims. It is her way of showing support, no matter what might be bubbling underneath in her own mind.

'I'd be lying if, I said okay there is so much going on at the moment, I can feel the old demon creeping back in.'

'That is not good, I suspect it's to do with knowing he is walking around the same town as you. Would you like me to take a trip up?' Roz living in Waterford, would mean taking a good eight hour drive, being at the opposite end of the country from Sarah.

'No...no, I wouldn't expect you to do that.' Sarah replies, grateful Roz would go to such a lengths on her behalf, but she cannot ask it of the other woman. 'A sympathetic ear is enough.'

'I'm always that girl, remember.'

'I know and thank you for the beautiful wreath and Mass card.'

'I can't get my head around your poor father being gone from this world. It was the shock I'd imagine, he needed to be with Jack.' Roz's words echoing Sarah's own thoughts.

'That's how I see it Roz, I knew you would understand. The only thing is I'm left alone missing them. I do have some positive news though, I'm training for the Dublin marathon in October. It was my nephew Matt's suggestion, he is doing it too.' She refrains from adding, Matt's physical attributes remind her so much of Jack. 'A fitting tribute to Jack, don't you think, I plan to get t-shirts and banners made up. I won't have my son forgotten about.'

'God bless Matt, isn't he great to think of it. I have a friend in the printing business, I'll find out if she'd donate the t-shirts or at least print them free.'

'That would be fabulous Roz, I appreciate it.'

'Not at all girl, we are all here for each other, which brings me to what I have been up to. Desmond's early release has prompted me to take action too, so I've been in contact with a local politician. Cathal Riordan, you won't know him, but he is big into cycling and sees first-hand the dangers on our roads from impatient and dangerous drivers. He suggested, we apply to the Seanad Chamber in the houses of the Oireachteas Seanad Eirean, for a hearing with the Public Consultation Committee. He is going to help me, would you be interested in coming too, telling them about Jack. It is personal, going over details you might not want to relive, but we are our children's voices and if we don't do it, who will? They certainly can't.' Roz is matter-of-fact, her expression one of conviction.

'Do you think it will help change the law and bring tougher sentences?'

'It's worth a try at least it will bring it to their attention. Cathal told me he had been contacted by a lady forced off the road when she was cycling. The driver never even stopped to check if she was alright. She was just left there with two broken ribs and that is only the physical scars. What it has done for her mortality, I daren't to think.'

'That's unbelievable, what is it with people and their ignorant mentality when driving? Okay, I'm in, what do I need to do?'

'Basically tell your story, make it full of facts but also we want to hit them with the emotional reality. These are our children not statistics, real people lives that matter.'

'I guess, I can do that when do you want it by?'

'As soon as you possibly can then email me, I'll consult with Cathal again see if we can arrange a date for a sitting. Now I must go, have to drop all these cakes over to the school.' She moves the laptop showing dozens of fairy cakes all beautifully iced. Roz partakes in voluntary work, filling her days as much as she possibly can.

'They look delicious, there are so many what are they for?'

'A fundraiser for the local school Natasha went to, they are planting a tree and putting a bench under it with a plaque in her honour. Half the money raised will be handed to the group towards raising awareness.'

'You're fabulous Roz, I don't know how you keep going.'

'I've you to thank for that girl, besides with Ray gone on his merry way, I need to keep busy. Rumour round the town is he is seeing someone which I find hard to digest, Ray with a new woman.' She scoffs throwing her eyes to heaven. Sarah can tell by her expression it's a front. 'He's too lazy to make the effort, I couldn't imagine him in anything other than those awful brown cords he always wore and who would look at him twice in them?' They both laugh, Sarah hoping for Roz's sake she is right. If Ray has met someone it would be another blow for Roz. It doesn't matter that they have been living apart for the best part of two years, it will still hurt her deeply. 'You keep your spirits up and best of luck with the marathon training, good for alleviating anxiety, running or so they say anyway. Nighty night.'

'Night Roz.' Sarah clicks off immediately opening a word document. Then stares at the blank white page wondering where to start, scared of reliving moments she has pushed to a compartment in her mind labelled "Devastation."

'You look serious everything okay?'

'Jesus, you scared the life out of me.' Sarah jumps up almost knocking her coffee over the keyboard. 'What are you doing sneaking in like that?'

'That's not much of a welcome.' He looks handsome dressed in jeans and a red shirt with the top two buttons undone, highlighting his sallow skin. Sarah unable take her eyes off his taut chest, wanting to sink into his arms as he sidles towards her with a swagger of confidence only he could have. His deep dark eyes fixed firmly on hers, he leans in kissing her softly on the lips while his hand slips with ease under her top. Inhaling his musky male smell makes her feel weak at the knees, his power over her unexplainable. In the midst of Sarah's elation, the warm tingly feeling running through her veins suddenly turns to ice.

'You can't be here.' She shoves him away, jumping back as though having been burned by fire.

'What? Why?' The disappointment etched on his face palpable, she had been too quick to dismiss him, and it came out harsh and unfeeling.

'Maggie is coming over she'll be here any minute.'

'You're kidding me.' His face turns red. 'Shit, that's what she was on about, wasn't really listening...give her a ring make an excuse and blow her off. Tell her you have a headache or you're tired.' He slides his arms around her waist.

'I can't do that. It wouldn't feel right.' She had never been good at hiding her feelings or lying, a fact which is ironic considering the large lie she has been harbouring for most of her life.

'Aw come on babe for us, I haven't seen you in ages and I thought now you're here alone, we'd get more of a chance you know. I'm mad turned on, you have an effect on my libido.' He places soft kisses on her neck, almost causing her to falter and succumb to his charm. A tingle runs down her body, her senses bewitched by his touch. The sensation of his hand touching her bare skin almost sending euphoria through her body, until she hears a car pull up outside.

'Shit, it must be Maggie,' she hastily pushes him away for the second time. 'You have to go before she sees you.' She grabs him by the hand pulling him into the hallway. 'Go out the front door, she'll come in the back, always does.'

'You know this is turning me on.' He is a natural flirt, making women drawn to his persona like a magnet. The close proximity of his body radiating making her flush, desperate to give in to the desire he is sending through her body, but reason takes over.

'Where did you park?' She whispers, panic rising in her chest.

'It's okay, I parked up behind the old barn, we had some magical moments in there do you remember?' He teases. Sarah can hear footsteps, magnified by her growing fear, all desire having been doused as though water had been thrown on a fire.

'Go.' She opens the front door shoving him outside. It does not deter Finn, as he leans over kissing her tenderly on the lips before walking away. Sarah closes the door leaning against the back of it, her heart beating wildly as the door into the kitchen opens literally seconds later. Sarah buries her head in her hands, emotionally drained.

Chapter 17

'I can't decide, whether I've come at a really bad time or I'm your saviour.' Maggie says, red curls tumbling across her shoulders. Holding a bottle of chardonnay in one hand and Chinese takeaway in the other, she looks ten years younger and less stern out of her Garda uniform. 'Gauging the look on your face, it is the latter.' She adds, causing Sarah to inadvertently burst into tears, Maggie quickly discards the bottle and food onto the table, pulling Sarah into her arms. This only makes Sarah feel worse, her dear friend Maggie as always offering a shoulder, unaware of the lie Sarah is hiding. Her lips still moist from his kiss, convinced Maggie could pick up on the lingering scent of Dior, left in his wake.

The deceit, had often been too much over the years, Sarah initially convincing herself, her actions were to protect Maggie and her daughter's, as well as Jack. Now she wonders, had she been kidding herself into thinking this while protecting her own reputation. Especially, since rekindling her affair with Finn after Jack's death. She had never intended too, but the loss had thrown them back together. Being with Finn, making her feel closer to a part of Jack, or at least this is how she rationalises her guilt.

'Come sit, tell me all.' Maggie says steering her towards a chair. 'I'm guessing Conor is the reason. Have you spoken to him since he employed that Desmond?'

'No...I think he has been avoiding me, even stopped coming into the café for his sourdough bread. His cousin, Alice who works in the office collects it on her way to work.'

'Good god you are shaking, let's have some food and wine you'll feel better, trust me.' Maggie winks, not generally the mothering type, Maggie perfectly capable of handling any situation without unnecessary fuss. 'Have to say I don't know what he was thinking, employing that lout....If it's any consolation, I think he still loves you. Maybe it's his way of getting you to stand up and notice, if he even needs to do that.' Maggie raises a brow, throwing Sarah a knowing look.

'Well it's a stupid way of going about it.' Sarah replies pretending not to notice, she takes the plate stabbing a chicken ball with her fork, hating herself for wishing Finn was the one sitting across from her. For years she had been happy to be on her own, still preferring her independence to a certain degree. There are times when she needs to feel loved, craving his touch and attention. She flicks a glance towards Maggie, trying to ignore the pang of guilt chipping away. 'It's silly, we are in the past...still, I thought our friendship meant more, especially as Jack adored Conor.' Sarah sighs. Had she really believed at the time Finn loved her, causing her to break off her engagement to Conor, breaking his heart in two? Finn told her she was the only woman in his eyes and she believed him. Until he had turned up in Kilmer Cove, with Maggie, married literally five months after leaving Sarah pregnant. Maggie had a natural beauty, she could see why Finn had fallen for her, had proposed to her after learning she was carrying his child. His new wife three months pregnant, wide eyed, beautiful and very much in love with her beau. Maggie immediately bonding with Sarah, through their shared pregnancies. How could Sarah tell her, their babies also shared the same DNA? It took him a long time to ask Sarah about Jack, and had only shown any real interest after his death. She has to wonder, why he keeps coming back to her since, when clearly Maggie adores him. 'It's not just about Conor employing Shanahan. I've barely had time to grieve Da, and our Aine is contesting the will, wants this house and some of the land.' Sarah reveals, knowing she would have to leave her guard down and tell Maggie about Aine. It would be around the town soon enough and Maggie would be hurt, if Sarah didn't confide in her.

'Jesus, seriously...selfish bitch. Hasn't she a life in New York, with her fancy job and apartment. What can she want with this place? Mind you she'd be after the money, it'd fetch a fair price now being on the Wild Atlantic Way. It's a goldmine with the business.'

'It's my home Maggie, my family home besides she can't sell, Da stipulated it in the will.' She has completely dropped her guard, the half a glass of wine and emotion getting the better of her.

'I'm your friend and honesty is my middle name, you know I will speak my mind, even if it's not what you want to hear.' Maggie says between mouthfuls of food, taking a large gulp of wine to wash it down. 'Would you not consider moving on from here? Not entirely, but this farm. I know Conor has overstepped the line but...maybe you two....' She takes another mouthful of wine, then refills her glass. Slurring slightly she continues. 'What is there not to like about Conor, you obviously still care about each other. He is hot, has oodles of cash, his own business, not something to be sniffed at. I can only dream of Finn looking at me the way Conor does you.' She adds, her eyes becoming dreamy before sobering and taking another mouthful of wine. Leaving, Sarah wondering where all this has come from, she doesn't get a chance to ask. 'Sarah, don't take this the wrong way, but you have put Jack's father up on a pedestal, a complete fantasy. You were young, university sweethearts of course it had been exciting back then. In reality, he is probably married, fat and generally not a very nice person.' Maggie takes another sip of her wine. 'Look, if this guy was the man of your dreams. Then ask yourself, why did you never contact him and tell him about Jack? I mean, Finn asked me to marry him as soon as I told him, I was pregnant. We were meant to be together, would have probably married anyway, nature or fate whatever you want to call it pushed along the inevitable. If you and whatever his name was, were fated to be together, he would be here now don't you think?' Sarah nearly chokes on her chicken ball, if only Maggie knew.

'I never put Jack's father on a pedestal, had never expected him to marry me, but it doesn't mean I have to make compromises either.' Sarah replies, trying to hide her underlying annoyance over Maggie's statement.

'Conor is anything but a compromise, don't you agree?' Maggie says, raising her voice slightly and hiccupping before downing more wine.

'I do wonder sometimes could we have worked...I think, I like my independence too much.' Sarah can feel her cheeks burn wanting desperately to change the subject.

'Mm.' Maggie raises a brow, clearly unconvinced. 'So you've never secretly rekindled the old spark...I mean we live in a modern world, friends with benefits and all that...., aren't ye two single people with needs.'

'Noooo....and don't look at me like that Maggie O'Driscoll.' Sarah scolds.

'Like what, sure I'm only stating the obvious.' Maggie laughs, 'here have more wine you look like you need it. Besides I'm curious, was it guilt over not telling your mystery, Trinity lover about Jack, or do you still have a flame burning?' The question coming unexpected as well as untimely, since Sarah is still emotionally dazed from Finn's visit.

'Shit, I'm meant to be meeting Dini in the morning for a training session on the track.' Sarah purposefully changes the subject, scared she will trip herself up with more lies. 'Drinking wine and eating Chinese, the night before is not a good idea.'

'You need to unwind, besides you'll be fine by the morning two glasses of wine won't do much damage.' She pauses, taking a sip from her glass. 'Look there is an ulterior motive for coming here tonight. I don't know if I should say anything now...after.'

'What is it?' Sarah asks, blood draining from her face. Wondering what else could be thrown at her within the space of a few hours.

'Just so you know, we are not taking it seriously at the station and have not made any record but the Serge said, I should at least warn you.' Maggie pauses placing her fork on the plate. 'Ger Shanahan came in the other day, complaining about you hanging around outside their house. Before you protest this is not an official warning, I'm your friend and I'm on your side.' Maggie points out. Sarah simply nods not trusting herself to speak. 'I have to ask though...are you sitting in the car outside their house most days?'

'No.' Sarah protests, launching into a white lie she feels guilty about. Ironic considering the great big one she has hidden since knowing Maggie. 'I was out running, training for my marathon and bumped into Ger, he went crazy. There is no law saying I can't pass their house.'

'I'm sorry, I had to ask. You're right, Ger Shanahan can be a bit of a grumpy old bastard at the best of times forget we had this conversation.' Maggie spoons a forkful of noodles into her mouth, washing it down with wine. Her gaze resting on Sarah, eyes wide darting between Sarah and somewhere beside her as they did the night she looked uncomfortable telling, Paddy and Sarah about Shanahan's early release. 'I better go, have an early shift again tomorrow.' Maggie suddenly announces taking her mobile from her pocket, becoming distracted her fingers tapping the screen.

'Oh...I thought.' Sarah surprised as to the sudden haste in which she is leaving. 'Are you tweeting that we are drunk, I'm definitely not up for a selfie tonight, say my face is red and blotchy.' Sarah quips used to Maggie taking her phone out and snapping a picture before putting it on social media.

'No you're safe tonight.' Maggie replies still engrossed in her phone. 'I really have to get going thought, sorry.' She stands up. 'Oh, have you had any more problems with damage to fences, or gates being opened. Ted was onto us again, he's lost a couple of cattle over the cliff.'

'No, but I'll mention it to Tommy.' Sarah gets up too.

'How is Tommy coping without yer, Da to help on the farm?' Maggie asks as she puts the wrappers in the bin.

'Leave those Mags, I can tidy them. Nothing much else to do for the evening. To answer your question, Tommy is fine we've taken on, Paul Quilty and the lad is a godsend.'

'Kitty mentioned it alright but I thought she'd gotten it wrong, you know mixed up which of the Quilty's it is. You know he used to knock about with Desmond Shanahan?'

'Used too.' Sarah points out, agitated Maggie could be so judgmental. 'Paul is a nice fellow and a hard worker. It's unfair to label him because he had once associated with Desmond.'

'You're right of course.' Maggie's face turns crimson, partly due to the wine and partly because she had only been looking out for Sarah, to have it thrown back in her face. 'I didn't mean anything by it, I'm glad Tommy has help. Your family have had more than their fair share of misfortune it doesn't seem fair, that's all.' Her comment leaving Sarah feeling bad, but she could not have allowed Maggie bad mouth, Paul or anyone unjustly for that matter.

'They say god only deals what we are capable of dealing with, sometimes I think there is no god.'

'Don't lose your faith that would be like giving up completely.'

'Thanks for tonight Mags, I really appreciate the company.'

'And the advice of a friend who cares, I hope.' Maggie hugs her. 'Take care and remember, I'm always on the other end of the phone should you need me.'

'Will I call a taxi or get Tommy to drop you home?'

'I'm grand, Finn should be pulling up outside any second now. At least, I think he is had a meeting for a new job earlier when I phoned him. Some extension or renovation of an old cottage over on the Byer way, I think he said. Most likely some rich American wanting it done up as a holiday home, we are getting more and more of them these days.' Maggie's face drops, clearly horrified. 'Jesus, I'm sorry that was tactless of me...look I'm sure you'll be able to resolve the house situation. If your, Da made a will what can Aine do?' Maggie places a hand on Sarah's arm, causing an eruption of guilt to surface again. 'Now I should really go, if Finn is waiting outside he won't be too happy.' Maggie places her glass in the dishwasher. It is on the tip of Sarah's tongue to ask why Finn wouldn't give a knock, also confused as to why he never mentioned this earlier.

'Thanks for the food, and the wine, you're a good friend I'd be lost without you.' Sarah says, with sincerity. Feeling badly for Maggie being caught up in the middle of their deceit. She is a good person, and doesn't deserve the way they are treating her.

'I'll pick my car up in the morning...chin up and think about what I said about Conor, be a pity to let him slip away, he's got a good heart under that cold exterior you know.' Maggie adds, being the beacon of comfort, she has often tried to be. 'Could be the answer to all your problems, a fresh start. You deserve a bit of happiness. Night.' She waves her hand in the air, as she disappears out the door.

Chapter 18

'So, how is the training going?' Dini asks Sarah, as she approaches. He is leaning on the railing observing Lucy Goulding sprinting around the track. 'Pace, pace, pace...or ya'll burn out too quickly.' He shouts at the younger girl. Sarah pauses next to him, her body becoming rigid, memories flooding to the forefront of mornings standing in the same spot watching her son train. She could almost imagine him gliding with ease, adrenaline flowing. The steady pummel of footsteps echoing in her ears, arms pumping a bead of sweat running down his forehead, as he gave it his all. Determination to be the best he could be, making her proud as any mother should be. Like a bird flying free, Sarah knew he was becoming a man and one day he would fly the nest. It wouldn't have been easy but she had already accepted her son had plans to travel, to compete, to go to university. It made her proud to think she had prepared him to be confident enough to follow his dreams. 'Watch Lucy's stride, I've been checking your progress on the Strava, you are slowing and what's with the regular stops?' Dini's voice cuts into her thoughts surprising her, having forgotten about wearing the running watch which had been Jack's. She didn't realise it linked up to anything in which Dini or anyone else could see.

'If you know how I'm doing, then why did you ask?' Sarah replies trying to sound blasé, hoping he'd not detected the quiver in her voice or at least put it down to her being cold. Her head beginning to pound, unsure whether it is the after effect of last night's wine or tension from being in a place, which reminds her so much of Jack.

'Gettin defensive with the coach gets ye nowhere, it only highlights yer weaknesses. See how Lucy is pulling her body up and sliding her foot. Gives a freer stride and ya end up less likely to have a hamstring. Are ye doing stretches and warm ups?'

'Yes of course.' Sarah replies throwing him a sideward glance.

'Good, within the next three weeks we need to be up to a half marathon. You also should be havin a rest day say every three or four days. Make it four, I need you focusing on a strict regime. On yer rest day, do a few stretches but no running. Nothing too physical or demanding on rest days, D'ya hear.'

'Nothing!' Sarah quips, making it his turn to throw the sideward glance and a wry smile.

'Paddy Connolly will never be gone as long as you grace Kilmer Cove, girl.' Dini smiles with bemusement.

'She floats around the track with such ease reminds me of when I used to come and watch Jack.' Sarah says as they watch Lucy, once again becoming immersed in memories.

'He had a natural talent that lad, Jack owned the track.' Dini coughs, clearing his throat. 'Lucy is good, in better shape than she has ever been but Jack…he was a true Olympic star in my eyes.' His eyes glaze over. 'Pure determination and dedication.'

'When are you setting off for the worlds?' Sarah suffocated by a need to break their spell before crumbling from the magnitude of their loss. Though she's mindful Jack should have been going too.

'In three weeks they don't start til 4th August, but we're headin over a week before, I need this one focused without distractions. Don't worry, I've plenty time to get ye on a proper programme before I leave. When I get back, I expect to not recognise the woman running round that track.'

'You trying to change me?' Sarah questions, raising a brow.

'Never in a million years, girlie but I will make ye into an excellent runner. I've been in contact with Matt, fair talented that boy too must be something in the Connolly genes. He's happy following a programme I've given him, making great progress I've noticed. Now let's get you started with a wee warm up, before we get down to some real training. ' He rubs his hands together, a wicked smile crossing his face.

'Slave driver.' She throws her eyes to heaven in mock exasperation. 'Better believe it, Jack would be proud of what ye're doing in his honour. I know I am.' His words sincere. 'I'll be waiting at the finish line and so will Kitty. She was blown away with pride, when I told her what ye're doin.'

'Thanks Dini and I appreciate you taking the time to do this.' Sarah replies with equal sincerity.

'Anything for you, girlie. I miss Jack, he was one hell of a special kid.' Dini purses his lips together, turning away to hide overcoming emotion.

'Yes he was.' She swallows back the lump which is beginning to form. Being at the track with Dini and without Jack, odd. Panic rising in her chest, with an overwhelming urge to escape from the clutches of invisible hands clawing their way up her body. She closes her eyes taking a deep breath.

'Are ye okay, ya look a little pale?' Dini asks looking around from where he had moved onto the steps, concern etched on his face.

'I'm fine.' She pastes a false smile on her lips, reminding herself of why she is there and why she must do this. The marathon would bring recognition to the forefront of peoples' minds, that a talented young man had his future stardom cruelly taken away, when his life was cut short by a mindless drug taking idiot.

'Hi Sarah, Dini said you'd be training with us.' Lucy stops running joining Sarah at the side of the track. 'It's good to see you.' She gives Sarah an unexpected hug, making her want to cry. Something she appears to be on the verge of regularly in recent times. Lucy had spent many an hour at the farmhouse, either studying or training with Jack.

'All ready for the World Championships'?' Sarah asks hoping to sound more enthusiastic than she is feeling.

'A little apprehensive about going on my own.'

'Dini will be with you and your parents.' Sarah replies, Lucy drops her gaze and Sarah realises what she had meant. 'He'll be there in spirit.' She places a comforting hand on the young girl's arm. 'You will be fine, we'll all be routing for you here.'

'Thanks Sarah, that means a lot.'

In spite of Sarah's initial reservations, the training session is successful. By the time she waves goodbye to Dini and Lucy, getting into her car Sarah is exhilarated, less weepy and more enthusiastic. Maybe Roz had been right about running being good for mental stimulation. Once she had got moving on the track, Lucy pacing alongside, Sarah had felt closer to Jack than she'd done in a very long time. The feeling alien and comforting all in one her body relaxing into a comfortable stride, it felt as though he was pacing alongside too, encouraging, almost carrying her body, legs becoming lighter heart lifting.

Pulling out onto the road, she drives towards the town centre keeping her eyes fixed on the road ahead. Passing by the end of Seaview Park and the Shanahan's, holding resolve not to turn and look in the direction of their house. The fact of Ger putting a complaint into the Garda, practically laughable. Nothing would knock her positive resolve, she would take a swim in the cove to revive her tired muscles, before heading up to the old stables. As it is Sunday, there would be no tour buses, Lily would manage without her. Planning to make use of the time to help Tommy and Paul, they are tiling the shower units on the campsite ready for it to open in forty-eight hours. An exciting prospect, also nerve wracking as they will be going against Alan's explicit instructions over the will being contested.

The water is cool and refreshing, leaving her exhilarated as she slips back on her dress. Distracted watching sailboats out on the bay, she does not hear his approach.

'You always look so sexy when your hair is wet.'

'Finn you can't keep doing this.'

'I miss you Sarah, miss being with you. It's been a couple of weeks, a man can't be kept hanging the way you tease me.' He flashes her one of his smiles melting her heart. She remains frozen to the spot caught up in their web of deceit as he snakes his arms around her waist pulling her close. 'I want you.' He whispers in her ear sending a shiver down her spine. All too easily she relents giving in to his accomplished persuasion.

'Not here, someone might see us.' She pulls him by the hand up the narrow pathway to the farmhouse.

By the time they reach inside they are completely absorbed in each other, the rest of the world doesn't exist. A tingling sensation running down her spine in anticipation, her body crying out for his touch wanting his strong arms around her, it takes all her restraint to make it up the stairs to her bedroom. The urgency heightened due to Finn placing soft kisses on the nape of her neck and bare shoulders, causing her skin to burn with desire. A gasp of pleasure escapes her lips as she pushes open the door finally alone with the only man she has ever truly loved.

Once inside, he swings her around to face him their eyes locking, now only they exist. It's times like this that makes all the pain and lies worthwhile, stolen moments locked in passion with the only man she has ever truly loved. Whispering her name he leans in teasingly, he knows how to play this, how to make Sarah feel like the only woman in the world. Her moist lips waiting in anticipation for his soft kisses, as they awkwardly try to undress.

Still in a state of semi-dress, Finn guides her towards the bed, planting gentle kisses on her breasts taking her erect nipples in turn, whilst watching her reaction, until she cannot take the anticipation any longer, begging him to enter her. Covering her lips with his kissing her deep and passionate, his tongue thrusting deeply their hot breaths entwining lost in each other, he does this making love to her slowly, sensually while she revels in his soft touch as though she is delicate porcelain. Their bodies become entwined as one in the shimmering light of the room each savouring the moment, lost in a heady trance of passion, fingers touching each other's skin as he moves, Sarah closes her eyes relishing the sensation, her body becoming rigid with euphoric trembles and warmth. They moan as he thrusts deeper becoming completely lost in each other, until their bodies explode in uncontrollable passion.

Moments later, lying wrapped in his arms their limbs entwined in the silence of the room wishing this moment would never end, Sarah is filled with overwhelming love for the man, who makes her feel as though nothing else matters when they are together. All too quickly, Finn leaps out of bed hastily dressing. It is part of their ritual, precious moments ending in his swift departure. Sarah doesn't protest or tell him how used it makes her feel. She has never begged or thrown herself at his mercy, she is not that sort of woman. Nevertheless, inside her heart is breaking in two.

'Have you spoken to Conor recently?' She tries to play down her feelings, making the question sound casual.

'Not since your, Da's funeral, I've been busy with a few new contracts, why?' He asks not meeting her gaze as he pulls on his jeans.

'He knows about us, I sent you a text but…did you know he has employed Desmond Shanahan to spite me.' Sarah slips a t-shirt over her head before getting out of bed, still elated and flushed from their lovemaking she entwines her arms around his waist.

'Don't pay any attention, he won't say anything. It's only a shallow jealousy.' He kisses her on the forehead. 'I have to go, I'll try and slip away again soon.' Sarah closes her eyes biting back an urge to tell him, she hates being his dirty little secret. 'It's handy you having the house to yourself now, no sneaking away down to the barn like a pair of teenagers.' Finn says as they walk along the landing, passing Jack's bedroom door. She flinches, willing him to ask to see their son's bedroom. He doesn't, leaving her fighting back raw disappointment.

Her mobile rings as she closes the front door, behind Finn. A welcome distraction, saving her from melancholy until answering. It is Aine on facetime, nothing could be worse. Her hair of course immaculately styled, makeup flawless if a little overdone, wearing an expensive Gucci top. Her disgust, obvious by her revolted expression over Sarah's dishevelled appearance. Hair damp and tousled from her recent lovemaking with Finn, though her face is glowing and flushed as she climbs the stairs, holding up the phone in front of her face.

'Jesus, Sarah you look like you've just got out of bed, isn't it noon over there.' Aine turns up her nose as though having caught a bad smell. 'Anyway, I'm calling because, you've been up to your usual tricks. How dare you, getting the boys to gang up on me.' Aine launches straight into an attack. 'Everything is always about you, Sarah. Have you ever considered the rest of us may have problems?' Aine continues, vibes of hatred crackling across the ocean. Years of pent up resentment bubbling to the surface. Sarah clenches the phone tight in her hand, wanting to wipe away her sister's smug expression.

'Now hang on a minute.' Sarah replies unwilling to be bullied. Feeling stronger than she had been a couple of weeks ago, when the shock of their father's death and Shanahan's release had been raw. 'You are the one trying to kick me out of my home.' Sarah's tone equally sharp. 'And for the record, I did not get anyone to gang up on you as you put it. This affects Tommy and Lily, if you are planning on taking our livelihood too. Oceanic temptation's is the reason this farm still exists, Da and Tommy had been under terrible pressure, where were you? Not here helping them and worrying about them, that's for sure. Lily and myself set the shop up becoming our lifeline.'

'Always with the over dramatic.' Sarah's protest falling on deaf ears. 'It's not just your home though is it, it's the family home. All I'm looking for is a fair split of land to live off, Dad did have four children not just you, and as for Lily...she's not family. Bloody sticks her nose in though.' Aine's reply heartless, fueling Sarah's anger.

'You cold hearted bitch, Lily has been more of a sister to me than you have ever been.' Sarah swallows back bile rising. 'I won't have you regarding her with disrespect.'

'Spare me the bullshit.' Her accent wavering from native to American. 'Going forward, I realise it was a mistake trying to reason with you, in future any contact can be made through our solicitors.' Aine takes on a patronising tone, a move to make Sarah feel outdone. Underestimating her sister as Sarah is not about to let her hang up without a fight.

'If you really want to add a property on the Wild Atlantic Way to your portfolio, then build your dream mansion. There is enough land for you to be far enough away so we won't cramp your style.'

'The farmhouse is my home, my roots and as the eldest... look there is no point, you wouldn't understand.'

'That is rich, if you loved this place so much then why did you rush off to America, you haven't lived here in nearly twenty-two years, whereas this has always been my home.'

'I thought you'd try that one frankly it's gone over my head. The simple fact is by rights the farmhouse should go to me. Of course, before I move back the house will need a total overhaul. I want to build a studio and sunroom, redesign and refit the kitchen.' Launching into her plans with bravado. 'Turn the bedroom at the back into a bathroom, so the existing one can become my en-suite. Luckily, it is next to daddy's room which is perfect.' Getting in vital points, aware of their effect on Sarah. Then the final twist of the knife as she reveals ultimate treachery. 'I've already commissioned Finn, to draw up the plans and the mock ups he has sent me are wonderful.' Her poisonous words resonate in Sarah's ears. Wanting to drop the phone as though being burned by it. Not sure which is worse, the house being pulled asunder ripping out Jack's bedroom to become a bathroom, or Finn's faithlessness. Aine's face however, is a depiction of satisfaction in the cat that got the cream, sort of way. 'That shut you up didn't it?' She sneers. 'Your precious Finn isn't as loyal as you thought. Though, I'm sure you learned that a long time ago, when he knocked up someone else and married her instead of you.' Her words cruel and unjust. Sarah clutching the phone, can barely take it all in. Her legs unable to hold her up, she shakily moves across the room, to sit on the edge of the bed where they had made love less than half an hour ago. Tears stinging the back of her eyes threatening to flow, Sarah regains her poise knowing, Aine is studying her face gauging the full force of her revelation.

'You have no right this is my home. You can't go making major changes or any changes for that matter, Da kept all mam's stuff the way she had it. The very essence of our family breathes through these walls. Happy memories, dad built this home for us, you can't knock walls down. Besides...I won't allow Jack's room to be changed.'

'Oh it hurts doesn't it, his rejection.' Aine says, clearly getting enjoyment from Sarah's angst. A thunderous silence filling the air, Sarah unable to find an appropriate reply. 'You had to take him from me didn't you?' Aine reveals. 'It wasn't enough being daddy's little girl, the centre of attention. Little Sarah, always needing protection hanging around her brothers' and their friends.' Aine taunts. 'They were all moving on with their lives, going to Uni, meeting girls and you didn't want to be left behind so you seduced Finn, because he was the only one around that summer. You took my boyfriend from under my nose and purposely got pregnant, you are so devious.' Blood draining from Sarah's body as she listens to Aine's bitterness. Each word choking her as though her sister's hands are clawing at her neck squeezing tightly, draining the very life from her. She grasps the neck of her t-shirt fighting for breath, eventually finding the strength to reply.

'What the hell are you talking about? You were never-'

'Yes I was.' Aine cuts her up sharply sounding like an adolescent child. 'We got together in Galway. He had only one year left so I got a job in Galway and rented an apartment, waited around like a fool. He went home to visit his parents that summer because his mother hadn't been well. I stayed in Galway because I couldn't get time off, besides I needed the money for rent. I couldn't wait for Friday, drove all the way straight after I finished work. It had been hot, I felt clammy from the drive and decided a swim in the cove was better than a shower, to refresh my body. I heard a noise as I passed the old barn, thought it was dad or Tommy working in there, so I went in to say hello. There you were practically naked on the hay, legs wrapped around his waist like some wanton slut. My boyfriend, my Finn, the man I was planning marry and spend the rest of my life with. You took everything from me and then you had his child. I know, Jack was his there was no one in Trinity, unless I'm giving you credit of course.' Her words sting, partially because what Aine is saying more or less the truth and partly because, Sarah genuinely never knew Aine had been involved with Finn.

'I don't know what to say…I never knew.' Sarah relents momentarily, until realisation kicks in. 'So you are going to take my home in spite. That's pretty low, even for you.'

'I knew you would be like this, you are far too selfish to think of anyone but yourself. Get a grip Sarah, life has to move on no matter how difficult, you can't keep living in a bubble.' Aine pushing too far, Sarah disconnects the call her body numb with anger.

Chapter 19

Pulling herself together Sarah finishes dressing, sweeping a brush through her hair, before walking down to the café. Her head still spinning from Aine's revelation and the discovery of Finn's betrayal. The fact he'd gotten Maggie pregnant within weeks of her own conception had been humiliating enough, but to learn he'd been seeing her own sister too, unforgiveable.

Luckily, Lily is too busy serving customers to pick up on Sarah's unrest, allowing her to quickly grab the food prepared, to bring up to Tommy and Paul at the campsite without indulging in conversation.

'It all looks fantastic.' Sarah says pasting a watery smile on her face, as she pokes her head round one of the newly refurbished cubicles, in what was once a stable block. Hoping the quiver in her voice would not give her away, because inside her heart has been shattered into tiny pieces.

Tommy is on his knees grouting the shower cubicles, while Paul is finishing tiles around the sinks.

'I'm at your disposal, the café is quiet and Lily has Rachel on standby. Here, I brought you both something to eat.' She holds up the bag containing freshly baked chicken pies and Lily's sour bread, thickly covered with butter. 'I'd say there's a piece of Lena's cheesecake in there too, knowing Lil.'

'Now you're talking.' Tommy wipes his hands grabbing the bag. 'Here Paul, take a break and get some food lad you deserve it.'

'So what can I do to help?' Sarah asks, in a chirpy voice.

'Any good at grouting?'

'I'll give it a go, how hard can it be?' The two men laugh at her reply. Sarah raises a brow. 'I used to make mosaics remember for the gift shop in Carraigbrin.' She protests, giving her an idea for a pastime to fill her evenings. 'I should start doing them again, for when we open the gift shop.' Sarah picks up the bucket Tommy had discarded, filling grout between the tiles.

'We need to get this finished tonight, otherwise it won't be dry enough for use.' Tommy says, finishing off his food and joining her.

'I should have the tiles around the sinks finished soon enough, then I'll fix on the mirrors.' Paul says.

'Good man, we've got a good bit done today,' Tommy replies, 'feels like we are making headway now.' '

Aye...I'll crack on.' Paul slopes away.

'You and Paul, have done amazing work, I only hope this site can keep the farm afloat. Maggie was over last night and said, Ted O'Neil reported losing two cows over the cliff due to broken fences again.' Sarah says in a low voice, not wanting to worry Paul, about the security of his job.

'The Garda would want to get their act together so and do something about it, catch the bloody vandals and charge them.' Tommy shakes his head in dismay.

'How are you?' Lowering his voice to practically a whisper, he adds. 'I saw Finn, slipping down the side of the house earlier. Be careful Sarah, I know you are an adult and what you do is none of my business, but I'd hate to see ya getting hurt.' His words of wisdom, opening the floodgates she has been trying to put a dam on. Tommy is not the type to give a hug, it doesn't mean he is uncaring. In fact quite opposite when it comes to family, just not a man to throw affection around easily. 'What has he done?' He asks, suggesting Finn is at the root of her upset.

'I keep telling myself it has to stop, then he catches me when I'm at a low ebb. It's pathetic I know and I hate myself for it. Aine rang before I came up here, did you know she'd been in a relationship with Finn, when they were in Galway?'

'Yeah sorry, though it was a long time ago and well...teenage days...you know yourself everyone is full of hormones and confusion. Why did she bring that up now?'

'She has spitefully commissioned him to do up plans to pull the farmhouse apart. Add an extension and turn Jack's bedroom into a bathroom. I can't believe, Finn would go along with that behind my back and not have the decency....to come to the house and pretend nothing....' Sarah gasps unable to speak, as fresh tears flow freely. 'How could he do that to me? All the years I protected him, never asked for anything towards Jack's upbringing, while he played happy families with Maggie. Believed him after Jack died that it was me, he had loved all those years.' The pent up tension of the past few weeks, unleashing in heavy sobs. Tommy awkwardly wraps his arms around her, showing every sign of a person out of his depth when it comes to women's emotions. Surprising, with a wife and two daughters' to contend with at home.

'I won't let that happen. They have no right to discuss pulling our family home apart.' Tommy replies, his face contorting showing his anger. 'This is our home Sarah and if anyone tries to bulldoze it, they will have to get through me first. No matter who they are or what the courts decide. The likes of Finn O'Driscoll don't deserve you, Sarah. You are too good for him and so is Maggie for that matter, he is a scoundrel who plays with women's feelings. Surely you've worked out what he is like.' He points out what is obvious to everyone else in the town, apart from Sarah and Maggie, it would seem. 'One day, Sarah the right person will come along, you deserve better than this.' Tommy adds, shaking his head, clearly unable to understand what his younger sister sees in the self-absorbed, pretentious Finn. She had been independent, bringing her son up alone after being treated badly. Had dealt with the situation with maturity only to falter after, Jack's death. Sarah deserves better than men like Finn O'Driscoll, preying on her vulnerability. 'You are a strong independent woman and I'm proud of you not making compromises to suit a man, most women would have gone for the easy option taking security over their own true happiness. You and I both know you could have.' Tommy's words both surprising and delighting Sarah, especially as he would never normally be so open. Unable think of an appropriate reply, she simply says.

'Thanks for putting it so nicely, in short I'm a stubborn cow.' She manages a weak smile.

'As for Aine, she's pretty messed up at the moment but it doesn't excuse her behaviour. If she wants to come home so be it, but fighting us for our homes and livelihood is low even by her standards.'

'Let's hope Alan is a good enough solicitor, to battle against this Fintan Power, from Dublin.' Sarah wipes her eyes feeling a little foolish. 'I'd hate to think she is contesting the will over a grudge, I didn't even know existed until today.'

'If that is her reasoning over contesting the will, it's low, even for her. You and I, both know the only woman who lost out as far as Finn is concerned, is the woman who ended up married to him.' Tommy sets down the grout float he'd been using. 'I know you'd never set out to hurt Maggie, but ya have to realise it would break her heart if she ever found out...not judging, just saying.' He picks up the grout float commencing with his work, indicating the discussion is over.

'Tom I've finished round the sinks and the mirrors are up, but need to set properly. Only thing left to do is check the tap in the laundry room. I'll come in tomorrow and wash everywhere with hot soapy water once the grout has dried properly.' Paul says, popping his head round the shower cubicle. Sarah can only hope he had not heard any part of their conversation, she'd practically forgotten he was close by.

'Fair play to ya Paul. You should get home, you've been here since seven this morning.' Tommy replies, to the younger man.

'Thanks Paul, we could never have gotten this finished if it weren't for you.' Sarah adds.

'Glad to get the work Sarah, thanks for giving me the chance, otherwise the mother would have kicked me back to Donegal University in September.'

'Not you're thing?'

'Never was one for books, I prefer a hard days graft. See ya in the morning, I'll be in early.'

'You've certainly done some job here and we've got a few bookings for next week, so here's to us. See ya tomorrow lad.' Tommy says. Once alone again with Sarah, adds. 'I was talking to Paul earlier about running the campsite, what d'ya think?'

'I think it's a great idea.' She hopes they were not being too presumptuous offering the poor chap the job with all the uncertainty surrounding the will. In hindsight, Alan said they should not open the campsite while Aine is in dispute, but Tommy will not be swayed.

A couple of hours later, Sarah strolls back down the hill towards the farmhouse, to the sound of birds twittering in the trees, before they settle down for the night. Dusk coming sooner than expected, the summer sunshine gone from the sky and the air beginning to cool. She breathes in the cool evening air, savouring the wonderful surrounding scenery. To her right, luscious green fields stretch as far as the eye can see with a backdrop of rolling hills. To the left, a perfect view of the Atlantic Ocean and the surrounding vegetation, an idyllic location for a campsite, offering tourists peaceful tranquility and breath-taking beauty. In retrospect of this, it had been easy to decide on a name for the campsite, Lily being the one to come up with the idea of "Elysian Farm Campsite" meaning paradise. To Sarah, this place is paradise, but it is also her home.

As she pushes open the front door, her senses are captured by the sweet scent of honeysuckle mingled with her father's prized climbing rose. How could anyone consider making changes and eliminating the house of its natural charm? It doesn't make sense, not to Sarah anyway.

Once inside, she climbs the stairs. In hindsight she should be tired but her mind is still buzzing, the day's events running through it like rush hour traffic. She pauses on the landing outside, Jack's bedroom door which sits slightly ajar, imagining him on the other side sitting at his desk studying. Head bent low, his nose practically touching the paper as he writes. In anticipation, Sarah places the palm of her hand on the door, slowly pushing it open. The room is empty as it has remained for over five years, disappointment engulfing every pore. Nothing has changed, nothing moved since that horrific day, the same bedclothes on his bed, which he had neatly made before going on his run. She lifts a t-shirt thrown on the back of a chair wanting to inhale his familiar scent, trying to picture his face but the memory is becoming faded bringing fresh tears to her eyes. Crumpling onto the bed, her whole body shaking with grief needing desperately to hold onto this house where, Jack had laughed and played. To keep this typical teenager room intact with posters on the walls, his medals and trophies proudly displayed on the bookcase. The view from the window overlooking the back of the farmhouse and garden, with its treehouse and swing made of rope and an old tractor tyre. Rolling out past the field giving a glimpse of the sea beyond, Jack had always declared how lucky he was to have such a wonderful view from his room. A room holding everything sacred which is the epiphany of Jack, and if it is changed Sarah is scared she will lose her little boy forever. Lily is always telling her, Jack will always live in her heart no matter what but Sarah needs physical memories too, otherwise she will be lost in purgatory. A place in-between where, Jack had physically existed and where she can be with him again. She could not cope with that, could not walk a path he had not walked on.

The sky outside is illuminated catching her attention, Sarah walks over to the window. Thick black smoke billowing in the sky above the barn, along with a deep orange fire flickering, sparks like fireworks cutting through the blackness veiling the sky. Sarah, rushes downstairs taking them two at a time reaching the back door meeting, Lily coming across the yard.

'The barn is on fire, I've called the fire brigade.' Lily shouts grabbing the hose and helping Sarah pull it out. Flames stretch high up into the evening sky as Sarah sprints down the narrow pathway towards the barn, hose reel clutched in her hand hoping it will stretch far enough. Lily at her heels screaming, fear in her voice as she calls out her husband's name. Sarah switches on the nozzle trying to douse the flames, the weak force of water from the hose a vain attempt, as the barn is already partially gutted. 'Do you know where Tommy is?' Lily asks, panic in her voice as she tries to push past Sarah.

'No...Lil...He's not in there.' She drops the hose grabbing hold of Lily's arms. 'He was finishing the grouting.'

'That was earlier, he said he was heading down to check the fences by the cove, and make sure the barn was securely locked due to these louts during the night.' Lily shouts, fear in her eyes.' A plume of fire explodes into the darkness, flames rolling outwards as the fire engine roars up the road.

Chapter 20

'Lil, Sarah, get back there is nothing we can do.' Tommy's rushes to their side as the firemen, pull out hoses dousing the fire putting it out in minutes. Lily, almost knocking Tommy, as she jumps into his arms visibly relieved to see her husband safe. The Garda car pulls up, Maggie and her colleague get out joining them. Soon the blackened building is surrounded by friends and neighbours coming to see if they can help, having seen the smoke and flames veil the sky.

'What could've started it?' Kitty asks no one in particular. 'That aul barn has been there for nearin forty years. Poor Paddy, would turn in his grave.'

'Be those fellows been damaging our fences and killing livestock.' Ted O'Neil adds removing his cloth cap and scratching his head. 'What are ye lot doing about it. Nothing that's what, someone could've been killed had they been in there.' He turns to Maggie, waving his cap face red with pent up anger.

'Now now, Ted we can't go attacking Maggie, tis not her fault.' Lily says, face still ashen from worry over her husband.

'But we do need to get these louts caught.' Tommy adds matter-of-fact. 'Ted is right, someone could have been killed. We've already lost some of our animals which is bad enough.'

'Look, I'll talk to the fire officer once they've done a full inspection of the barn. Apart from us sitting in a ditch all night there isn't much we can do.'

'We could set up CCTV cameras on any buildings might be safer for the campsite.' Paul suggests.

'Good idea but it'd cost a fair packet.' Tommy points out.

'I'll look into getting a security company out and price it up.' Sarah adds. 'Paul is right it's not worth the risk, tis costing us more losing livestock and buildings like this.'

'No need for that Sarah.' Paul protests. 'They charge a fortune and you're building a business. We could buy the equipment for a fraction of the price, I'll set it all up.'

'You sure, no offence but...'

'I worked for Alpha Tech for eight months.'

'Aye, amongst others.' Ross intervenes, receiving glares over his unwanted input from all the Connolly's.

'That would be great Paul if you don't mind.' Sarah interjects. 'You organise what equipment we need for the CCTV and let me know a price.'

'Looks like your fire was definitely started on purpose, we came across this discarded behind the barn.' One of the fire personnel joins the little group holding up a metal petrol can. 'The fire officer will be along...eh...tomorrow bein a bank holiday it'll probably be Tuesday morning. He'll do a full inspection, so in the meantime I suggest everyone stay away from here. We'll cordon the area off, I'd be worried about the building collapsing. I'll be along myself tomorrow just to check everything is alright.'

'Who would do that ta ye.' Kitty gasps.

'Hum...there is plenty scum round here, one or two-' Ross is abruptly cut off by his wife Mel.

'Ross.' She gives him a warning stare.

'Here, I'll take it as evidence see if we can get any prints off it.' Maggie grabs the can, passing Sarah adds. 'You alright, you look pale?'

'I'm fine thanks Mags, just the shock kicking in I guess.'

'Don't you worry I'll find out who did this, an believe me they'll be sorry.'

'I know you will.' Sarah tries to sound grateful while adding a weak smile for effect.

'Come on down to ours, tis good of ye all to come and so quick. I baked a fresh batch of scones and soda breads, a cup of tea is needed.' Lily says linking Sarah's arm. 'Come on lads you come and join us too.' She shouts across to the firemen. Anyone would think, Lily started the fire to bring the town to her table, of course she would never have done that. The question on everyone's lips as they drink tea and indulge in Lily's home baking, who would want to sabotage the Connolly's barn.

By the time Sarah finally slips between the sheets catching a faint hint of Finn's aftershave, reminding her of their earlier lovemaking and his deceit, she is weary from the day's emotions, yet sleep evades her.

Her mobile bleeps on the bedside locker as dawn breaks, a text from Conor having heard about the fire wanting to check she is okay. Unable to stomach the thought of walking down passed the burnt out barn for a swim in the cove, she decides to go for a run to refresh and wake her body up. Instead of the usual route, she veers left heading out the coast road avoiding going in the direction of Seaview Park, if nothing else. Keeping this momentum of focus, she passes the rest of the day by helping Tommy and Paul finish off the tiling and cleaning. No one really talking, as mentioning the fire might douse the euphoria of the progress they have made in such a short time. By the end of the day the campsite looks like an oasis of tranquility, with Sarah feeling light-hearted for the first time in weeks in spite of recent events. The amenities having turned out fantastic, better than she had ever envisioned. Natural stone buildings, sourced from a local quarry, uniquely designed to blend in sympathetically with the surrounding countryside. Teamed with spectacular views and nearby attractions to visit resulting in a perfect getaway, Paddy would have been thrilled with the result. The stables, no longer a run-down disused building, but a viable business.

For reasons unknown to Sarah, she falters and the following morning finds herself parked outside the Shanahan's house again, unable to recall getting there. A little voice in her head urging her to start the engine and drive away, but her limbs do not correspond. Hands clasped tightly on the steering wheel, she stares aimlessly at the old fashioned net curtains on the front windows.

The knock on the window startles Sarah, she glances up gauging Agnes Shanahan. Prematurely grey hair and a pinched expression, added to by fine lines on her face, making her look considerably older than her years. It is the glazed empty look in her eyes which captures Sarah, a resemblance of what she sees in her own reflection each time she looks in the mirror. Unthinking Sarah presses the button to open the window.

'Come inside I'll make us a cup of tea.' Agnes says surprising her. 'Come on, I'm not going to beg. There is no one else in the house unless you count the dog.' The invitation unexpected, something about Agnes's expression resulting in Sarah following her, as though she is a child following the pied piper.

Once inside, Agnes directs Sarah to sit at the kitchen table which she does with caution, while Agnes undertakes placing mugs and a plate of fruit cake on the table. The kitchen itself, presents a warm and homely atmosphere, though a little tired and dated. Sarah glances around the overcrowded room, units, a cooker and fridge dominate one side of the room. Beside the stove the fluffy little white dog, Ger walks every day lying on its bed, sizing her up with great interest. Everything in the room screams out a normal family existence, from the world's best mum plaque on the windowsill, to the montage of photographs' grouped on the wall. Various pictures of two young boys, ranging from babies to their teenage years. A couple of pictures have been removed, obvious from the precarious spaces and different colour wall, indicating a clear imprint of where they had been.

'I had to take them down to change the photographs.' Agnes says as though reading her mind, the words sharp and cold startling Sarah. 'The ones that were there....I have a granddaughter, my son Phillip lives in Edinburgh now. He sent some pictures of her...Amelia, to my phone.'

'Can I see, would you mind?' Sarah asks. With a shaking hand Agnes hands her mobile to Sarah. 'She is beautiful, how old?' 'Two weeks today. I would give anything to see her.' The older woman's voice laced with sadness. 'I don't know how

I'll get them printed, everything is on our phones these days.' She pours weak tea into the mugs. Sarah hates weak tea and tries not to focus her attention on it.

'They have a machine in Phelan's Chemist, have you bluetooth?' She suggests.

'Ah…yea, I think so.'

'All you have to do is bring your phone down, switch on the bluetooth select the photograph you want printed, Tess will do the rest. It's really easy, be lovely to have Amelia's pictures up there next to her father's.' Sarah casts her eye over the photographs on the wall again. Gaze fixing on one of Desmond, possibly taken when he was a teenager. Due to the large age gap, Sarah had never gotten to know Desmond growing up, apart from seeing him around the town occasionally. Enthralled in the photograph, she doesn't notice Agnes's stiffening demeanour.

'The cheeky one is Desmond.' Agnes says sitting down across from Sarah. 'He was a good boy, Desmond. I know what you think, but he has a soft heart.' Sarah abstains from answering, too polite to inform this woman in her own kitchen what a misguided mother she is. Has Agnes forgotten her precious son had taken drugs and got behind the wheel of a car killing another human being? Not the actions of a soft hearted man. 'He lost his life too, I know it doesn't appear that way on the surface.' Agnes says, confirming for Sarah she has. Agnes on the other hand had invited Sarah in, on a foolish impulse, wanting to alleviate the tension Sarah sitting outside most days, is causing between Ger and Desmond. 'We all lost something that day Sarah, I wish I could fix what has happened but I can't. I'd like to reach out to you, there is so much pain and all I can see is my family falling apart, I have no way of stopping the avalanche.' Words of a desperate woman, wanting her life back even if it had never been perfect in the first place. Sarah realises, she'd made a mistake. Swallowing back a lump the size of a golf ball forming in her throat, she views the older woman with caution.

'I should go, I'm sorry, I should never…' Sarah hastily pushes back her chair bolting for the door, wondering what the hell had possessed her to agree to come inside in the first place.

Arriving back at oceanic temptations to work her shift, joining Lily, Lena and Olive. The café, thankfully busy due to the first coach tour having arrived earlier than expected. This saves Sarah from being questioned by Lily, clearly having picked up on Sarah's unrest, due to the frequent concerned glances she receives throughout the day. A day which continues being busy, with a coach arriving as soon as another had departed. Sarah grateful for the distraction, otherwise her earlier interaction with Agnes might fester until it explodes.

When things finally quieten down, Lily has to rush off to collect Lauren, thankfully leaving them little chance of conversation.

'Are you sure you don't mind locking up.' Lily asks as she grabs her bag in preparation to leave.

'Go.' Sarah replies sounding as blasé as she can, so not to rouse Lily's suspicions any further to her underlying desolation.

'Thanks kid. I'll not be long, come over for your tea won't you. Are you ready Olive? I'll drop you home, bye girls.'

'Bye Lil. See you tomorrow Olive.' Sarah says, then turns to Lena. 'Come on let's have a cuppa and take the weight off our feet.'

'You look weary Sarah, I hope you don't mind that a say this.' Lena says, as they sit sipping lattes. 'It's can't be easy all the sadness you carry around. I know because I used to be the same.' Sarah jerks her head up giving Lena a quizzical stare.

'Malik and I, had a daughter, she got very sick pneumonia and she died. Aleksandra would have been thirteen today.'

'Oh Lena, I am so sorry.' Sarah places a comforting hand on the other woman's.

'Thank you but I do not tell you this for that reason. I tell you because I see your pain. It is like...how you say, I see in your eyes what I saw when I once looked in the mirror. My eyes like yours emptiness....I don't mean to offend.'

'You're not, it's a relief to speak with someone who understands. Most people apart from, Lily and Tommy of course think I should be over it. I had learned to live with my loss but recent events....'

'You never forget your child and shouldn't have to, but focusing your negative energy will at least make life bearable. You are doing the marathon in October yes.'

'Yes.'

'Don't make it your last one, focus on a new challenge each time you complete one. Soon you will feel better with each goal you reach. You are not forgetting your son you are making a life he is not in. It's not ideal, but it makes each day easier because each day is about you. Your well-being, I hope you don't mind I say this. I do triathlons, I don't forget my Aleksandra, but I can look in the mirror now and see myself again. I am a different person from the one before, I accept that.'

'How old was she, do you mind telling me?' 'No I don't mind because now when I speak of her, I feel happiness instead of pain. Joy for the precious time I got to have with her. She was four, when she got sick, always a healthy child you know...had never been sick before not as much as a cough or cold. She was a smiler, always she smile a happy child you know. She had this dolek, how you say in English...a...dimple, here.' She points to her cheek. Sarah noticing how her eyes light up with love and pride as she speaks about her daughter. No sense of sadness or anger for her loss.

'She sounds like a wonderful little girl.' Sarah smiles. 'The triathlons, you do these a lot.'

'I like to do about four or five each year, I enjoy the bike the most but my swimming needs much improvement.'

'I can help you with that, I was a swimming instructor and life guard for years in the adventure centre. Fully qualified, I renew them every two years even though I haven't worked there for many years now. It's nice to keep up the fitness.'

'You already have a good sense of focus so.'

'Yeah, I do try Lena, really I do. Sometimes it feels like every time I take a step forward, I'm pushed back two. Something comes along landing me a heavier blow...I get tired, I admit to that.'

'I understand, when you are down it is hard but you are a strong person Sarah. Remember your son would not want you to be unhappy.'

'He was an amazingly talented young man.'

'So I hear, make him proud. Every time you run, he runs. Every time you achieve a goal, he does too.' She stands up, 'sorry I must go, but I will take you up on the swimming coaching if you don't mind. In return, I will help you train with the running. Deal.'

'Deal, thanks Lena.'

'I bring you some of my Poleski tomorrow, our last indulgence before we train...yes.'

'You are a bad influence but I will not refuse.'

'Good, oh did you get any news on the fire, how it was started?'

'No, Lena but it was definitely deliberate according to the fire officer. Paul is going to put up cameras, should act as a deterrent at least. I know the Garda think its fellows coming in lamping, but it's usually dark winter nights and never damage like this. Not starting fires anyway, a few broken fences alright which in itself is a nuisance.'

'What is this lamping, you say?'

'Men seeking out rabbits with torches using lurcher dogs, they trespass on farm land damaging fences, endangering animals. They class it as a sport, it's a disgrace in my eyes and an opportunity too if you get my meaning.'

'It sounds cruel, these people have no respect for your property or the wildlife. Take care, see you in the morning Sarah.'

As Lena exits, Finn slinks through the door with a confidence only someone like Finn could have.

'I wasn't sure if ye were still open, Maggie asked me to pick up her bread as she is working late again.' Unsure whether this is a hint he is free and at her disposal, Sarah choses to purposefully ignore his bewitching stare along with his advances. Slipping from his imminent grasp, she quickly moves behind the counter creating a barrier between them. His lean frame and magnetic smile will no longer fool her into falling for his charm.

'It's not here, Lily must have brought all the uncollected orders down to the house. She should be back from dropping Lauren at the bus station if you want to call down.'

'So I guess we are alone.' His expression brightening, he pushes his luck further than he realises, whilst working his way round to her side of the counter and snaking his arms around her waist. In response, she hastily shoves him away resulting in his face becoming a mask of confusion.

'You have some nerve.' She says voice low and even, determined to remain poised and in control. 'Think you can use me and discard me like a piece of trash. You didn't even bother to ring to check if I was okay after the fire.'

'I didn't know til late when Maggie got in, I thought you'd be asleep besides it was the barn, I knew no one was hurt.'

'I suppose if it was the house that might cause a problem for your plans with my sister.' Sarah imparts, unable to hold back any longer.

'Oh...I...a...look Sarah.' Finn blusters causing Sarah to bristle further. Her patience has finally run out, wondering why she has never seen through him before now. 'You have to understand it is nothing personal. None of this changes how I feel about you and Jack. My business was in a mess when your sister offered me work along with a promise, she would be recommending me. I saw a rare opportunity.'

'I'm sure that's not all she promised.'

'What–'he almost chokes on his words to be abruptly cut off by Sarah, no longer able to restrain her anger.

'Did it feel good? Drawing up plans which would mean pulling, Jack's room into crumbling pieces erasing every memory, I have left.' Sarah lashes out. Finn drops his gaze to the floor as he backs away. 'I never expected anything from you. Hated lying to my son when his father was right here in this town, now I am glad because you never deserved his love.'

'I saw your car pull up.' Tommy hastily opens the shop door, face red with fury indicating the depth of his anger. 'Here's your bread, now leave you are not welcome around here.' Finn, takes the loaf from his outstretched hand without uttering a single word or any further acknowledgment of Sarah. He simply slips away kicking up a trail of dust as he drives down the path and out onto the main road. 'Come on kid, as they say; when times are tough you find out who you're real friends are.' He wraps a comforting arm around her shaking shoulders.

'I'm glad you interrupted.' She replies with sincerity grabbing her keys. If Tommy had not intervened, she is not sure how she would have dealt with learning of Finn's feelings for Aine. How, he had never really loved her making the conception of their son a sad and sordid experience.

'That can't have been easy.' Tommy says. The walk outside with Sarah locking the door of the shop behind them.

'Like you said, you really do find out who your friends are.'

'He should count himself lucky, Lily is out back hanging washing.' Tommy winks bringing a smile to his sister's face. Dealing with Lily would be another matter, both well aware of this fact. She would chew Finn up and anyone else who dared to hurt her family, Lily a pussycat loving and kind, one of the nicest people you will ever meet. Would bend over backwards to help others and give her last crumb to anyone, unless they threaten her family's happiness. Anyone of sound mind does not want to experience that particular side of Lily. 'That's better, hungry?'

'A little.' She admits truthfully finally aware of, Finn's true personality. The only person he truly loves being himself. Tommy, had been right the only real victim is Maggie, the woman who married him. For the first time Sarah is grateful she never told Jack, the true identity of his father.

'I believe there is a fine pot of stew on the stove, one of my darling wife's culinary delights though we will have to fight for a spot at the table.'

'Why is that?' Sarah asks confused, they link arms striding down the laneway towards the house.

'We've adopted young Paul, and boy that kid has one hell of an appetite, god only knows where he puts it.'

'He's certainly not inherited his father's build, a sound lad and a good worker though.'

'I'll second that, he's as strong as an ox and quiet!' Tommy replies in a matter-of-fact way.

'Now that suits you down to the ground Tommy Connolly.' Sarah teases, entering the kitchen as he holds the door open, a true gentleman.

'What suits him?' Lily asks, dishing spoonful's of streaming hot stew onto plates. Sarah smiles, a full on radiant gleam as she and Tommy join Paul, sitting at the table as though he has always been there. 'Now that is good to see.' Lily says placing a large plate of food before Sarah.

'What is?' Tommy questions his wife, his brow furrowed.

'Seeing Sarah smile.' She replies with a wink. It is times like this, wrapped in Lily and Tommy's unconditional love, Sarah is grateful for at least having them, even if it doesn't banish the loss felt for those who were absent. Lena is right, she needs to focus and make changes and there is one way she can. A way which might save Tommy and Lily from losing much needed income for the farm.

Chapter 21

As soon as the lunchtime alarm has sounded, Desmond hastily makes a quick exit, keen to avoid Jimmy who had spent the morning harping on about his growing friendship with Alice. Although Des is enjoying her company, he is not sure he could call it a relationship yet. Unclear, whether she sees him as good company or something more. He would not overstep the mark, not with a girl like Alice, preferring to take it slow, after all he has been burned once and once is enough for any man. They had gone to the movies the previous night to watch, Cat on a Hot Tin Roof.

'Who did you say the heroine in the film is?' He asked as they strolled amiably round Carraigbrin afterwards, neither wanting to end the evening.

'Elizabeth Taylor, she was beautiful but Marilyn Monroe is my true heroine. Women were sexier then, don't you think? The way they dressed with more style and sophistication.' Not knowing how to answer without saying the wrong thing he simply nodded and smiled. The film something, Des would never have considered watching before or even entertained the idea of going to the cinema, but thoroughly enjoyed it all the same. Mainly due to sitting in close proximity to Alice for a long period of time. The fruity scent of her perfume and cute dimple on her cheek every time she smiles, melting his heart in a way he never expected. Afterwards they went out to dinner, chatting easily, he'd never felt so at ease before with a woman. She had asked about cars showing genuine interest, even added a few comments showing more knowledge than she originally claimed to have. Evelyn had never been interested in what he did, always immersed in what she wanted, even when it came to their wedding plans. He had assumed it was because weddings were a woman's big dream day. Now he realises she was completely self-absorbed.

'You didn't think I saw ya, but I did....strollin through the town with Miss Posh, from the office.' Jimmy said a little too loudly attracting unwanted attention, when he had arrived into work that morning wearing one of his goofy smiles. 'She'll be high maintenance, don't say I didn't warn ya.'

'What is this high maintenance?' Malik had asked, clearly bemused by the whole scenario, obviously making his working day more interesting.

'Don't listen to him Mal, Jimmy has a habit of talkin out of his backside.' Came Des' disgruntled reply wanting to silence Jimmy, in retrospect it had the opposite effect, because he carried on teasing.

'She's an uptown girl like the Billy Joel song, Mal. Looking for a bit of rough and Des here fell for her, the eejit.'

'I think, Jimmy you are being unkind, this girl she most likely picked Desmond because she like his company.' Thankfully, Malik's comment ended the conversation temporarily. Des aware, Jimmy will not leave the subject lie. In truth, Des is beginning to find Jimmy a little tiresome, especially his immature behaviour. Besides, at this particular moment he needs space and time to think, having never in his life met anyone like Alice before. Level headed, gentle, beautiful, yes he is becoming more and more smitten by her. Never in his twenty-six years has a woman had such a profound effect. Not even, Evelyn the woman he had planned to spend the rest of his life with at one time. Nevertheless, his fondness for Alice also highlighting there still being unfinished business with Evelyn, something he cannot completely erase from his mind. The fact she has a five year old child and her unorthodox hostility towards him, since the accident. If he is to take things further with Alice, then he must clear up lingering doubts about the past first.

He sits on a low wall overlooking the harbour, taking out the roll he had purchased on his way to work. From here, Desmond watches fishing boats in the harbour, seagulls circulating over them waiting in anticipation for a fish head, or any spare morsel of food. They do this with great expectation and a constant stream of noise. The view, which stretches out towards the salmon farm and beyond, exhibits the beautiful outline of the coast. With the early afternoon sun casting light across dancing ripples, making the sea glisten and sparkle, looking truly magical. He missed this more than he realised while in prison, the freedom and smell of the salty air, things so often taken for granted. To his left, is the water adventure zone, popular with locals and tourists alike, having an abundance of activities such as kayaking, small sail boats amongst others. Further up the coast is a sandy beach almost tropical in appearance, with soft silky sand and a boardwalk stretching outward to the crystal clear water. Just past that on the far side of the village is a real hidden gem, Glanvisce Cove referred to by villagers as surfer's cove. This particular beach can only be reached through the Connolly's farm land or when the tide is fully out through a small inlet under the cliff face. Desmond had not been much of a surfer when he was younger, due to lack of balancing skills but he often indulged in a swim by the cove, being one of the most beautiful spots in the area, as well as being private. So enthralled in his thoughts and surroundings, Desmond doesn't hear her sneak up behind him.

'So this is where you are hiding, I was looking for you in the canteen.' Alice's cheery voice makes him jump, spilling his drink. 'Are you avoiding me Desmond?' She asks, throwing him an inquisitive stare. He glances up taking in her angelic vision, blonde curls shimmering in the light, framing her perfect pale skin and cherry lips. Desmond finds himself staring at her dumbfounded, face flushed with embarrassment.

'Here sit on my jacket, the rocks can be a bit cold.' He mumbles, almost tripping over his words. What he really wants to say is "go away and stop teasing, me." Surely she must know the effect she is having.

'A true gentleman, I am impressed.' She replies seemingly oblivious to his plight, as she carefully fixes her skirt before sitting down. 'Your little friend Jimmy is holding court in the canteen. Unusual for him to hang around, he normally slips away at lunchtime.' Her comment casual, if not a little probing.

'He's not my friend.' Des replies a little too gruffly, then immediately regrets his harsh response. Embarrassed and unable to meet her quizzical stare, he watches a seagull swoop down to one of the fishing boats, cleverly acquiring a fish in its beak, before bringing the food to a nest on the steep incline of the cliff face. Its partner, then takes flight to find more food, once contented their offspring are safe and being fed. The interaction between these two parents fascinating, their focus on family showing more dedication than any human being.

'Sorry I didn't mean to...' She eventually says still staring at him, appearing forlorn.

'I shouldn't have snapped....got a lot on my mind.'

'Look, I know I'm speaking out of line.' Alice hesitates before continuing. 'Jimmy...he attracts trouble and what might be a slap on the wrist for him could land you back in prison.' Desmond remains silent, still focused on the family of seagulls. Alice takes this as a rebuff, she stands up handing him back his jacket. 'It's not my place to judge who you hang around with sorry, I shouldn't have-' Des leaps up, grabbing her arm.

'No.' He cuts in, 'you are right about Jimmy...stay, please.' He begs in a way he never thought he would again. Had never intended to allow his affections be so free again. 'I didn't mean to...like I said, I have a lot on my mind, and...can we start again.' He pleads, sounding desperate and foolish. There is no response, Alice simply leans forward kissing him tenderly on the lips, and Des revels in the wonderful sensation of her touch.

'I really like you Des, but I want you to know.' She points out when they eventually pull apart. 'I don't make a habit of throwing myself at any man who comes my way.' The sincerity in her voice evident, which makes him feel bad about doubting her. He'd been cautious, wanting to be certain before wearing his heart on his sleeve. After all, he had been badly burned once and isn't about to be anyone's puppet again, but everything about Alice screams sincerity. He pulls her close, kissing her this time with more intensity and passion. His only concern being, would she notice the stirring in his trousers?

'Get a room Shanahan.' Jimmy calls from somewhere behind, breaking their spell. Des wanting to throttle him, especially when he adds. 'The heat you two are giving off, no wonder Connolly's barn went on fire Sunday night.' He laughs at his own stupid comment, adding a little snort. This causes the hairs on the back of Desmond's neck to stand on end. 'Word is…it was arson, better have a tight alibi.' Jimmy adds for good measure, making Des flush deeply from the neck up.

'I better get back to the office.' Alice says pulling reluctantly away. 'If you're free later, we could meet up.'

'I'd like that.' Des smiles trying to ignore the fact, Jimmy is still loitering, watching them. 'I'll meet you in the Falcon bar in Carraigbrin, say eight. I've something I need to do first.'

'Perfect, I'll see you later.' She walks away, leaving Des staring admiringly after her.

'You'll get burned badly by that wan mate. Ha…get it, burned.'

'Fuck off, Jimmy.' Des bypasses him, about to follow Alice into the building when a familiar voice calls out.

'Hey Dessie, heard you were out.' Brian says as though nothing had ever gone between them. Des halts swinging round, noticing Jimmy has become very edgy. Shifting uncomfortably from one foot to the other, kicking at the ground with his head down avoiding eye contact with either of the other two men. 'I thought you weren't due out til January, what ya do bribe someone?' Brian's words underhanded and crass. A couple of older men from the factory, pass by throwing a look of disgust in their direction. Des, no longer wishing to be associated with the likes of Brian Lennon. Not that they had been close friends before, but it had still been unforgivable to discover the man had bedded his fiancée, so soon after the accident. 'It's good to see you Des.' Brian winks, giving a nod. 'Call round for that later Jimmy alright.' He adds, before turning his back and walking away. Des remains rooted to the spot watching him get into a gleaming gun metal silver, newly registered BMW and drive away. Brian's presence having made him edgy and restless, but the reason why, he cannot fully work out. Possibly it's the nagging doubt which has haunted him for the past week, having toyed with the idea he could be a father and Brian is bringing up his child.

As soon as Des gets in from work, he takes a shower and changes eager to catch the six-thirty bus to Carraigbrin. He is about to rush out the door when.

'Will you not stop and have your tea?' Agnes asks, disappointment etched on her weary face. Des halts in the doorway, caught between desperation to get away and guilt over not stopping to talk to her.

'Sorry Ma, I'm meeting Alice, don't want to be late.' He replies, catching a glimpse of the pictures of Amelia, placed in the old frames on the wall. 'How did you manage to get them printed?'

'You don't mind do you?' She asks, her voice laced with renewed excitement. 'I took the bus into Carraigbrin and got them done in a chemist, takes seconds. Very clever, don't you think. I thought now you and Evie have both moved on. You'd not want it up there, if Alice came round.' She is making an assumption, while excusing taking his pictures down, rather than those of Phillip. 'I haven't thrown it out, it was your graduation after all.'

'No, best to put the past where it belongs. The pictures of Amelia are perfect.' Des agrees, wanting to ask, has she kept the other photograph too. The one of him sitting on the bonnet of his Subaru. The only picture taken of his beloved car, refraining when it quickly becomes clear Agnes is upset. Phillip would not be bringing his daughter home to visit any time soon.

'They're all, I have of her.' Agnes sighs. 'She'll be grown up and won't know us. He says with Skype and video call, an whatnot, I'll talk to her as if we are in the same room. It's not the same though is it? I'll have to get your Da to have a word with Phil, see if he'll come home for Christmas maybe.' The revelation leaving, Des, feeling guilty, knowing the reason his brother won't come home, is because of the shame, over the accident. His parents have no savings, as all their savings went on solicitor, and barrister fees. Helping him out when his own cash flow had dried up. After the charges had been brought, Des had to pay a bond, while awaiting trial, or spend the time in prison.

'I'm sorry Ma, really I am.' He glances at the clock, feeling wretched and torn. 'I should go, if I'm going to catch the bus.'

'Of course love. You get off.' His mother pastes a forced smile on her withered face. 'I'd like to meet Alice, do you think she might like to come to tea one night?'

'I'm sure she'd love to Ma. I'll ask her tonight and let you know. You'll love her.' he replies eyes shining, delighting Agnes to see him so happy.

'G'wan, you'll miss your bus have a lovely evening.'

Roasters' sign can be seen from the coast road, causing unanticipated jitters. His stomach beginning to churn like a washing machine on rinse cycle, yet his resolve remains is fully intact. As the bus nears the town of Carraigbrin, Des presses the bell. This time he is prepared to face her, planning to find out the truth, without considering the prospect of her not being on shift. Luckily for Desmond, she is there when he walks inside and the place is almost empty of customers. Taking a deep breath, he strides up to the counter depicting an air of confidence that is certainly not reflected on the inside, his only hope being she does not see through the façade.

'I need to talk to you.' Des says, keeping a poker face.

'I'm working.' She retorts. There is s look of fear in her eyes he has never seen before, arousing his suspicions further and confirming she is hiding something.

'When do you have a break?' He asks, fighting to keep resolve as backing down is not an option now he has come this far, easier in theory, less simple now he is standing face to face with her.

'Not for half an hour or so.' She offers reluctantly, aware her supervisor would not like a scene. Already on a warning for being late twice this week, when Brian wouldn't drop Danny to school.

'I'll have a coffee, make it a cappuccino....I'll sit over there and wait.' Des points to a table by the window, unsure why he had added this fact.

Her discomfort is obvious by the way she constantly flicks her gaze in his direction, while serving customers, no doubt hoping to find he'd given up and left. Des is going nowhere, the only way to move on with his life and possible relationship with Alice, is by settling the past.

Forty-five minutes and two coffees later, making him even more jittery, Evelyn slips into the seat opposite him. Her close proximity and the adverse effect of too much coffee almost bringing him back to a version of his former self. The Des who had been her fiancée, doing everything he could to please her and had somehow failed for reasons unknown. Working two jobs to enable indulging her with gifts, while saving for their wedding and future, had treated her like a princess to have it all thrown back in his face.

Sitting across from the same woman is seems somehow surreal, especially as she appears to be a contrast to the girl he'd fallen in love with. Though still attractive with her long strawberry blonde hair, even if it is no longer as silky in appearance. Her face is considerably thinner, eyes lacklustre and lifeless having lost all radiance, with deep dark shadows underneath giving her a haunted aura. His gaze rests on a large yellowy purple bruise on her right arm, prompting her to hastily pull the sleeve of her cardigan down, averting her eyes from his inquisitive stare. All the time flicking a watchful look towards the door, as though she is frightened prey watching for the moment her attacker will pounce. It saddens Des to see her like this, for whatever has gone between them he would not wish any bad on her. He almost loses the resolve he has built up over the last few days.

'Evie, I need you to be honest with me.' He says, eventually searching her eyes for a sign of the love they had once shared. It is completely gone, lost somewhere in an abyss of betrayal and fear. Des hesitates once again, unsure how to proceed, wanting to avoid any accusation as a stand-down is not what he's looking for, simply straight forward answers. 'Were you seeing Brian when we were still together?' He takes a sip of the now cold coffee, mainly to quash the urge to cough, as his throat becomes restricted.

'This is ridiculous, why are you asking me this.' She hisses back, immediately defensive. 'We are in the past Des....you need to move on, I have.'

'I am well aware you have moved on.' Des replies, keeping his voice low and even, though more determined now not to falter, 'but I need to know the truth, so I can move on too.'

'You were always so deep.' She seethes, turning accusation around. 'Everything had to be black and white with you, Des. What is the point in going over old wounds, you know very well what happened.' This does not surprise him, only highlighting a reminder of how it used to be. Their relationship one sided, him giving while she took, sucking the life out of him while constantly blaming him for their pitfalls.

'No Evelyn, I don't. So please, I'm asking you to fill in the blanks, you owe me that much at least.' He hisses back, having completely lost all patience.

'Are you saying you don't remember anything about....?' She begins, eyes wide indicating her surprise over this revelation. Jamming a thumb into her mouth, teeth crunching down on its nail. A habit he had hated and whether she is aware or not it instantly gives away her apprehension. It is obvious, he has pushed her into a corner. She would always bite her nails when trapped in a situation, where she had been in the wrong, eyes glazing over hand immediately going to her lips. Lips he had once kissed, once loved the sweet taste of, lips that planted soft kisses on his neck as they made love. He turns abruptly away brushing aside the memory, annoyed at himself for faltering. This woman is not the woman, he had fallen in love with and planned to marry.

'I heard you have a son.' He blurts, all polite awkwardness gone along with the need to ask in case she announces having to get back to work, before he establishes what he'd come for.

'Who?' She asks, hand shaking, as she nibbles nervously on the practically non-existent nail. 'Bloody Jimmy, who else.' She spits pulling the hand from her mouth and shaking her head. 'He has a big mouth.' It takes her all of two seconds to grasp, why Desmond has asked. 'If you think...he is not yours.'

'How old is he?' 'He was five on Saturday.' She avoids eye contact, thumb this time slipping between her lips.

'That means...how can you say?'

'He was two and a half month's premature.' She confirms in a way which should explain everything, but it doesn't and they both know this.

'We would have still been together.' He points out, voice now laced with conviction. 'At least for two maybe even three months before the accident.' Desmond's voice raises another octave, revealing his true vexation. 'Evie, we were still together when you conceived.' He retorts, receiving a look in return which knocks the wind out of his stomach. 'You were seeing Brian.' The penny finally dropping. 'You were sleeping with him, an allowing me to think we were getting married. Christ sake Evie, we were looking at houses to buy, you were trying on fucking wedding dresses and making lists.' A couple sitting on the next table stare across, Evelyn's face flushes red.

'I don't need this Des.' She pleads, 'You should go, we're finished, it's in the past so let's just leave it there, what use is dragging it all up again?' She stands up hastily scraping back the chair. He grabs her hand out of desperation because nothing is resolved in his mind. She flinches and there is a fear in her eyes he has never witnessed before, it is upsetting to think she could be frightened of him. Unaware, her fear is not of him but the abusive relationship she has gotten herself into.

'There is still a possibility he is mine, have you thought about that...Just because you are happy with-'

'Des see for yourself,' she cuts in. Evelyn never needed a paternity test. A stranger could work out who Danny's father is, if they stand side by side. Des follows the direction of her gaze and her warm, loving smile. Evelyn's mother, Gillian is heading in their direction, a little boy by her side. His hand clasped tightly in his grandmother's, until spotting his mother and gleefully running into her open arms. With his blonde almost white hair, he is a miniature version of his father, there is no doubt in Desmond's mind, not anymore. Des rises from the table, walking away without uttering another word or giving a backward glance. Evelyn is not the person he thought and it's possible, he never really knew her. She is right, they are in the past and he doesn't need her in his life, he has Alice now a warm and honest person, life moves on.

Chapter 22

'He looks well considering.' Gillian says, as soon as she and Evelyn are in the sanctity of her kitchen, later on in the day. 'You two looked as though you were having a serious discussion when I arrived.' She probes further. Evelyn knows deep down she should tell her mother the whole truth, but can't bring herself to. Losing her mother's respect, would be unbearable, especially as she is the only person who truly cares about her and Danny. Maybe one day she will, once she has figured out a way to leave Brian and make a new life.

'He wanted to know if Danny is his son.' Evelyn says in a low voice, her watchful gaze darting in the direction of the lounge, where her son is watching television. Brian had asked the same question the first time she endured his short temper. She had been in bed asleep, he'd come in drunk spouting about Des', something about his imminent trial at the time. She'd been in a daze, still half asleep the whole thing a haze. Then remembered the letter from Des, solicitor requesting she attend the trial and go on the stand as a character witness. Brian had gone spare and stormed out, leaving her desolate and torn. Drunk and fueled by his jealousy, on return he grabbed her by the hair and pulled her from the bed. The force hurling her body upward causing it to slap off the wall, as she landed with a thud on the floor the bleeding starting almost immediately. Even when she woke in the hospital, to learn her baby was in the intensive care unit, Brian declared he wanted a paternity test. Yet, she still convinced herself all would be different, once she proved they were a family. Seeing Desmond again is opening floodgates of painful memories, signifying the first signs of her relationship with Brian being not as perfect as she'd originally thought. The last thing she needs right now, is Desmond making life harder than it's already become in recent times. Opening up wounds which never really healed. She had noticed him eyeing the bruise on her upper arm, it is nothing compared to the bruise on her back from where Brian had shoved her against the table after his cruel attack. Discarding her like nothing but a piece of dirt, declaring she better get pregnant if she knew what was good for her, before slinking upstairs to bed. The rose tinted specs are now off, Evelyn seeing Brian clearly for the brute he is. She would not tell anyone, not even her mother the true depth of Brian's volatile treatment. She realises far too late, her involvement with him has ruined not only her life, but Desmond's too. 'He realised as soon as he saw him...how much Danny looks like Brian.' Evelyn simply tells Gillian, wishing she could find the nerve to admit what is really playing on her mind.

'It's not stopped Brian giving you a hard time.' She says, putting her hand up to quash, Evelyn from defending a man who does not deserve her loyalty. 'I try to hold my tongue, you must realise that, but I fear for your safety love. There I said it.'

'So do I, which is why I plan to leave him.' She finally admits, getting up to check Danny, she pushes the door too while keeping her voice low. 'I haven't got a definite plan yet, but I've been putting aside a little of my wages when I can. Have managed a bit more since, Brian is flush and throwing money around the place.'

'I've been hearing talk you know, about him dealing. In itself it's bad enough, but he is going up against that Murphy family. They take no prisoners that lot, he is putting you and Danny in danger.' Referring to the fact they retaliated against a business rival in the past, by threatening his family.

'I know, look will you keep Danny tonight. I've been talking to Lexi and well, we might have a way.' The look on her mother's face, along with the stray tear down her cheek, heart-breaking. Lexi has a cousin in the Garda, if Evelyn could find out where Brian gets his supply and they catch him, he'd get arrested. Nothing could be traced back to Evelyn, but once he is in prison she would be free to pick up her life and move away, be long gone with Danny before his release. The only problem being Brian never discusses anything with her, keeps his cards close to his chest, and if she asked it would raise suspicion. Her mother of course does not need to hear all this, only keep Danny safely away from the house.

'You don't have to ask, I'll keep him here, but what about you? You're my daughter Evelyn, I need to protect you too. Jesus, your father would turn in his grave.' The extent of Gillian's worry suddenly very clear, as Evelyn has never in her life heard her mother use the lord's name in vain before. It isn't a thing Gillian Priestly would do.

It's a horrible feeling, where your heart sinks down to your toes. Chest constricting leaving you with a feeling of being suffocated, body being pinned down, as though held by an anchor. Of being, literally unable to pick yourself off the ground, from shock. That is how Evelyn is feeling, as she stares dumbfounded, watching Brian sink to his knees before her proposing marriage. A laughable scenario, if the prospect not so frightening considering Brian is the least romantic man on this earth. He opens a ring box, revealing the biggest diamond she has ever seen. Her eyes fixated admiringly as it sparkles before her. Already she is thinking of the Instagram post she would put up with a picture of this magnificent piece of jewellery. "My beau's romantic proposal as we strolled along the banks of the Seinne. Surprised and delighted, what a lucky woman I am. Of course I accepted." Reality strikes a cruel blow, how can she accept when the last thing on her mind is to marry this monster, she's allowed into her affections. On the other hand a refusal would gain her a few broken ribs, along with arousing his suspicions. He could never know of her plans, so for now she must play along. After all engagements can be broken and she will have the ring to sell.

'Oh Brian,' she gushes, flashing him a beaming smile, one deserving of an Oscar. 'Of course I'll marry you.' Her arms wrap around his neck for added effect, body tensing at the thought he will want sex. Since the night of Danny's birthday, she cannot bear his touch, his smell. Each time he has instigated wanting sex, she freezes, body becoming rigid, mind somewhere far from the room while submitting to his groans as he invades her body. It is hard to believe she had once enjoyed his touch. Silent tears sliding down her cheeks as he ejaculates, emptying his load inside of her thinking he is getting her pregnant. Evelyn has already made sure she is one step ahead of him, keeping a supply of contraceptive pills safely in the back of the drawer with her second mobile.

'Great, I've already gone to the town hall to sort the license. There is a slot available with the registrar next week.' The anchor is being tugged, making her head spin, his need to have total control submerging her to new depths. Desmond's early release, obviously unnerving him more than she had realised. Either that or he has noticed the change in her since the night of Danny's party when he had crossed the invisible line. Needing to buy more time, as panic sets in she pleads.

'But darling, surely we are going to have a proper wedding in a church, like. I've always dreamed of walking down the aisle in a flowing white wedding gown, our friends and family watching us seal our love for each other.' Maybe she had gone a little too far with that last bit, made it too Mills and Boon for his liking, but what other choice does she have.

'Jaysus, Evie. Yer so fecking dramatic. What family? Your mother, and my lot like. I'd hardly think yer brother will fly back from Canada.' She'd gone too far with the whole romantic approach, of course he didn't buy it. Not about to give up, she adds.

'Well why not, I'm sure your sister would be delighted to be my bridesmaid, and her little Sally a flower girl walking up the aisle alongside Danny....Jimmy for your best man, what about that?'

'Aw, I don't know....well...I suppose we could go see.' He relents, pleasing her, 'but I'm not waitin month's mind, I want you as my wife.' Of course he does, wanting control over her.

'I'll go with Mam and talk to Father O'Shea in St Declan's.'

'Why yer mother an not me, Jesus she is always interfering...you said it yerself.'

'She knows Father O'Shea, might get us to jump the queue, it's what you want isn't it....to get married as soon as possible.'

'Fair enough, I've invited everyone over tonight, so we can have an engagement party....make it official.'

'Tonight!'

'Ya sum thin wrong with that?'

'No, it's just...I'll need to have something to wear and sort food.'

'Here, there's a few quid, buy yerself a new dress. We can order takeaway, be grand.'

'Mam has got Danny couldn't we go out.' She doesn't want everyone coming to the house, drinking smoking and taking god knows what. Tired of getting up in the mornings facing stale smells and having to clean up discarded cans, bottles and leftover food.

'No I want to relax in me own home...stop feckin whining about everything. I don't know what's got into you lately, anyone would think I'm not good to ya. An here I am, givin ya money, doin the house, put a fecking ring on yer finger and ya still whine in me ear.' Brian screws up his face in displeasure. Without replying, realising he hasn't expected sex in return for the ring, Evelyn grabs her car keys and makes a run for the door before he makes any advances.

With a heavy heart, Evelyn drives into town to buy some new clothes. A task she would normally love, only today she searches through the rails of Chic, without really looking. The prospect of marrying Brian terrifying making her want to throw up. She pulls her mobile from her bag, sending Lexi a quick text desperate to find a way out of the situation she has gotten herself into.

'Big rock, flashing the cash about, I see.' Evelyn nearly drops her phone, not having heard Janine Murphy's approach. 'Little edgy, aren't we.'

'No, I didn't see you....I was texting...' 'The light blue one is nice, would suit your colouring.'

'What?'

'I take it you are looking for a dress to wear.' Janine raises a perfectly shaped brow on her line free face, from too much Botox. Framed with newly styled platinum blonde hair. Her lips swollen like balloons, glistening under the lights of the boutique.

'Ah yeah...I guess.' Evelyn stammers, she'd never really liked Janine. Although Evelyn hasn't had much dealings with her before now, she's conscious of Janine's track record for being a bully.

'Nathan really enjoyed the party last week. He and Danny get on very well. Maybe Danny could come over to ours, you know for a playdate.'

'Ah, yeah...I'm sure Danny would love to.' Evelyn replies, in a honeyed tone, suddenly becoming an expert in acting nice. When really all she wants to do, is tell the likes of Janine Murphy what she really thinks of her. Classing this woman, every bit as evil as Brian.

'Good, cause we're all friends here, right, and friends don't take liberties, if you get my meaning. You're a smart woman Evelyn, so maybe you could have a little word with yer fella, cause I'd hate to have any misunderstanding between us.' Janine walks out of the shop, leaving Evelyn feeling worse if at all possible at this stage. She grabs the blue dress, quickly paying for it. Safer to go home with something, rather than nothing.

Chapter 23

A last minute change of plan by Brian, means going out much to Evelyn's relief. Chrystal nightclub is crowded when they arrive, Evelyn wearing the blue dress. Janine had been right, it makes the blue in her eyes more prominent, while complimenting her sallow skin. She should feel like a superstar, wearing her large diamond ring as they strut towards their usual table in the corner. Jimmy and Jackson are already there. Jackson with yet another new girlfriend, even younger than the last one, if legal, chattier too, to the point of becoming annoying.

'Congratulations.' Jackson jumps up, giving Evelyn an overly affectionate hug. A gesture which immediately riles, Brian causing a bad start to the night.

'Just remember she is spoken for mate, alright.' Brian shakes his hand, keeping a tight grip for longer than necessary.

'Hi I'm pixie, Jackson's girlfriend.' The overly enthusiastic girl says in a syrupy tone, temporarily defusing the situation. 'I love your dress.' She adds, staring at Evelyn for a little too long. 'Have we met before, I feel like I know you from somewhere?'

'No, I don't think so.' Evelyn abruptly replies, agitated by the girl's voice grating in her ears.

'Ya probably seen her behind the counter of Roaster's.' Jimmy chides joining the conversation without invitation. His pupils large, Evelyn unable to tell if he is actually looking at her.

'Well...she won't need to be working there for much longer. Once we are married and the patter of tiny feet come along, Evelyn will have enough to keep her occupied at home. Besides as my wife, she won't want for anything.' Brian offers another unwelcome announcement. Roaster's is one of the worst places to work, but in retrospect it is her little bit of freedom. The thought of not having that miniscule piece of independence. Not being able to sit and chat with Lexi, her one true friend these days, filling her with dread. If she doesn't break free from Brian's clutches soon, she may as well be dead, because that is how a life being his wife will feel, as though she is spiritless inside. With a heavy heart Evelyn squeezes into the booth next to Jimmy.

'I know.' Pixie almost screeches in her baby doll voice. 'Are you on social media, twitter, snap chat, Instagram or even Facebook, though that one's for older people really?'

'No, I've never bothered with social media sites, don't have the time for that sort of pretentious stuff.' Evelyn aware her face is flushing. Thankfully, hidden in the dimly light club, or so she hopes.

'Are ya sure, cause you look so familiar. I'm on all the sites, I have over a thousand followers on twitter. I follow all the stars, actors, actresses, supermodels–'

'Like Jimmy said, you've probably seen me in Roaster's.' Evelyn cuts in, aware Brian is eyeing them with a curious look. Nervously, she shoves a finger in her mouth, biting her nails. Luckily, Brian quickly shifts his attention elsewhere, jumping up and striding in the direction of the bar. Evelyn watches with interest as he stops to talk to a guy called Mark Walter's, a known drug dealer in the area, making her wonder if this is where Brian is getting his supply from. Unfortunately, she doesn't get to study them too closely, as Pixie, starts talking again.

'Instagram.'

'What?' 'Instagram, OMG you look so much like her, you could almost be twins.'

'What are you talking about?' Evelyn retorts, fixing a scowl on Pixie, aware Jackson is studying her with interest.

'Lynn Priestly the fashion designer, I follow her on Instagram. She has just designed this amazing wedding dress and put a picture up on her page. I've never seen anything so beautiful, it's a silk slim line gown with the most amazing detail.'

'I never posted....I mean, I don't know anything about Instagram or fashion for that matter.' Jimmy's attention seems to be on the two women, leaving Evelyn grateful Brian is out of earshot. 'Oh gosh, you could never design anything like this, I mean this girl is way out of your league. I'm only saying you look like her, wow it's just mad like.' Pixie rattles on, Evelyn wanting to strangle her. 'What do they call it, a doubler or something when two people are a mirror of each other, but have never even met?'

'Doppelganger.' Jackson pipes in. Jimmy is still silent, his eyes intently fixed on Evelyn and there is no questioning their focus this time. 'Bit of a coincidence having the same surname too....could be a relative eh, Evie.' The room becomes very hot, all three pairs of eyes are fixed on her. An overwhelming need to escape, urges Evelyn to make a bolt for the ladies room, hoping Pixie will have shut up before Brian's return and Jimmy won't mention any of this.

Once inside the sanctity of the ladies room, Evelyn stares at her reflection in the mirror, pale faced, eye makeup too dark and heavy, adding to the pitiful sight. Gillian is right, she does look like shit these days.

'You okay?' A woman she vaguely recognises asks.

'Yeah, thanks.' Evelyn replies, acknowledging her through the reflection in the mirror, unable to let go of the sink or turn around for fear of fainting. Beads of perspiration have formed on her forehead, the blue dress sticking to her clammy body making her wish she could pull it off and throw it in the nearby bin.

'Here,' the woman passes a dainty make-up purse. 'Better fix yourself up before going back out.'

'Thanks.' Evelyn takes the bag, managing a weak smile. She flicks some blusher on her cheeks, after dabbing her face with tissues from a dispenser.

'Whoever he is doll, he ain't worth it.' The woman says, with a raised brow as she replenishes her own lipstick.

'No...you're right, he's not.' Evelyn replies when she hands back the bag before turning to leave.

Back outside, feeling less wobbly and a little more positive, Evelyn glances across at the little group round their table. Jimmy and Jackson aimlessly watch the goings on of the dancefloor, evidently oblivious to Pixie's non-stop chatter. It comes to her notice, Brian has not returned to the table and is nowhere to be seen. Without giving it a second thought, Evelyn makes a bolt for the exit uncaring of how Brian will react.

'Evie love, what's happened?' Gillian jumps up from watching the television when her daughter arrives into the lounge.

'I don't know, I feel very tired mam.' Evelyn practically collapses into a chair, her feet no longer able to hold her up.

'I'll make you a cup of tea.' Gillian, about to get up suggests. 'I don't want tea.' Evelyn replies a little too sharply. 'Sorry mam, I didn't mean to snap. None of this is your fault, I shouldn't be taking it out on you.'

'It's alright love, I understand...more than you realise.'

'Dad would never have...' She stares at her mother aghast.

'Not yer father, he would die rather than lift a hand to a woman. No, my own father was an alcoholic and a bully. Growing up, I witnessed my mother, god rest her soul being beaten black and blue. Eight children she had, not including the three miscarriages due to his beatings. I couldn't wait to get out of that house as soon as I was old enough. Seeing you going through the same as her, pains me....Evelyn you are a beautiful talented girl and times are different.'

'Mam,' she protests. 'I can't just walk away it's not that simple when it comes to Brian.'

'You're wrong you can. You and Danny can stay here for a start, that leviathan will not darken my doorstep. We can get an injunction against him.' Her eyes rest on the engagement ring.

'Oh please tell me you don't intend to marry him.' Her eyes become watery with tears.

'No...no...I only agreed so as not to arouse his suspicions. Once Lexi's cousin arrests him everything will be okay. I need you to play along for the moment with a false wedding.'

'Wake up Evie, he'll get bail. You can't stay with him a minute longer, he's winning, gaining more and more control and it's draining all the fight from you, can't you see this. Please I beg you stay here tonight.'

'No mam, I can't drag you and Danny into this. I need you to keep him safe here for me, where Brian won't suspect anything....' Evelyn's mobile bleeps. She rises from the chair with renewed strength. A text from Lexi, having helped. 'Mam, did you take a picture of the dress?'

'I wouldn't have, if I'd known you were planning to wear it to marry Brian. I should have known. I saw your Instagram profile, thought if I put a picture of the dress up, you really would get noticed. You have an amazing talent and deserve a chance to shine.' Gillian's eyes light up with pride, amidst her tears.

'I don't deserve it mam, I already told you that. I had my chance with Desmond and I ruined his life, so why should I get a second chance when he won't. Killing that boy will follow him around for the rest of his life and it wasn't his fault.'

'What are you talking about?'

'I should go, before Brian comes banging on the door and waking Danny.' Evelyn wraps her arms around the older woman. 'Promise you'll say nothing, just go along with whatever you hear. I'll tell Brian, Danny has a temperature, he won't want a sick child around. Keep Danny off school too, will you.'

'I hope you know what you are doing.'

'So do I.' Evelyn mutters under her breath, as she leaves her mother's house. She walks the short distance across to her own house, to find the lights are on and music blaring which can be heard from out on the street. Taking a deep breath, she opens the front door. As usual the house is full, this time with people she doesn't even recognise.

'Where the fuck did you go?' Brian hisses getting up, forgetting to put on his fake persona for the benefit of his friends. Not that anyone seemed to notice they are all out of it, he grabs her roughly by the arm steering her into the kitchen out of earshot.

'I got sick in the club and needed air.' Evelyn's tries to think quickly, her head spinning. Most men would ask is she alright? Not Brian.

'An you expect me to believe that. Why didn't ya come back, at least have the decency to tell me. I was worried.' His nostrils flare. If they were alone he would have hit her by know of that she is sure. If he was so worried why didn't he come looking for her she wonders, knowing the answer? 'Where have you been all this time?' He bellows instead, face contorted, spittle flying from his mouth landing like a shower on her face.

'I walked home, couldn't find a taxi.' Realising she is getting nowhere, she adds. 'Look I'm sorry, I didn't think. I was so excited about the sickness, you know like the last time, I went looking for a late night chemist.'

'Are you telling me? Fuck why didn't you say, where's the test.' His features softening, apart from the hint of disbelief still evident in his eyes.

'I threw it in a bin. I wasn't putting it in my new bag, had piss all over it.'

'So we're...I'm going to be a daddy.' She refrains from reminding him he is already a father.

'Yeah, isn't it great news.' Easier to lie, and keep him mellowed for the moment saving her from a beating, for now at least and possibly even having to endure sex.

'That's my girl, come on.' He sweeps her up in his arms. 'You being pregnant with my kid is such a turn on.' How wrong had she been?

'What about all them,' she nods towards the lounge door hoping to quash his libido, as he carries her towards the stairs.

'Ah they're all out of it, won't even notice were gone.' He replies, causing Evelyn's heart to plummet.

Just as they reach the bedroom there is loud thumping on the front door, accompanied by raised voices. Brian drops Evelyn, with a thud she hastily falls to the floor. He disappears downstairs, within seconds her ears are met by the sound of a scuffle and raised voices. Through the unclosed curtains she can see the lamination of the blue lights. She pulls herself up and watches from the window, as the Garda bring Brian and all their unwanted guests, out to the awaiting patrol van.

Chapter 24

It surprises Des when he leaves the house for work, to find Sarah Connolly is absent. Her little Corsa, having become a regular feature in recent weeks on the street. Alice's words the previous evening once again resonating in his ears. Suggesting he try and talk to Sarah, apologise for what happened and make her aware of his remorse. The idea of approaching Sarah filling him with renewed dread. Apart from Sarah Connolly, Agnes's continued unhappiness over Amelia is causing concern. She had waited up, eager to know if Alice had agreed to come to tea, making it more and more apparent her need for bonding with their family unit.

'I'm being pushy, I know, but I'd love to meet her. I suppose it is too this early in your courtship?' Agnes had said, with an agonising sadness in her eyes. Agnes had never been a social person, dedicating her life to her husband and bringing up her sons'. It has left her with nothing only a gaping hole, from her loneliness.

'Ma what sort of word is courtship.' Des had teased, delighted they were alone. Ger had gone to bed early, giving the opportunity to sit and have a cup of tea with Agnes, cheering her endlessly 'You will love her, and Alice will love you, but tea with Da might be a bit too much.' Des had stated the obvious, which thankfully Agnes understood.

'Fair point.' She replied though her smile had instantly faded.

'Maybe you could come out to tea with us.' Des suggested. 'I'd like to take you out, you deserve it.'

'That's very kind, I don't want you to feel obliged.' Agnes managed a weak smile. 'It's great having you home, I missed having you pop in with a cheery quip, if it weren't for you I don't know what I'd do.' Her words unleashing guilt, since Des had spent the previous evening with, Alice discussing going back to college or even university as a mature student. The up side being, he would still live close enough to visit. 'Don't mind me I'm feeling sorry for myself.' Agnes added, as though reading his thoughts.

'What is it, Ma?' Des questioned, detecting her sadness went far deeper. 'Is it the aul fella, has he been given you a hard time?'

'If only that was all. No, I'm used to dealing with him. You should get some sleep, it's getting late an you have to be up in the morning. Don't mind me at all.'

'Ma.' He'd protested, loathed to accept her brush off.

'I got to thinking after you went out. Me an my ideal's, who am I kidding.' She finally opened up, the depth of her strain carved on her face. 'I rang Phillip and suggested coming home with Amelia for Christmas. I'd imagined us all sitting around the table together.' Desmond could imagine his brother's reaction, far quicker than visualising, them all playing happy families for Christmas. As he pushes open the door of the Garda station, it dawns on him what he can do to help his mother.

'You're too early, either have a seat and wait til nine, or come back.' Garda O'Driscoll barks at Desmond, clearly not in a frame of mind to be challenged. It doesn't stop Des from trying.

'I have to be in work for half eight, and don't want to be late. Can I sign now....please?' He presses, doing his best to remain calm and polite. Hoping to appeal to her softer side, while doubting she has one.

'Your signing time is between nine and five, come back later.' Maggie's tone firm, before turning her back, to indicate the matter is not open to discussion. It had been the wrong thing to do, tired of being treated like a common criminal Des remains rooted to the spot.

'Look, all I want is to adhere to my parole conditions, and prove myself by holding down a decent job. If I'm late for work it won't look good will it. If I leave it til after work, I'll be breaking the parole conditions, I don't finish until five. Surely you can see the logic in me signing now. I'm here, give me a break will you.' All politeness diminishing as frustration takes over. Maggie gently places her pen down, eyes fixed on Des, she lets out a heavy sigh. He had got through the previous week, without her patronising glare. It had been Sergeant Collins himself on the desk, and he saw no problem with Des signing early before work.

'That's not my problem, now is it? If you are so keen to stick to your parole conditions then you will sign between the hours of nine and five each Tuesday. We can't go making special allowances for people, conditions are made for a reason.' Her antiseptic stare bloodless, sending a chill down Desmond's back. 'I hope you have a solid alibi for the Sunday evening of the bank holiday too. There has been a couple of incidences in the town since your release.' She adds, to antagonise him. Desmond can see right through her façade. Garda O'Driscoll, a pure ice maiden, worse than any of the prison officers in Castlerea, and they were a force to be reckoned with. Desmond remembering how it had been a cold and wet January afternoon, when he arrived into the prison reception, where they took his clothes and personal belongings. Replacing them with cheap jeans, a white t-shirt, cheap shirt and underwear. He was also handed clean bedclothes, a towel, soap and a toothbrush before being brought to the cell by a burly prison officer, who spoke in monosyllables' and barked at him in much the same way as Garda O'Driscoll. 'I'm keeping my eye on you, remember I can have you back in prison so quick your feet won't touch the ground.'

'Are you accusing me of something? It sounds very like a threat, and I'm sure your superior wouldn't be too impressed. ' Having survived the past couple of weeks working in the factory, deeming it more soul destroying than his time in prison. Most of the other prisoners may have looked hard, acted hard, but no one bothered you really. They were more intent on getting through their time without extending it unnecessarily. Nobody wanted to be cooped up in their stifling, mind numbing cell for longer than needed. The yard, where they walked around for a couple of hours each day supposedly getting fresh air and exercise no better.

'Words of someone with something to hide, in my experience.' Maggie leans forward, green eyes piercing him. Des bolts from the station, exasperated by her resistance. Head bend, he texts Gary as he walks out onto the road unaware of the jeep driving down the street, until hearing the screech of its brakes. Only then does he look up.

'Des what the hell...I could have killed you.' Conor shouts, alighting the vehicle, his face ghostly pale. Maggie appears on the steps behind them.

'What's going on?' She demands in an accusatory tone, glower firmly locked on Desmond.

'It's nothing Mags, everything is fine all my doing.' Conor says, regaining his composure.

'Are you sure?' Maggie challenges placing her hands on her hips, evidently disappointed by this reply.

'Yes, I am.' Conor replies in an equally firm tone, turning to ask Des. 'Are you alright?' A bristling Maggie, slams the door behind them. Leaving, Des with no doubt she will up her acrimony towards him.

'I'm sorry, I was distracted.' He apologises, to a distinctly shaken Conor. 'I need to sort out signing at the station, but it's clashing with my work hours.' The incident leaving him with little choice but reveal the reason for his thoughtless behaviour.

'Why didn't you tell me?'

'I don't want preferential treatment, if I come in late or leave early, it will be noticed by everyone, you know same time every week. I want to slot in, not stand out. I was texting Gary hoping he could sort it, as they won't let me sign now.'

'By they....I'm guessing you mean Maggie.' Conor shoves a hand through his perfectly combed hair, disheveling it. Maggie's displaced loyalty to Sarah, causing her to overstep her mark. 'Come on.' Conor suggests. 'Let's, you and I go sort this with the sergeant.'

'But...' Des hesitates, as it may rile the red headed Garda further.

'No buts.' Conor opens the door to the station, waving Des ahead of him. As soon as they step inside, Gary rings. A relief, to have to answer the call. By the time he comes off the phone, Conor has mellowed Garda O'Driscoll and she allows Des to sign his sheet. It does not prevent her from throwing him a glaring look.

'My parole officer will arrange for the times to be changed officially.' Des offers.

'I'm sure Gard O'Driscoll understands the predicament you were in don't you Mags.' Conor interjects causing her to bristle further, leaving Des with no doubt she will find a way of making him pay for this. She will do anything to put him back behind bars.

Chapter 25

She didn't want to be seen sneaking out of Alan O'Sullivan's office after their meeting, which is how Sarah ends up almost colliding with a man walking hurriedly along the path, due to her distracted state.

'Sorry...I,' she mutters absently, 'wasn't looking...' Struck dumbfounded when met with a pair of deep hazel eyes, Illuminating intense sadness to the point the light has completely gone out of them. Her heart lurches, feeling partly responsible until remembering their last encounter.

'I seem to be making a habit of this today.' Conor says in an attempt to defrost the chill between them even though the sun is radiating down. 'Sarah...have you...could we maybe go for a coffee?' His uncertainty clear.

'I...sorry,' unable to handle any emotional discussion, after the decision she's just made. 'I have an appointment in Carraigbrin and I'm already running late.' The lie flows easily from her lips while dropping her gaze, unable to look him in the eye. She is only going to the cash and carry to get supplies for the campsite and is in no rush at all, could easily spare the time for a coffee but something about the way Conor is looking at her suggests she would not like what he has to say. Maybe, if it wasn't for the day that's in it, she might have had the strength.

'Of course.' His response one of defeat, along with a look that suggests seeing through the fabrication. Without another word, he carries on his way leaving Sarah with the bitter taste of disappointment. Expecting him to have at least tried a little harder.

'Thanks for your text.' She calls after him, wondering why she felt the need to say this.

'You're welcome,' the smile not reaching his eyes. 'I'm just glad no one was hurt.' He adds, and then he is gone, disappearing round the corner without a backward glance. The encounter leaving Sarah apprehensive, along with an unexpected longing, to visit the graveyard. Soft raindrops begin to fall, landing on her face as she climbs the hill towards the final resting place, of those she has loved and lost. Reaching the top, she discovers the reason for her yearning. The stonemason has written on the tombstone, below her mother's name.

Patrick Thomas Connolly
15th January 1951 – 16th June 2017
Loving husband, father and grandfather

Sarah clears any wilted flowers, rearranging some of the wreaths, proceeding to do the same on Jack's grave, wishing she had brought some fresh flowers to replace the decayed ones. A soft wind whistles through the trees and for a moment she's convinced she can hear his boyish laughter rustling in the leaves. With a heavy heart she rises to leave when her mobile buzzes, a message from Dini asking how the training is going.

'Are you trying to tell me something Jack Connolly?' She whispers, fighting back emotion.

'Good day to you Sarah.' Father Kennelly greets her as she is crossing the car park. A soft spoke man in his late fifties, father Kennelly has been the parish priest in Kilmer Cove for over twenty years. Considering his age, he has a clear understanding of the modern world and a good inside knowledge of all his parishioners'.

'Good day to you father. Davy has done a lovely job on the gravestone.'

'An artist in his own right is Davy, and how are you doing? I know you feel god and the church has deserted you, it's understandable after all you've been through. Remember my door is still always open if you'd like to talk. Keep faith, Sarah, time will heal and may I add, try to keep an open mind. It's hard to see families in this town broken, shared pain can bring understanding.' His well-intentioned words doing little for Sarah, having long felt god has deserted her, possibly deterred by her sins. Thou shalt not commit adultery. Not on the same level as thou shalt not kill, but none the less seemingly devoid of absolution.

'Thank you father, I'll bear that in mind.' She replies simply, before hastily getting into her car, to avoid further conversation. After all, it's not the priest's fault she's had a falling out with his boss. That somehow god the almighty decided her son would not live a full life.

After picking up everything on Paul's list from the cash and carry. Sarah is drawn towards the shopping centre, finding herself walking into a sports shop for the first time in years. Initially, gripped by an uncontrollable sense of suffocation and an immense longing to be brought back to the last time she'd been in here with Jack. He had wanted a very expensive pair of running trainers and Sarah had questioned the extravagant price, encouraging him to opt for the cheaper pair the assistant was offering. Jack had not questioned, only accepted she could not afford the trainers he had desired. If only she could change that day, buy him the ones he had wanted, unaware it would be the last thing she would ever buy her son.

'Can I help you?' An assistant asks. 'Ah...I'm looking for a good pair of running trainers.' Sarah replies.

She eventually leaves the shop with not only the trainers but running pants and vest. The soft rain from earlier now heavier and unrelenting, a typical Irish summer shower, the type that leaves you with little hope of it easing, she makes a run for her car. Driving out of the car park onto the road, visibility is limited as the windscreen-wipers make a futile battle against the robust rain. As she drives along the now deserted street, her gaze is drawn towards a forlorn figure huddled at a bus stop. Recognising, Agnes drenched to the skin with bags of shopping by her feet. Slamming on the brakes, Sarah swerves pulling impulsively to the side of the road. The manoeuvre causing the driver behind to sound his horn and irately shake a fist as he drives past.

'Agnes.' Sarah shouts jumping out to be hit by a torrent of rainfall. 'Here let me help you, your soaked.' She grabs hold of the heavy shopping bags, as though it is the most natural thing in the world to do, help out a neighbour in need. Agnes showing every sign of a person wishing to protest, but Sarah has already loaded her shopping bags into the boot of her car. Leaving, Agnes with no choice but to get into the car, since Sarah is holding her groceries hostage.

'You're soaked through...and your car.' Agnes says, trying to hide her discomfort as Sarah gets in and starts the engine. 'I really don't want to put you out.' She continues to object, landing on deaf ears.

'Not at all, sur I'm practically passing your door on my way home.' Sarah insists. Hair, flattened against her forehead from the rain. 'Here, I'll put the fans on, it may not dry you out completely but at least it'll warm up the car.' She adds, less confident now they were trapped in the close proximity of the car. It would have played on her conscience of she'd driven home, knowing Agnes was standing in the rain. So here they are, in a confined space together, both women feeling the suffocation. 'Good ole Irish summers.' Sarah adds shivering slightly from nerves rather than cold. Checking her mirrors as they turn right onto the coast road from Carraigbrin to Kilmer Cove, the road seeming longer than it normally is.

'Thank you...I don't want to be any trouble.' Agnes eventually mumbles. Her face tight, as she stares aimlessly ahead.

'It's no trouble at all, Agnes.' Sarah replies, knowing she is becoming a seasoned liar. 'Are you warming up a bit?' She asks in desperation. Small talk between the two women quickly becoming stilted and forced, stuck in a situation, they would rather not be in.

'Yes thanks...though I'm dripping all over your seat.'

'It's only water it'll dry.' Sarah replies nonchalantly, while keeping her gaze firmly on the road ahead. The rain is beginning to ease, making visibility somewhat clearer. 'Those bags were heavy, must be a struggle on the bus for you.' Sarah says by way of filling the lingering silence beginning to ferment. A pitiful attempt because she is unable to think of anything else to say, and Agnes' continued lack of communication becoming frustrating. Before Jack's death, Sarah knew little about Agnes and possibly not much more since. Not the type of woman to pop into the café for a coffee, or the Nook of an evening for a drink. Never joining an evening class, or getting involved in the local committee. A woman who in general kept to herself.

'I manage...it's a case of having too.' Agnes responds, a hint of sadness etched in her voice.

'Would you not wait until Gerald got home from work, to drive you into Carraigbrin? The supermarket is open late most nights, sign of the times we live in.' Sarah's suggestion opening up a can of worms, she'd not expected.

'No...' the reply sharp. 'It would be too much trouble, he's tired after working all day, besides Ger hates shopping.' Agnes exhales a heavy sigh, indicating her frustration, turning to look out of the passenger window. 'Desmond was always the one to take me before, nothing was ever too much bother for him. Even when he moved into Donegal and then to Carraigbrin with Evelyn, he would come and pick me up every Saturday morning.' The dig causing Sarah anguish, Agnes conscious of what she is doing, by saying this. Generating, a stagnating atmosphere in the cramped space of the car. Even though the vehicle has warmed from the fans blowing out warm air, Sarah shivers suddenly cold. Beads of rain water dripping down her forehead, as she grips the steering wheel. Concentrating on the road ahead, so as not to reveal her simmering displeasure. Compelled to allow Agnes witness her anguish, having already bared her emotional state too freely up until this point, unwilling to be a victim anymore.

'Doesn't Leo do a special service with the minivan once a week?' Nerves causing her mouth to run away with itself, ignoring the caution screaming in her head. 'I think he picks up a few locals and takes them to the supermarket, waits while they shop, and he loads their shopping. Mrs. Burgess uses it, I remember her saying how great Leo is, taking her straight to her front door and carrying her shopping. You should ask him, I'm sure he doesn't charge much.'

'I don't think, he would.' Agnes's reply abrupt, surprising Sarah.

'I'm sure he-'

'No, you don't understand.' She cuts Sarah short, distinct agitation evident as she continues. 'No one in Kilmer Cove will allow me avail of their service.'

'I didn't mean....' Sarah flushes genuinely mortified.

'I shouldn't have said...' Agnes retracts. 'I'm happy getting the bus that's all.' Unshed tears glistening in the older woman's eyes.

'Agnes...I'm sorry you've been having difficulty. To set the record straight, I didn't ask people to shun you. I might resent your son, but on a whole, I'm not a spiteful person.' She'd never purposefully cause this woman unnecessary pain. 'If it would make a difference, help change other peoples' minds. You would be welcome at oceanic temptations, I'd be happy to serve you, but only you.' Unsure why the need to voice the latter fact, already an unspoken certainty.

'Your offer is a little pointless, in that case.' Agnes replies, seeing things differently than Sarah. 'You have to understand Sarah, it hasn't been easy for my family. It's why Phillip doesn't come home to visit anymore, he is ashamed of his brother. I am aware my son took your sons' life, there is not a day goes by...Nothing can ever change what happened...I have prayed to god each day.' Her face contorting with anguish. 'In my heart, I know Desmond is not a bad person, he would never have deliberately set out to hurt anyone. I still find it hard to believe, he knowingly took drugs and got behind the wheel of his car. It felt like I lost my son that day too, I'm only grateful, Conor O'Dowd has compassion. It's given Desmond a chance to prove his worth, and meeting Alice....As a mother you understand, I want to see my son happy again. I could not have turned my back on him, no decent mother would.'

Fortunately, they reach Seaview. Sarah pulls up at the kerb, allowing Agnes to get out of the car. Sarah closes her eyes, fighting back tears, until hearing the boot bang closed, allowing them flow freely. Streaming down her cheeks, matching the streaks of rain outside running down the windscreen. She not a cold hearted person, if anything she has an understanding of Agnes's maternal instinct to protect and stand by her son. It doesn't make Sarah's loss any easier, or her resentment of Desmond any less. They are simply two women sharing the pain of that dreadful day, affecting their lives forever after, albeit in different ways. Some could say they had both lost a son that day. Sarah would never get to see Jack's smile again, due to his physical absence. Agnes would never see her son smile, or be truly happy, due to the sadness inside. To the outside world, he hides it well, but she knows, how he's unable to sleep at night, due to the nightmare repeatedly torturing his mind.

Chapter 26

Later on in the day, Sarah is sitting in the farmhouse kitchen, still unsettled by her encounter with Agnes. The only person who would fully understand her unease is Roz. She fires up her laptop connecting to skype. As usual her friend is willing to be a supportive lifeline.

'Lily and Tommy are wonderful as you know.' Sarah explains, wanting to reiterate how supportive her family are. 'But...I did something, I know even they might find hard to understand.'

'Spill girl, I'm all ears.' Roz encourages in her usual cheerful tone.

'After Desmond's release, I took to sitting outside his house in my car. Mainly early in the morning, sometimes late at night too. I sound like a desperate stalker.' Voicing her actions sounding pathetic, even to her own ears. Her only reprieve being the knowledge Roz would never judge her actions, and she is right.

'Oh my poor girl, you are anything but.' Roz peers at the screen, with a look of horror. 'There is no protocol for how we deal with life after...' she pauses, searching for the right words. Her own loss, overshadowing her prematurely aging features. 'When you become lost it's hard to know what to do. Hearing of his early release is bound to have an adverse effect. Knowing he is free to fulfil his life, while you are left in limbo. Remember, Sarah you are entitled to feel aggrieved, he murdered your son.'

'He looks like a normal young man...I can't.'

'Nothing changes the facts, girl.'

'I know and the resentment is eating me up. Last week his mother came out, you know as I was parked outside the house and invited me in for coffee. I don't know what made me go in, curiosity I guess. The house was a normal warm welcoming family home with photographs on the wall of Desmond and his brother, as little boys. Agnes, that's his mother, said they have suffered too.' Sarah wavers, taking a drink from a glass of water, her throat dry.

'The woman couldn't begin to understand how you feel. Jesus girl...how dare she insinuate such nonsense' Roz almost screeches, indignant by the suggestion Agnes's pain is ranked with Sarah's loss.

'I...I...' Sarah takes another drink from the glass of water to try and ease the fact, her throat feels like it is constricting further.

'Go on Sarah let it out, it's the only way.' Roz gently encourages, placing the palm of her hand on the side of the screen. A gesture of encouragement, in which Sarah reciprocates by placing her hand on the screen in the same way.

'I panicked and ran out that day, suffocation overwhelming. Today, I was driving home from Carraigbrin when I saw her standing at the bus stop in the rain. I gave her a lift, could see pain etched in her face. I've tried to divert my focus by training for the marathon and putting every hour I can into the shop and new campsite, but it's beginning to consume me.' These words revealed to a person who truly understands, equally broken by the loss they share.

'I know it's hard but Agnes still has her son, you don't, that's the difference.' Roz points out. Her advice different from Lena, who has been encouraging Sarah to achieve peace of mind, Roz wanting Sarah to rise above the Shanahan's. Both wanting her to find a way of living in the same town as Desmond. Each looking at it in a very different way, the latter not entirely the most ideal for Sarah, as the underlying resentment and pain is consuming her, though Roz's sentiment bona fide. 'Inside you may be crumbling, but paste a smile on your face for the audience. They will not make us their victims too. Still aim for the Dublin marathon in October. We'll make sure to let everyone know, a wonderfully talented young man, had been deprived of representing his country in the Olympics. No matter how hard Agnes may think this has been for her, it will never compare to the loss of your child.' A simple nod in agreement is all Sarah can manage in return. 'Sarah, when I read your email with the outline for our case in the Seannad. Even though, I already know every detail I cried, girl. Your loss is real and you have every right to be angry. You ring anytime the dark destroyer comes a knockin, you hear.' Roz adds with conviction. Sarah simply nods again, not wanting to tell Roz she doesn't agree. Agnes Shanahan's face conflicting this, yes the woman still has her son, but she has suffered too. Drained of emotion and not wishing to discuss it further, Sarah averts the conversation, asking about Roz's son.

'How is Vince did he get the job?'

'He did, aw you wouldn't believe how happy he is, better hours. I'm delighted for him, he deserves it.'

'Good, I'm pleased. How are you doing, are you still keeping busy helping in the charity shop?'

'Ah sur...like you pet, good days and bad. Ray has met someone, the rumours were true. He's filed for divorce, says I can have the house...that's big of him.'

'I'm so sorry Roz.' Sarah frowns, conscious rejection from the very person you'd expect to support and understand your loss, is painful.

'Oh well, what can you do? Life goes on for some people whether we like it or not. I better go, girl, Vince will be in soon, wanting his tea. You mind yourself, and remember I'm always here. Nighty night.'

'Night Roz.' Sarah remains staring at the blank screen after they disconnect. Roz had been her usual supportive self, but something about her demeanour, suggesting she is trying to convince herself as much as Sarah to keep positive. Sarah closes her laptop and climbs the stairs to bed, where she struggles to find sleep. The day's events running around in her head, trying to make sense of it all. Roz always claimed the apology she'd received had been fake, a ploy to get away with what he had done. Sarah having no doubt in her mind this is true. An apology will not bring back a lost son or daughter, but at least it would show some sort of remorse for what had happened a simple acknowledgment of what they had done in taking another person's life. Desmond had never said he was sorry, had never come to Sarah's door and apologised, showing any emotion over taking Jack's life. A fact which swirls around in her head, fueling her resentment. Even Agnes never apologised, as far as she can remember, when defending her son's actions. Trying to think back over their two brief conversations recently, to find it becoming a haze. Throughout the trial, they had passed her in the corridor, each time burying their heads, a saddening fact but true. Eventually she drifts into a pitiful sleep, everything still going around in her mind, reliving the events of that fateful day, again in her slumber. Maggie's pale face, travelling to the hospital in the back of the police car. Passing the mangled car mounted on the pavement, its bonnet embedded in a lamppost and the unforgettable smell of burning rubber. That smell will never leave her, causing nausea to rise every time, she even thinks about it. Jack, already rushed into surgery when she reached the hospital. She had begged and pleaded to see her son, only to be instructed to wait in that small waiting room. The one with magnolia walls and not much else. The very room she collapsed in when they broke the news her son was dead.

Bolting upright, Sarah can barely breathe, the wretched feeling of suffocation overtaking her body once again. Drenched in her own sweat, clasping her hand on her chest, due to the crushing sense of the room closing in on her. Disorientated her eyes search into the darkness, waiting for the fear to subside, and her breathing return to normal. When it eventually does, she slips from the bed on wobbly legs, heading downstairs to the kitchen, waiting for dawn to come. When it does, leaving behind the gloom of the night, and the previous day's rain, giving away to blue skies and a humid sticky heat. Grabbing a towel, Sarah rushes out to the shed. Grabbing her surfboard, she walks down to the Cove, desperately needing the sense of tranquility the sea normally gives. There she sits on a rock, her bare feet caressing the sand. Reveling in its touch, while inhaling the salty air and listening to the sound of waves crashing against the rocks, finally causing her to relax. It is all she needs to breathe again, away from the suffocation of dealing with life, allowing her to absorb and indulge in memories of happier times. Feeling a little rejuvenated, Sarah strolls back up through the narrow pathway. Surrounded by the heady natural scents of honeysuckle and wild roses entangled in the ditches, on either side of the path. The sounds of young birds twittering in the trees, summer being her favourite time of year, living on the farm. As she reaches the burnt out barn, her resolve wobbling. Tommy and the fire officer convinced the fire had been started deliberately. Though holding doubt about it being fellows' lamping, as it would not be something they would partake in doing. Leaving a big question mark over who and why. Brushing doubt from her mind Sarah continues on her way, she would have just enough time for a quick shower before opening the café. Lena would be arriving at eight thirty to do the early shift with her. They planned to get all the food prep done along with some of Lena's beautiful pastries Kremowka, which are puff pastry layers separated by whipped cream, sweet cream, pudding or meringue (made of egg whites), and the top sprinkled with powdered sugar or covered in icing. This along with her wonderful sernik, the café offering a wide variety of food to the tourists, becoming more and more popular. The only downside being Sarah also enjoying indulging in these tempting delights. Conscious since her fortieth birthday in recent months, everything has been speedily heading southward, beginning to sag. Apart from the threat to her already fading figure, she loves working alongside Lena, enjoying her stories of her home land and her adoration for her husband Malik. The couple much like Tommy and Lily when it comes to devotion. She unlocks the door of the café, about to push up the shutters on the front window, her mobile rings.

'Sarah...this iz Malik...I'm in the hospital...Lena was in an accident...she won't be coming to work.'

'What happened? Is she seriously hurt?' Sarah can feel panic rising in her chest.

'They say, her arm is fractured from the fall...and she has to have stitches on her head, but she will be okay...a little shaken maybe. She say a car came from nowhere, it overtake and come at her...forcing her off the road...as she cycle to work....I'm sorry I must go the doctor wants to speak with me.'

'Tell her...' he has already hung up, Sarah can feel bile rising in her mouth. She immediately rings Maggie to find out if they had news of the accident, to be told the driver had driven off. 'Isn't that classed as a hit and run?' Sarah probes.

'They didn't hit her, exactly.' Maggie sounds irritated by her question. 'Look we will look into it Sarah, I can assure you....It is our job, I hope Lena will be okay.' She disconnects, leaving Sarah with a sense of helplessness wanting to visit Lena in the hospital, only she has to open up.

◆◆◆

Over in Carraigbrin, Evelyn is sitting up in bed having barely slept too. Nothing has changed and she is no closer to making an escape from Brian's clutches. Beside her, Brian is snoring gently seemingly unperturbed by the events of the arrests. An incident which has left a lasting effect on Evelyn, one she is unlikely to forget. As she had been watching Brian's arrest through the bedroom window, armed Garda very quietly ascended the stairs. Frightening the living day out of her when they suddenly burst into the room brandishing rifles. Evelyn, literally wet herself from the shock. Ashamed and cold when they bundled her into the back of the Garda wagon with Brian, Jimmy, Jackson, Pixie, whom at least had shut up temporarily and two other individuals, Evelyn didn't recognise.

On the journey to the station, no one spoke, all fearful of why they were being brought in and conscious of having excessive alcohol and drugs in their system, all apart from Evelyn of course. At the station they were quickly separated, Evelyn initially taken to an interview room. Whereupon, two Garda, one male and one female the scarier of the two, a burly woman with eyes like a cats, that appeared to be looking into her soul, hurled questions about firearms. Throughout the whole ordeal, Evelyn expected Lexi to pop her head round the door and assure her everything would be alright. That she had only been taken in as to not arouse Brian's suspicions, or even for the young male Garda to start laughing and call off the Rottweiler of a colleague, revealing himself as Lexi's cousin. It didn't happen, Evelyn could feel her body becoming hot and clammy, could even smell her own perspiration, along with the urine from her damp knickers. It had been the most humiliating moment of her life, and neither Garda seemed to notice her anguish.

Instead, when they weren't satisfied with her answers they hauled her down to one of the holding cells. A tiny grey room, made entirely of concrete, with a thin bed along one wall, and a steel toilet in another corner. No windows or natural light, the only sliver of illumination in the room, a single dim bulb high in the ceiling. As soon as they locked the door behind her, the sound of the key turning in the lock, causing panic to rise. Enlightened to the fact, she may not be released any time soon, desperately wanting to see Danny and Gillian. Her only comfort being, she had asked her mother to keep him that, he didn't have to witness the terror of their home being raided by armed guards.

Sitting on the hard single bed she shivered, alone and scared, with the perception of being trapped. Dawning on her, it was how Desmond must have felt the morning he was arrested for killing Jack Connolly. Guilt over that tragic event, ripping through every pore and coursing through her veins. Immersing herself in self-hate over what she had done, fully comprehending how terrifying it must have been.

She had blanked him, moved from their flat without a word of explanation, and then proceeded to ignore his calls and texts. It had been a cold and calculating thing to do, too self-absorbed in her relationship with Brian and their expected baby. Thinking life would be far more exciting, not realising the excitement was of a different kind. Even when his solicitor had sent the letter asking for her to appear in court, she refused. Contacting Des solicitor telling him, she had no ties with Des and could not offer any help with his case. Luckily, the Garda did not subpoena her as a witness to the accident, since she'd not been there. She had turned her back on him, when he needed her support. Could have easily stood up in court and saved him from a prison sentence, by revealing the truth.

'Hey baby, don't cry.' Brian's sleepy voice, bringing her back to the sanctity of the bedroom. Having not realised tears are streaming down her face until Brian's arms wrap reassuringly around her. Causing further guilt, as he's been gentle and kind towards her, under the illusion she is carrying his child. Along with a guilt complex over the arrest, and their home being dismantled while the Garda carried out their extensive search. Happily agreeing to allow Danny stay at her mother's for safety, now he thinks someone is out to hurt them. At one stage, even insisting she go to her mothers, his renewed kindness barely recognisable. 'We will find out whoever did this to us, and make them pay. I promise you. I have a pretty good idea, who the sorry son of a bitch is.' Of course, he is convinced the Murphy's are behind it, and is possibly right. She had phoned Lexi, when they were released from prison without charge, because the Garda couldn't find any drugs or firearms in the house. Lexi knew nothing of the raid, as her cousin was waiting for the name of a possible supplier, to catch Brian away from the house, when he is dealing with his buyer, as planned. 'We'll get the house fixed up too babe, I promise you.' Brian continues to comfort her kissing her forehead, acting like a caring boyfriend.

'The cell, I can't get it out of my head, trapped and frightened. I didn't think, I'd ever get out again.'

'I'm sorry you had to go through that, Evie.' He nuzzles her, pulling her closer to him. 'He must have been terrified.'

'Danny is fine, your mam has him, he doesn't know any different.'

'Not Danny! Des, when they arrested him, after crashing and killing that boy. Locked in the cell, he would have known, he wouldn't get out for a very long time.' Brian shoves her away, his face changing to one of fury, the vein on his temple pulsating, teeth clenched.

'What the fuck are you whimpering on about Desmond for? Are you seeing him again?'

Chapter 27

'Oh, Dessie you shouldn't have, I'd never put you down as an old romantic. Must be all the old movies, I have you watching.' Alice teases when Desmond slips into the passenger seat of her little mini, carrying a bunch of flowers.

'Ah...they're for yer Ma.' He admits flushing deep red.

'I'm only kidding, she will love them. You are very thoughtful.'

'You sure?' He has never been as nervous, as he is tonight over the thought of meeting Alice's parents for the first time. He'd known Evelyn, since he was fourteen and couldn't even remember the first time he'd met her parents. Her Da had been a great man, Des getting on better with him than he ever had with Ger. Hopefully Alice's parents will be the same, though he'd understand if they were wary of their daughter seeing someone who'd served a term in prison. In the short time he's known Alice, he has also grown to learn she is close to her parent's and cherishes family values.

Alice, met Agnes the previous evening, when they took her out to dinner at the Malaren Hotel. It had not been easy excluding Ger and making excuses, something Alice had been clearly uncomfortable about. Des could not afford for her to have been insulted by him, at this early stage in their relationship, or worse, belittle Des in her presence. Otherwise the evening went very well, Alice and Agnes chatting like old friends. It had been wonderful to see Agnes relax, as she had been extremely on edge beforehand. He put it down to nerves, just as he is now when it's his turn to be in the spotlight.

'Don't look so worried.' Alice says, as though reading his mind. He leans across, met by the subtle sweet scent of her perfume he plants a soft kiss on her beautifully enticing cherry red lips.

'What if they don't like me?' He says suddenly, hands shaking as he tries to fasten the seatbelt. Wondering for the hundredth time why he'd agreed. 'Do they know about-?'

'Shush.' She gently places a finger on his lips. 'Yes Dessie, they do and they will love you as much as I do.' Her voice laced with sincerity, making Des want to pinch himself. Worried he will wake up one day to find it all a dream, even if it is a happy one, unlike the nightmares which torture him each time he closes his eyes to sleep.

'Do you?' He asks, surprised and elated, hoping it had not been a flippant figure of speech.

'What?' She questions, lucidly enjoying teasing him. Not the type of woman to give her heart easily, seeing something in Des the day she had gone down to the factory floor.

'Love me.' He dares to question, heart pounding in his chest, awaiting for her reply.

'I love you Desmond Shanahan, start believing in yourself, believing in us.'

'I love you too...I just can't believe...' a raised brow from Alice, stopping him mid-sentence. She switches on the engine and once again he wonders how he has fallen so lucky, still not quite believing he deserves this amazing girl sitting next to him. 'Oh...I almost forgot, I got accepted for the course.' He says, as they drive out of Kilmer Cove.

'Des that's fantastic.'

'It's all thanks to you...I'm looking forward to it, you know excited.' He beams. 'I'm grateful to Conor for giving me a chance when no one else would, you sure he won't mind...you know, rebuffing his offer of staying on.'

'Don't worry about offending Conor, I guarantee he'll be delighted too.' Her reply pleasing Des, having never felt happier, not even before the accident. For a brief moment he worries it could all come crashing down around him, as it had done so easily before. Immediately banishing the thought, if prison has taught him anything, it is how precious life and the freedom to live it is.

'Desmond come in, we have heard so much about you.' Elizabeth Richards is a stout woman, enjoying nothing more than to cook and look after her husband, children and grandchildren. She has six children in all, four of them married, the only ones left living at home are Alice, and her youngest brother Sean. Elizabeth, is very different in personality than her older sister Gloria, whose only child is Conor. Conveniently falling pregnant to trap the very rich and handsome Quintin O'Dowd. 'You are as handsome as Alice, said you are.' This comment from her mother causing Alice to flush, her cheeks turning pink, secretly pleasing Desmond.

'Mum!' Alice squeals, in mock horror.

'Here Des, come and meet my dad.' Alice takes him by the hand into the warm homely kitchen, where pots of vegetables and potatoes are boiling on the stove.

'Nice to meet you son.' Maurice stretches his hand for Desmond to shake, his grip firm. His welcome sincere, finding Des wishing his own father could be as amiable.

Dinner turns out to be just the four of them, Sean has text Elizabeth to say he is running late. Over the course of the meal, roast lamb with all the trimmings, Desmond, learns where Alice gets her no nonsense, but caring ways from.

'So Des you're in the factory with Ali.' Maurice says. 'I hear Conor is looking to expand the business. He's all work that one, no wonder he hasn't settled down.'

'Dad,' Alice protests. 'We shouldn't be discussing Conor's business.'

'Aye, or his lack of love life.' Elizabeth adds, with a wry smile. 'Living with my sister and Quinten would put anyone off marriage. How do you like working in the factory Des?' She shifts the subject slightly. Luckily Des doesn't have to say he hates it and sound ungrateful, as Sean arrives in.

'Hey guys, hope ye kept some for me.' Sean bursts in the back door, as though there is a fire. 'Traffic was crazy coming out of Carraigbrin. I'm bloody starving.'

'Where's yer manners lad.' Maurice says, as Elizabeth immediately rises from the table to dish him a plate of food, while voicing her own protests over his manners.

'Sean at least say hello to Alice's guest. Then sit yerself down, I've a nice bit of roast lamb.'

'Sorry, lad, pleased to meet ya, Desmond isn't it.' Sean beams. 'I've heard all about you.' His words causing the room to fall deathly silent. Des convinced he can hear Alice's sharp intake of breath. 'You're a whiz with cars. Did you remap Paul Quilty's Celica a few years back?' Sean adds, seemingly not having noticed the sudden chilly atmosphere. This comment though receiving a round of gasps of relief around the room.

'Ah....ya, I did. Nice car that one.' Des replies, relieved to be chatting about his passion. 'She was a nineteen ninety-seven model. Does he still have it?' He launches into his comfort zone.

'Yeah, it's been off the road cause he couldn't afford insurance, but he got a job recently so's hoping to get her back in use again.' Sean informs him. 'Hey, do you want to come out to the garage and see the old Celica I'm restoring.'

'What year is she?' Des asks eyes lighting up, wondering why Alice has not told him about her brother's shared passion for cars.

'You promised not to badger Des about cars.' Alice warns, her face crumpling with displeasure.

'But Ali,' Sean almost pleads like a child. 'Des has to see it. He's the only person I know, who will appreciate the beauty and the three litre engine.' He points out, in a literal manner. 'It's deadly, man, she's rare, nineteen seventy-five, not many around anymore, had to get her imported.'

'Looks like you've lost him love. Can you not see the passion in the man's eyes?' Maurice winks at Alice, resulting in her sighing heavily while throwing her eyes to heaven.

'What about yer food? I thought ye were starving.' Elizabeth protests placing an overfilled plate of food on the table.

'Would you mind?' Desmond throws Alice pleading look, showing every sign of his excitement etched in his gaze.

'Ah, Ali sur leave the lad have a look.' Maurice intervenes again, leaving her with little choice.

'Go on.' She replies with a heavy sigh, knowing she has already lost him to her brother and their shared passion for cars.

'Great stuff.' Sean beams, 'sur, I can warm me dinner up in the microwave, mam. We won't be long.' He kisses his mother on the cheek as he passes by, leading Des outside. Elizabeth shakes her head, having to put the plate back on the counter, her warm smile indicating bemusement rather than annoyance.

To the rear of the Richard's bungalow, stands a large purpose-built garage. The type of thing Desmond would have once dreamed about owning, on his own plot of land. Being able to pop out and work on a project whenever he wanted. Sean unlocks the door, pulling it open to reveal, a 1975 Toyota Celica GT2000, recognisable in its form to many even if they aren't aware of its origin.

'Isn't she a beauty?' Sean beams with evident pride. 'I've had her about six months now, she was a bit of a wreck, but I've been slowly restoring her. Spend any spare cash, I have on parts. Put in 40mm dual throat Mikuni Solex Carbs, which help the 18R-G make 145 bhp. She purrs, I can tell ya.' Desmond slides his hand over the shining paintwork, caressing the curve of the bumper. Sean is right, she is a true beauty. 'Sit in and switch her on, feel her power. Better than sex,' he declares with a wry grin. You can have a drive if you like, go on sit in she has leather seats.' Sean insists, his eagerness evident. 'I worked and saved to buy her, man, I always dreamed one day I'd own one, still can't believe she's mine. Here take the keys.' Sean opens the driver's door, Des hesitates for a moment before sliding into the driver's seat and caressing the steering wheel, inhaling the smell of the leather interior. He is in heaven, a feeling he thought he would never experience ever again. He inserts the key turning it halfway, listening to the fuel pump kick into life, waiting in anticipation as he primes the carbs before finally turning the key the rest of the way to be engulfed in the cocoon of her growl, his own heart fluttering in time with the warming revs and sound from the intake.

'Des, what are you doing?' Alice stands silhouetted by the garage door, brow furrowed, angelic face etched with horror.

'Relax, Ali. He's only sitting in to listen to the engine.' Sean says, but when Des looks out of the windscreen it's not Alice he sees, it's Jack. Beads of perspiration form on his forehead, he is back in the Subaru can see the scenario clearly like watching a film, only in slow motion. Deafened by the sound of metal meeting concrete and glass shattering, the seatbelt tugging at his skin before the impact of the airbag. Then everything stops, a resounding silence until the sound of sirens.

'Des are you alright?' Alice is by his side, her gentle voice filled with concern, eyes wide searching his.

'He came out of nowhere, I didn't see him.'

'Des it's okay.' Alice assures him. He focuses on her as though seeing her for the first time, tears blurring his vision. She wraps her arms around his neck pulling him to her. 'I know you wouldn't hurt anyone, not intentionally.' Words he badly needs to hear.

A little while later, Desmond and Alice say goodbye to Elizabeth and Maurice, leaving Sean scoffing down his food in the kitchen. Seemingly unperturbed by Desmond's breakdown in the garage, having slipped quietly away leaving the couple alone, to talk. There had been no mention of Desmond's meltdown from Sean, when they went back inside the house. He simply, patted Des on the shoulder indicating in a manly way his understanding and compassion. A gesture Des has dreamed of getting from his own brother.

'Your family are lovely.' Des says, slipping into the passenger side of her mini.

'They liked you, I can tell.' She replies. 'Not everyone judges, you know. Some people realise things happen out of our control and are willing to make allowances.'

'I don't know what, I would have done if it weren't for you over these past few weeks. Was beginning to think, I would be carrying my prison sentence around like a flashing light over my head warning people.' He leans over, kissing her on the lips.

A car pulls into the yard breaking their spell. Alice's facial expression changing to one of apprehension.

'You must be Desmond.' A tall thin man, leans in the open widow of the mini. His demeanour far from friendly.

'Yeah...n...nice to meet you.' Desmond raises his hand to shake in the same way Maurice had done, to find it not reciprocated.

'Des, this is my older brother Adam.' Alice intervenes. 'We can't stop, our movie starts in less than half an hour.' She turns the key starting the ignition to highlighting their need to leave. Adam on the other hand is not perturbed and speaks his mind.

'You better take care of my sister, or you'll have me to answer too. And don't think this is some idol older brother threat. I know all about you, and that friend of yours Brian Lennon.'

'Adam, mind yer business, mam told you not to be coming round and spouting off.' Alice replying to her brother in a way, Des has never heard her speak before now.

'Brian Lennon, is no friend of mine.' Des, barely seizes a chance to stress this as Alice puts the car into gear, driving away. The encounter leaving him unsettled, especially, as Alice is unusually quiet for the rest of the evening. Giving him a quick peck on the cheek, claiming to be too tired when he suggests coming in, as she drops him home.

Agnes is sitting at the kitchen table wrapped in her dressing gown staring at the mug, her hands are wrapped around.

'Taken to reading the tealeaves Ma.' Des cajoles, trying to regain his earlier bravado as much as lift his mother's spirits. She tries to hide her grim expression with a weak smile. 'Everything alright?' He asks, concerned. The glow of happiness she had been wearing the previous night when they were out, long faded.

'Evelyn called round tonight, said she needed to speak to you. Asked for your number, but I refused. I assume it was the right thing to do.' He could imagine his mother's hostility towards the woman who had deserted her son in his hour of need. 'I told her you've met someone, you don't need her disrupting your life again.' Agnes continues, asserting her motherly protective instinct. 'Kept, insisting she had something important to tell you. In the end, I agreed to take her number, she wasn't leaving otherwise. Told her I'd pass it on, but not to expect a call. She has some nerve, I'll give her that. You're well shot of her Des.' Agnes warns, having witnessed Des' slump into depression after the accident. By the time he had been released on bail pending a court hearing, she'd packed all her stuff and moved out of their flat. No contact whatsoever, the move cold and uncaring in Agnes' eyes.

'You were right, she's in the past, Ma.' Des takes the piece of paper, scrunching it up he pops the lid of the bin, throwing it in. Relief evident on Agnes's face as he does so. 'Time to move on with my life.' He adds, giving his mother further reassurance. He'd considered ringing his ex-so many times, when in prison. Had hoped she would have at least wanted to visit, and find out what had happened, see if he was alright. In light of the recent discovery, extending the depth of her treachery, Des is glad he had not been foolish enough to.

'Good, how was your night?' Agnes asks, her face having brightened considerably.

'Grand.' Which isn't a complete lie. He fills her in on the important details omitting his meltdown and meeting Adam.

'I'm delighted things are finally working out for you. It's good to see you happy again...something I never thought.' Tears shimmer in her eyes.

'Ma.' He places a hand on hers. 'Ya have ta stop worryin about me. I'll be fine.'

'You're a good lad, Des....always were.'

'I have a good Mam...an she brought me up well.'

'I know, I never asked at the time or throughout the trial....I don't want you to feel under pressure now, but if you need to talk about what happened...I can handle whatever it is, if it helps you. You know, to sleep at night.'

'I wish I could remember, Ma...it would be a lot easier if I could. I see his face, the rest of it, what happened beforehand, what I was doing there is a blank. The doctor in prison gave me tablets to help me sleep. They didn't do anything, so I gave up. Believe me, I've gone over it a million times in my head and none of it makes sense.'

Chapter 28

Des takes a cold shower to wake his body after yet another sleepless night. Each time he closed his eyes, Sarah Connolly's face flashed before him, sat behind the wheel of her car, contorted with hatred as she drove straight at him.

He wanders downstairs, hair wet and dishevelled, to be met by the aroma of fresh coffee, toast, bacon and sausages.

'You didn't sleep.' Agnes says, placing a cafetière of coffee on the table. 'I hope it's nothing to do with Evie calling round, I should never have told you. Alice is a lovely girl, she respects and cares for you, something Evelyn never did.' Her words blunt, but true. Desmond aware of this as much as his mother. Mindful of his feelings towards Alice, her company refreshing in contrast. With Evelyn, it had been about what she wanted in life. A house, career, suggesting they get a new sensible car. The lavish wedding she had wanted, looking back, everything about her had been materialistic, a show for her friends. Alice has a zest for life, wanting to enjoy every moment as she lives it rather than planning and wanting material things.

'Don't worry Ma, I have no intention of risking what I have with Alice for Evelyn. I told you last night, she is in the past. You have nothing to worry about.'

'Good, now get this into you before a day's work.' By the time he arrives at the factory, his spirits' have lifted considerably. Nothing could knock what he has now, Des accepting, Adam had been rightfully concerned for his younger sister. As for the nightmares, he should be used to them haunting him, as they have done for over five years. Though, it had always been Jack's face he'd seen in the past, not Sarah. Since his release, seeing Brian, remembering what he was like when they were all hanging out, Des has questioned, could he have been drawn in to temptation? Considering all the pressure he had been under from Evelyn, the toll it was taking on him, both physically and mentally. As he takes up his place on the line across from Malik, he brushes the notion away.

'I think someone iz very happy today, yes.' Malik says, his smile wide. This pleases Des, as he had been quiet in recent days.

'Lena ask if you, and Alice would come to dinner Friday night. She likes to cook for friends, her Bigos, served with homemade rye bread, pyszne. She's how you say it getting cabin fever, being at home. I say she should rest but Lena is not a woman to sit still for long.'

'Thanks Mal,' the invitation delighting Des. 'I'll say it to Alice, I'm sure she'd love to.'

'Lena, she meet Alice many times when she work for Mrs. O'Dowd, they become good friends. Mrs. O'Dowd, she leave for Spain, so no work for my Lena. Mrs. Connolly, she offer Lena job in Oceanic Temptations....dis is better for my wife, she like it there. Mrs. Connolly, she let her cook food from our country...customers' say it very good!' Malik informs him, clearly proud of his wife. 'Mrs. Connolly much nicer to work for...she has been so good to her this past week specially, Lena say this is her way of thanking our friends. There'll be eleven or twelve for dinner...I'm not sure if Paul, he has a partner.' Not being the type of person to indulge in idol gossip, Malik has no idea mentioning the Connolly family causes a problem. Never mind inviting Des to a dinner they are also invited to. Des also oblivious to Lena's recent accident, as Malik is not normally so forthcoming about his personal life.

'Oh...right.' Des simply replies, to the subject of Lena being employed by the very kind Mrs. Connolly, not sure what else to say. Not wanting to indulge in discussing the Connolly's, either directly or indirectly and voicing events he has tried so hard to bury deep in the recess of his mind. Des carries on working, hoping it is the end of the discussion. Beside him, Jimmy has remained unusually quiet up until this point, a factor which rapidly changes.

'Ah, now Mal, did no one tell ya?' He blurts loudly, indisputably happy to offer his opinion. 'Ya can't go mentioning the Connolly's around Des here. It's a bit of a sore subject.'

'My apologies Desmond, I did not realise, you have...how you say....bad feeling. I did not mean to offend anyone...I will talk with Lena, we can make other arrangements.'

'You haven't Mal.' Des responds, throwing a warning look in Jimmy's direction. Not wanting to offend Malik and have the man thinking badly of him, Des tries to smooth the situation. 'There is no need to apologise.' He adds, voiced etched with sincerity while keeping his gaze fixed on Jimmy, who appears to be jittery. Beads of perspiration have formed on his forehead, unusual in light of the cool conditions they work in.

Following Malik's example, Des returns to his duties, keeping his head down and concentrating on work. It should have been the end of the discussion, but Jimmy is not about to let it lie. Knowing by smearing Desmond and presenting him in a bad light, it would tarnish his friendship with Malik. A trait of Jimmy's personality, Des has forgotten about. There was many a time had he played Brian and Des against each other, if there was a way of building conflict Jimmy would find it, then stand back and watch it all crumble. Little did Des realise at the time Brian could not be trusted either.

'Yeah, Des ran her son down an killed him...did time inside didn't ya Des.' Jimmy puts this in a context, as though it is something to be proud of. For Desmond, it's a chapter of his life which haunts him more and more each day. Throwing a pleading look in his direction, does not silence Jimmy, who is now delighting in having become the centre of attention. Not only is Malik listening but everyone on the floor has stopped what they were doing to stare at them. A dozen faces, along the line focus on Des, knives still in their hands. Curious to hear any titbit of detail they had not heard before, regarding the death of Jack Connolly and imprisonment of Desmond Shanahan. The whole scenario causing Des to inadvertently perspire from apprehension. 'Sarah Connolly doesn't think it's enough, she'd like to see our Dessie burned at the stake, wouldn't she Des?' This comment is followed by one of Jimmy's hideous laughs, amusing no one but himself. 'Having the two of them at the same dinner table, I'd advise ya ta hide any sharp objects.'

'Dis is not appropriate time to speak of this here Jimmy.' Malik speaks in a stilted tone, Des sensing his disgust. 'I'm sure it is very painful to have lost her son.' A grief cutting deep for Malik, which no one else listening would know about and why would they, Malik is a private man.

'Jimmy put a sock in it.' Des hisses, feeling the pressure of everyone's eyes anchored on him, their expressions similar to Malik's, making him feel sick in the pit of his stomach, wishing the ground would literally swallow him up. 'It was an accident, I never killed anyone.' Des seethes, trying to redeem himself in Malik's eyes, above anyone else's. His words only fueling Jimmy with more ammunition.

'Ah lad...sur you were givin it nearly a tonne...I heard. Didn't they have to scrap the Scoobie, fecking waste of a class car that. I tell ya Mal, Des here used to polish it every weekend like a nonce....not a scratch it had before whacking it.'

'Driving dangerously and taking a life is no joke Jimmy. Only last week my Lena was knocked off her bike. This impatient driver, she overtake a tractor forcing her into zee ditch and she ended up in hospital. It is the reason Lena wants to thank everyone for their kindness, Mrs. Connolly in particular. We had no idea...' The penny finally dropping with Des, in an odd way grateful for Jimmy's intervention as turning up and facing Sarah is a situation he could not imagine. Malik's eyes bore into Des, emanating his own pain. 'It is very sad that Sarah son die. We cannot begin to understand the grief and loss a mother must endure. For a parent to bury their child....part of them is buried too.' Malik's blunt words bringing a deathly silence, in their wake. Des swallows back bile, seeing the hatred he'd become engulfed in. Every person on the factory floor would feel empathy for Sarah and blame towards Des. Apart from Jimmy, he does not know what true emotion is. The only good thing being he has finally shut up.

'It's not lunch time yet.' Mossy, the supervisor appears. 'Why have ye all stopped working? 'We don't pay ye, ta stand around doing nothing.' His face stern, immediately inciting everyone to put their heads back down and continue with their work in silence. 'I'm tellin ya, Duggan yer on a short leash.' Mossy levels Jimmy a glare. 'I been hearin stories lad, an Mr. O'Dowd wouldn't be too pleased, so ya better start keepin yer head down from now on.' Jimmy does not furnish Mossy with his usual protests, instead his face turns sickly pale making Des wonder, what he has been up to, riling Mossy.

When the lunchtime bell finally sounds, Malik walks away keeping his head down. Des certain the other man's eyes are brimming with tears, leaving him with the same feeling he had, when Charlie had refused him, his job back. Ashamed, Des flees outside keeping his own head down, avoiding eye contact with everyone, especially Jimmy. The last person he wants to spend his lunch hour with.

'There you are, I thought we were meeting in the canteen.' Alice says, a frown on her soft features. Des is sitting in his old spot around the side of the building, staring aimlessly out at the sea as though expecting to find answers. 'What's up?' she asks immediately sensing something was wrong, resulting in Des feeling worse, if at all possible. Convinced he is unworthy of her kindness and definitely undeserving of her love, his reply is cold and blunt.

'I want to be alone.' He declares sounding like a petulant child, expecting her to walk away without question. Alice is made of more than that, she is no fool, having heard the gossip in the canteen and enduring hushed whispers as she passed by. Small town pettiness is not something she would either belittle herself to partake in, nor would she let it get to her.

'Don't push me away Des.' She says with conviction. Not a person to beg, rather wanting him to realise he does not have to deal with this alone. 'I had no idea, they would invite us to dinner along with the Connolly's. Lena and I, we never talk about...I would never discuss your business behind your back. There are enough people already judging you unfairly. I didn't tell you about Lena's accident because, I didn't want it raking up painful memories.' Her reasons may be genuine, but they highlight cracks beginning.

'Please Alice.' He pleads. 'Why are you interested in me? It doesn't make sense, you should be with someone....' He doesn't know who she should be with, but it isn't someone who had been in jail like he has. Someone, who people would view as a murderer. Unfair, to allow Alice be painted with the same brush, shunned and ending up broken like his mother. He couldn't live with that on his conscience. 'Please, go away.' His tone harsh and cold, he stares at the concrete ground avoiding her expectant gaze. Preventing him from witnessing, silent tears streaming from her eyes, smudging her mascara causing blue streaks down the side of her face, as she reluctantly slips away. He might think, she does not deserve to be with someone like him, when realistically, Alice doesn't deserve his brutal rejection.

The afternoon drags with a deafening silence, causing an uneasy atmosphere. Not a single attempt is made to ignite conversation, not even from Jimmy. Working like a robot, getting more salmon gutted in one afternoon than he normally got done in a week. Mossy noticeably passes up and down the line, with increased regularity throughout the afternoon. His cold gaze constantly fixed in Des' direction, casting further unsettlement.

Des is relieved when the evening bell sounds, indicating the end of the shift and working day. The expectancy of receiving a cold shoulder from Malik, does not ease the rejection when it happens, only leaving a cruddy taste in Desmond's mouth as he walks up the hill towards Seaview Park.

'I haven't anything for your tea.' Agnes says, as Desmond walks through the back door. 'I wasn't expecting you home.' She frowns, 'didn't you say, you were going to Donegal with Alice?'

'I'm not hungry Ma.' Des replies, as he places an envelope on the table. Avoiding the latter part of her question. 'This is for you and Dad.'

'Has something happened love?' Agnes dries her hands on a towel. Seeing in her son's face, the sadness that had been there every time she visited him alone in the prison. The visible change from hope to desolation. This is not the same man, who had been filled with optimism less than twenty-four hours ago. Strongly suspecting, Evelyn has something to do with the change and regretting informing him of her visit.

'Everything is fine Ma, I'm a little tired that's all. Think I'll have an early night.' He make's for the door, with the intention of hibernating away from local incrimination. Just as he had cocooned himself in the flat, away from the prying world after the accident. If he lay down on the bed and closed his eyes, then he could possibly pretend to be back in Castlerea. Listening to Cecil talk of plans for a future business adventure. Of living somewhere, no one would know your past, could judge you by your mistakes only able to take you at face value, a fresh start.

'What's in the envelope?' Agnes questions, stalling Des from his planned quick exit.

'Plane tickets to go to Edinburgh, and see your granddaughter. I've squared it with Phil, he's looking forward to seeing you and Da. There's a bit of cash too, for taxis and spending money, should be enough to see you through.' It is everything he had put by over the past few weeks. His escape fund, in retrospect his parents need it more than he. They are the ones who have endured alienation in the town, for over five years. He had witnessed it in every one of their faces today, their disgust. It was Malik's brush-off, which clawed deeply bringing with it a clear awareness.

'I don't understand.'

'What is there to understand? Des questions, becoming impatient. 'Phil won't come home because of ...besides travelling with a new-born is not ideal. It makes sense, you and Da get the holiday you both deserve. Time away from here, and what better way to spend that time, than with Amelia.' Des forces out a weak smile for encouragement. 'Gina has the spare room made up, sounds like they have plenty room. They are both really looking forward to seeing you.'

'I don't know what to say.' Tears brim in her eyes, threatening to overspill. Her fingers touching the envelope, without lifting it from the table, scarcely able to believe its contents.

'About what?' Ger asks, in his usual gruff manner, returning from walking Roxy. Des planned to be upstairs in his bedroom before his father got back. His rebuff, the last thing needed right now, not expecting, nor wanting any praise.

'Des has bought us flights to Edinburgh to stay with Phillip and see Amelia and money to spend, look.' Agnes picks the envelope with a shaky hand, passing it to her husband. Ger stares at its contents for a moment, bewilderment stamped on his leathery, weather beaten face. Des is about to slip silently away, this time stopped by his father's unpredicted words.

'You gave all this for us?'

'Yes...yes I did. You both deserve a break, it's not much consolation for all I've put you through.' Des shifts restlessly, still positioned at the threshold of the room, wishing to escape upstairs. 'I want you to know, I'm sorry for everything I've put you through, with the accident. I realise exactly how hard it's been, and hope you both enjoy seeing your granddaughter, and Phil of course.'

'I...' Ger is deemed speechless for the first time, Des can remember. If he didn't know any better, he'd swear there are unshed tears in his father's eyes. Des turns to make his exit. 'Thanks son.' It is the nicest thing his father has ever said. Two simple words meaning a lot, leaving Des with an overwhelming sense of emotion, as he climbs the stairs to his room.

There are two missed calls and a text from Alice, on his mobile, he switches it off. Blocking any communication from her is for the best, she might hate him now but will soon be thankful. It'll be hard to avoid her for the remaining weeks in the factory, without wanting to relent. Harder than the cold shoulders, he will have to endure from his peers on the factory floor. Planning to treat it the same way as, his last few weeks in prison. Survival had been his focus then, a sentiment he did not expect to become a necessity on release. He could do it, keep his head down and finish his parole.

'Des, can I come in.' Agnes voice comes from the other side of the closed door, along with a gentle knock.

'Sure Ma.'

'That is a very generous gift.' She says, on entering. 'Dad is bowled over by your generosity, though, I do think myself the amount is a little too much.' Agnes raises her hand slightly indicating for Des to hear her out, having opened his mouth to protest. 'Don't get me wrong, it's not that I'm ungrateful. It must be everything you have earned, over the summer and I thought you are planning to get an education. Surely you'll need a bit put by.'

'Ma, I have enough.' Des insists, 'or will have by the end of my parole. I...I've decided not to study after all. I rang a friend earlier, there's this job, bit of an opportunity really, so I'd be mad to pass it up. It means moving away but I think it would be better in the long run. Eventually, Kilmer Cove might forget me and allow you an Da get on with your lives.' seeing her expression darken he quickly adds. 'You and Da can come visit when I'm settled.'

'I see.' Though she clearly doesn't, as sadness creeps back into her lined face. 'Where exactly are you thinking of moving to?'

'Spain.'

'Jesus, Mary and Joseph, that's further than Edinburgh. What's happened Des, and don't say nothing? Have you and Alice had a falling out?'

'No nothing like that,' he decides to be honest. Since there was no easy way of doing what he has to do, but if anyone deserves the truth, Agnes does. 'Alice, is a wonderful person, makes me happier than I've ever known but she deserves better than me, Ma. I realise that no, and if you and Da have any chance of resuming a normal life, then I should not be around as a constant reminder of what happened.'

'You're a good boy Des, you always were.' She takes hold of his hand fighting back unshed tears. 'I know you think, because I'm your mother it's easily said. I'm proud of the way you've faced everyone here. I can't pretend to be happy you are leaving, especially so far away, but I do understand. Don't ever forget I love you, and you have a home here if it doesn't work out in Spain. You are always welcome back.'

'Thanks' Ma, I couldn't ask for a better mother, you've stood by me, I'll never forget that. You have to remember to put yourself first sometimes. Now get packing, enjoy every minute you get to spend with Amelia. Leave Kilmer Cove and the cloud of the past five years behind, even if it's only for a short time.'

'You'll be alright when we are gone?' Her boys, might both be in their late twenties, Agnes would never stop caring and being a mother.

'I'm grand Ma.' He hugs her, struggling to maintain a poker face. As soon as, Agnes closes the door, Des pulls the posters from the wall, shredding the pictures of his beloved cars and the cruel past into tiny pieces.

Chapter 29

With a couple of free hours to spend Sarah decides to go for a run, as she is desperately trying to fit in her training for the marathon, with the growing demands of the campsite's welcome success. The only dark cloud still hovering over their success is the unsettled dispute with the will. Aine's silence, along with no communication from her solicitor, becoming a growing concern. A silent demon, neither herself, Tommy nor Lily wish to mention aloud, for the reality of what they might lose kicking in. At least since the barn fire there has been no further damage, or problems. Paul's CCTV proving to be a valuable deterrent for any would be vandals.

Sarah picks up her pace a little, cutting down through a laneway, which runs between the primary school and a residential property. Catching the scent from sweet peas in the garden as she glides passed. The school adjacent, much bigger than the days when she had attended. The school had housed three classrooms, and barely much more when Jack had attended. With the growing population in Kilmer Cove and its surrounding areas, the school has quadrupled in size, in recent years.

Her reasoning for taking this new route having an ulterior motive, as Lena's accident two weeks ago is still causing underlining annoyance for Sarah. Though Lena has made a fantastic recovery to the extent of treating everyone who supported her to a wonderful meal at her house last Friday evening. The perpetrator who hit her has still not been found. Sarah, unbeknown to either, Lena or Maggie has been keeping her ears peeled in the café, which to her credit has paid off. Having overheard a group of local mothers, who gather in the café each day during term time once they have dropped their children to school. The group returning to the café last week, as their children are attending a summer camp at the school for the next couple of weeks.

'Why is Ariana not joining us?' One of the mother's had said. A tall thin girl with dyed blonde hair and an annoying habit of looking you up and down with distaste, before answering when being served.

'Let's just say, she's a bit weary after her little ding the other week, and is keeping a low profile as far as driving up here is concerned.' The heavy woman, who generally appears to be the leader of the group, or maybe it's the fact she is the loudest, taps the side of her nose with her index finger. 'She drops Chloe to camp and drives straight to the gym in, Carraigbrin for a spinning class. Says she needs to lose the weight, Terry made a comment about her love handles. I told her my Freddie loves a bit of something to grab hold of.' She let out a hideous laugh similar to a hyena.

'Bloody cyclists, shouldn't be on the road.' Piped up the red haired, (definitely dyed too), one. Throwing her peers a distasteful look, as though having caught a bad smell. Sarah had wanted to spill the latte she was serving all over her floral print, lace designer dress. These women being the type Sarah loathes, not through jealousy, but the fact they go around thinking they are better than everyone else, driving SUV's looking down their noses at women who work. With their fake eyelashes, fake tans, and fake nails. Depending on men to supply them with their fake lives filled with possessions. In Sarah's eyes these women are slaves to their own frivolity.

The whole scenario got Sarah to thinking this woman who is avoiding the café must be the same person who hit Lena forcing her off the road, hence the reason she is taking her run by the school, at the exact time the women will be dropping their children to camp. As she the rounds the corner, the street is filled with cars parked on the pavement and anywhere they can fit basically. Some of the drivers stopping on the middle of the road and allowing their children jump out before, ramming the car into gear and taking off at speed. No regard for whether the child makes it safely into the school. One car practically clears the speed bump and lands on the other side with a thud, scraping the front bumper.

'Aye, it's an eye opener isn't it?' An elderly gentleman appears at Sarah's side. 'I live in the bungalow here, my driveway is blocked, an I'm supposed to have my wife at the clinic for her check-up. We'll miss her appointment now. Used to be in term-time, we'd look forward to the summer, then they started up these summer camps. Ya'd wonder why they have kids, can't wait to get rid of them they can't. Throwing them out of their cars, they do. Of course when we bought the house over forty years ago, it was a quiet street, everyone walked their kids to school.'

'I know, I used to go here myself and my son, he loved walking up here. There used to be a field where those houses are and when the blackberries were out, we used to pick them on our way home after school.'

'Aye, those were different times.' The clicking of central locking and lights flashing on the car blocking the man's driveway, alerting them to its owners return. Sarah wastes no time in approaching the owner, whom she recognises immediately.

'Excuse me, you are blocking a private driveway and denying access to residents. You do realise apart from being inconsiderate, it is illegal.'

'I was only dropping off.' Blondie, eyes Sarah up and down, then waves her hand in dismissal.

'That car has been there for nearly half an hour, I needed to get my wife to the clinic.' The man chides, visibly delighted to have a strong back up. His protest met with a dismissive flutter of the woman's eyes. Sarah is not about to let her off easily, and blocks her as she is about to open the driver's door.

'You are preventing me from getting into my car.' She protests without meeting Sarah's glare.

'Now you know how it feels.' Sarah retorts.

'My wife is in a wheelchair you know.' The elderly man points out, fueled with years of pent up angst, now unveiling and brimming over. 'Ye park on the pavement preventing her from being able to leave the house, causing her distress.' His face red, indicating his frustration. Sarah detecting, a possible flush of embarrassment wash over the woman's face.

'Maybe you will think, before parking next time,' she points out spotting a white SUV pull up, the driver's side wing mirror broken. 'I bet that was sickening, to come back to your parked car and discover the mirror broken.' Either the woman doesn't recognise Sarah instantly, out of her normal context or she is playing the game as cleverly as Sarah.

'Oh it's fine I don't use them, I don't know why my husband insists we replace it. It's the third one I've broken off the gate post going into our driveway.' She replies, breezily.

'I know, it's the whole idea of having to bend to check my mascara hasn't run. I find the rear-view mirror so much better for that don't you?' Sarah mocks, but seemingly the other woman has not realised this.

'Ah...yeah...I guess. Though I have mine turned, so I can keep an eye on Chloe in the back when I'm driving. I used to turn round, but I spilt my coffee doing that one day. And coffee stains are a demon to get out of a white lace top. I'd only worn it once.' This prompts Sarah to throw back her head, animating a fake laugh.

'An accident waiting to happen, just like this ole wing mirror, when you're in a rush.' She points out, not wanting to lose sight of the whole point of this conversation.

'Talking of rush, it's been lovely to chat but I'm late for my spinning class.'

'Oh god forbid.' Sarah's tone darkens, unable to keep up the charade any longer. 'Couldn't have that, suppose you'll have to drive a little faster, hope you don't get stuck behind any tractors.' The other woman's face turns ghostly pale, people around them are beginning to stare, prompted by Sarah's voice rising an octave. All willing to stop and take time from their busy lives, to witness a juicy piece of gossip.

'I better...' She reaches for the door handle, to be side stepped by Sarah. 'What are you doing get out of my way.'

'No...not until you admit you ran Lena Janowska off the road last week causing injury and didn't have the decency to stop. She could have been dead for all you knew.'

'I don't know what you're talking about. Get out of my way, you have no right to stop me getting in my car. Making false accusations who do you think you are anyway.' Her facial expression changing as the penny finally drops. Only this woman has less compassion with her realisation and launches into a verbal attack. 'You cannot go around harassing people, just because your son was killed by some kid on drugs. I am a respectable member of the community there is a difference.'

'So you are suggesting, all young people on the roads are a liability and you are entitled to drive erratically because you're what? Older? A woman? Which is it, because my understanding is, anyone who drives dangerously regardless of age or gender shouldn't be allowed behind the wheel of a car.' She cannot believe she is standing up for Desmond. Technically she is not, she is standing up for good young men, like Paul who had fixed Lena's bike, putting a new front wheel on at his own expense. Paul who loves and respects the car he drives and has every right to be on the road, as this woman in her thirties with her SUV. 'Who you are and what you drive is irrelevant, it is the person behind the wheel cocooned in the safety of their metal tank, uncaring of anyone else on the road, especially cyclists' and pedestrians. To people like you, they are a nuisance and in the way of you rushing to the gym or picking your kid up from school. God forbid anyone getting in your path. After all the road belongs to you, and the pavement for that matter, judging by the way you are all parked here this morning. You have no regard or respect for anyone else.' Sarah's face red from her frustration, but not as red as the woman standing shamefaced before her.

'Okay Sarah, you've had you say, come on I'll deal with this.' Maggie says, her tone abnormally cool. One of the onlookers having called the Garda, over the commotion.

'Mags, thank god you're here.' Sarah says, as she turns to her friend. 'This is the woman who hit Lena. Her broken wing mirror is proof, she can be charged with dangerous driving causing harm.'

'Sarah, I said, I will deal with it, you can go.' Maggie's tone cold and detached. Sarah's heart plummets when Maggie does not meet her expectant gaze.

'What the hell Maggie-'

'Sarah are you okay?' Conor interrupts, pushing his way through the gathered crowd. Luckily he'd been passing by on his way to a meeting. Sarah doesn't get a chance to furnish him with a response.

'Conor, could you give Sarah a lift home please. Everyone else go about your business, there is nothing to see here.' Maggie's backlash practically knocking the wind out of Sarah, as does the look of contempt on her freckled face. Confused by the rejection, Sarah willingly allows Conor's steer her towards his car.

'What was all that about?' Conor asks, when they are safely inside the sanctity of his car.

'I think, I just opened a can of worms instead of helping.' The crushing pain in her chest leaving her feeling as though she cannot breathe properly. 'I miss my little boy so much. Lena's accident, shook me up. I keep thinking if I could change things, make a difference. Stop others from suffering the way I have, then at least it would be something. I wouldn't wish my loss on anyone. Not even...' She pauses, staring straight ahead.

'I don't know what to say to you Sarah, I've been so caught up...punishing you instead of being there...especially recently after Paddy's death.' He says appearing jaded and drained of emotion, brow furrowing, revealing a tiny sprinkle of lines on either side of his eyes. 'Jesus, why do I always get it so wrong?' He pulls the car to the side of the road, burying his head in his hands. 'I think I'm the one who made a mess of it all. I should have told you, I knew about Finn, the minute you broke off our engagement and insisted on bringing Jack up as mine.'

'You have nothing to apologise for, I am the one who should be filled with remorse. All the years I thought I was protecting Jack from rejection, filling his head with a fantasy. When the midwife placed my baby in my arms, I decided he didn't need a father. He had me, and I had enough love to give. I understand, my revelation was a shock, a lot to take in. You trusted me, and I let you down. Jack was everything to me, and I let him down too.' Sarah declares, shivering, not from cold but emotion. 'You don't ever get over losing a child, not because he was so cruelly taken but because he was my son, my whole life. From the moment I saw the first scan, I fell in love. A love so unexplainable, it doesn't compare.' Fond memories of Jack causing, Sarah's face to light up, imagining his cheeky grin. 'If we'd married, it wouldn't have changed losing him. He still would have been out running that morning. Jack was an amazing boy...determined to succeed.' Her smile wide, though not quite reaching her eyes. They've glazed over, her mind drifting to another time and place. 'I sound like any mother, I guess.' Her pride evident. 'From the moment he learned to walk, he would run around. His energy knew no bounds, from sunrise to sunset. When he was little he loved nothing more than to go up on the farm and help Grandpa and Tommy. He would come into the kitchen throw his muddy wellies next to my fathers, the pair of them purposefully ignoring my horror after messing my clean floor. Launching into a tale of their mornings' work, barely taking a breath between words.'

'You were a fantastic mother, he was a credit to you.' Conor's eyes glistening from unshed tears. 'Are you okay, you look a little pale?'

'I need some air, do you mind?' she opens the passenger door, before he has a chance to reply.

'Here we can walk down to the park, sit on the bench overlooking main street and the harbour from there.' Conor suggests jumping out too.

'We used to sit there after climbing the hill, eating chips from Quilty's remember?' She reminisces, taking his outstretched hand as they cross the road.

'It's been a while, since I've had the pleasure of your company, Miss Sarah Connolly. I'm not going to let the chance pass by.' The dramatic change in Conor's facial expression unmissable. There is a glint in his eyes, Sarah has not seen in a long, long time. They stroll along the path in an amiable silence, one they had often shared in their youth. Content being in each other's company, yet both knowing they are purposefully avoiding certain subjects. Conor, still holding the barrier he had long put up, and Sarah possibly doing the same. 'You've done some job with the campsite, without spoiling its natural beauty.' Conor says, eventually breaking the silence. 'It appears to be doing well and bringing business to the town.'

'It is pretty special alright.' Sarah replies, swallowing back the thought of leaving, if Aine doesn't agree to the proposal, she had brought to Alan. It has been weeks since she'd spoken to the solicitor. Two more weeks of Martin being under duress unnecessarily, and the farm hanging on by a thread. The only communication from Alan, a warning not to proceed with any more plans of expanding the, campsite until the matter is resolved. Paining Sarah, as they could easily double their bookings each night, if they could start work on new pitches being hooked up.

'Aine wants to take it all away from me in revenge for taking Finn from her, sad isn't it. Considering I never knew they were...'

'Jesus, are you serious.' Conor gasps, clearly shocked by this revelation. 'How can she though?'

'As the eldest, she thinks she should have inherited the house and some of the farm and is contesting the will, Da left.'

'Christ that is low even for her. It's not as though she needs the money or wants to live here...does she?' He glances across at her, deep concern etched on his face.

'I don't understand my sister or her intensions. My only worry now is, what this is all doing to Tommy and Martin.'

'Surely Tommy is entitled to the farm, and what about you? That house is your home, you've never lived anywhere else.' He points out the obvious. 'Look Sarah if there is anything I can do to help. Give you money to buy her out, then...I want to help.'

'Thank you, I appreciate it, though it's not about money.' A tear escapes down her cheek. He automatically reaches out, gently brushing it away. 'Why are you still single Conor O'Dowd? Lots of women would give their right arm to find a caring man like you.' The words flow without thinking. His reply catching her by surprise.

'No one like you.' His voice laced with sincerity, making her want to cry fresh tears all over again. Instead holding restraint, as god only knows what he would think if she turned on the waterworks again. 'I know it sounds corny but you were always there in the back of my mind, sometimes the forefront.' He nervously shoves fingers through his hair. Sarah unable to find the right words to respond, only able to walk in silence by his side. They reach the bench sitting in silence, taking in the view over the back of Kilmer cove Main Street, stretching out to the Atlantic, and the vegetation surrounding. From here, there is a glimpse of the Farm to the left, and Conor's own house to the right. A house he had built overlooking the sea with ample surrounding gardens, hoping to have made it into a home with Sarah.

'Maggie was acting very strange, don't you think?' Sarah says, breaking the spell.

'In what way?'

'I don't know, she was different...cold and distant.'

'Maybe she was just stressed, not often you get a couple of grown women brawling in the town, and one of them her best friend. She wouldn't be used to dealing with it.' Conor replies. Joking and making light of a situation, does not suit the ever serious Conor, deeming Sarah unable to reply. That and the nagging concern over the way Maggie had practically looked right through her. 'I know you said before, protecting Maggie and her marriage, was your reason behind keeping Finn's parentage to, Jack a secret.' Conor reverts to his sensible self, breaking into her thoughts. 'Maybe it's time to tell her the truth, she deserves to know what her husband is really like.' His suggestion may been logical. Sarah aware Maggie would never speak to her again, especially as the lie is far bigger than Conor realises.

'She would hate me for what I've done.'

'There's no denying she would be upset, feel as though everyone has been laughing behind her back, and rightly so. It won't be an easy thing to get past, but be honest Sarah. In light of all the recent secrecy with Aine, it's only fair.' Conor is right of course. If honesty is what he appreciates, then she would need to tell him the truth first.

'Since we are being honest. I need to tell you something, which will put me in a bad light in your eyes.' She turns to face him, sensing his sudden intensity, or is it her own. 'The day after Jack's funeral.' Sarah clears her throat, from somewhere behind she can hear a dog barking and footsteps, willing Conor not to look around and break her resolve, knowing the consequences of her revelation will be irreversible. 'Finn rang in a state over Jack....Maggie was working and his girls were staying with their grandparents, so I stupidly agreed to call over. When he said he'd missed out on Jack, I thought he was sincere. It left me with a terrible guilt that I had not only denied Finn, but like a slap in the face realised, I'd denied Jack. He was gone and I couldn't make up for what I'd taken from him.' Sarah closes her eyes, shivering now from cold. The sun gone from the sky, hidden by dark clouds threating. A gentle rustle of leaves from the trees framing the pathway 'I...we ended up.' Even the thought filling her with shame, expected Conor to hate her, turn away in disgust. Instead he surprises her by wrapping his arms around her, fueling the underlying guilt.

'You're grief was raw, he took advantage, men like him do.' He whispers into her hair, causing Sarah to allow herself sink into his arms sobbing like a child. The tension and grief of the past few weeks, unleashing like flood gates opening. They sit wrapped in each other's arms staring out at the sea, watching life go on as it always does. Watching fishing boats enter the harbour, seagulls eagerly circulating overhead. Delivery vans to and froing from the factory, as Sarah and Conor slip into a comfortable silence. One they had often had before together, when they would sit and study, or read side by side. 'It's beautiful here.' Conor whispers.

'Yes it is.' Sarah replies, unable to banish a feeling of guilt for how happy she is at this moment. 'I didn't end it there.' Unable to lie any longer, years off pressure and guilt unfolding. Opening her soul for the first time in her life, letting him in wholly. 'Do you hate me?' The desire to know truthfully, hating herself in recent times. His body stiffens next to her as he abruptly pulls away, staring out at an abyss. The comfortable silence, now stilted and icy. He eventually stands up turning to face her, looking at her in a way she doesn't recognise as being him. His obvious disgust filling her with shame. Once again, she has crushed his respect for her. Conor, her one true friend who would have done anything for her. Had bared the scars of her rejection for years, now filled with repulsion because of her actions.

'There are little white lies, and then there are seriously destructive ones. I don't think I will ever understand your reasoning, but for now, I need time to let this sink in.' He walks away leaving Sarah desolate and broken.

Chapter 30

'Sorry Paul,' Sarah apologises an hour later, having walked back to the farm, devoid of any energy to manage running.

'No worries it's quiet enough, Tommy has gone up to see Ted O'Neill. There was a few fences damaged bordering the farms last night.'

'Seriously? I thought we'd done with all that, at least the cameras are working around the campsite and outhouses, thanks to you. We'd be lost without ya Paul.' She replies, with sincerity.

'Tommy said it was your idea to give me this job. Thanks for giving me a chance.' His words surprising Sarah. She looks up from checking tonight's booking sheet.

'Paul why on earth wouldn't I? We worked well together at the adventure centre, I knew you'd be perfect.'

'I just wanted to say....don't want you to think.' He hesitates, shifting uncomfortably. 'Well since, I used to hang around with Des Shanahan before...' he clears his throat. 'The way we had cars in common, you know.'

'Paul, I hope you haven't got the wrong impression of me.' Sarah replies, concerned he may think she would see him in this light. Making her wonder is this how the whole town sees her. 'I have no objection to people having an interest in cars. It's not about cars, it's about people's attitudes and irresponsibility behind the wheel. No matter who they are or what car they are driving. My issue with Desmond is his carelessness and taking drugs while driving. If it was a genuine accident then maybe I could find forgiveness, even if it doesn't make my loss any less. If he was in his sixties and did the same thing, in a Micra. It's his actions I'm against.'

'Thanks Sarah, I'm surprised at Des myself to be honest. He used to come across as very sensible, never even used to drink. It's none of my business but taking up with the likes of Brian Lennon and Jimmy Duggan, was his downfall. I didn't keep in touch after he got engaged to Evelyn, our lives were going in different directions by then.'

'I appreciate you being honest with me, Paul.' Sarah flops onto the leather couch which they had delivered the previous day, along with a chunky wooden coffee table. Housing a display of magazines and brochures to give the reception area a luxurious and welcoming edge.

'This business with your sister.' Paul drops his gaze, a clear sign he is threading on territory he is uncomfortable with. 'I know it's not my place to...well I love the farm and campsite. For the first time in my life, I genuinely enjoy getting up in the morning an coming to work.'

'Ah Paul, I'm sorry, we should have been more open with you. I can assure you, your job is safe. The farm is belong to Tommy, no matter what happens he needs to make a living and keep it going. He can't do that on his own as you very well know. You will always have a job here, as long as you want. You have my word.'

'Thanks Sarah, I hope you don't think I'm only concerned about myself. I like working with you and Tommy.'

'And we love having you.'

Later that evening, Sarah ventures into the front lounge, a room she has avoided since before the funeral. The room is dusty, opening the window with the intention of giving the room a polish and vacuum, to keep her mind off her interaction with Conor and Maggie's odd behaviour. The text she sent earlier still unanswered, unusual for her friend. She picks up Jack's communion photograph, carefully rubbing the glass with a soft cloth before replacing it. Next to it a picture of her parents on their wedding day, Paddy gazing lovingly at his new bride, expecting to live a long life together. Moira in a long slim elegant gown, beautiful as any movie heroine. Moira married the man she truly loved, had planned to spend a lifetime with him, bringing up their family, she would never have gotten herself into the mess Sarah had. Convincing herself she was protecting her son, giving Jack a stable home her life's goal. Claiming the love of one parent was enough, because it had been for her. Yet she held the biggest secret from him, the true identity of his father. She felt the absence of her mother growing up. Paddy had been a wonderful father, but Sarah often fantasied about what Maura would have been like. Had Jack done the same, wondered what his father looked like, how he spoke? He didn't even have photographs to look at, or siblings to fill the unanswered inquisitions.

'Caught.' Lily teases entering the kitchen an hour later, catching Sarah eating a tub of chocolate ice cream. 'Thought you are on a strict nutritional diet for your training?'

'Ah, I've another few days before Dini is back. I'll be on form by then he'll never know I faltered, unless of course someone tells on me.'

'Would I?' Lily askes raising a brow. 'I guess you won't be needing any of the chicken curry I've made for tea.' Lily adds, waving a covered bowl around, the aroma wafting enticing Sarah's senses. 'Thought you'd have come in for your tea, since you didn't, Mohammad came to the mountain so to speak.' Forgoing one of Lily's curries would be hard, but she needed to get a run in later after the disastrous attempt earlier.

'Here, I'll go for a run tomorrow.' Sarah jumps up grabbing a fork from the drawer.

'You have no resolve at all, have ya.'

'Not when it comes to food.' Sarah replies savouring the taste of the lovely food. 'Mm...I swear it tastes better every time you make it.' The back door opens again, this time it's Tommy. 'What's this, you two worried I'm in need of company?' She glances from her sister-in-law, to her brother and back.

'Did you go and see Alan last week?' He asks, in an accusatory tone, only Tommy could use and no offence would be taken.

'Yes, well more like nearly three weeks ago, and before you say anything. I couldn't see you lose the businesses. The campsite is a success and will save the farm.'

'Giving up your home, though. Where will you go?'

'What is all this about?' Lily questions, aghast. 'I thought you had spoken to that Fintan Power.' She turns to her husband. 'You said he was nice, and would put our offer to Aine.'

'What offer?' 'A section of the farm and one third equal share in the campsite, along with her original inheritance money to build a house.' Lily informs her.

'What?' Sarah barely able to believe she is hearing this pushes the curry aside, having suddenly lost her appetite.

'We couldn't see you lose your home or it been torn asunder.' Lily points out. 'Why would you give it up?'

'Martin is in a bad way with his mortgage, the inheritance would save his home. I can't have you all suffer because of me. After all, I am the reason Aine is doing this.'

'Sarah, we appreciate what you are doing, what you've tried to do but we can't let that happen. The farmhouse was my home too and Martin's. We won't see it being pulled apart. Let Fintan put our offer to Aine, it's not an ideal solution but it's the best for everyone.'

'A third share in the campsite?'

'As a silent partner, she doesn't get to boss us around, as well as reap from the profits.' Tommy purses his lips together, agitation evident. 'Working alongside you is bad enough.' He winks, indicating to Sarah it is a joke, albeit a very weak one.

'Get out of here Tommy Connolly.' Lily warns jovially. 'We may not be like Paul, the strong silent type but we work hard.'

'Ye sure do, ladies. I'm one helluva lucky man.'

'Take him home, Lil will ya.' Sarah says. 'I should really get my training in and thanks guys...I appreciate you trying to keep the farmhouse for me.'

'It's your home. Let's hope Aine will agree to our suggestion, luckily Alan Sullivan was more interested in his new extension and I managed to stop him from offering yours in time.' Tommy gives her a hug, a rare gesture from her composed brother. 'I can't believe you suggested it, but I do admire why.'

'Let's hope, Aine has some heart.'

'Now you are being ridiculous. Good luck.' Lily squeezes her hand following Tommy outside.

As Sarah is climbing the stairs to bed, exhausted after a rigorous work out and looking forward to a hot shower, her mobile rings. Expecting it to be Maggie, she is surprised to find its Roz's son Vincent.

'Sarah, I didn't know who else to call, you are the only person who understands. I don't even know what to say to her anymore, it's like...she's...'

'What's happened Vinnie?' 'It's mum...she's...' His voice breaks, as though he is trying to catch his breath. 'She's in hospital...I can't bring myself to....she took an overdose.'

Chapter 31

'Are you sure you'll be okay when we are gone?' Agnes asks, placing enough home cooked meals in the freezer to last Des, and possibly half the residents of Kilmer Cove, a month. 'I've labelled all these, make sure you defrost thoroughly before sticking them in the microwave. Can't be too careful, especially when it comes to meat and chicken.' She adds, as though speaking to a child, forgetting Des is very capable of cooking his own meals. Had done when he lived in Donegal and later with Evelyn in Carraigbrin. Des, a dab hand at making delicious omelets, with various fillings.

'Ma I'm twenty-six not six,' He reminds her, trying to hide his impatience. 'I can cook, and use the washing machine, so I'll be grand. You enjoy your holiday and get plenty of hugs with Amelia.' He replies with an edge in his voice, while inconspicuously glancing at the clock on the kitchen wall.

'I wouldn't feel so bad if you hadn't split up with Alice.' Agnes pushes her luck, by veering on shaky territory. 'I don't understand...she's a lovely girl.' Agnes protests, unwilling to accept his feeble excuse of them being incompatible.

'Ma please,' Des sighs, tired of having to explain. His mother's intentions may be good, but she has a terrible habit of making him feel like a six year old. 'We have been over this. Realistically, it wouldn't work between us, with her going back to university in September and now I have this job opportunity in Spain with Cecil. The guy I told you about, we shared a cell in Castlerea....don't look like that, he's sound mam, honest. I'll be heading out there in a few weeks, once I get the money together. Be better all-round if I move on from here, surely you understand.'

'I'm still not convinced you know.' She shakes her head in dismay. 'What exactly is this business he is setting up? It's a lot of money to invest into something you know nothing about.' She searches through her handbag, as though having lost something.

'Ya have the tickets, haven't ya mam?' Des asks, trying to hide his exasperation.

'You have my mobile number don't you. In case you need me.' She sighs reaching for her glasses, popping them in their case and into the bag. 'I wouldn't be able to read the tickets, if I forget them. You should be coming with us anyway.' She protests. 'Now that you and Phil have bridged the gap, you should be coming to see your new niece too.'

'You know it's important, I stay and finish my parole and stick to the rules. Besides, you don't need me tagging along.' Des taps the table with his fingers, silently wishing the taxi would arrive soon. 'This is a holiday for you and dad. A long overdue and well deserved break. Go...have fun...make this time about Phil and Amelia, I'm fine Ma.'

'The taxi is outside.' Ger announces walking into the kitchen, smartly dressed in a new jumper and trousers, Agnes had insisted he buy for travelling, along with a few new shirts for their visit. He'd also gone into a barber's when in Carraigbrin, to have his moustache trimmed and a haircut. 'Here, I'll carry out these cases, while ya do yer mothering thing. I'm sure the boy will appreciate not being smothered for a couple of weeks.' Ger lifts the two heavy cases. 'Christ woman, what the hell have ya got in these? They'll never let us on the plane.' He doesn't wait for a reply. 'Cheers Des take care, while we're gone.' He drops one of the cases with a thud, to pat his son on the shoulder, before hauling the heavy cases out to the awaiting taxi.

'There's a stew in a bowl in the fridge and a Lasagne, that'll cover tonight and tomorrow. Then you have the stuff in the freezer. I know you didn't listen the first time, so I'm reminding ya to make sure and defrost them before you pop them in the microwave. They'll need about three minutes, be sure they are piping hot all the way through.' Agnes fusses, stalling.

'I will, Ma.' Des hugs his mother.

'Thanks for this Des.' She wipes a tear, which has slipped down her cheek. 'I know he hasn't said, but your father is grateful.'

'Aye, and he can speak for himself too.' Ger appears unexpected in the doorway. 'Thanks son.' He shake's Des' right hand, bringing round his left to slap him on the shoulder. The unanticipated gesture taking both Des and Agnes by surprise, causing Agnes to shed more tears. 'Come on woman, or we'll miss the flight. Leave the lad have a bit of peace.' He urges her towards the door. 'We'll ring ye, when we get there.' Ger follows Agnes, having shown more affection towards Des in that moment, than his whole life. 'Oh,' he pauses at the threshold. 'Ye won't forget to take Roxy for a walk, every day and only give her the food I've left. No treats, as they upset her stomach.'

'Sure dad, I'll take good care of her.'

'Right son, I'm sure ye will.'

Des checks his watch, he would have to walk Roxy when he gets back from Donegal. Having refrained from mentioning to his mother, Gary had phoned the previous day and asked him to come into his office for a meeting. Gary had been vague, as to why. Des assuming it to be a formality, due to being more than halfway through his parole period. Possibly a review of some sort. Pulling on his jacket, Des grabs a key and sprints to the bus stop. To his dismay, Jimmy pulls up alongside while he is waiting.

'Where ya off ta?'

'Donegal.'

'Hop in, I'll give ya a lift.'

'It's grand J, the bus I'll be here any second.'

'Feck sake, Des get in will ya.' Jimmy insists making it impossible to say no. An old couple also waiting, eye them with obvious distaste.

Working in the factory had been awkward over the past week. Missing being with Alice more than Des expected, although not wanting to admit this to himself. Having passed her a couple of times in the hallway, the sadness etched on her face almost causing him to crumble and relent. They will soon be following their own separate paths in life. Des having no doubt a girl like her, would meet someone more worthy of her affection. Des is also missing Malik's friendship, since the day Jimmy had told him about the accident, Malik has taken to offering polite hellos and goodbyes, all other conversation completely ceased. The only person who talks non-stop each day is Jimmy, seemingly oblivious to the change in atmosphere around him.

'Where ya plannin on goin?' Jimmy asks, as soon as Des gets into the car. Jimmy shoves the gearstick pushing his foot heavy on the accelerator, he spins the wheels as they pull away from the kerb. Why he regularly performs this, Des has never quite figured. Knowing Jimmy, he has seen it in a movie thinking it cool. In actual fact it makes him look like an idiot, while wearing the tires unnecessarily.

'I'm heading into Donegal, have a few things to do.' Des replies, avoiding sharing too much information. 'Just drop me off in the centre, when we get there.' He adds, wishing he'd stood his ground and waited for the bus.

'I have ta stop off in Carraigbrin on the way, it won't take long.' Jimmy announces, instantly making Des feel apprehensive. The last thing he needs is to be late for his appointment with Gary. Seemingly, oblivious to Des tense demeanor, Jimmy rattles on. 'Did ya hear, Benzo bought a WRX, feckin lovely in satin white pearl with 17" gold alloys?'

'What year and spec?' Des asks, relaxing slightly due to finding common ground.

'I don't know....Jesus, Des it's a WRX, what d'ya need ta know, lad?' There is no point in answering the question, Jimmy's microscopic brain would never be able to understand. Des on the other hand, would have been interested in what torque she has and how many cylinder's she runs on, the engine capacity. The body style, aspiration, and whether it had a catalytic converter, along with its performance stats. 'Feckin nice, I tell ya.' Jimmy pulls into a housing estate, Des recognises as being where Evelyn's mother, Gillian lives. He gets a further surprise when Jimmy stops outside a house, where Evelyn herself answers the door, and is clearly unhappy to see Jimmy. During what appears to be a heated discussion, she glances in the direction of the car, gauging Des. Her expression immediately changing to one of horror. Des swallows hard, regretting allowing himself to be bullied into taking the lift. Unable to tear his gaze from her, he watches the scene play out. Evelyn being pulled inward, replaced by a sullen looking Brian. He and Jimmy chat animatedly, laughing before Brian hands over a small packet. They knuckle bump and Jimmy returns to the car wearing one of his cheesy grins.

As they drive away, Des catches a glimpse of Evelyn peering at them from one of the bedroom windows upstairs. A ghostly silhouette of the girl she had once been, he almost has empathy for her. A reality check, soon quashes his foolhardy sympathy, reminded of her deceit. Jimmy turns right, as they exit the estate.

'Donegal is that way.' Des points out.

'I have ta drop this package to Jodi, only take a sec.'

'Drop me off in the town so, I'll get the bus from there.' Des suggests, trying to sound calmer than he is feeling. Glancing at the clock on the dashboard.

'Chill lad will ya. It won't take long, sur I'm heading in ta Donegal meself. Ya don't want ta be sittin on a smelly bus, that stops at every town on the way.' His reply leaving Des with little choice. Jimmy's eye twitching involuntarily the way it always does when he is nervous about something. Usually, something which ends in deep trouble. Des has already worked out what is in the package picked up from Brian. Brian used to dabble a little in taking drugs, Des knows this and had never agreed, but it was Brian's choice. Dealing however, is another matter in which Des didn't think Brian would be stupid enough to get himself involved in, especially with the likes of Jodi. Although, Des has already learned that Brian is not the person he had thought him to be. With all this in mind it is no wonder, Alice's brother, had been weary of him, possibly thinking he has some involvement too.

Entering the estate where Jodi lives is nothing in comparison to Brian and Evelyn's. Half the houses are boarded up, their tenants long moved on to brighter pastures, and who could blame them in retrospect. It is obvious a couple of the vacant houses are used for drug users to hit up somewhere dry and out of eye sight. Others where teenage gangs gather to drink and have sex with girls whose morals have long departed, along with their virginity. A shiver runs down Des spine, unnerved by the eerie feel of the street, even in broad daylight the place is scary. A far cry from the quaint and tranquil Kilmer Cove only ten kilometres down the road. Even the Garda refuse to come in here if called out, declaring it beyond the duties of an officer, and would rather be sacked than risk their life going into the barren estate as it is referred to. As for Des, it is the last place he wants to be seen. No doubt Jodi would know he had been in prison and why, Jodi made it his business to know everything about everyone. If he spotted Des in the car with Jimmy, he would order one of his many children to bring Des into the house. Des would be ordered to sit on the stained sofa, where they would all stare at him. Jodi, his wife, their children his brothers. About a dozen pairs of eyes, boring into him, each owner clad in more ink than skin flexing their muscles, women included. Bile rises in Des' throat at the thought.

'Stop the car Jimmy.' Des shouts.

'What the fuck is wrong witcha Des.' Jimmy complains.

'Stop the car, I'm going to be sick.' The threat works as he knew it would. Jimmy slams on the brakes, causing Des to hit his head on the windscreen, having already taken off his seatbelt.

'You are a feckin lunatic, ya know tha.' Jimmy shouts, as Des alights the car.

'I'll get the bus Jimmy.' Des replies, catching a breath of air. 'On ya go, I'll see ya later.'

'Please yer feckin self.' Jimmy's eye twitches as he slams the car into gear, spinning its wheels as he speeds off. From where he'd been dropped it takes Desmond half an hour to walk out to the main road to catch a bus to Donegal.

By the time he walks across town to the dull grey building he is twenty minutes late for the meeting with Gary.

'Come in have a seat.' Gary offers, non-discretely glancing at his watch, without mentioning Des' unexplained tardiness. It doesn't take long for Des to figure out why Gary refrained from starting their meeting on a bad footing. 'How are things at the factory?' He asks, leaning back on the chair, perceiving the meeting to be casual. 'Mr. O'Dowd is very happy with your work, from his report.' Gary eases the conversation along gradually with small talk.

'I won't deny the work is boring, but I'm grateful to Conor for giving me a chance when no one else would.' Des replies, wanting to be upfront and honest.

'I see, so you don't intend staying there once your parole period is up.' Gary probes. 'If I might say....I'd like to advise you, it won't be easy getting employment. Jobs aren't exactly plentiful in the current climate and the factory isn't the worst place to work.'

'Don't get me wrong, like I said I'm grateful and Conor is sound, but it's not exactly what I want to do in life.'

'I understand it's not a career, but it is well paid and the conditions are fair.' Gary continues, leaning forward in the chair, resting both his arms on the overly crowded desk. 'With regard to your parole time nearing an end, Mr. O'Dowd has stressed, he would like to keep you on a permanent basis. He did offer the job in the first place, with the intention of keeping you on.' Gary points out. There is a stain on his shirt, bolognaise sauce or something similar. Desmond's eyes are drawn to it no matter how hard he tries not to look. 'I don't mean to belittle you Desmond, but you may find it hard seeking employment elsewhere with your record.' He'd hit a nerve, without realising, Desmond's face darkens, lifting his gaze to meet Gary's.

'I appreciate your concern Gary.' Des replies, trying to hide his irritation by keeping his tone light and his voice low. 'I already have a job opportunity lined up for after my parole period lapses. As I've absolutely no intention of staying in Kilmer Cove for the rest of my life. The town always suffocating, everyone knowing everyone else's business. I hated it before the accident, and loath it now. The place is full of smallminded, judgmental people. Besides, I'm a constant reminder to the Connolly's as are they to me, so it's not an ideal situation.'

'You've not had any bother from them have you. I couldn't imagine they are the type of people-'

'No nothing like that, but like I said. The knowledge is there among the locals, I'd like to start fresh, somewhere new.'

'Somewhere like Spain you mean.' Gary slips the comment in casually so it takes Desmond a few minutes to grasp, what has been said. Des' face turns a bright shade of crimson, it is now clear why Gary has asked him to meet. 'You spent a lot of time with Cecil, whilst in prison. I would have thought you'd be aware of his track record.' Gary doesn't waste any time making his point now the subject has been thrown open. 'As a person, Cecil is a nice man but investing with him in a business you know nothing about. I'd have to suggest caution.' Des opens his mouth to speak, Gary holds up his hand. 'Please hear me out.' He pleads, face etched with genuine concern. 'I'm not advising as your parole officer, I'm talking as a friend so to speak. Someone who realises and dare I, be blunt about this. You get pulled in and trust others too easily. People like Cecil can spot that a mile away.'

'You have got it all wrong.' Des pushes back his chair getting up. 'I know what you are suggesting, I'm gullible.' He retreats to the door, pausing in the threshold. 'Fair enough, I've made bad choices in the past but I'm no idiot. Cecil only ever ripped off rich people, who to be honest had too much in the first place and deserved what they got. I know what I'm doing, thanks for your concern.' Des exits without giving Gary a chance to reply.

Leaving the grey building, Des hastily rushes down the street without paying much attention to where he is going. Agitated by those who shun him, along with those who treat him like a child. He made a mistake, a stupid lack of judgement, one which will follow him around forever. As he makes a sharp turn to his right, intending to go into the town centre rather than home. Des literally collides with a woman causing her to drop one of her shopping bags.

'Sorry.' He blusters, at the same time as she makes her own apology. Des glances up from picking scattered groceries from the pavement, to be met with her angelic blue eyes and flushed pink cheeks. 'Alice.'

'Des.'

'Here, I think....am...nothing seems to be damaged.'

'Thanks.' She replies, clearly as uncomfortable as he is. 'Mam slipped and sprained her ankle the other day, I volunteered to pick up this lot. I didn't think there'd be so much.' She avoids his lingering stare.

'Here let me carry it, where are you parked?'

'Over on new street carpark.' Her tone apologetic, as it is a good ten minute walk. 'Like I said, I didn't realise it would be this heavy.' The conversation stilted as they begin to walk. Des searching for something sensible to say, while Alice walks silently alongside, an intensity radiating between them.

'So how did your mam sprain her ankle, then?' Des asks, feeling the need to instigate a conversation.

'Ah it was silly really.' Alice begins, her lips curl into smile. A gentle breeze, slices through the air carrying with it the sweet scent of her perfume, making Des want to drop the shopping bags and pull her into his arms. Only he doesn't, he simply listens to her tale in silence. 'She was walking along, not looking where she was going. Auntie Glo said, mam was talking away, you know the way she does non-stop. Didn't notice she had come to the end of the pavement. In a split second down she went, her foot rolled underneath her leg. Glo said she heard a crack, then mam roared with pain. She got such a fright, she was paralysed to the ground. Anyway Glo got her to the hospital, she'll be fine, nothing broken they said, just needs to rest it for a few weeks.'

'I'm sorry to hear, give her my regards.' He says, as they finally reach her car. She unlocks the boot enabling Des to put the shopping in.

'Can I give you a lift, are you going back to Kilmer Cove?' Alice offers, her eyes settling on him in a pleading fashion, causing his stomach to flip, being in such close proximity is becoming too much.

'I...ah.' Des hesitates, about to refuse knowing it is a bad idea. Then realises, Roxy has been locked in the kitchen most of the day. The last thing he wants is a stressed dog due to being unfed and needing put out to the toilet. The next bus to, Kilmer Cove isn't due for another half an hour and it would take an age to get home stopping in all the towns and villages on the way. 'Yes, that would be great, if I'm not putting you out.' He replies against better judgement.

'Not at all, hop in.' She replies, face instantly brightening, causing his heart to sink. Knowing he has falsely built up her hopes, only to disappoint her again.

Alice pulls out of the car park, slipping the car into the left lane to bring them out onto the N56 to Kilmer Cove. They shift through traffic with ease in total silence, both wondering how to fill the noticeable gap. Eventually it is Alice, who breaks the silence. 'Your mam and dad, did they get away okay?'

'Yes...yes they did, went this morning.'

'It is a lovely thing you did. I bet Agnes was excited at the prospect of seeing Amelia.' Alice continues, keeping her eyes fixed firmly on the road ahead.

'It's the least I could do for them.' Des replies staring out of the passenger window, extinguishing any further conversation.

Finally, after what appears to have been the longest journey ever, Alice pulls up outside the house in Seaview.

'Thanks for the lift.' Des reaches to open the door, avoiding her expectant gaze.

'What did I do to turn you against me?' she asks, hands clasped tightly on the steering wheel, her knuckles white. Of course she would ask, he should not have expected any less. Alice is an open and honest person, it had been the reason he fell so easily in love with her in the first place.

'You didn't do anything, Alice.' He replies, hoping to sound sincere rather than patronising. Too late, his use of words already sounding like a pathetic cliché. If nothing else, Alice deserves the truth. 'You are the best thing to have ever happened to me. In the few short weeks being with you, I...' wavering, cautious of wearing his heart on his sleeve, after being badly burned in the past. 'People in this town will never accept, it was an accident. I had no control over what happened and I can't have you tarnished with the same brush. It's better if we accept it wouldn't work, besides you are going back to finish your studies and I'm setting up a new business with Cecil. Once my parole period finishes, I'll be moving to Spain.' His announcement obviously a surprise, as it takes a moment for her reply.

'You are never coming back are you?' She asks, remaining dignified and poised, making him love and respect her more. Also making it harder to walk away, knowing he'd most likely never see her smile again. Unable to falter, not for a second, he changes his tone coming across as cold and uncaring.

'Not if I can help it. I finally understand why my brother, Phil feels the way he does now and in a weird way it has bridged the gap which had formed between us. Goodbye Alice.' He gets out before she can see his heart breaking in two.

Chapter 32

'What's going on?' Des asks the following morning as he joins the group gathered outside the factory.

'I don't know the Garda were here when we arrived.' Says a man, Des recognises from working on his line, having no idea of his name. 'O'Dowd told us to wait out here, while they search the premises, that's all I know.'

'I hope we'll be paid, if they're shutting the place.' Another says. 'Can't afford to be out of work, the missus will go spare.' His comments, instigating a few nods and grumbles of agreement.

'Mister O'Dowd is a fair man, he will pay us I'm sure. It is the worry of what all this is for making us edgy, I think.' Malik says, making conversation for the first time in over a week. Even if it's not directly intended for Des, it gives him a lift.

'Rumour is, Jimmy Duggan has been arrested for drug dealing. He and his buddies have been using the salmon farm and factory as a way of smuggling them in.' Sam Jacobs, who also works on their line joins the group. 'Not a brain in his skull that fella. They raided a couple of houses over in Carraigbrin last night after a tip off. Few fellas arrested, then they caught Jimmy's buddy what's his name...mouthy lad, tall fair hair, his missus works in Roaster's.'

'Brian Lennon.' The first man says. Des can feel his face flush, hoping no one will make a connection. He falls back, trying to become invisible in the group.

'That's him, he got arrested taking possession of drugs down at the old pier, from a boat.' Sam's gaze rests on Des as he speaks. 'Hope you haven't anything to do with it. Didn't you used to hang around with that Lennon fellow, and Jimmy, sur.'

'Used to.' Des tries to point out, but the frog in his throat causes his voice to sound weak. Receiving disgruntled stares from everyone around him in return, reiterating their disbelief of him. Des tries to catch Malik's eye but he turns his back, the expression on his face saying more than words. Des is hurt by the lack of trust from them all, he has worked hard since being in the factory, has lived by the rules for over two months and still they view him as the man who killed, Jack Connolly whilst high on a substance. A label he will wear for the rest of his life. He would soon be far away from, Kilmer Cove making a fresh start where no one could judge him by the past.

'Desmond Shanahan, I'd like you to accompany us to the station.' Garda Maggie O'Driscoll appears at his side, wearing a solemn expression as always, one which could freeze hell over. About to protest Des thinks better of it, she does not look like a woman in the mood for any shenanigan's and resisting would only make the situation worse, drawing more attention.

'What are you taking me in for?' He calmly asks getting into the patrol car. He at least deserves to know why all eyes are on him, making judgement. A sickening panic rises in his chest, almost crushing him, a reminder of the morning he had been arrested.

'You can't do this.' Alice shouts pushing her way through the gathered crowd. 'Dessie has done nothing, this is harassment.' Her outburst alerting Conor to the little scene, which is beginning to erupt. Des can feel his face burning, not only from the fact everyone's attention is now focused on his arrest, but the impression he is unable to stand up for himself.

'What are you doing Maggie?' Conor asks, placing a hand on Alice's shoulder to calm her. 'I can assure you, Desmond has no involvement in this. He has worked hard and proved his worth.'

'It's Gard O'Driscoll to you.' Her tone harsh. 'I'll thank you to not intervene in police business, or any other business that has nothing of your concern.' The latter comment, clearly having an underlying meaning, only Maggie and Conor know about. 'Mr. Shanahan is not under arrest, we are simply asking him to accompany us to the station to help with our enquiries. He has a connection with a suspect in this case, whom we arrested earlier this morning. I simply wish to interview him and confirm some details we have taken. Now if you'll move back out of the way, I have a job to do.' The reply curt allowing no regression, leaving Des with no doubt she would try and pin something on him to land him back in prison.

'Sur that's the thanks ye get for helping the likes of him.' Someone shouts from the crowd, having misinterpreted.

'All of ye, get back to work.' Conor shouts, disgruntled. 'I'll ring Gary, Des.' He adds. Maggie closes the door of the car. Des closes his eyes, bowing his head as they drive out of the yard, having never expected to live through this scenario again.

At the station to his surprise, he is brought into the small interview room and not down to the cells.

'Can I get you a cup of tea or coffee?' Gard O'Driscoll asks, receiving a look from her colleague. Her harsh persona dropped, having become almost human in Des' eyes. Her watery smile is not quite reaching her eyes, yet, she's still revealing a side to her, he's never seen before. 'The sergeant has asked us to wait until he returns from Carraigbrin. Wants to interview you himself, has a few questions he wants to ask. I think we might have a few chocolate biscuits to go with the tea.'

'Why am I here?' Des asks, feeling brave due to her softer demeanour. Gard O'Driscoll wrinkles her nose, forehead creasing.

'I'll go an get that mug of tea for you.' In what feels like hours, moments later she returns with a mug of tea and plate of biscuits, making Des worry. She is followed into the small, suffocating room by Sergeant Collins. A small man in his late fifties with grey thinning hair and a moustache.

'Des, before we start, I want to make it clear you are not under arrest. We have a few questions, so if you'd be more comfortable with a solicitor present...though it would slow things down, I must point out.'

'Why am I here?'

'Early this morning we arrested Jimmy Duggan and Brian Lennon, for receipt and distribution of cocaine. They are currently being held in Carraigbrin station.'

'What has that got to do with me?' Des interrupts, becoming increasingly agitated. He slumps back in his seat, rolling his eyes like someone half his age would do when being scolded. Tired of everyone's treatment of him lately.

'Were you with Jimmy Duggan yesterday?' The sergeant asks, seemingly not having noticed Des' discontent.

'Well....yes...but only because, he offered me a lift when I was waiting for the bus.'

'So you went to Brian Lennon's picked up a package and delivered it to...' he pauses looking at a sheet of paper. 'Jodi Garner.'

'No...I mean...Jimmy said, he needed to stop off on the way to Donegal. He called to Brian, I stayed in the car. When he said we were going to Jodi's, I realised it was not good, especially since Jimmy had put the package in the car. I got out, told him I'd catch the bus instead.'

'So you admit, to going to Brian Lennon's house and picking up a package.' Collin's persists, his voice sounding impatient.

'No, I told you Jimmy picked up a package from Brian.' From the corner of his eye, Des gauges Gard O'Driscoll's watchful gaze, her brow furrowed. It makes him wonder was her kindness all a show because she'd finally gotten her wish to see him back behind bars. Visualising her telling Sarah Connolly of her great achievement. Picturing the smile of satisfaction pasted on Sarah's face.

'You accompanied him.' Collin's reiterates in a bid to make the facts clearer.

'Yes, but I didn't know we were picking up any substances. Once I realised something wasn't right I got out of the car.' Des points out, aware any attempt of claiming innocence is falling on deaf ears, yet still states his case. 'I do not associate with Brian Lennon, and haven't done in over five years. I have never had any dealings with Jimmy Duggan, apart from working together in the factory.'

'That's not entirely true though is it, you have been seen in Mr. Duggan's car on many occasions.' Collin's equally points out. The older man's face darkening, tired of hearing feeble excuses over his many years in the job. 'You also admitted to being with him yesterday, am I correct? You admit you picked up a substance from Mr. Lennon, whilst in the company of Mr. Duggan.'

'No.'

'You said, a moment ago you did.'

'I was in the car, but I didn't know what was in the package. I swear. Jimmy never opened it or mentioned anything about a substance. If you are accusing me of something then maybe I do need legal representation.'

'Do you need a solicitor Mr. Shanahan, is there something you would like to tell me, you must have had some idea what was going on. You admit yourself to getting out of the car.'

'My point exactly. The minute Jimmy mentioned going to Jodi's, I realised something wasn't right and I got out of the car. Everyone knows Jodi Garners rep and now you are trying to twist thing around to blame me.'

'So you knew there was drugs involved. You knew the package you picked up from Brian Lennon's, contained an illegal substance.' Collin's persists, thinking he is breaking Des.

'Yes...I mean no, I didn't know, I simply worked it out.'

'We've been here nearly an hour now and it's getting us nowhere. Why don't you cooperate Mr. Shanahan, it would make life a lot easier for us all.' The sergeant says, his expression dull. There is a knock, the young Gard who'd allowed Des to sign late on occasion pops his head round the door.

'Sir, might I have a word outside.'

'Is it necessary?' Collin's tone sharp.

'Yes...sir.' Whilst they are alone, Gard O'Driscoll simply stares at Des, giving the impression she wants to say something but hasn't summoned the nerve. It makes him edgy, her phony sympathetic smile, eyes glittering in the dim light of the room, probably delighted.

'Desmond Shanahan, I am charging you with possession of an illegal substance.' Sergeant Collin's says bursting back into the room. Horrified by these words Des shoots a glimpse in the direction of Gard O'Driscoll, catching a look of pity or maybe he is mistaken. The shock causing Des to zone out as he is read his rights. Facts he is very much aware of, remembering being read his rights with the smell of burning rubber and blood all over the broken windscreen, causing bile to rise in his throat.

◆◆◆

In Carraigbrin, Evelyn has received news of Desmond's arrest. Lexi having already warned her she must pack her bags and get to Belfast, as soon as she can. Only, Evelyn's conscience won't allow her leave until she has laid a ghost from the past to rest.

'Mam will you watch Danny, I have to go to Kilmer Cove.' Evelyn rushes into her mother's house, practically dragging a disgruntled Danny by the hand.

'What on earth for, we have to get on the road, Evelyn we can't miss our chance, you heard Lexi's cousin yesterday, if they haven't enough evidence to charge Brian he will be released. He will want to find out who grassed him up. It won't take long, not even for an imbecile like him to work out who tipped off the Garda.'

'Mam, our bags are packed an ready in the car. I promise this won't take long, I have to do this. I can't let Dessie go to jail unfairly again.'

'What's all this about?'

'Desmond has been arrested. I think Brian and Jimmy have set him up.'

'Honey, I know you want to think better of Des, Your father and I thought highly of him too but he is no different than his friends. Face facts, you have the chance of a new life for you and Danny. Your brother is arranging flights and visa's so we can join him, you can have the career you always wanted.' Gillian pleads with her daughter, desperation etched on her tired and fast becoming withered features. 'We have to get out of here, because if Brian is released, he will kill you this time.' Gillian stops Evelyn before she escapes out the door. Pulling up her top to reveal her bruised torso.

'Mam.' Evelyn protests, flinching from the pain. Ashamed her mother has worked it out once again.

'Sorry love, but I need to get you and that little boy in there away from him.' Gillian's eyes flicker in the direction of the lounge where Danny has settled himself playing with a truck. Tears stream down Evelyn's face. Brian had beaten her through jealousy, accusing her of still having feelings for Des. Deep down, she is not in love with Des or Brian for that matter. It's the guilt of having ruined his life she cannot get over.

'Mam it's all my fault.' Evelyn blurts, sadness clouding her features. Wet tears sting her cheeks, unveiling the bruise down one side of her face, she had tried to mask with concealer and foundation.

'What's your fault pet?'

'If I had the courage to speak up, to defy Brian then Des would never have gone out in his car and Jack Connolly wouldn't have died. I should have done something.'

'Evie you're not making sense.'

'Dessie was working two jobs remember to save for our wedding. He'd taken on a couple of nights in Autoblast, stocking shelves and filling online orders. I stupidly had Brian over, an...well we fell asleep after-'

'Spare me the details.' Gillian cut in, shaking her head in dismay. 'I'm a big girl I can work it out thank you very much.' Her face hardening.

'I woke up when, I heard the front door slam. Des was home and Brian still in our bed. I'm not proud of what I've done mam, I'm a horrible person and there are days I think, I deserve...'

'Deserve what? That fecking bully slapping ya around.'

'Now who's swearing?'

'He has that effect. Look love, no one deserves a man like that. Your, Da god rest his soul, Christie was my saviour in life, a good husband and father as you know. I think his sudden unexpected death took it out of us. Too wrapped up in my own grief, I didn't see you were hurting too, and with our Frank having to go back to Canada right after the funeral. Well, I was lonely and I think you were too, I'm sorry I didn't see it. Desmond working all the hours' god love him, he was doing it for the right reasons but you needed affection and Brian saw his opportunity. You're not a bad person Evie, you were going through a rough patch and you were vulnerable. He took advantage of that. As for Des...I don't know what to say, I was shocked, surprised by what he did. I guess he wasn't who we thought he was either, forget them Evie.' Gillian pleads. 'We have to go...think of Danny.'

'Not til I've put things right, mam. I can't live with the lie any more, not when there is a chance Des could go to prison again.' She places a hand on her mother's. 'Des was in the kitchen making coffee, I went in to distract him thinking Brian would leave but he had other plans wanted, Des to know about us. There was a row, Des...I'll never forget the way he looked at me. I told Brian to leave so we could talk but he refused. I saw him slip a pill in Des' coffee, when Des was pacing the kitchen all hyped up and angry. He picked up the mug and downed the coffee before grabbing his car keys and storming out. I tried to stop him but Brian grabbed me, told me he'd calm down and the pill was only to help him. I believed him, just like I believed him when he told me that, Des wanted nothing more to do with me after the accident.'

'Oh sweet Jesus.' Gillian buries her head in her hands.

'Have Danny ready, we'll be on the road in an hour, I promise.'

Chapter 33

'You are free to go Desmond.' Garda O'Driscoll says, her face puckered as she stands in the doorway of the cell. Des rises from the hard bed he'd been lying on, contemplating how his life had gotten so fucked up.

'I'm not free though am I, not really? Next week it'll be something else. There'll always be something until you break me.' He replies, meeting her cat like stare.

'Is that what you think?' She retorts pursing her lips together. Weeks of pent up angst over her treatment of him finally brimming over, Des speaks his mind.

'It's the truth isn't it? You're Sarah Connolly's friend and in your eyes I am scum, because I am the person who knocked down her son.'

'Maybe that's how I saw you before Desmond, but I know better now.' She replies taking him by surprise, though Des is not about to let his guard down, not even when she adds, 'and for the record, Sarah Connolly is not my friend.' There is an air of hopelessness about her, all spark and fiery spirit gone from her eyes. It doesn't change his opinion of her, nothing ever will.

Des walks out of the station where the warm sunshine brushes his cheeks, yet a cold shiver runs down his spine. He spots her sitting on the low wall, shoulders hunched perceiving her to be old beyond her years. When her tearstained ghostly pale face glances up displaying red rimmed eyes and the shadows of the beating she'd received, it tugs on his heart strings. The knowledge, one human being could do this to another, Brian Lennon had done this to Evie, his Evie, breaking something inside of him. Seeing the sadness in her eyes, unyielding and sorrowful as fresh tears begin to flow. Yet, he cannot bare to touch her, to do the simple humane thing of wrapping his arms around her for comfort. It suddenly dawns on him, what is she doing here anyway?

'Des.' She rushes towards him wrapping her arms around his neck, as though it is the most natural thing in the world to do. He can feel her bones through the thin top she is wearing. 'I've made everything right, told them it wasn't your fault.' Like a switch being flicked, it all comes flooding back. Brian in their kitchen, him having returned from working all night. Flinching, he harshly pushes her away.

'Go home to your family Evelyn nothing has changed, I know why I left but it doesn't explain everything else.'

'It was Brian...you didn't know.' She pleads trying to pull him back to face her.

'Did Brian get Jimmy to put those drugs in my locker, so I'd be put back inside?' Des questions, narrowing his eyes.

'I don't know anything about drugs in your locker, I'm on about the accident, when you hit that boy.'

'What are you saying?' He swings round finally willing to acknowledge what she is trying to tell him.

'Brian put a pill in the coffee you were drinking that morning when you came in....I'm so, so sorry, I never suspected til after I'd heard about the crash it was too late by then. Brian said it was harmless to help you calm down.'

'Fuck.' Desmond drops onto on the cold steps of the Garda station, burying his head in his hands. He sobs loudly and openly, relief flooding through him until adrenaline kicks in.

'I am so sorry.' He can hear Evelyn pleading, her hot breath close to his cheek. 'I would never have left you drive away if I'd known. You were so angry with me and I don't blame you, I was a fool. I told the Garda, made a full statement, I know it won't give you back the past five years but at least it'll clear your name.' She says between her own sobs. 'It's over Des, this whole thing is behind us now we can both move on with our lives. I'm taking Danny and making a fresh start knowing you are okay now.'

'What the hell Evelyn! This will never leave me and I'm not talking about having a prison record. Nothing will erase the fact, a young boy is lying up there in a cold grave instead of living his life. Nothing will erase the nightmare, I relive every night when I close my eyes. I see his broken body lying on the ground and smell the sickly burning of rubber tyres. Nothing will ever make me forget that, nothing, it will haunt me until the day I die.' Des glances up, through blurred vision from tears he spots Alice.

'I rang the station, they said you'd just been released.' She says shifting uncomfortably, glancing from Des to Evelyn.

'I need to tell her how sorry I am, I took his life.' He replies, giving Alice the cue she's been waiting for. 'Will you walk with me?' He asks fighting back tears. 'I'd like to walk up to Jack's grave.'

'Yes Dessie, of course I will.' Alice gives him one of her radiant smiles.

Evelyn walks away having done what she'd come to do. All she has to do now, is get away and become Lynn Priestly, single independent career woman and mother. If there is one thing she has learned in recent weeks, it is her worth. Men like Brian Lennon can rot in jail where they belong, with the added assault charges she's pressing along with the knowledge of Desmond's case, it should be enough with his drug smuggling charges to put him away for a long time. Lexi's cousin said she can give evidence via Skype when the trial goes to court, saving her from ever having to return.

'I'm sorry, I pushed you away. I didn't think I was good enough for you. You deserve better than all this.' Des declares as he and Alice walk hand in hand, Des carrying the teddy bear he'd picked up in the shop.

'So do you, Des.' She replies matter-of-fact, reminding him of why he had fallen for her in the first place. The afternoon sun casts over the graveyard as they walk up the hill. Des' stops by the grave of Jack Connolly with trepidation. Working out the dates, Jack should have been twenty-one earlier in the year, the same age as Des had been when he took his life. He had been young and naive, two young men died on that day, he can only hope the man he has become will live a life for both of them. Des places the bear next to a posy of flowers now beginning to wilt.

'It's sad to think, this is it when we are gone.' He stares at the black marble stone with its gold lettering. Taking in its details. Beloved son, grandson and nephew. Talented Athlete.

'You alright?' Alice whispers.

'He was only sixteen, had his whole life ahead of him and I took it away.' Des replies with sadness in his heart. 'He was destined for the Olympics, to think he would have represented Ireland.'

'We could do something you know in honour of his memory, a monument in the park maybe. So people visiting would know how special he was. Do you think you'd be okay with that? I could talk to Conor as town councillor...he'd have to square it with Sarah of course but...'

'That is a lovely idea.' Des manages a weak smile. 'Thank you for sticking by me.'

'Well that depends.'

'On what?'

'Are you going to be sticking around here, or are you still planning on taking off to Spain?'

'I'm not great with heat, I don't think Spain will suit my complexion.' Des replies with a wink, they make their way over to a bench, situated under a hawthorn tree where they sit in comfortable silence staring out at the sea, Desmond wondering if Sarah sits in this very spot thinking about her son. Alice slips her hand in his, it's all he needs as fresh tears begin to flow unleashing genuine remorse.

Chapter 34

'Mum's awake, but she is distant, I don't think she recognised me at first when I went in.' Vincent informs, Sarah when she returns to the intensive care unit, having sat all the previous day by Roz's bedside watching her friend sleep. It was all there written on her waxen face the strain, loss and desperation. Things, Sarah herself has felt again since Paddy's passing. Not realising until now, how much her father had held her up after, Jack's death. Of course, in the beginning it had been impossible the grief unbearable. After Jack's death she had cocooned herself in a bubble of grief and denial thinking the pain would swallow her up, wondering how life could continue without him. With the help of her father, Lily and a prescription of Valium from Dr. O'Brien, she learned to take each day, one at a time. Sometimes the pain sat at the back of her mind like a pulse. Other times it pushed itself to the forefront shredding her heart into tiny pieces. It was on those days she did not want to live anymore, incapable of even getting out of bed. The insufferable sensation of drowning and being unable to breathe making her understand Roz's desperation for it all to end.

'It's been hard for Vinnie, he is good to his mum.' Aisling, Vincent's girlfriend says breaking into her thoughts. Sarah having taken to the gentle spoken girl, the moment they met on Sarah's arrival in Waterford. Aisling made up the bed in the spare bedroom and cooked a meal, her presence bringing a new lease of life into the O'Reilly household. An injection which is badly needed. Delighted to learn of Vincent and Aisling's plans to marry after spotting a gleaming engagement ring on the young girl's finger. Saddened by the fact, Roz had never mentioned this, during any of their calls, a proven fact life is moving on and she could not accept this. Ray in some respects had been right, the house having become a complete shrine to their dead daughter, Natasha. Every room containing pictures of her, especially the lounge where Roz has a large framed photograph on the sideboard surrounded by her medals from Irish dancing. Half burnt candles stand either side of the mahogany frame, an indication they are lit regularly. The sight sending an eerie chill down Sarah's spine. That and the fact there is not one picture of Roz's other children, not even Vincent who still lives in the house.

'Yes, sometimes we are so consumed in our grief, we forget the loved ones who are there supporting us.' Sarah's reply opening her own mind.

'We'll leave you speak to her on your own, its better if we don't crowd her.' Vincent says in a shaky voice, showing his apprehension. Gauging his anxiety, Sarah places a comforting hand on his shoulder receiving an unexpected hug in return.

'Thanks Sarah, you are the only one who really understands.' His lips quivering.

'Don't go beating yourself up, this hasn't been easy for any of you. You especially, being the only one living at home and having to bare the load of her grief on top of your own. Unfortunately, she has depended on you without realising how much.'

'You're a good friend Sarah, I hope she will see how much she means to us all, I'd be lost without her. We thought she had seemed to be coping better recently. She was always doing something, busy with helping in the charity shop and talking about getting this hearing in the Seanad.'

'She booked a hotel in Dublin for October, and was excited about sorting t-shirts for your marathon.' Aisling adds. 'Said I'd go with her, you know for support.'

'The only thing I did notice, which is odd.' Vincent pauses face flushing, as though ashamed at having missed a vital sign. 'She had been chatty non-stop, even when watching the telly. Like she was on a high, it's hard to explain but it was odd, you know. Making loads of meals and freezing them too. Every evening, when I got in home from work there'd be loads of home cooking. She seemed to be so positive about everything, I don't understand.' He shakes his head in dismay. Sarah sighs heavily knowing there is nothing, Vincent could have done. He could never have predicted Roz doing what she did.

'There is nothing you could have done.' Sarah's comments causing Vince's lips to finally curl into a glimmer of a smile.

'She's still very groggy and a little frightened, she also has a tendency to switch off, regressing into herself.' The nurse, a pleasant soft spoken woman, informs Sarah when she enters the intensive care unit. It's overly familiar antiseptic smells making her feel a little nauseous. 'I think it upset her son earlier. I tried to explain.'

'It's tough, he needs time to get his head round it all.' Sarah points out, adding. 'What about Roz...her metal state, I mean? Is it possible she could try and do this again?'

'The psychiatrist will be visiting her later this morning to asses her fully. There is no denying, she is very fragile still and lucky to be alive with the cocktail she took.' She loses her serious tone, adding a smile. 'No pressure but, Vincent said if anyone could get through to her it would be you.' She raises a brow. 'I'll leave you alone but I'm close by if she gets upset.'

Sarah pastes her best fake smile on her face, the one she often uses for Lily and Tommy, for the customers in the café, and had tried in vain many a time to fool Paddy with. Gauging Roz's waxen appearance, the strain far more visible now she is awake. Making it hard for, Sarah to accept this broken woman before her is usually the crutch to hold Sarah up.

Roz is propped up by pillows staring in Sarah's direction as she nears the bed, her gaze however, is somewhere far beyond the room eyes devoid of any life. To Sarah, Roz is barely recognisable as the woman she had coffee with when they had met up in Dublin just before Easter. It had been the anniversary of Natasha's death, a ritual they slipped into without either of them verbally saying so, each travelling to Dublin on the anniversaries, Jack's in October and Natasha's in April. They would sit in Starbucks and talk while watching the bustle of the city through the window. Then they would part ways and travel home, having satisfied passing the day in the company of someone who truly understood.

'Roz are you up to a little visit?' Sarah draws closer, realising the only sign of life coming from Roz's body are silent tears streaming down her cheeks, the sight sending a bolt through Sarah's tattered heart.

'Sarah what are you doing here?' The question unexpected from a voice sounding very unlike Roz's, unaware Sarah is visiting for the second day due to being in a coma for three days. Roz's eyes regain their focus, fixing on Sarah. 'Silly question, Vince...I wish he hadn't, I don't want anyone seeing me like this. You must think-'

'Shush now, I think nothing.' Sarah cuts in, keeping her voice low and gentle in hope of reassuring this broken woman before her. 'Vinnie told me, you were unwell and in hospital. Of course, I would visit one of my dearest friends.' Sarah pulls a chair to the side of the bed, she reaches out to hold Roz's hand. 'You don't have to tell me, I'm happy to sit with you but I found talking, especially to someone who understands, helps.'

'Whether you realise it or not, girl, our conversations have been the only thing preventing me doing what I did, a long, long time ago. If it wasn't for your courage and fight Sarah, I wouldn't...I'm lost without her. I look at photographs' and her life stopped days after her thirteenth birthday. She was so full of life, a sparkle of energy, always smiling and enthusiastic. Now the house is quiet, the heart has been ripped from my home. How can Ray move on as though she had never mattered? How can he do that?'

'Everyone deals with grief differently. It's not that Ray doesn't love Natasha any less or has forgotten her.' Sarah choses her words carefully.

'Hum.' Roz's expression hard, as she speaks of her estranged husband. 'He claimed, he couldn't live in a shrine anymore, a mausoleum. I think those were the words he used. It was like looking at a stranger, and yet it was the man I had walked down the aisle to, had five children with. A man I thought, I would grow old with. Instead he walked away because he could not cope with my grief. I tried, I really did try to pretend it wasn't happening. These things only happen to other people, right. We had everything, a good life, raised five wonderful healthy children. There is no time limit for grief, not when it's your child your flesh and blood. I did try ... after Ray went...keeping busy...trying not to think about how much I resented that man ruining our lives. Then the free paper came through the letterbox. I had made a cup of tea....picked it up to read it like I would have in the past. A resolve to pretend my life is a normal one...hah, who am I kidding... his face was staring at me. Front page news, local businessman Donald bloody O'Toole, shaking hands with the mayor. My blood ran cold, seeing his big fat balding head staring at me. He's a bloody murderer an there he was being made look like some local hero...I'll tell ya girl, it was the last nail in my coffin.' Roz's words shocking Sarah, but not as much as the angst in her face. Lost for words, Sarah instead wraps her arms around the other woman. Silent tears streaming down both their faces. Finally, Sarah pulls away.

'You once told me, we had to be our children's voices now, do you remember?' Sarah says, brushing tears from her cheeks with the back of her hand. 'This is why we have to find the strength to go to the Seanad, together we will get this bill passed and stop people like Donald O'Toole and Desmond Shanahan from ruining lives, then walking free without a care.' Even as she gives her speech of encouragement, Sarah knows they have to stop fighting. Having made their children's memory about how they died, and not the real people they were. Matt had been right about doing the Marathon to honour what Jack stood for as a person. An athlete, a talented young man with dreams of representing his country. Just as Lena has focused positive energy into her daughter's memory, Sarah realises she must do the same for Jack. Take up marathon running, wear t-shirts bearing his name and face, not as a campaign against how he died but as a celebration of his life. Raise money for athletic clubs, so other children will have the opportunity to compete. Jack would be proud of her for doing that, a great believer in helping others. A weak smile crosses Sarah's lips, assured it is the right thing to do.

'It haunts me.' Roz sobs, bringing her back into the hospital room. 'Those last moments, before Natasha left the house that day. I never spoke about it to anyone, couldn't bring myself to admit the guilt I'd been left with. If only I could turn back the clock and have that last conversation with her again. If I had known, it was the last thing we would say to each other.'

'You're being unnecessarily hard on yourself.' Sarah points out.

'What was the last thing you said to Jack?' Roz asks, taking Sarah by surprise.

'I've thought about this so many times.' She admits, having relived the scenario in her head, yet each time the words are slightly different leaving uncertainty and fear. 'I think, I asked him if he would be warm enough in shorts. It was silly and...' Sarah's voice trails away, wishing she had told him, she loved him with all her heart, that she was proud to be his mother.

'You were being your usual caring self and Jack felt your love from that simple question.' Roz points out, Sarah had never thought of it like that before. 'Me and Natasha...well...we rowed that morning.' Roz reveals for the first time. 'She wanted to go to Bagley's with her friends after school and I told her, she needed to come straight home and study for her exams. I'll never forget it, she slammed the door with a merciful shudder on her way out that morning. Screaming that she hated me because, I was ruining her life.'

'Roz these are words of a teenage girl.' She'd heard it so many times with Lauren and Rachel. Luckily, Jack had never given her such strife but she would not say this to Roz. Choosing her words carefully. 'Your words were no different than my last words. They still conveyed a concerned mother, someone who loves their child and cared for her wellbeing. I'm sure once she had calmed down, she was aware of that fact.'

'How do you do it Sarah? Keep going each day.' Roz throwing the most difficult of questions her way, each time Sarah mindful her words must be chosen carefully, as well as being completely honest with Roz. This frail woman lying in her hospital bed looking vulnerable and old beyond her years, their friendship has meant everything to Sarah. 'I came close many a time, thought a life without Jack in it isn't worth living. Every morning I'd wake to realise he's gone and the insufferable knowledge to much to bear. Then, I'd go downstairs see my father sitting at the table....he'd give me this look of...I don't know how to explain it.... I couldn't leave him alone, he had been there all my life and loved Jack too. Just as Vincent, is there for you. He hasn't gone anywhere because he loves you and remember, he has lost a little sister too. You have each other Roz, you still have him. He is your strength and so is Aisling. She's a lovely girl, clearly in love with your son and fond of you. They are your reason for living, share their happiness with them, it's what Natasha would want.' Sarah would need to push Roz into this way of thinking too, as it is the only way they will both survive their loss, in a bearable way.

An hour later, Sarah is sitting in a café in the city centre, drained of emotion. Seeing Roz so lost and broken had been hard, seeing young Vincent baring the load of his sister's loss even more heart-breaking. The fact, none of his siblings live locally and don't seem to be in a rush to return and see their mother, also a hard truth to swallow. She pays for the coffee and walks through the town towards the medieval museum. Inside she views the mayors wine vault, then upstairs the art of devotion, along with models of Waterford. Her visit inspiring her to take a visit to

Tramore, reminded of the conversation she'd had with Martin the day of their father's funeral.

Arriving in the seaside town nine kilometres from the city, she parks the car before getting out to walk along the prom. Taking in the family atmosphere, visualising Paddy walking with his four very young children, missing his wife. Wanting to walk on the sand, hand in hand or swim in the sea while she sat on the beach watching the children build sandcastles. Paddy had never given up, no matter what life threw his way, a strength to be admired.

The lure of the sea prompts, Sarah to return to the car and grab a bathing suit and towel from the boot. The urge to swim and feel the watery embrace, making her feel closer to home.

After a refreshing but decidedly cold swim, she sits on the prom eating chips and watching families walk by. Children on cycles or scooters, happy to go in front of their parents' who advise them to stay close and not go too far ahead. Dog walkers, runners, groups of friends and couples out for an early evening stroll. Occasionally, people would stop and strike up a conversation with those coming in the opposite direction causing an eddy, in which walkers would veer round with ease.

Life goes on no matter whether we wish it to or not, no one knows if the lady with the solemn expression walking by herself has lost a loved one, or is simply taking time to decipher how to tell her family she has cancer. Or maybe the couple wearing frown lines and false smiles, are worried about how to pay their mortgage and give their children a secure home. The pregnant woman, filled with so much love for her unborn child is secretly worried everything will go well with the birth, as she has already endured a miscarriage and still birth. Everyone, carries unspoken pain knowing life has to go on and no one knows this fact better than, Sarah.

Back at the house, Vincent and Aisling have left a note saying they have gone back to the hospital and a plate of food for Sarah to reheat in the microwave, leaving her feeling guilty for having the chips. Tired from the emotion of the past two days, she heads upstairs to bed. Sarah fluffs the pillows and sits prompt up against them in the bed, ready to video call Lily, missing her brother and sister-in-law. Tommy of course does not possess a mobile phone, unwilling to succumb to life's modern ways.

'Hey you, looks like you have a house full as usual.'

'Yes, Tommy thinks I'm avoiding empty nest syndrome by having half the town here every night for tea. Say hello.' Lily turns her phone, so Sarah can see Tommy, Paul, Olive, Lena and her husband Malik all sitting around the table eating Lily's delicious home cooking. Instigating a pang of homesickness, Sarah wishing to be there among them.

'Hi, Sarah.' They all say in unison.

'Hi guys. Lena you've had the cast taken off.'

'Yes, I am fully functioning again.'

'It is a relief as she was trying to cycle to work with one hand.' Malik adds, giving his wife an affectionate smile.

'I was bored at home, you do not understand.' Lena protests, in an equally affectionate way.

'Come home soon kid, we all miss you here.' Olive adds, making Sarah smile, realising she is surrounded by wonderful friends.

'Here, here, I'll second that.' Tommy adds, her big hearted brother, rarely showing outward emotion looking glassy eyed.

'I miss you all too.'

'Now down to business.' Lily cuts in, moving out of the kitchen into the lounge, barely able to contain her excitement. 'I have some news, but firstly I must ask, how is Roz? I didn't want to discuss her business in front of the others, though I'm sure none of them would gossip.'

'In a bad place unfortunately, but the staff at Waterford university hospital are good to her. She and Vincent will receive support and counselling, though Roz is not keen. Hence why she never had it before. Her daughter Orla is arriving in the morning, I'm not sure about the others', which is saddening.' Sarah informs her sister-in-law. Lily nods, showing her understanding.

'I know this sounds like a strange thing to say but you look brighter, like something has changed.' Lily tilts her head, a quizzical expression on her face.

'Seeing Roz like that has made me think how close I have come to...' Sarah admits, 'if it weren't for Da and you, and even Tommy...I'm sorry I've been so selfish putting you through so much with my grief, when I see Vince and the strain he is under it makes me realise.'

'You have nothing to be sorry for, we are family and we love you, loved Jack. I was worried, I admit, after Paddy died, he always knew how to pull you back. I'm glad you are seeing things in a different light though.' She says with sincerity. 'Now, I can't hold back any longer, I have some fabulous news which should put a smile on your face, altogether. Aine has dropped the case and is willing to accept her original inheritance. On the condition, she can build a holiday cottage over on the far side of the cove with its own private drive and a decent surrounding plot. Isn't that great news?'

'What changed her mind?' Sarah dares to ask, barely able to believe what Lily is telling her.

'She and Chad have an arrangement. They are getting married for appearances, so his first wife won't find out the truth and stop him having access to the children. Chad gets to be with his lover in secret and Aine gets, well the magazine apparently, along with inheriting all his money.'

'Wow...I guess if it makes her happy.' Sarah screws up her nose. Lily immediately picking up on her displeasure.

'Each to their own, I say.' Lily laughs. 'At least you have your home and that's all, Tommy and I care about.'

'And Martin gets his inheritance to sort out his finances.'

'Win, win.'

'Yeah, win, win. Did you manage okay today?'

'Oh I think we just about kept everything running in your absence. No major catastrophes.'

'I feel terrible running off, when we are so busy.'

'Sure, I'll get my payback when, Tommy and I go away in September.'

'You know about that. How?'

'Your brother is terrible at keeping anything from me, I worked it out when he let a comment slip. It's what happens after being together so long. I'm blown away he has gone to such lengths, I don't need it to be a surprise, I can look forward to going. Talking of which, I have bread in the oven and I doubt anyone else will check it. You get some sleep, what time will we expect you home tomorrow.'

'I want to visit Roz in the hospital before I leave, so it may be quite late.'

'Give Roz my love. Drive safe and ring me, you know I worry.'

'Yes mammy.' They both laugh.

'Oh, I almost forgot, I had a coffee in this most beautiful tea room this afternoon, it had this fab vintage theme. Oh, Lil you would love it, quaint and...like, oh it's so hard to describe. I took some pics on my phone, I'll message them on. It's given me great ideas for things we could do in the winter when the tourist season is over, you know to keep the business healthy.' Sarah's face animated with excitement, as she speaks. 'I went out to Tramore for a swim, apparently Da took us there when we were small. Tommy might remember, he'd have been older than me. It made me realise we have to keep going no matter what, like Da did after mam died.'

'Yes, life has a way of forcing that on us and whether you realise it or not, you have survived.' Lily replies, misty-eyed.

'How was the water?' she brushes the melancholy away, by briskly changing the feel of the conversation.

'Would you believe, colder than in Kilmer Cove?' They both laugh. 'It was lovely though.'

'Night kid, get some sleep, looking forward to see you tomorrow.'

'Night Lily.' Sarah hangs up, and snuggles into the soft pillow, feeling happier than she has in a long while. She easily drifts off to sleep, engulfed in a warm fuzzy feeling.

Chapter 35

Sarah pulls into the drive late the next evening tired from a long eight hour drive. She has barely alighted the car when, Lily comes running out almost bowling her over with a welcoming hug.

'Good to have you back kid.' She exclaims, 'come I've made dinner, you must be famished.' She leads Sarah across the yard to the dormer bungalow. Inside, Sarah is greeted not only by her brother but the same people who were there the previous night. The table filled with variations of food cooked by Lily and Lena.

'Welcome home Sarah.' They shout in unison. The scene before her, filling her with emotion causing her nose to tingle, tears threatening to spill not from sadness but due to the feeling of love surrounding her. Captured in the bosom of her family and friends, Sarah sits at the table. The atmosphere light, as they discuss future plans for the expansion of the campsite and addition of a gift shop.

'You used to do fabulous mosaics, if memory serves me right.' Olive addresses Sarah.

'Yes, I did, you know I'm thinking we could hold classes for the tourists. Ceramics and painting, we have some wonderful scenery round and about. People might like to create their own pictures, rather than photographs'. What do you think Paul about doing some advertising on our website?'

'Sounds good to me.' Paul replies, his smile not quite as wide as she'd expect. There something not right by way he is not meeting her gaze.

'We could also do walking tours, how you say it...hiking.' Lena suggests, causing further enthusiasm round the room.

'Great idea Lena, we could encourage scout groups early in the year before the tourist season kicks in.' Sarah replies, eyes dancing in the light of the room. Tommy winks across at her, for the first time in months they are all feeling positive about the future. The conversation rolling late into the night until, Tommy announces he and Paul have to rise early as the farm still has animals needing to be fed.

'We should have petting and feed the animals.' Lily says as they shuffle about tidying the kitchen.

'I like that idea.' Malik says. 'I'm beginning to feel left out...Lena is enthusiastic about going to work each day.' When all eyes are on him he retracts. 'I don't mean to suggest...I am ungrateful for my job, it is not as much fun.' Omitting adding, being uncomfortable working alongside Desmond in recent weeks. Paul has picked up on his unease, knowing the gossip which has been doing its rounds. A subject which should not be voiced in Sarah's company, not yet anyway, not until she has had time to settle back home.

'Once things pick up, we will need more staff and you will be the first person we will come to.' Tommy adds, 'at the moment, I couldn't offer you anything more than a casual position, it wouldn't be fair to expect you to give up the factory.'

'Thank you, I appreciate.' With a flurry of hugs and goodbyes, everyone departs.

'Thank you for tonight, you two.' Sarah says, once alone with Tommy and Lily. 'It's good to be home.' It certainly does feel good to be home, back in the sanctity of the farmhouse knowing it will stay as her home, Sarah sleeps soundly after sending a text to Roz, telling her to stay strong too.

The following morning Sarah rises early to get her training in, a few light stretches and she is on the road her feet light, striding with an ease she has never felt before. Passing by The Nook, Dini is outside stacking barrels, when he lifts his head she receives the brightest of smiles making her almost want to stop and talk, as though suspecting this he shouts.

'Great stride keep moving.' As she passes by, Sarah is sure she can hear him mutter. 'Jack would be damn proud.' Sarah swoops along Main Street, on the side where the path curves along the Atlantic. After all, she could never imagine living anywhere but on the idyllic North West Coast of Ireland. She heads out on the other side of town making a loop of six kilometres and back towards the bottom of Seaview Park, gliding passed the GAA pitch without glancing to her left. Coming back towards Main Street she decides to stop and use the wall for some light leg stretches. The sun now risen in the sky, casting a warming light over the harbour below.

'I heard you were training for the Dublin marathon.' She glances up, met by Conor's unequivocal stare. He shoves a hand through his thick mane of hair, disheveling it from its previous immaculate style. Sarah recognising this as a clear sign of his discomfort. Knowing he will be deciding if it is, he, who is in the wrong or her. It surprises her how much she knows this man before her and still, she cannot love him in the way he desires. She also realises, her life is not the same without his friendship. 'Sarah...I'm sorry for the way I've been treating you.' Hand combing through his hair once more, leaving a piece spiking up awkwardly. Sarah, stifles the urge to reach out and fix it, an action she would have done in the past without thought. So much pain has gone between them, the barrier, never to be fully taken down again. 'I get frustrated by the fact you pull me in, then push me away. I know you value your independence, but it's like no man is ever good enough for you because, Paddy was on such a high pedestal. At first, I was jealous of your feelings for Finn, for the fact he was Jack's father. The truth be told, you didn't love him any more than me, if you did then you would have told him about Jack from the beginning. You weren't protecting Maggie, you didn't want Finn.' His face crimson, eyes wide, one of them twitching. For the first time in all the years she has known him Conor, has admitted what is on his mind.

'So this is your apology.' She simply replies, the truth a bitter pill to swallow. There is no crime in having high expectations, or wanting independence. Paddy had been a good father, better than most, so why should she accept less in the man she would marry. If she thought about it logically, Conor looked up to Paddy, he came close to the barre. 'We are lucky to live in this beautiful place, I could never imagine living anywhere else.' Sarah side-lines him by saying. A fisherman passes by, nodding a cheerful morning greeting. Bag thrown over his shoulder, most likely containing thick crusty sandwiches, hand cut by his wife, lovingly made along with a flask of hot tea. The bond of marriage, Sarah could never imagine sharing. A wife comforted, knowing her husband will have something to keep him from growing hungry, whilst out on the boat for hours trying to bring in a good catch of Tope or Pollack.

'Morning to ye, tis a fine one.' Years of enduring harsh winds etched on his face, the sea a beautiful enchantress, also capable of being a deceptive mistress.

'Morning.' Sarah smiles back, glad of the intrusion on their conversation.

'Good day for a fine catch, are ya heading out George?' Conor asks, stating the obvious. His eye twitching again from discomfort.

'Aye. Good for a bit of Pollack at the moment.' He waves a hand, continuing on his way.

'I don't know where to start.' Conor says, when they were alone again. 'I shouldn't have spoken to you like that. I knew Finn used you, had treated you badly, and still I throw it back at you.' He sits up onto the wall overlooking the pier. 'I have been annoyed with myself over the years, for letting you go without a fight.'

'I didn't sleep with Finn to spite you. You were away and I found his attention flattering. He had a way with words, I was a fool to be sucked in, for the record maybe you're right about me' Sarah's heart sinks, as though being pulled to the bottom of the ocean. Trapped in a shipwreck unable to break free from suffocation. Conor had got it wrong, in truth she was smitten by Finn, sadly it took twenty-two years to see though his fecklessness. 'It's easy to live with regrets, Jack isn't one of them. I'm happy for the time I had with my beautiful son, even if it was cruelly cut short.'

'You normally frown when you speak of Jack's death, there is something different about you today.'

'I've finally learned to accept it. Roz, my friend in Waterford, remember you met her when she came to stay with me a couple of years back.'

'Yes, she does a lot of campaigning with you.'

'She tried to take her life, couldn't face being without her daughter. I went down to see her.'

'I'm sorry, is she alright?'

'I hope so....seeing her so lost and vulnerable....I realised, it's time to stop fighting.' She gazes out at the sea, 'the water was colder down there, when I went for a swim, wouldn't have expected that.'

'You wouldn't...ignore me...stupid to even think it.' Conor's face creases. 'I was worried when you'd disappeared without a word. Lily was cagy about where you'd gone, when I asked.' Good ole Lil, who'd also informed her about the commotion at the factory and Desmond's arrest, surprising Sarah that Maggie had not called to tell her. Lily hadn't been certain of any facts, only overhearing whispered mutterings in the café from customers about his release again. It doesn't matter to Sarah now, she's pushed Desmond from her mind. After all, life is about honouring her son's life now. 'I often thought about it over the years, how we could have been a family. I wished Jack was my son.' Conor admits, surprising her. 'I miss him...I don't know how you cope.' He turns his head away. She reaches out placing a hand on his arm in a gesture of understanding.

'If we are being open and honest, truth is I haven't coped at all, the only way to get through each day has been to pretend. Some days it's easy, other days less so. I often considered doing what Roz did, if it weren't for my father and Lily.....now I realise how selfish I've been.' He turns to face her, with watery eyes. 'I'm sorry for how badly I treated you.' She slips into his open arms.

'It's taken me twenty- two years to accept we will be nothing more than friends and I finally realise, I want that more than not having you at all.'

'Good, cause I need a friend, especially one who will not allow me fall back into my old ways.'

After they part Sarah slowly jogs back up the hill, today she is helping Paul on the campsite, as they want to spend time going over revamping the website and discuss ways of expanding now that Aine has finally settled.

'We're fully booked again tonight.' Paul beams enthusiastically, when she walks into the reception. 'Have you seen the website?' He turns the monitor to allow her, see the screen. 'We've been given some fabulous reviews.'

'Couldn't have done it without you.' She replies reading all the kind words, delighted to think this is their business people are referring too. 'The cameras have done the trick too.' Sarah adds as her mobile buzzes in her pocket.

'Actually, I need to talk to you about that.' Paul's voice a little shaky, his face turning pink. He doesn't get a chance to explain, with a wave of her hand Sarah answers her phone.

'Maggie, it's so good to hear your voice.' Sarah says, turning away from an unusually disgruntled looking Paul.

'I'm having a few people over for a barbecue tonight. Nothing too big, Marion next door, you know Marion don't you. Well she was flabbergasted when she realised I, wasn't doing anything for my fortieth. Talk about being a true friend, she's organised the whole thing, even ordered a cake and got some little favor's made up. Anyway, if you can't make it at such short notice, I'll understand. I heard you've been away and I've been busy at the station.'

'Jesus, Mags, I'm so sorry, I was away...have had so many things on my mind lately...you must think...' When Maggie doesn't reply and an unusual atmosphere crackles on the line, along with a lingering silence, Sarah adds. 'Sure Mags I'd love to come, what time?' Glad they are not on facetime or in the same room. If they were Maggie would see the wounded expression Sarah is wearing.

'Oh...ah, pop over around half-six.' Maggie blusters down the line.

'Great I'm looking forward to it.' Unsure why she has said this as Maggie does not sound like her usual self, leaving Sarah anything but excited by the prospect of going. 'Would you like me to bring anything, a bottle of wine maybe?'

'No, we've got it all organised, I went to the cash and carry on Saturday.' Another bolt of admittance the party has been organised for some time and Sarah's invite is last minute. She may have been away but in the modern world of mobiles, everyone is accessible all of the time within reason.

After she hangs up the thought stays with her for some time. Luckily, a family had arrived into the reception area when she was on the phone. Meaning, Paul had to bring them to their pitch, giving her time to gather her composure before the next tourists walk through the door. The day going quickly with a succession of people coming and going, leaving no time for Sarah and Paul to indulge in any sort of conversation. Probably as well, Paul's demeanour changed having become jittery and distracted, eyeing her on a regular basis with an agitated expression. Sarah glad to finish up for the day grabs her bag, shouting over her shoulder.

'I'll see ya tomorrow Paul sorry to run.' Her sudden hasty departure, causing him to whip his head round so quickly, he could cause himself whiplash.

'Sarah, I need to talk to you about something.' Paul says in a pleading tone, his gaze shifting uncomfortably between Sarah and the German couple he is dealing with.

'Sure, tomorrow.' She flippantly replies, misreading his unusual behaviour.

Back in her bedroom in the farmhouse, Sarah showers, changing into a pair of tight black jeans, and a new top she had picked up in a boutique in Tramore, blown away by the lovely clothes and the friendly owner. As she carefully applies her makeup, her mobile buzzes on the bed indicating a new message, before she gets a chance to retrieve it there is a second message. Sarah reaches across grabbing it, the first message from, Roz thanking her for travelling all the way down to Waterford and letting her know she is home. The second text from Finn, her heart flipping like a washing machine on a spin cycle as she reads the words. "I love you, always have. We should be together Finn X" While initially taken in, sensibility takes over and Sarah deletes the text flinging the phone back on the bed.

'You look stunning, where are you off too.' Lily asks, catching Sarah as she is heading to her car.

'Maggie is having a barbecue for her fortieth.' Sarah omits telling Lily, Maggie had left it until the last minute to invite her or about the text from Finn less than half an hour ago.

'Oh…I thought she hated celebrating birthdays.' Lily drops her gaze to the ground. 'Have you spoken to Paul today about the cameras?'

'Yeah, I've been working with him all day.'

'Excuse me, is this the campsite?' A man asks approaching them, having parked his VW Camper at the bottom of the road.

'Yes, yes it is.' Lily answers uncharacteristically flustered.

'I should get going, I'll catch you later.' Sarah jumps into her car.

'You know, Tommy and I are always here don't you?' Lily shouts, still wavering between Sarah and the expectant tourist.

'Always a mother hen,' Sarah mutters smiling, misinterpreting the reason for Lily's caution. 'You're the best, have I ever told you that.' Sarah shouts through her open window, before pulling out of the driveway.

Chapter 36

Sarah makes a small detour on the way to Maggie's. The graveyard is quiet as she walks up the hill, apart from Dan the grounds man who maintains the flowerbeds and keeps the grass neatly manicured. Taking great pride in his work looking after the long forgotten graves, possibly because there is no one left in the family to visit. On her approach to her own family plot, she immediately spots the little soft toy placed carefully in front of Jack's headstone. A puppy with long dangly long ears and doleful eyes, wearing a shirt, on which someone has written in neat capitals the words sorry. It spooks her a little, she glances around the empty graveyard as though expecting to catch whoever had put it there, lurking behind one of the trees or a gravestone.

'Dan,' she calls out to the old man stooped over a grave pulling out weeds. 'You didn't see who put this here did you?' Sarah holds up the little dog.

'Na sorry love, ain't noticed anyone visitin those graves apart from you and Tom.' He tips his cap before returning to his weeding.

'Thanks anyway,' she carefully places the dog back in its place. Stopping for her usual chat, clearing leaves and dead flowers before walking back down the hill.

She spots, Finn coming out of the local grocery shop as she unlocks the car, leaving her wondering had he put it there, possibly as part of a little game to get her back on side. In retrospect, it would be his personification, wanting to charm his way out of the situation he has gotten into. Sarah would not be seduced by his immoral behaviour, something he would find out soon enough. Not wanting to arrive at the barbecue at the same time, she lingers for a few minutes. Sitting into the car, she watches him through her rear-view mirror as he drives up the hill and out of sight.

Nearly half an hour later, after wavering between backing out and going several times, Sarah pulls into Maggie's driveway. Taking note of Conor's car parked next to Finn's, along with a car she does not recognise, parked behind Maggie's. Her chest tightening, as she walks round the side of the house to the sound of chatter and laughter ringing through the air. An indication, there are far more guests than the cars out front portray. Sure enough as she rounds the corner, Maggie's neighbours the Jenson's, a youngish couple. Well, younger than Sarah and the O'Driscoll's by about ten years, are sitting round the fire pit with bottles of beer clutched in their hands, listening intently to Finn spinning one of his great yarns. Making her wonder is she the only one to see through his veneer, his eyes are intently fixed on Carol Jenson's cleavage. Each time she laughs, her chest wobbling, barely covered by the extensively low cut of her top.

'Sarah, I though you weren't coming.' Maggie exclaims feigning surprise, hugging her like a long lost friend. There is a desperation in Maggie's face Sarah has never seen before, making her wonder should she have been honest all those years ago and saved Maggie from the fate she has ended up with.

'These are for you, happy birthday.' Sarah kisses her friend on the cheek as she hands her a bouquet of flowers and bottle of prosciutto, catching Finn watching them before quickly averting his attention back to the Jenson's, Carol in particular.

'You shouldn't have...Will you have a glass of wine or a beer?' Maggie offers seemingly oblivious to her husband's behaviour. 'I better put these in water, I suppose. You know Marion don't you, she's been wonderful organising all this.'

'Hi.' Sarah graciously greets Maggie's neighbour, who throws Sarah a disdainful glance in return. 'You have gone to a lot of trouble.'

'Yes, Maggie deserves it, she's a good neighbour and friend.' Marion replies in a clipped tone before turning to address Maggie. 'Here I'll put those in water for you.' Marion takes the flowers before swiftly disappearing inside the house, the scenario leaving Sarah bewildered.

'Right, that drink.' Maggie says, seemingly not having noticed the icy atmosphere, Marion has left in her wake.

'Maybe just half a glass of wine, I'm driving.' Sarah relents, needing something to ease her nerves.

'Ah let your hair down, girl. You know Carol and Liam, don't you and Conor is here somewhere, went to get burgers out of the freezer for me.' Maggie, carries on talking without taking a breath. 'A...here's Conor now, I'll get your wine.' Maggie swoops quickly away before Sarah can answer.

'Just in time to help me cook these.' Conor grabs her by the arm steering her towards the barbecue. 'Something is seriously wrong, it's like being an extra in Stepford wives.' Conor whispers out the side of his mouth as they place meat on the lit grill.

'Stepford what?' 'It's a programme my mother used to watch, probably used to model herself on it now I think of it, the way she overly pleased my father.' Conor, being no good at humour, Sarah is faintly aware this is a jibe towards his parents for never being around when he was growing up. Spending every summer in Spain, leaving him in the hands of a housekeeper, entailing in him spending all his time at her house, no wonder she sees him as an extension of her brother's, she decides knocking back the glass of wine in practically one mouthful. Maggie is at her side almost immediately filling it again. This invokes an "I told you so" look from Conor. Maggie, draining her own wine in one swallow, refills the glass.

'Won't be too long Mags, want to make sure they are cooked in the middle, hope your guests are hungry...how did I get roped into this anyway, isn't Finn meant to be doing the cooking?'

'If we wait for Finn, we'll all starve too busy entertaining the guests.' She flicks back her glossy red hair before taking another gulp of the wine, while throwing a despondent look in her husband's direction before moving away. Sarah dares to glance across to where, Finn is still locked in conversation with the Jenson's. Carol fluttering her eyes and laughing, hanging on to his every word.

Another couple arrive, prompting Maggie to leave the little group she had been talking to, greeting her new arrivals. It dawns on Sarah, Finn has not moved from his group to acknowledge any of their new arrivals.

'How many people has Maggie invited do you know?' Sarah asks Conor, viewing Maggie and seeing a stranger walking around tonight, her behaviour unexplainably odd.

'A lot it would seem, I thought it was only us and the Ross's from next door.'

'When did she invite you?' Sarah has to ask.

'A few days ago, just after De....here will you hold this.' He hands her a plate, unsuccessfully trying to steer the conversation from unsafe territory. Luckily for Conor they are interrupted before Sarah can react.

'Hi Sarah.' Niamh, Maggie and Finn's younger daughter greets her with a hug. 'Matt told me you are going to do the Dublin Marathon in October with him.'

'Yes.' Sarah takes a moment to reply, not realising Niamh and Matt are in contact, of course social media possibly the reason. 'Will you be coming along to support us?'

'Yeah, I plan to if I get a place in Trinity, I'm still waiting to hear back.'

'I'm sure you will, I went there myself it's-'

'I'm not sure if that would be wise, I'd hate Niamh to end up pregnant and wasting all her hard work.' Maggie quips, having appeared by their side without Sarah noticing. 'Niamh, will ya come and help me with the salad and make sure Catherine and Bernard have a drink will you.' Maggie throws her daughter a warning look, before turning on her heels and heading back to the house. The whole incident leaving Sarah with a bitter taste in her mouth, from the expression on Conor's face, he felt it too.

'Which does she want me to do? I swear, she's in a bitch of a mood, has been for weeks. This party is only a way of getting at dad and it's already backfiring, sur look at him. Why they stay together is a bloody mystery, it certainly isn't for our benefit anyway. Be a relief if they went their separate ways since they hate the sight of each other, always fecking arguing resulting in him storming off an her hitting the wine, she's drinking way too much.' Niamh declares, offering far too much information. 'Don't mind her, besides she is no one to talk when she did exactly the same. I'm sorry she said that to you Sarah, can I call over some evening, you can tell me all about Trinity.' Niamh asks before making a reluctant retreat.

'Wow, what was all that about?' Sarah says, as soon as she and Conor are alone again, still wounded by Maggie's harsh words.

'It doesn't make what I want to talk about any easier to say, but I need to. There is something I need to run by you and the thing is I don't want it to spoil the fact, we are back on good terms.' Conor says, placing cooked burgers and sausages on plates. 'Fact is, I can't put it off any longer.'

'I'm guessing this has something to do with Desmond.' Sarah eyes him with suspicion. 'I heard something happened while I was away.'

'I wouldn't bring it up if I didn't think it was important, you should know that-' the conversation goes no further, they are interrupted by Finn. Sarah acknowledging the pained expression on Conor's face.

'You taking over my job there, Conor.' Finn, pats him on the shoulder, before Sarah gets the chance to walk away, not wanting to indulge in conversation with Finn. 'Looking pretty good Sarah, nice top...the colour suits you brings out the sparkle in your eyes.' He leers, waggling his eyebrows. The comment prompting Sarah to walk away in disgust, wishing she had made an excuse and not come to the barbecue after all.

Slipping in through the back door she overhears, Maggie and Niamh having a heated discussion in the kitchen. Not wishing to intrude on mother and daughter, Sarah instead slips upstairs to the bathroom, the wine having taken effect on her bladder very quickly. Alighting the bathroom a few minutes later to find, Finn standing in the hallway. His head tilted slightly to the side eyes blazing with desire, a look she knows too well, the one he has used many a time when trying to get her back on side after she has told him, they must end their affair.

'I meant what I said, you look amazingly sexy this evening.' He snakes his arms around her waist, Sarah retracts pushing him away. 'Babe, don't be like this,' he slurs slightly from too much alcohol. The flirtatious smile he is trying to convey, sleazy and lecherous making her wonder why, she could never see through his guise before.

'You have some nerve Finn O'Driscoll, I'll give you that.' She attempts to push passed him.

'We're good together, don't tell me you don't feel it.' He pleads. 'I love you, Sarah, we had a child together.'

'How dare you, for twenty-one years you have been happy to stay on the side-lines. The sad thing is, after Jack's death I was so vulnerable, so consumed in grief, I was willing to believe your lies to get me into bed again. You never loved me or Jack, so don't try laying claim on being his father now. Do you think I'd be fooled by a pathetic little bear, saying "sorry" on his grave? Too little, too late Finn. It takes a lot more to be a father.'

'What are you talking about, what bear? C'mon Sarah, you were never like this before, why so demanding now?'

'Jesus, Finn you just don't get it do you?'

'Maybe it's you who doesn't get it.' Maggie is standing on the top step of the stairs, her face a mask of anger. 'I didn't think you'd be brash enough to seduce my husband in my house. I thought maybe burning down the barn and getting rid of ye're love nest would have put paid to the treachery. Guess I was wrong.'

'Maggie, I never meant for you to...what did you say?' Sarah stares at the other woman as if seeing her for the first time.

'Spare me the bullshit, for nearly twenty-two years you have pretended to be my friend, while all along you have been laughing behind my back. How could you Sarah? Him' She jerks her head towards her husband, who has gone deathly quiet. 'I'm used to his lies and deceit. Have put up with more than you'll know over the years. Oh, don't think you were the only one he's cheated with, but no more. You though, I would have expected more from...thought you were a friend.'

'How long...how?' Sarah takes on a stutter, she's never had before.

'The morning of Desmond's release from prison. Like a fool, wanted to be the one to warn you, so I rushed over to the farm as soon as I knew. There was no one at the farmhouse, guessing you'd have gone for a swim, I walked down towards the cove. That's when I spotted the surfboard outside the barn and heard voices. Naturally, I assumed it had been Conor, how wrong had I been, should have worked it out then really, but maybe I just didn't want to.'

'Maggie, I-'

'Don't Sarah...I will not listen to pathetic excuses, please give me some dignity.' It is clear she is fighting back unshed tears. 'The night we had the Chinese, I gave you every opportunity to tell me you and Conor were back together, because you would never betray our friendship...some fool I've been. Thanks to your delightful sister ringing me last week and gleefully filling me in on the details, I'm enlightened to the fact my husband was Jack's father.' The pain evident in her eyes, causing Sarah to reach out only to have her gesture rebuffed. 'It all fell into place, the picture of Jack on the mantelpiece above the Aga, I'd seen it a thousand times maybe more over the years...thought there was something about his smile...told myself I was being silly, god you Connolly women are something else. Can you leave, as I don't want a scene, not tonight? Tonight is my night, all about me for a change, not Sarah's problems or Finn's infidelity. Me, Maggie, so go, I want to enjoy celebrating life beginning at forty, as they say. I'll say you had a headache because I'm sure Conor will ask. I always said, Conor was one of the good ones. Finn,' she turns to address her soon to be ex-husband. 'You will stop flirting and see to our guests, then when the last one leaves, I want you to pack your bags and go.' She stands pokerfaced allowing Sarah to pass by. Sarah pauses at the top of the stairs opening her mouth to speak, but the right words won't come. Besides, Maggie probably wouldn't listen anyway, she has already turned her head away in disgust.

Silent tears stream down, Sarah's cheeks as she slips out the front door to ensure no one sees her departure. She should go home, but shame stops her from wanting to face Lily and Tommy, the idea of having to explain to Lily what has happened? Not that they would judge, but having been through so much recently, standing by her no matter what life had thrown their way. It makes her wonder, why each time she has tried to pick her chin off the ground and battle on, another punch is thrown. Is this how Roz had felt, when she decided life is not worth living without Natasha in it?

It's a horrible feeling, having driven your car and pulling up to park realising there is no acknowledgment of how you physically got there. It is only when Sarah gets out of the car gasping for air, the full comprehension of where she is, kicks in.

There is a memorial stone where a lamppost once stood. A vivid memory of Lily and Paddy discussing putting one here, but Sarah had never before now come to see it. The pain always raw, denial preventing her from wanting to see the last place he had breathed life. On many occasion, Sarah had gone out of her way to avoid travelling this road after that fateful day, the one where her son's life tragically ended. In many ways, her own life ended that day too. She slumps to the ground next to the stone, its carving simple. "Jack Connolly, 12th October 2011, sleep peacefully." There is a bunch of fresh flowers next to it and a bronze medal, London 2017, draped across the stone using a green ribbon.

'Lucy.' She whispers through her tears. 'She did it for you.' A soft breeze brushes over her face, warm and soothing. Voices carried on the wind telling her not to cry, yet she cannot hold back, instead allowing tears flow freely.

The sun has gone from the sky, Sarah shivers from the cold unsure how long she has been sitting there. Tiny droplets of rain splash onto the marble stone, but she remains motionless under an invisible veil shielding her from the rest of the world, until the rain becomes heavy and relentless urging her to give in and get back into the car. Driving on autopilot towards the farm there is a hollow emptiness within, hands clasped tightly to the steering wheel as the wipers fight against an unrelenting force of nature.

Eventually, Sarah pulls onto the narrow road leading up to the farm, driving in an almost robot like form, mind devoid of concentration she almost misses the turn into the house. Twisting the steering wheel at the last minute, she hastily swings the car barely missing the gatepost or so she thinks, the sound of a thud bringing her back to her senses. It is only when she alights the car does the full force of her actions sink in, Buster, Jack's Labrador is lying unmoving on the ground. Sarah lifts him into her arms, barely able to carry his heavy mass across the yard and into the warmth of the farmhouse, where she gently places his body in front of the aga, before fetching a blanket to wrap him in. As she lifts his head, he lets out a weak whimper his breathing fluctuating, taking his last breath before she can get through to the vet.

Shaken and wrought with uncontrollable guilt, she is reminded of the glass of wine she'd drank earlier at Maggie's or was it two glasses, the memory now blurred. Sliding onto the stone floor beside Buster, brings a cold realisation her actions are no different than Desmond's, as she pulls his lifeless body into her arms sobbing into his soft wet fur.

Eventually, the early morning sun shines brightly through the kitchen window, almost blinding with its cheery façade. With Her body cold and shivery from wearing damp clothes all night, Sarah rises from where she had laid beside Buster's lifeless body, now gone cold and stiff. The overwhelming feeling of suffocation from guilt urging her to rush from the house down to the cove, the only place she has ever found comfort.

There she strolls aimlessly along the water's edge deep in thought over her recent actions, her feet caressed by the gentle flow of water sweeping in on the sand. The tide being out allowing passage through a hidden crevice in the rocks bringing Sarah across to Kilmer beach, which stretches from the Connolly's farm across as far as the adventure centre. Expecting it to be deserted at this early hour, she rambles as far as the boardwalk, to find there is someone getting ready for a swim in the calm and inviting water.

Not wishing to engage in small talk, she turns to sit on the soft sand, staring out at the sea's mesmerising beauty. An amazing sight, especially at this time of day when the morning sun dances on its soft ripples. Sarah shivers, her body cold even though the warm sun is kissing her cheeks as she watches nature at its best, her saviour in hard times only today the effect is useless.

Catching another glimpse of the man on the boardwalk as he stands up ready to dive into the water, she realises it is Desmond. In the early days of his release, she had sat outside his house going over in her head the words she would convey to this man in order for him to understand her pain. Today her emotions are devoid of feeling as she observes him gliding through the water with considerable ease, like a knife slicing through soft butter.

Her mind drifts to a time when she would walk down to the beach with Jack for a swim, afterwards they would stroll up the narrow path to the house. Life had seemed so simple then, his cheeky smile as he ran head to pick grandpa's strawberries before the birds pilfered their share. The sweet smell of fresh strawberries will always remind Sarah of Jack's cheeky smile, only her heart will be lighter for the fond memory of her beautiful son.

As Sarah glances up again, Desmond has stopped swimming and is waving his hands in the air. She glances around to see who he is waving at, but there is no one else on the beach. Gauging him once more it becomes clear, he is not waving rather flailing. The man who'd taken her son's life, ripping her heart out is in trouble and at her mercy.

An unexplainable force takes over her body, there is no questioning or hesitation. She rushes to grab a nearby lifebuoy making her way to the water's edge, swimming towards him with an unrecognisable determination pulling her along.

'Here, grab onto this.' Sarah calls out the moment she reaches a distressed looking Desmond, whereupon he clasps onto the lifebuoy still flailing and breathing too heavily. 'I need you to relax, slow your breathing. I know it's easy to say but the key is not to panic.' Sarah instructs calmly. 'Hold tight... ...you're safe now.'

'Thank you...I cramped up and I'm afraid, I panicked.' He manages to reply. It is a strange moment for both of them, time freezing as they grasp onto the lifebuoy, their eyes lock, his filled with pain and fear. 'I'm sorry.' A statement often gone unsaid when needed or too easily spoken dispassionately, it is the pained expression etched on Des' face showing real remorse. Before her is a young man filled with anguish whom she now realises, has lived with the pain just as she has.

After their watery encounter, Sarah finds herself sitting beside Desmond Shanahan on the soft silky sand, a scenario she could never in her wildest dreams have imagined. Absorbing the surrounding beauty, lulled by the sound of the sea rolling onto the shore causing a calming stillness to encircle them, finally at peace with the world and comfortable in each other's company. The sky above is a blank canvas of clear blue, not a cloud in sight. The only feature, an aeroplane flying overhead, inside three of its passengers are finally free, destined for a new beginning as it disappears over the Atlantic.

A note from the Author

Thank you for reading, "A Sweet Smell of Strawberries." This Book is dedicated to all the young people tragically killed on our roads. When a child's life is tragically taken too soon, it not only takes away their future but devastates the lives of family and friends.

A report in January 2018, showed 30 pedestrians and 15 pedal cyclists killed on Irish roads in 2017. OVER 2,600 CYCLISTS were hospitalised in road accidents in 2015 and 2016. The story is fictitious as are the characters portrayed, I was inspired to write, "A Sweet Smell of Strawberries" after hearing of a particularly tragic case on the news of two talented teenagers, athletes out training early one morning, killed by a negligent motorist high on a cocktail of drink and drugs after an all-night party. The story pulled on my heartstrings and sat with me so much I felt compelled to write this book. However, I am also aware sometimes incidents can happen outside of our control. Like Desmond, there are people who respect and have a genuine interest in cars. We all have a responsibility to be mindful of each other regardless of age/gender or what type of transport we use when on public roads.

Printed in Poland
by Amazon Fulfillment
Poland Sp. z o.o., Wrocław